THE LOST CITY

MW00977177

Earthly Trinity

By Daniel Blacraby

elevate

Published in Boise, Idaho by Elevate Publishing
Web: http://www.elevatepub.com

This book may be purchased in bulk for educational, business, ministry, or promotional use.

For information please email info@elevatepub.com

ISBN (softcover): 978-1937498566

Printed in the United States of America

Dedication

To G.R.S. Blackaby.
For a contagious love of books
that transcends generations.

Table of Contents

Prologue

Her eyes glistened as three tears slid down her cheek. She stepped another inch toward the ledge, the vast chasm below her stretching out into oblivion. The heels of her feet hung suspended over the ridge. She wobbled for just a moment before regaining her balance. Her face conveyed both fear and determination.

Cody felt his own eyes moisten. "Don't...there has to be another way...please..." His voice trailed off. He stretched his arm toward her. She raised her hand, the tips of her fingers brushing against his. "I'm sorry, Cody. It's the only way. The price must be paid." Her gentle voice was laced with unwavering conviction.

Realization hit Cody. The words that had haunted his every nightmare echoed again in his mind: *The one closest to you must pay that price.* He had known from the beginning that the words had only one meaning: Death.

Cody's heart slowed to a near coma. It all made sense. For weeks he had done everything in his power to prevent The Prophecy's required bloodshed. He had vowed not to let it happen. But he had failed.

Now she had to die.

Cody shook his head. "I don't care about The Prophecy. I don't want it. I want *you*. Don't leave me...*please*." He knew every eye in the room was staring at him but he didn't care. He let the tears stream down. Her smile was full of sorrow.

"Precious Cody. One day it will make sense. I promise." She took a deep breath. "Be strong."

Then she spread her arms and stepped backwards off the ledge.

"Noooooooo!" Cody lunged forward. His fingertips brushed against the fabric of her dress—and then she was gone.

Her hair streamed around her calm face like a halo as she fell. The light illuminated her silhouette with an angelic glow. She was beautiful. She gave one final smile before a blazing pillar exploded from the bottom of the chasm to the celling.

Cody shielded his eyes from the blinding light. A burning pain pierced his chest. He collapsed weakly to the floor. "I'm so sorry," he whispered. "I'm sorry. It should have been me, not you." The column of spiraling light erupted in a final flash, faded, and vanished. *The price has been paid in blood.*

A soft humming rang in his ears. Then there was a collective gasp. Cody wiped his eyes and looked up at the metallic podium jutting out over the abyss. The humming increased to a deafening siren. The simple ivory book was glowing, a beam of energy shooting from the cover. The crowd around the Book backed away nervously as a laser scorched an image on the ceiling. An image of an upside-down arrow framed by a sun—the sign of The Earthly Trinity.

Thirteen Days Earlier...

Cody stared down the hollow of the pistol barrel as it leveled to his face. Dunstan bowed. "What are my orders, my Master?"

In shock, Cody turned to Jade's father. Mr. Shimmers reached to the desk and lifted a large, polished sword. "Welcome to the headquarters of CROSS."

PART ONE:
THE JOURNEY BACK

1

Mr. Shimmers

———————————

Arthur Shimmers' imposing frame cast a long, narrow shadow across the room. His face was accented by the sharp angles of his pointed nose and deep-set, mesmerizing green eyes. The hilt of his majestic double-edged sword was formed of crystal and adorned in jewels. Engraved writing marked the blade's silver surface.

Cody Clemenson stared at the man with a mixture of awe and fear. The moisture in his mouth evaporated. "You? *You're* the Master of CROSS? I don't understand." He tried to step backward but felt a tingle as the cold metal barrel of Dunstan's pistol brushed the erect hair on his neck.

"Father!" Jade joined Cody's side. Fair-skinned Tiana appeared at Cody's left in a crouch, as though ready for combat. Mr. Shimmers withstood the outburst with absolute stillness. He allowed the uncomfortable silence to linger.

Leisurely resting the sword against the side of the desk, the well-postured man replaced it with a cigarette. "This is an unexpected opportunity to finally meet you face to face, Master Clemenson." His voice held the warmth of a Canadian blizzard.

Cody braved a step forward, the sound of Dunstan's knuckle tightening on the trigger as he did. "Who are you? *All* of you," he said, motioning to Dunstan. "Why do you keep helping us? What is CROSS?" Mr. Shimmers inhaled another slow puff.

"Ah, like so many others, you cannot even begin to grasp the depth of your ignorance." He tapped the ash from his cigarette onto the floor. "Helping you? Is that what you believe?" Cody nodded uneasily. Mr. Shimmers seemed to grow larger with each passing moment.

"It was CROSS who warned me about the dangers in Atlantis," Cody said, "and provided The Prophecy on that stone tablet; and rescued Xerx and me from the Garga; and..." Cody's tongue was bogged down by the sticky saliva filling his mouth. His cheeks burned. Mr. Shimmers' eyes narrowed into snakelike slits. His lips curved in amusement.

"My dear boy, I'm afraid you are terribly mistaken." He turned his back to them. "It has been *you* who has been helping *us*." His hand gently stroked an unseen object on his desk. Silence hung like a dense fog in the room. Cody strained his neck. He caught a glimpse of a book with a simple wooden cover. "It is late. So if you will kindly hand over *The Code*."

Cody instinctively grasped his backpack. "Never!" He could feel the heat of the Book's energy radiating through the fabric of his bag. He caught Tiana's eye in his peripheral. She nodded slightly. He glanced to Jade who returned his gesture. They would not go down without a fight. Cody began discreetly motioning with fingers.

Three...

Two...

ONE!

Cody opened his mouth to shout the High Language.

Tiana hurled herself at Dunstan.

Jade lunged for her father's sword.

Mr. Shimmers turned.

The shrilling clang of a gong shook the room. Cody grabbed his ears. The lamps in the chamber flickered and streams of bright colors flashed like strobe lights. Cody stumbled, disoriented by the fluorescent bursts that were swirling around him. The sonorous gong continued its deafening assault. The floor seemed to ripple beneath Cody's feet, tossing him off-balance. His knees buckled and he crashed face-first onto the wood floor.

Silence.

Cody lowered his hands. His ears still throbbed but the gong had ceased. He stood, a wave of nausea sweeping up from his stomach to his throat. His eyes leveled to the barrel of Dunstan's gun. The British henchman had not moved. Cody turned. Mr. Shimmers was still standing in place and he was holding *The Code*.

Cody's posture stiffened. "You just used the Orb's power. You're a creator! *How?*" Mr. Shimmers held the Book in his outstretched hand. Instantly a hooded figure appeared from the shadows. A circular blade hung from the man's belt and another glimmered in his hand.

"Bring this Book to the Table Room." The cloaked man took the Book, nodded obediently and disappeared from the room.

Jade clenched her sweaty hands. "Father, what have you done?" Her father turned, returning his gaze to the prized object on his desk.

"Dunstan, show our honored guests to their room." The British underling used his pistol to lead the three captives from the office. The last thing Cody heard as the door shut was the diminishing sound of crazed laughter.

2
Puzzle Pieces

The room was poorly lit. Against the far wall was a gothic styled, four-post bed; a veil canopy draped over it from the high ceiling. A floor-to-ceiling bay window looked out over the dark forest three stories below. The décor did nothing to cloud the truth: the chamber was as much a jail cell as if iron bars had lined the perimeter. Cody gripped the doorknob and twisted.

It was locked.

Tiana stood at the window gazing at the starry sky while Jade sat in a high-backed chair twirling a strand of her charcoal hair. Her eyes rose to meet Cody's. "I'm so sorry. I shouldn't have brought us here."

Cody dropped to the floor beside her chair. "There was no way you could have known that your own father was the leader of CROSS. But maybe our coming here will help us answer some questions..." Jade raised an eyebrow. Cody reached into his backpack and pulled out a familiar ruby pocket-sized clock. It had one short red hand and three long hands colored red, gold, and purple.

"Wesley's old pocket-watch." Jade muttered.

Cody pointed at the clock-face. "Except we know it's much more than that. It's a *compass*. The short hand always points toward the Orb. The tall red and gold hands aim to the two Books of power…"

Jade perched forward in the chair and cut in. "Yes, but the purple hand remains a mystery."

Cody grinned. "Until today." He handed her the ruby-coated device and watched as her eyes widened. The purple hand was steadily looping in a counter-clockwise circle.

"What do you think it means?"

"I have no idea. When we were in your father's office, there was a book with a wooden cover on his desk. When I approached it the purple hand started going crazy. I don't know how, but I just *know* all of this, CROSS, and that book, are part of something more than we realize."

Jade let out a cavernous yawn. "You are probably right." It was clear exhaustion had overtaken her. Cody noticed the weight of his own eyelids. As always, she was right. He stood and helped Jade to her feet.

Walking to the window, Cody stopped by Tiana's side. Her eyes were mesmerized as she gazed out at the night. The trees below swayed gently in the breeze.

"You never told me that Upper-Earth had an Orb as well." Tiana said softly. Cody traced the path from her blue eyes to the bright full moon hanging in the night sky. He smiled and squeezed her shoulder.

"You need some sleep." For once Tiana didn't resist, a testament to the depth of her fatigue. He turned and found Jade staring at the bed in alarm.

"There's only one bed." Her cheeks were glowing red. Cody grabbed a pillow and tossed it onto the floor.

"I'll sleep here. You and Ti can share the bed." The two girls locked eyes. Tiana snarled. "If any part of your body touches me during the night, I'll chop it off."

Jade rolled her eyes. "If any part of my body touches you during the night, I'll chop it off myself."

Cody ignored the bickering duo. Some things were not for the male species to understand—quarreling woman topped that list. He lay on the floor and pulled out the pocket-watch. He watched the purple hand as it moved in slow, plodding circles. The pieces to the puzzle were starting to come together. He just hoped they would like the final picture.

3

A Pierced Heart

Why does she have to be so bloody beautiful even when she's sleeping? Jade glared bitterly at Tiana's peaceful, reposing features. She rolled over to face the opposite direction of Sleeping Beauty and exhaled a prolonged sigh. There had been a time once when she had felt beautiful, too.

She had fallen in love with a perfect prince in a perfect fairytale city. For a short time her life had been just that— *perfect*, like a surreal dream. But, like all dreams, eventually you have to wake up. She had, and everything had turned out to be a big fat lie.

She took a deep breath. *I'm used to being disappointed.* Her entire life was a domino chain of letdowns. Now her own father, a man she had looked up to with unabashed admiration since her childhood, was holding her prisoner.

It was an odd thought. Somehow the memory of once having been a carefree little girl felt like a myth, as though it, too, had been some long ago dream.

Snap out of it! Now is not the time to mope. Cody needs me to be strong. She snickered silently to herself. Cody *always* needed her to be strong and bail him out of trouble. *Needy little brat.*

Jade opened her eyes. The room was still dark. She had dozed off but wasn't sure for how long. Beside her Tiana still slept soundly. Jade felt a restless ache in her legs. She slipped out from the covers and stretched her feet over the side of the bed. The moon was still high in the starry sky. *What time is it?* She rubbed her eyes. *I could use a sip of water.* Crawling out of bed, she tiptoed toward the bathroom. Her attempted stealth was abandoned when she reached Cody.

He was sprawled out on his stomach with his arms flopped out like a bearskin rug and had his left knee tucked in toward his chin. A substantial flow of drool drained from his open mouth. A nuclear bomb couldn't wake him.

Jade stepped over him and entered the bathroom. It was comforting to be in a regular bathroom again. She filled a glass with cold tap water. As she took a sip she looked back to Cody—and frowned.

How can he sleep so soundly when it's his *fault we're in this awful mess to begin with?* She took another drink. The more she thought about their situation the deeper her scowl became. *If Cody had just listened to me for once and not returned to Wesley's bookshop and that blasted book none of this would have happened.* She tightened her grip on the glass. *It's all his fault. It's* always *his fault.*

Cody coughed, gagging on his copious drool. With a groan he rolled over and returned to unconsciousness. The disgusting sight was the final straw. It suddenly clicked in Jade's mind. *I hate him.*

She smashed her water glass against the counter. The glass shattered, leaving only jagged edges. She stepped toward Cody and dropped to her knees. *You won't ruin my life anymore.* Then, without hesitation, she rammed the serrated glass into Cody's chest.

4

A Murderous Trance

"Jade!" Tiana screamed. Her face was white in panic. "Jade, stop! What are you doing? What's wrong?" Jade gasped as Tiana grabbed her shoulders and shook her.

Her entire body was coated in a layer of sticky sweat. She sat up from the bed. On the floor Cody lay graceless and undisturbed. *It was just a dream.* Jade rested her head in her hands. Her forehead was feverous and throbbing. She rubbed her eyes, trying to wipe away the lingering residue of the experience. *It felt so real.*

"Are you okay, girl?" Tiana asked.

Jade nodded absently. "Yeah. Sure. It was just a nightmare."

"Just a nightmare, indeed!" Tiana said. "You were screaming Bloody Mary for well over a minute! I kept shaking you but you wouldn't wake up. It was like you were in a trance." Tiana frowned; then she swatted Jade across the top of the head. "That's for scaring the spit out of me! I'm going back to sleep."

Jade rested against the headboard. She glanced over to Cody who was still unconscious. She exhaled, releasing the tension in her shoulders. *Cody, you really* could *sleep through a nuclear bomb.* She needed to rest. Exhaustion was taking its toll. Her eyes lifted to the bathroom—and her heart skipped a beat.

Sitting on the counter beside the sink was a half-full glass of water.

5

Caged

———————————
—————————

Cody squinted one eye open, fearful of what he might see—and groaned. His worst fears had been realized: it was morning. He had long held the philosophy that the best defense against a miserable day was to simply sleep though it. At peace with his decision, he rolled over and began to doze off again. His bliss came to an end in the form of a sharp kick to his ribs.

"Get up, you sloth!" Jade yanked him up to his feet by his collar. Whatever she said next never registered in Cody's mind. His senses spiked and pulled his attention to the table by the bed. A fancy tray was steaming with the most glorious smell of a hot breakfast. "Where did that come from?" Cody was at the tray in an instant. He lifted a bowl of oatmeal to his mouth and began devouring it like a dog.

"The food was here when we woke," Tiana said. "I don't know how they came in and out of here without me hearing anything. It might be poisoned." Cody's sloppy chomping drowned her words out. "Although you apparently do not share my concern," Tiana finished flatly.

Tiana's expression seemed almost pleasant next to the utter disgust Jade displayed as Cody shoved two whole pancakes into his mouth and washed them down with a hearty swig from the syrup flask.

"Good heavens, Cody! Can't you at least *pretend* to be charming sometimes?" Her own stomach groaned. *When's the last time we ate?* An equally loud gurgle echoed from Tiana's stomach. *Far too long.*

All grace and manners were abandoned as the three savagely assaulted the breakfast tray like a pride of lions surrounding a hippo carcass. Several moments later, in a heap of crumbs, they sat holding their bloated stomachs.

"Well, now what?" Jade asked. Cody shrugged and deflected the question to Tiana with a belch. Tiana had already positioned herself in a crouch by the door. She cracked her knuckles.

"We wait."

Their waiting amounted to jack-squat.

In the early afternoon, the elderly butler briefly appeared, but only to bring them lunch. The caretaker nearly had a heart attack when Tiana pounced up behind him. Other than that event, they had been completely ignored. The last rays of sunlight began to disappear behind the horizon, casting a bright pink haze across the sky. Jade pounded her fist against the wall. "We can't wait any longer. I don't know what my father...what *Mr. Shimmers* thinks he's doing," she said, over-enunciating the name, "but we're wasting time. We don't even know if our friends below ground are okay. By all accounts the escape plan from El Dorado was a disaster. Did Dace and the others manage to escape or did they wait for us? And why didn't Randilin show up? I'm worried sick about him."

"Jade's right," Tiana said. "By now the Golden King will have begun his march toward Atlantis. We can't afford any more delays."

They were interrupted by the sound of knocking. Their eyes shot toward the door as it slowly opened. Dunstan stood smiling in the doorframe.

"Cody, if you will please come with me." His blue eyes danced between Jade and Tiana. "Unfortunately, ladies, *only* Cody." Without waiting for a response, he tipped his fedora, turned, and departed down the hallway.

Cody gulped. Jade and Tiana each grabbed one of his hands and squeezed. Jade looked him in the eye. "Promise me you'll be safe." Cody touched his forehead to hers. Without a word he began following Dunstan down the lengthy corridor.

Some things weren't in his control to promise.

6

Doors Ajar

Neither spoke a word. Only the old wood floor creaking beneath their feet resonated as Cody trailed behind Dunstan. Flickering candle lanterns provided meager lighting for the seemingly endless matrix of passageways. If the mansion had looked large from the outside, inside it was even more massive. Doors and hallways branched off to dozens of unknown locations. Cody maintained the brisk pace as they climbed a winding flight of stairs. Every footstep loosened a cascade of dust from the steps beneath. Full suits of armor stood as sentries at the top, guarding another lengthy corridor. The walls were ornamented with faded artwork of every imaginable style. Cody looked down—and leapt.

A gray rat scurried across the corridor in front of him before vanishing within the refuge of a hollow suit of armor. By the time Cody regained his composure Dunstan was already at the far end of the passageway. The middle-aged man disappeared around a corner.

Cody scampered to catch up, but paused at the sound of voices. There were people speaking on the other side of the hall's lone door. The rich mahogany of the doorframe was carved in the striking image of a fire-breathing dragon. Cody tiptoed toward it. The door was ajar.

He stretched his neck to peek inside. The sizable room was oval shaped. A crystal chandelier hung from the low ceiling and wielded thirty flickering candles. The rounded walls were plastered with hundreds of maps, newspaper clippings, and pictures. Acting as the room's centerpiece was a giant, circular table made of aged, cherry-toned wood. Additional maps and documents lay strewn across its vast surface.

Several hooded CROSS agents sat, spaced sporadically around the table facing a man in a slightly larger chair with his back to the door. "The *Day of Reckoning* is upon us," the man declared. "Tomorrow, at long last, we make our move. We will finally regain our stolen glory."

As Cody leaned closer, his hand slipped on the smooth wooden frame and propelled him forward. His shoulder hit the door, causing it to creak open. Every hooded face looked up at him. The speaker in the larger chair turned his head. Mr. Shimmers' piercing gaze locked onto Cody.

7

Checkmate

The room's temperature seemed to plummet as Mr. Shimmers' icy stare cut through Cody's skin. No one in the room moved or spoke. Like silent wraiths, they sat expressionless, all eyes fixed on the intruder.

Cody dropped his gaze to the floor. Without a word he grasped the handle, pulled the door closed and darted away. He had no intention of waiting around long enough to see what happened next. His heart was still racing when he caught up to Dunstan.

The British gentleman was reclined in a tall-backed chair beside a crackling fireplace. Before him was a small table showcasing a wooden chessboard. "Fancy joining me for a match?" Dunstan motioned to an empty chair on the other side.

Cody sat slowly, keeping his eyes fixed on his old acquaintance. "What's the catch?"

Dunstan chuckled, removing his fedora and resting it on the table.

"Golly, you remain as untrusting as ever! Cannot two old friends engage in some friendly sport?"

Cody leaned in, his finger harpooning toward the older man's chest. "We are *not* friends!" Dunstan's face fell. He appeared genuinely hurt by the remark.

"Very well, very well. Then I offer you this: naturally, as a principled Brit, I'm a betting man. What say we throw in a friendly wager?" He leaned back in his chair. "If *I* win, you owe me one favor, sworn on the name of your dear mother, *no questions* asked. If *you* win, well..." he leaned forward and folded his long, skinny fingers together, "I will tell you *everything* you want to know about CROSS." Dunstan held out his callused hand. "Do we have a deal?"

Cody's palms were sweaty as he grasped the out-stretched hand. "Deal."

A devious smile contorted Dunstan's face. "White moves first."

Cody peered down at the board. He was a competent chess player. He and Jade had played on occasion and he had always finished victorious. Jade's mind was too pre-dictable. She always played the most logical move, never thinking outside the box. Thinking outside the box was Cody's specialty. He slid his first pawn forward.

Dunstan immediately pushed his own pawn forward. Cody bit his lip in frustration. Jade always took a calendar month to decide on her move. After some thought, Cody moved his next piece. Once again Dunstan countered without hesitation. Cody grimaced. *I need to distract him.*

"So," Cody began casually, "have you known Jade's father for long?" His next move was followed quickly by his opponent's. Cody grinned as he examined the board. Dunstan was crowding the left side, an obvious all-out offensive. *He underestimates me.* Cody slid his Bishop up to counter.

"Indeed, I have. He raised me," Dunstan replied.

Cody's concentration shattered. "What? He's your father? That would make you...Jade's *brother*!"

"Oh, no-no-no," Dunstan replied. "Good heavens, I'm old enough to be her father. I had my own family once. Good chaps they were. But as I once told you, I had an early hankering to find the Holy Grail. As a young lad I ran away to pursue my crusade. Don't you see? When I first saw you aboard that Las Vegas-bound train I knew we shared a connection. You were fleeing your deadbeat town in search of greatness just as I had once done. You and I are the same."

"I left because I *had* to," Cody shot back. "To stay alive. To protect the Book. *You* left for glory. We are *nothing* alike!"

Dunstan nodded thoughtfully. "Perhaps, perhaps." He moved another piece. "But you *desired* greatness nonetheless, did you not? Tell me, if given the choice to do everything over again...would you? Could you truly give up the chance to become a Book Keeper? A *hero*?"

Cody remained silent. *Would he?* He wanted to say yes, but something deep inside prevented him.

"What happened after you ran away?"

Dunstan didn't appear to mind the deflecting question. "I ended up as a street rat in London, living off of scavenged food scraps and pickpocketing tourists. That's when *he* found me."

Cody retracted his initial move, noticing his exposed pawn. He slid over his rook to protect it. Dunstan claimed Cody's pawn anyways with his knight. *Amateur,* Cody sneered as his rook captured Dunstan's valuable piece. "And then what?"

"Mr. Shimmers took me in. He raised me—in a manner of speaking."

Cody lifted a questioning eyebrow. "I lived in this very house for a portion of my childhood. But in all the years I stayed here I rarely saw Mr. Shimmers. He is not an... *affectionate* man. Dangerous men seldom are." For just an instant, a pained expression flashed across Dunstan's face.

Cody slid his queen across the board to claim Dunstan's second knight. "How did you end up following him? Why did you join CROSS? What happened for him to earn your loyalty? What..."

Dunstan chuckled. "Easy lad. You are full of questions tonight. I believe our bargain was that I answered your questions only *if* you *won*..." Dunstan stood. "Checkmate."

Cody inspected the board in disbelief. "That's impossible. I've been beating you this entire match!"

Dunstan replaced his fedora on his head. "*Ah,* but perception is an untrustworthy devil. You'd be wise to remember that, lad. You tasted success and became distracted. You were so focused on the diversion that you allowed me to saunter through the back door and steal the victory." He winked. "Good night." He departed down the corridor.

"Wait, what about the favor I owe you?" Cody called after him. Dunstan paused, flashing a mysterious grin.

"All in good time."

8

An Open Door

Jade struggled to keep her eyelids from drooping. She rubbed them, trying to correct her blurring vision. Tiana was asleep in the bed beside her and Cody had yet to return from wherever Dunstan had taken him.

Despite Cody's physical absence his presence was suffocating. Jade refused to succumb to exhaustion. Her nightmare still haunted her. She could feel the warm dampness of his blood on her fingers and obsessively wiped them on the bedcovers to clean the invisible stains.

Abruptly the door swung open. Jade's heart jumped. Cody entered, quickly closing the door behind him. "We need to get out of here." Tiana was out of the bed and ready so quickly Jade was suspicious whether she had been asleep at all.

On the other side of the door, they heard the latch being locked. Cody lifted his finger to his lips to motion silence and retreated to the far side of the room. Even in the darkness Cody could see the rings under Jade's eyes. Noticing his stare, she blinked several times. "What happened out there?"

Cody absently ran his fingers through his hair, lost in thought. "I don't know. I think Dunstan was trying to *warn* me about something."

"Warn you about what? Why would he help us?"

"I don't know," Cody admitted. "But I trust CROSS as much as I trust Wolfrick to drink responsibly. I'm getting the feeling there's a game being played and we're just the pawns." He glanced back to the exit.

"We bust out of here at the first open door we get."

Cody woke to the sight of Jade's worried face. She pressed her finger to her lips. *"Shhh."* She motioned toward the door. A faint noise sounded from the other side.

Creeeeeak. Creeeeeak. Creeeeeak.

The doorknob was turning.

It jiggled for only a moment before stopping.

Tiana glided to the door, forming a sword with her hand and readying to strike. Cody grabbed Jade's hand. They held their breath—and waited.

Silence.

The handle remained motionless and all noise from the hallway ceased. They waited a moment longer but nothing happened.

"Do you think they were eavesdropping?" Cody suggested, the tension in his shoulders persisting.

Tiana was unconvinced. "Eavesdropping on what? Jade's snoring?"

"Or..." Jade muttered to herself. She released Cody's hand and stepped toward the door.

"Wait, what are you doing?"

Jade continued toward the entrance. With a deep breath she grabbed the doorknob and twisted. The door swung open with a high-pitched rasp.

The hallway was abandoned. Discarded on the floor was the key. Tiana poked her head through the doorway and scanned both directions. The corridor was empty.

"Either we have an unknown ally...or it's a trap," she concluded. Clearly she believed it to be the latter. Cody nodded.

"Agreed. But right now it doesn't matter which. We've quite literally found our open door." He tossed his backpack over his shoulder. "Quick, grab your stuff. We're breaking out of here."

9

House of Horrors

The ancient manor was shrouded in a silent trance. The soft moonlight washing through the vast bay windows was all that illuminated the unending corridors. A sudden rhythmic tapping caused the three escapees to stop in unison. They clustered together, scanning the dense shadows for whatever lurked within. A gust of wind blew in through an open window, making the blinds sway and tap the wall like a dreary offbeat metronome.

Cody exhaled. They resumed their silent procession down the hall, the nipping chill from the breeze stinging their faces. Cody closed his eyes, trying to recall the route Dunstan had taken.

Mr. Shimmers had ordered that *The Code* be taken to the Table Room. Cody was confident the room he had glanced into the previous night was the same room. Once they located the Book he could create a portal out of the haunting house.

"*Shhh!*" Tiana's hiss cracked like a whip as she glared at Jade. "You move with the grace of a rockslide. Are you *trying* to wake up the whole house?" Jade's eyes narrowed but she remained silent.

The corridor branched off in two directions. Cody glanced at both options, and then dashed quickly down the left passage. He didn't tell the girls that he was merely guessing and praying for good fortune. Right or wrong, to linger was to be caught.

The end of the hallway opened into a rounded room with an exaggerated ceiling. Displayed on the walls was an abundance of ancient weapons befitting an earlier age: swords, axes, bows, halberds, maces, javelins, and other instruments of death. Standing in the middle of the room, directly in front of them, was a man.

Cody skidded to a stop, causing Jade and Tiana to plow into him from behind. At the sound, the man turned. The startled elderly butler dropped his cleaning rag. Jade pushed herself in front of Cody. "It's just me. Little Mari, remember? You must be the one who unlocked our door." She flashed the best innocent and charming smile she could manage. The flustered chamberlain stuttered non-sensically as he bent down to retrieve the rag. He grabbed his chest for support—and pulled out a gun.

"Down!" Tiana tackled Cody and Jade as a bullet splintered the wall behind them. The aged butler moved with shocking agility. He lowered the gun and fired again. Cody rolled to the left. The floor sparked as the bullet hit. Cody smashed into the wall, trapping himself against a dead end. The butler's finger tightened on the trigger.

Tiana somersaulted forward. She whipped her feet in a swift arc, taking out the man's legs. The next shot discharged into the ceiling as he tumbled backwards. Tiana slammed her heel against the butler's chin, knocking him unconscious.

"We need to move!" Sweat streamed down Cody's face as they sprinted from the room. At the end of the hall was a winding staircase. Cody could see the familiar suits of armor at the top. "This way! Come on!" They darted up the stairs. The commotion from other parts of the manor told them they didn't have much time. Reaching the dragon-framed doorway, they found it was once again ajar. Cody stepped inside.

The room was vacant. Cody's eyes were drawn to a cluster of snapshots tacked to the wall. The photos were of faces, his own included. Joining his portrait were images of Jade, Tiana and all the royal family of Atlantis. Others, such as Levenworth, Dace, and Silkian, were also represented. There was even a picture of the Golden King. Accompanying each picture were various clippings and notes. "They're keeping tabs on us. *All* of us."

Pinned to another area of the wall was a massive world map. Or at least it *looked* like the world. The territories had unrecognizable labeling as though from another era. Purple cross-shaped markers were affixed to different locations on every continent. Strings stretched from each of the purple markings and joined together at a singular location. Cody frowned. That location was in the midst of the North Atlantic Ocean: the Bermuda Triangle.

At the top of the map was written: ***Phase Three: The Day of Reckoning.*** Tiana voiced the words forming in Cody's mind. "CROSS is on the move."

"Guys, you have to see this." Jade held up a document folder. "It's all written in a weird language I've never seen before. But look at *this*." She pointed to the front of the folder. On it was a three-crown crest and the letters: C.R.O.S.S. "It's an acronym!"

Tiana's eyes flashed toward the door. "We don't have time for this. We need to *go!*" Cody glanced around the room and spotted *The Code* on the table in front of the head chair. *That was easy.* He grabbed the Book and felt the Orb's energy flowing through him.

"Okay. Let's go!"

"So soon? But you've only just arrived," said a chilling voice behind him.

10

A Bullet to the Head

───────────

$\mathcal{M}$r. Shimmers stood in the doorway flanked by five subordinates: Dunstan; the man with the circular blades; the skinny crimson-haired woman; the bearded seven-foot titan; and another unknown agent. Every one of them had a weapon aimed toward the trio.

"If you desired a tour of my home you had but to ask." Mr. Shimmers stepped forward and raised his hand. The CROSS agents lowered their weapons. "I'd have thought my daughter would have been raised better than this."

Jade's face reddened. "No thanks to you, *Mr. Shimmers*."

Cody had never seen such burning defiance in his best friend. It was frightening. Mr. Shimmers, however, seemed amused by her rage.

"You surely *do* have my blood flowing through your veins. You lack your mother's weakness. She crumbled under the truth of who—*what*—I really am. A pity. She used to be rather pretty."

"Don't you dare say another word about my mother. You're no father to me." Jade scowled, although her resolve seemed to be weakening.

Tiana stepped forward to stand beside her and cast a vexed stare at the CROSS master. "If you're so proud of *who* and *what* you are, then tell us. We're not mindless children to be fooled by silly games."

Mr. Shimmers leaned forward, his angular nose prodding Tiana back a step like a spearhead. "Oh, but you *are* children. Swaddling babes strung along by pretty lights." He paced back toward the unmoved agents.

"We've been known by many names. Each century has its own title for us. The Society is immortal. We *have* and will *always* exist. The world will regret the day they stopped recognizing that. *The Day of Reckoning* is coming." His eyes were like snow globes struggling to contain a blizzard. He snapped his fingers. Instantly Dunstan's pistol was aimed at them again.

"But as you said, no more games."

Cody's eyes shifted to the British assassin, the same man he had played chess with only a few hours earlier. Cody was convinced he had been trying to tell him something. Dunstan's face was void of expression. *Would he really pull the trigger on me?* Cody bit his lip. If he could buy enough time to create a portal they could escape before any shots where fired.

"You may be a raging psychopath, but I don't believe you would murder your own daughter pointblank." The madness behind the man's eyes made Cody unsure of his claim, but he continued. "And if you truly wanted me dead you could have killed me a hundred times already." Cody laughed with feigned confidence. "You should have watched your tongue. You *need* me. You confessed that yourself. You can't kill me." Cody locked eyes with Mr. Shimmers.

"No, I suppose not," the older man muttered indifferently. He nodded toward Dunstan. Without hesitation Dunstan pointed the gun at Tiana's head.

Bang!

Tiana's head whiplashed as blood sprayed against the wall behind her. Her body crumpled to the floor, a scarlet bullet wound dotting the center of her forehead.

11

Set in Motion

---

single stream of blood trickled down Tiana's forehead. Her lifeless eyes gazed straight ahead. There was no movement of her chest. Her final breath had been spent in a gasp of shocked panic.

Cody dropped to the floor and pressed his fingers to her neck. There was no pulse. Tears coursed down his cheeks. He shot a venomous glare at Mr. Shimmers just in time to see him motioning again to Dunstan. The murderer's gun pivoted to Jade. He pulled the trigger.

"Spakious!" At Cody's command the air split down the center of the room. The bullet flying toward Jade vanished through the hole. "Go!" Jade dove headfirst through the portal. Cody lifted Tiana's limp body onto his shoulder. He cast a final glance to the CROSS leader. Mr. Shimmers was smiling.

With a grunt Cody hurled himself through the opening. *"Gai di gasme."* The wormhole closed.

Mr. Shimmers watched as the children disappeared. He stood motionless until the final ripple of the wormhole had disappeared. His lips curved into a grin, as though laughing at a joke only he had heard.   Dunstan bowed as he approached. "Master, do you think it worked? Will he do as he must?"

"Of course it worked. *I* was personally involved," Mr. Shimmers snapped. Dunstan bowed again.

"Yes, of course. Forgive me, Master." The other agents parted as Mr. Shimmers moved toward the door. Only the skinny redhead stood her ground.

"We've been planning for *years* for this opportunity and you allowed them to just walk away! I think it's time we had an explanation of this grand plan of yours. You can't expect us to..."

She never finished her complaint. Mr. Shimmers grabbed her throat and squeezed, snapping her neck and crushing her vocal chords. She collapsed to the floor. Mr. Shimmers turned to the remaining agents.

"Agent One and Two, return to your posts below ground." Dunstan and the blade-wielding agent nodded and left the room. To the bearded giant he ordered, "Agent Seven with me. Agent Nine..." he glanced down to the lifeless body of the woman, her final terror frozen in her eyes. "Clean up this mess." He turned and left the room.

At long last, matters were set into motion and could not be stopped. After so many years of planning, it was time to return to Under-Earth.

12

Death and Life

———————

The wind was crushed from Cody's lungs as he plummeted ten feet through the air where the portal had opened, and landed hard on his stomach. The dirt smeared on his face turned to mud as it mixed with tears.

The haunting words from the Thirteenth rattled in his head: *The one closest to you must pay that price.* He had been *convinced* it would be Jade who would be ripped away from him. He stared down at the beautiful, still face of Tiana and his sobs deepened. *I should have warned you.*

He felt Jade's hand on his shoulder. He looked up, seeking comfort in his best friend. She looked as he had never seen her before. Her eyes were ablaze and her face had contorted, forming deep wrinkles on her grime-stained forehead. She looked like a warrior with a bloodlust.

Her grip on Cody's shoulder tightened. With surprising strength she shoved him aside.

"What are you doing?" Cody protested, but Jade had tuned him out. She placed her hand on Tiana's forehead and pressed down forcefully.

"Jade! Stop!" She tilted her head back and began speaking with frightening zeal.

"*Uylesso, hortana, seamour, extrinca.*" She continued muttering the strange words with increased pace, her tongue entering into a rhythmic dance as it glided between syllables. Tiana's veins began to bulge, forming a dark blue matrix across her pale face.

"What are you doing to her!?"

Jade traced her fingertips along the swelling veins, which looked ready to burst. Her nails arrived at the bullet's entry point on Tiana's forehead. She placed both hands over it. Jade was screaming the words now and her body was shaking.

Then it was over.

Jade removed her blood-soaked hands from Tiana's forehead. The wound was gone. Only a faint white scar marked its place. Jade started to teeter.

Cody sprang forward and caught her before she hit the ground. Her eyes were dilated and her face was ashen. Cody brushed her sweat-soaked hair from her face. Her breathing was ragged.

"What...just...happened...*how?*"

Cody's eyes were bugged as he looked on his friend in awe and confusion. "Jade, you were using the *High Language.* What you just did should be impossible even for Master Stalkton. Jade...*How?*" Before Jade could respond there was a raspy cough behind them. They spun around. Tiana was propped up on her elbows.

"What in the bloody name of all that's precious just happened to me?"

"You're alive!" Cody and Jade tackled her back to the ground. She entered into another coughing fury.

"Easy, guys. I feel like death."

Tears of mirth streamed from Cody's eyes.

"Oh, Ti, I thought we'd lost you. This is a miracle." Even as he said it he knew there was something more. His eyes drifted to Jade. Her green eyes were glazed as she stared off into the distance.

Tiana fingered the scar on her head. "Well...where the blazes are we now?"

Cody examined their surroundings for the first time. He knew the answer instantly. He had lived there for years.

They were home.

13

A Cough Decision

The peaceful town of Havenwood lay at the base of a valley, a wall of trees crowning the ravine, shielding it from the outside world. The familiar community looked as calm as it always had; yet somehow it seemed foreign. Cody and Jade stood side-by-side staring at their old hometown. They had lost track of how much time had passed since they had fled on the horrible night of Wesley's murder. How many weeks? Months? It seemed like years had come and gone.

Cody looked at Jade from the corner of his eye. He lacked the courage to address the thirty-ton, purple elephant wedged between them: moments earlier Jade had used a power she didn't understand or believe in to resurrect the dead.

There's something she's not telling me. The thought did not anger Cody. After all, when *he* had been informed by The Thirteenth that Jade was destined to die in order for The Prophecy to be fulfilled, he had not told *her*. Nor would he. *I won't let it happen. I won't let them take you from me.*

"Mom knew about dad." Jade said softly. "That's why she left. That's why she's miserable. That's why she drinks." She brushed her cheek, although no tears wet it. "I blamed her. I idolized my father. The same man who just ordered me shot. My poor mother. I wish I'd known." She took a deep breath. "We need to go back."

"I agree. My mother will be worried sick, too."

"No, Cody," Jade said, turning toward him. "I mean we need to go back to Atlantis."

Cody's posture went rigid. "What? *Why?*"

"What do you mean *why*?" Jade snapped. "Because we *must*."

"But *why*? This is our home. We're finally back! We only left because we were in danger. What about our mothers? Not long ago I was begging you not to leave Atlantis and now you want to go *back*? We could just stay here in Havenwood."

Jade sighed. "Do really think we could return to our old lives after all we've been through? Do you think CROSS, *my father*, will leave us alone? What about the Hunter? That demon will never stop hunting us until the Golden King is destroyed."

"And..." Tiana interjected, leaning against Jade's shoulder, "don't forget about the underlings."

Jade nodded adamantly. "Yes, she's right. We can't forget about Dace, Tat, Chazic, Randilin, Xerx and the others. They *need* you Cody. Atlantis needs their Book Keeper when the battle begins."

Tiana laughed. "I meant *me. I'm* an underling. And *I* need to get home. I'm not spending the rest of my life stuck up in this awful place." She blushed, and then was quick to add, "but I agree with what Jade said about the others, too."

Cody's head swiveled back and forth between their two determined faces. His shoulders slouched. "Since when did you two become allies?"

They grinned in unison. "Only when you're too pig-headed to do what you must," said Jade. Tiana chuckled again.

"In that case, it's a miracle we didn't become best friends months ago." Abruptly Tiana's smile faded. She wobbled and fell to her hands and knees. She coughed, projecting a thick glob of blood to the ground.

"Ti!" Cody dropped and cradled her head. Her fair skin was pallid. A deep blue bruise marked the spot where the bullet had punctured her forehead. Enflamed veins branched out from the spot like tree roots. "What's happening to her?" He placed his hand against her sweaty forehead. It was an inferno.

Jade pulled on her ponytail. "I don't know. Maybe her wound is infected. She needs help, and quick. Cody—I think she's dying."

Cody felt his heart pulsing in his temples. He inhaled deeply and gazed back over the peaceful town of Havenwood. He would miss it.

They had no choice.

They must return to Atlantis.

14

Returning to a Murder Scene

"**S**he's going to die if you don't!" Jade said in exasperation.

Cody tossed up his hands. "I *can't* do it. I'm not strong enough to create another wormhole back to Atlantis. I'm not sure how I managed to transport us above ground in the first place. Somehow I drew on Tiana's strength. By all accounts using that much of the Orb's energy, even *with* the Book, should have killed me."

"But it *didn't* kill you!" Jade snapped, instantly regretting her outburst. "You're right. It's much too dangerous. But that means we're trapped up here and Tiana dies."

Tiana lifted her head. "Have you dimwits forgotten that you once made the journey before Cody had any knowledge of the Orb or the High Language?" Cody and Jade locked eyes.

"The Second Passageway—Area 51." Cody's face lit up. "Sally could lead us to the Wishing Well!" His excitement tapered off as fast as it had come upon him. "It's risky, too.

We were seen last time. I doubt we can count on such lax security again. I don't think it's a good idea."

"Then we take another passageway," Jade said with a grin. Cody was all too familiar with that mischievous look. Her expression implied she was already three steps ahead of him and shamelessly proud of it. "Dace told us that there are *many* access points into Under-Earth."

"But the other passages could be anywhere," Cody countered. "We don't even know where to start looking. We don't have time to waste." Jade's grin only widened.

"I think for the first time we've learned more from CROSS than they intended." All at once Cody's brain caught up to his companion's. His lips formed a matching smirk.

"The map on the wall. All the markers led to the same location—the Bermuda Triangle."

"Exactly. *Something* is going on there and I'm willing to bet my first edition *Anna Karenina* that it would be worth paying it a visit."

"Have you been there before, Cody?" Tiana asked.

"No."

"Then it won't work," Tiana said. "You can only make the exit of the wormhole if you can see where you are making it, either physically or in memory. If you can't see it and have no recollection of it, the portal would open at random and be disastrous."

Cody sighed. Why did he still think anything could be simple? He opened his mouth to utter a gloomy, defeatist pronouncement but paused. Jade had begun walking down the valley toward Havenwood. She peered over her shoulder and waved them on impatiently.

"Well, *come on*. I have an idea...."

Though it was only late afternoon, Havenwood was a ghost town. The streets were abandoned and only the eerie tinkle of wind chimes filled the hushed air. Cody scampered across the clearing to where Jade and Tiana crouched behind a building.

Tiana was breathing heavily. Her skin seemed more ashen every time Cody looked at her. Jade gasped. From their vantage point they saw a lone woman walking the streets. It was Jade's mother.

Cody restrained Jade. "She can't see us. Not yet." Jade didn't respond, but remained still. Cody watched as Mrs. Shimmers staggered up a few steps and disappeared into the town pub.

"Come on." Jade skirted from the alleyway and headed down another back alley. No one knew the back streets of Havenwood better than they did. They stopped, looking at the familiar building across the street:

Wesley's Amazing Used and Rare Antique Book Store

The ancient building had changed drastically. Like a cat wearing a ferret costume, the old store had been transformed and dressed up in an ill-fitting and unfamiliar guise. Where once there had been yellow crime-scene tape was now a pink, flowery sign reading:

Lady Anna's Book Shop.

"We need to be quick," Jade said. "We get in, find a book about the Bermuda Triangle, and use one of the pictures to make a portal back to Atlantis. It's important that *no one* recognize Cody or me. Got it?" Cody and Tiana nodded in consent. "Let's go!"

The three dashed across the road and up the entryway to the bookshop. Cody peeked over his shoulder to confirm the coast was clear.

Bang!

His head rammed into the hanging store sign. Jade giggled. Maybe things hadn't changed as much as she thought.

Standing in the shadows, the man watched as three children entered the bookstore. He had seen those faces too many times not to recognize them. The sickly blonde girl was unknown to him, but the other two...

He lifted a poster with both faces on it under the title: **Wanted for the murder of Wesley Simon.** He pulled out his phone and hit the speed dial.

"Sheriff Messiner. You're not going to believe this. They're back."

15

It's In a Book

Cody felt a touch of disappointment. The bookstore was utterly spotless. Not a single grain of dust floated in the air and the stacks of books that had once formed mesmerizing labyrinths throughout the store had been picked up and neatly placed on shelves. Cody frowned. An organized used-bookstore was a sinful oxymoron.

"Welcome dearies," said the woman, presumably Lady Anna, behind the desk. Her plastic-toned face was evidently as artificial as the two-inch eyelashes drooping over her eyes. As a whole, the woman had as much natural beauty as the manufactured *Rephaim* warriors in El Dorado. Cody looked past the slightly frightening lady to the wall behind her. A hole in the wood was still visible from where Wesley had used a dagger to attach the note for Randilin.

Cody shook his head. He didn't have time for sentiment. "Let's split up," suggested Jade. "I'll take Tiana. We must be *quick*." Cody nodded and veered off toward the staircase. Reaching the second floor he turned down an aisle of books and stopped. The hidden door through which he had first discovered the Book was now a sealed wall.

He wove his way through the rows scanning the book spines for anything useful. He stopped when he came across an atlas. He pulled the book down—and screamed. Staring back at him through the shelf opening were two gaping, lid-less eyes.

Cody dropped the book. The grimy, eyelid-less hermit tilted his head, his dilated eyes piercing Cody's. Then he turned and disappeared from view. Cody sprinted down the aisle and around to the other side. The spot was empty.

That's impossible. He looked behind. The store was empty other than an elderly lady reading *Twilight.* Cody rubbed his eyes. Had he really seen the man? Or was his lack of sleep catching up to him? A hand appeared from behind, the fingers curling over his shoulder.

"AHHH!"

"*Shhh!*" Jade said, standing behind him with Tiana. "I think I've found something."

Cody took the book from Jade's hands: Conspiracy Theories of the 40s. Jade flipped the book open to the middle. The chapter was titled: **The Devil's Triangle: The True Story of Flight 19 and What the Government Isn't Telling You About the Bermuda Triangle.**

Cody skimmed the text, which recapped stories of military airplanes that went missing over the famed water body and the plethora of government lies concealing the truth: that the Bermuda Triangle was a portal to an alien dimension. At the bottom of the page was a single, faded, black and white photo of a convoy of airplanes flying over the ocean. Jade pointed to the photo. "*There.*"

Beneath her finger was a small, rocky island—a dot in the water. Cody shoved the book back into Jade's hands. "*No-no-no.* The answer is definitely *no.* We need to keep looking."

They went silent as Lady Anna's voice sounded below. "Well, hello Sheriff, how can I help you?" The conversation dropped to inaudible muffles. Jade's face registered panic.

"Blast! It's Sheriff Messiner. Someone must have recognized us. We need to go *now!*" They heard footsteps ascending the stairs and the click of gun hammers cocking. "Cody, *hurry!*"

"This photo is decades old! We could drop into the middle of the ocean and drown!"

The muffled voices were closer now. Three long shadows stretched across the outside of the aisle.

"We don't have a choice!" Cody stared at the picture and whispered.

"*Spakious.*" With a popping noise the air unzipped, leaving a black wormhole in front of them. The policemen shouted and rushed forward. Jade and Tiana hurled themselves through, disappearing into thin air.

Cody had no time to reconsider. Taking one last look behind, he saw the haunting eyelid-less hermit staring from behind the bookshelf. Cody turned and jumped through the portal.

16

Under the Sea

Rain pelted relentlessly against the agitated sea as thick, foggy clouds churned above. Colossal waves swept across the water's chaotic surface before breaking with thunderous roars.

A fierce blow of water hurled Cody through the air. Blinded by the splash, he reached out desperately and felt a firm grasp on his wrist. He held on tight in the game of tug-o-war against the raging water. A moment later he was on his hands and knees. He pressed against the solid surface beneath him. It was smooth. *Had it worked? Had they reached the island?*

He shielded his eyes and forced them open. Towering waves rolled across the dark ocean as rain continued to crash down like an artillery barrage.

Jade stood beside him, holding his wrist and fighting to maintain her balance. The sky ignited as lightning flashed. A deep rattling boom immediately followed the flare. The resonance knocked Jade off her feet.

Cody squinted and yelled, *"Where's Ti?"* His voice was muted by another crack of the waves. He saw that Jade's mouth was silently moving, too.

He scanned the water for any sight of Tiana but the dark clouds stole the light. "Tiana!" Suddenly a large object pierced through the fog like a spear. Water splashed thirty feet high as a boat crashed down against the wave. As the large vessel rode the waves Cody faintly made out the flag with a triple-crowned crest. It was the symbol of CROSS.

Jade squeezed his arm. Six more ships emerged from the fog. "We need to get out of here!" Cody screamed, knowing Jade couldn't hear him any more than he could hear her. That didn't stop him from trying. "Tiana!"

The ground shook beneath them, sending him tumbling into Jade. She was yelling and pointing at something behind him. Off in the distance was a dark shape—a rocky island.

If that's *the island…*. The ground shook again. *Then what are* we *standing on?* Another rumble knocked him to the ground. Cody pressed his ear to the smooth surface and banged it with his fist. Through the vibrations he heard the clank of steel.

Oh, no! Bright lights flashed, illuminating the *island* they were on.

It was a submarine.

Bubbles began billowing up from the water. *The submarine is submerging!* Cody looked to Jade helplessly as the water rose up over their feet. He grabbed Jade and pulled her into a tight hug. The water reached their knees, leaving only the tower of the submarine still visible.

Cody could feel the fatigue in his muscles. Creating the portal had sucked him dry of energy. He looked at Jade. Her soaked hair was pasted to her face and her skin was wan from the cold. Her green eyes sparkled. She looked fearless—she looked beautiful.

Cody smiled. *I'm sorry, Jade. I couldn't keep you alive like I promised. But at least I'm going with you.* His lips pressed against hers. They were still locked in a tender embrace as the water climbed above their heads and swallowed them.

17

Of Conquest and Torture

The Hunter's tongue rolled across its black lips, lapping up the residual of blood. The air was saturated with death. The ground was littered with bodies; fallen soldiers, having forfeited their lives in defense of Flore Gub. A fortress once full of courage and determination was now full of rotting skin and death.

The Hunter unleashed a piercing squeal. The sound silenced the battlefield and sent golden golems and Dark-Wielders scurrying from sight. The Beast cared nothing for the taste of dead bodies. It hunted and it killed. Only then did it feast.

Its head retracted as a solid gold hand stroked its snout. It snapped its iron jaws at the hand. The handsome prince accompanying the gold-handed man retreated a step. The Golden King merely grinned. "My precious pet, do not be anxious. There is much hunting yet to do. And, much killing." The Beast's scarlet, slit-like eyes locked with the matching red ruby eyes of the King as though reflecting in a clear pond.

"I know what it is that troubles you, my beloved. But fear not. The time is upon us." The snowy-haired King stroked his lengthy fingernails down the underside of the creature's jaws. "Go now. Do what must be done."

Two giant wings stretched out. The Hunter shrieked again, and with one powerful sweep of its wings, it propelled into the air. The King watched the creature disappear into the distance. Not until the Hunter was completely lost on the horizon did the King turn to face the two men standing behind him.

The first was a titan of a man, covered from head to toe in black, jagged armor. Six spikes jutted out from the helmet like a nightmarish spider, and two pincers extended from the sides and curved around the mouth, the only exposed area of the armored man. He was El Dorado's High General—*The Impaler*.

"General, begin your march." The Spider-General nodded silently. The ground trembled beneath his feet as he departed. The King turned to the second man. "My son, what of our prisoner?" The broad-shouldered Prince Hansi directed his eyes toward a door on the other side of the courtyard.

"He remains defiant. I fear he lacks the strength to be pressed. Further interrogation could kill him." The Golden King's hand struck the Prince across the cheek.

"I do not deal in *could*. There is only that which I *have* and that which I *will* have."

"Yes, Father." Hansi's cheek throbbed but he did not allow the pain to affect his stony face. "I will question him again tomorrow."

"No. *I* will speak to him *now*." With a single word the door exploded off its hinges. The King stepped over it and into the room. The small, stone- walled chamber was empty except for the lone man strung up with chains around his wrists.

The man's naked body was bruised, scarred and swollen. The capillaries in his eyes had burst, coloring them a hazy red. The captive weakly lifted his head to see the visitor.

The Golden King's face pressed an inch from the prisoner's. "Your willpower is admirable. But I am a man who gets what I want. If I so desire, I can have even the strongest man curse his own mother." He rested his long fingernail beside the prisoner's bloodshot eye. "This will not be pleasant." The King sneered. "At least not for *you*."

Prince Hansi looked away in disgust. The sound of the captive's inhuman wails could be heard echoing in every part of the fortress. The howling continued well into dusk. When the torture session finally finished the Golden King leaned forward.

"Now, Chazic, why don't you start by telling me everything you know about The Earthly Trinity…."

PART TWO:
THE
APPROACHING STORM

18

Coming

The fireplace crackled like dead leaves, flinging a con-fetti of sparks toward the ceiling. The flame blurred to an orange haze as Prince Kantan's raven-black eyes peered through it. His presence was in body only. His mind soared across desert wastelands, over the smoldering Fiery Plaines, to arrive at the mighty fortress dwarfed within the rocky crevasse of the Labyrinth Mountains. However, he found only a black chasm of nothingness, as though the Divine Creator had blotched it out on the map with a glob of ink.

A distant voice called his mind back across the wasteland to his chamber and reconvened with his body by the fireplace. "Lord Kantan." The speaker was a bulky man with a weathered face and a gray beard as thick as sheep's wool. "May I enter?" Kantan nodded absently and motioned to an adjacent chair.

"Levenworth, forget the formalities. Our friendship runs deeper than titles and distinctions. You've known me too long for that." The General took a seat.

"Be that as it may, you are still my lord and I your loyal subject," Levenworth said, stroking his bearded chin thoughtfully. "Though, you have changed a great deal from the ambitious young man I once knew. You smiled more back then. Arianna had a way of drawing that joy to the surface."

"Memories best left in the past, *General*." Kantan's words pierced like a dagger thrust. "I trust you have reasons for this visit other than reminiscing old times?" The Prince's voice softened, but the directness implied that the vexation had not retreated far. "Indeed, my lord. The Company—or what's left of it—has returned." The Prince's slanted eyebrow rose.

"I wish to see them immediately." As Levenworth departed, Kantan clasped his hands behind his back and strolled to the tower window. He strained his eyes toward the faded backdrop of the Labyrinth Mountains. A mass of black clouds hovered above the Borderlands. The clouds had been first spotted early that morning. The Prince understood what they meant. He had seen them once before as a young boy. El Dorado was coming—and was bringing war and death.

He heard the men enter the room behind him and turned to greet them. A month ago Atlantis had dispatched a company of twelve—now only two stood before him: the master scout Tat Shunbickle and the Captain of the Outer-City Guard, Dace Ringstar. Conspicuously absent was the Book Keeper.

Kantan inspected them as one would a prized racehorse. "Captain Ringstar, report." Dace's face was filthy and marked with scabbing wounds. He looked like a man whose soul foraged ahead long after his body had given in to death. The Captain bowed. "I have urgent news for Queen Cia." Kantan's eyes narrowed.

"There has been an...*incident.* My sister is no longer fit to rule. I am acting King of Atlantis. *Report.*" Dace's face stiffened slightly.

"With all due respect, our mission was commissioned by the Queen. It would be only proper to report first to Lady Cia."

"With all due respect, Captain," Kantan sneered. "You were the sworn blood protector of the Book Keeper. His glaring absence implies he was either killed or captured by the Golden King. Both outcomes suggest your failure as his protector to *protect*; a failure punishable by death. So, *Captain,* you will speak your report to me."

If the threat troubled Dace his face was too weary to show it. "There is much of our mission to detail when time permits. But to pressing matters first. I come bearing grievous news—Flore Gub has fallen. *The Impaler* leads a formidable force, at least fifty-thousand strong, no less." Kantan's face remained vacant, although Dace saw his Adam's apple rise.

Levenworth grunted, "We are aware of the magnitude of the enemy's force. We have but ten thousand able men remaining in Atlantis, with hundreds more refugees from the outer regions of the kingdom pouring into the Capital each day. However, our advantage lies in our fortifications. To speak freely, I had feared worse."

Dace nodded. "Then let me give you worse. The forward offensive led by *The Impaler* is a diversion. A second force has crossed the Great Sea of Lava by ship. They march under the command of Prince Hansi. As we speak they are circling up from the West and will strike the city from behind."

"A wise tactic. How many men?" Dace exhaled a deep breath.

"No fewer than two hundred-thousand."

"*Impossible.* El Dorado cannot have amassed that many men unless they siege the city with infants!" Levenworth turned to Tat, but the scout nodded silently in affirmation.

"We'll be outnumbered twenty-five to one," observed Kantan. "How long do we have?" Dace glanced out the window at the growing storm clouds in the distance.

"Not long enough. They will be at the walls by week's end."

19

An Unwelcome Return

The world spiraled into view. Cody's vision came into focus to the sight of a massive wall of water bearing down on him. He cried out, throwing his hands over his head. The wave never hit.

He peeked open one eye. The entire sky above him was a swirling, blue expanse of water. The gravity-defying sea sparkled as soft ripples glided across its surface. The silhouette of a sea creature swam gracefully by. *The conspiracy theorists were right,* Cody thought in relief. The Bermuda Triangle was indeed a passageway into another dimension. They had returned to Under-Earth.

The portal had dropped him into the middle of an immense junkyard. Gigantic towers of debris jutted from the ground like a crumbling city skyline. Among the scrappiles were rusted airplane wings and propellers. In the distance, the large stern of a ship teetered uneasily in the air. Along the hull, faded and rusted, were the words: *U.S.S Cyclops.*

Cody heard the sound of muffled coughing in the distance. *Jade? Tiana?* He rushed in the direction of the noise, circling the bases of the scrap mounds. Something crunched under his feet and he looked down at a full-bodied skeleton laying half covered in dirt.

Cody resumed his dash, led by the sound of the coughing. Barreling around a tarnished freight-tanker, he found Tiana. Her soot-covered body was partially buried beneath the rubble. Cody dropped to his knees and dug through the junk. Tiana's eyelids fluttered, struggling to stay open.

The scar on her forehead had vanished. However, the black spider web of swelling veins now consumed her whole face and was rappelling down her neck. Her fair skin was glowing red. Cody could feel the heat radiating from her forehead. "Hold on Ti, I've got you. We need to find Jade and get you to Master Stalkton. It's going to be okay." Tiana grunted a weak response. He pulled her arm over his shoulder and helped her to her feet.

"Jade! Jade! Where are you? Jade!" He moved slowly to a clearing, supporting Tiana beside him. Before he could call again a voice responded.

"Cody!"

His head perked up. "Jade, I'm here! Follow my voice!" An instant later she came sprinting into view, running straight toward them. She was flailing her arms above her head.

"Run!"

The next instant thirty Garga warriors appeared in pursuit behind her. The combatants were armed with spears and simple bows readied with stone-tipped arrows. "Jade, run! Faster!" One of the Garga reared his head and released a guttural war cry. Suddenly the whole junkyard was echoing with cries from all directions.

They were surrounded.

"Faster, Jade!" Jade's pursuers closed in on her. One of them cocked his arm and launched his spear at her back.

Jade screamed.

20

The Price of Dishonor

"*Fraymour!*" The spear burst into white-hot flame and fell to the ground in a pile of dust. Cody glanced around and spotted the shell of a small aircraft protruding straight up from the ground. He thrust his hand toward the vehicle. *"Byrae!"* A heavy wind whooshed over his shoulders and caught the plane's propeller. The accelerating rotor produced a high-pitched whistle.

CRACK!

The airplane dislodged from the earth and came crashing down into the path of the charging Garga. The front line had no chance to slow before the whirling propeller appeared before them.

Jade continued her dash toward Cody and Tiana, slowing only to reach down and scoop up two fist-sized stones. Twisting her waist, she hurled the rocks at the still spinning propeller. The stones ricocheted off the twirling blades with cracks like gunfire. A Garga collapsed as one of the rocks struck his skull.

Cody heard the *hissing* flight of arrows. A group of Garga stood atop a junk hill, already refitting their bows. A dozen stone-head arrows arched through the air toward him. Cody threw his hands above his head.

"Spakious!"

Swallowed by air, the arrows disappeared just an inch from Cody's head. The sky rippled above the Garga archers—and their own arrows appeared from thin air, raining down on them. All but one of the warriors were turned into pincushions. The lone survivor sneered, bellowing a savage cry. Cody turned and whispered over his shoulder, *"Duomi."* The junk mound exploded, scattering debris and flinging the bowman twenty feet into the air.

More assailants continued to flood endlessly into view. Tiana had dropped to one knee, panting heavily. In her hand was a blood-stained piece of sharp debris. Three Garga lay dispatched at her feet but five more encircled her.

Before Cody could use the High Language to stop them a hand clamped over his mouth. He struggled to break free but more hands seized his limbs. It was no use. The fight was over.

The Garga escorted Jade and Tiana to Cody's side and pressed jagged rocks against their necks. A warrior with a fierce, dust-smeared face appeared before Cody.

"Book Keeper...infidel...*murderer!*" The Garga leader lifted a large cleaver and traced the tip down Cody's cheek and across his neck. Cody tried to suck in his throat, pulling his flesh away from the honed blade.

"I am not a murderer. We were only trying to defend ourselves."

"Silence!" snapped the Garga leader. "Several weeks ago you intruded upon our territory on the east side of the Caves of Revelation. You encountered a scouting party and you slaughtered them. Is this not true?"

"No! Well, yes, but that's not how it happened! We were..."

"Enough! The leader of that party was Yugar-Kir-Hugar—the Chief's son. You have dishonored the Great Garganton." The warriors began flinging angry words at Cody in an unrecognizable language. The Garga flashed his stone teeth, which had been filed to sharp points. "For your sins you must be brought to the Mouth of the Great Garganton—and cast inside."

21

Eaten Alive

Darkness.

The Garga had covered Cody's eyes and bound his wrists. Only the pinch of the spearhead prodding his back guided his blind march forward. He didn't know how long they had been gone, but the cramps clenching both legs suggested the journey had been lengthy. At long last, the procession came to a stop.

The Orb's light blinded him as his eye covering was removed. Towering mountains encircled a massive canyon. The flat ground, stretching as far as he could see, was riddled with holes the size of sewer openings. Hundreds of Garga moved in and out of the hollows.

"The Garga live underground?" asked Cody. His answer came in the form of the spear goading his back and urging him a step closer to the nearest tunnel. His foot slipped and dirt spilled into the pit. If it ever reached the bottom Cody heard no sound. "Where do these openings lead?"

"Everywhere," the Garga said. "If you know the correct entrance you will find the dwelling of the Garga." The spear nudged Cody again. His toes now hung over the ledge.

"Where do all the others lead?"

"Death."

Cody gulped. "Which of the two is *this* hole?" The Garga laughed. The act was mimicked by the others. Soon the shrill sound filled the whole valley. The Garga pushed the spear forward and sent Cody tumbling into the hole.

Cody pressed against the tunnel's wall to slow himself but found no grip on the rounded border. He picked up speed as the endless slide led him deeper and deeper into darkness.

CRASH!

His face slammed against solid ground. Cody stood slowly, spitting the dirt from his mouth. The slide had dropped him into a large domed cave. A low rumble provided just enough warning. Cody jumped out of the way as his Garga escort dropped from the holes, landing softly on their feet.

As soon as all the Garga had arrived the spearman began corralling Cody, Jade, and Tiana through the matrix of tunnels. They trekked for what seemed like hours. In the dark every passage looked identical, but the Garga navigated effortlessly as though by feel rather than sight. Cody quickly abandoned his futile efforts to memorize their path.

At last they emerged from the tunnel into an inner chamber similar to the first. A hundred torches lined the cavern filling it with a swaying, eerie light. Stone pillars jutted out around the perimeter of a large chasm in the center of the floor like sharp teeth. A wall of dense steam rose up from the pit and clustered against the cave's ceiling. The booming voice of their captor declared, "BEHOLD! *The Mouth of the Great Garganton!*"

Cody looked back toward the crowd behind him. Jade looked anxious, ready to follow his lead: fight or yield. Tiana, on the other hand, remained standing only by the strength of her captors. Her glazed eyes stared straight ahead. Her skin now matched the damp gray color of the stone walls. *She can't hold on much longer.*

Cody pleaded. "Please, my friend needs help. She will die unless we get her to Master Stalkton. *Please.*" The leader of the Garga party tilted his head. His expression was blank as he examined Cody. He turned to the others and spoke gibberish in a throaty voice.

Cody surveyed the twelve warriors. If he caught them by surprise he might be able to overtake them with the High Language. But if he gambled and lost he knew it would cost Jade and Tiana their lives.

Finishing their quick exchange, the Garga held out his hand. Cody grasped it hesitantly. "The Garga will listen." The warrior brushed the dust off Cody's shirt.

"Thank you," Cody said, the tension releasing from his shoulders.

"You can plead your petitions to the Great Garganton himself; may he be ever merciful." With a violent shove the Garga sent Cody screaming into the pit

22

Corn Pages

Eva Morningstar felt the chill enter through her fingers. It slowly spiraled up her slender arms and wrapped itself around her neck. The sensation tightened around her throat, its long fingers smothering her airflow. Her face turned a light shade of purple as the pressure against her neck bones increased tighter and tighter and tighter...

Air flooded into her lungs as the feeling vanished. Eva collapsed against the wall. The room was twirling in crazed circles. She stepped toward the window but staggered, disoriented by the wobbling chamber. She lost her balance and tumbled forward. Her neck twisted as her face collided hard against her bedpost.

She gazed up at the ceiling, lying helpless on the floor, too feeble to stand. She could feel a damp stream of blood running down her throbbing cheek toward her bottom lip. *"Thank the Orb,"* she whispered. These sensations were all she had. Her sand bowl, *The Speaking Sands*, had been silent for weeks. Every seizure meant one thing: *There's still hope.*

She pulled herself across the room and heaved her wardrobe-dresser aside. Her fingers traced along the stone wall then paused. Using the sleeve of her dress she brushed away the grime before removing a brick from the wall.

The brick thudded to the floor. Eva reached into the opening and retrieved a small box. She blew off the coating of dirt, coughing as the dust reached her nose, and opened the box. Inside was a lone object: a single, carefully folded sheet of paper.

There was no need to read the paper's finely printed inscription. She had memorized the words long ago. Across the top, in neat cursive writing, was the title: ***The Prophecy and the Search for The Earthly Trinity.***

The paper fluttered to the floor from her trembling hands. *It's almost time.*

23

The Mouth of the Great Garganton

Falling...

Cody plunged deeper and deeper through the haze. His arms flapped, desperately grappling for something to break the endless plunge. His fingers caught only air. On he fell, and fell, and fell. Without warning, the haze thinned and the bottom appeared.

Crash!

The wind squeezed from his lungs. Every inch of his body, from his forehead to his toes, ached. "Ouch." His groans echoed upward as he rubbed his hands across the sandy surface of the pit's bottom. The smog above obscured any view to the top. He wondered how far he had fallen. Even an expert climber, which he definitely was not, would be unable to scale these walls. *They've thrown me down here to die.* Cody turned to search for another way out—and encountered a giant.

The man was a walking mountain. His broad shoulders were as wide across as Cody was tall and his head looked as though a boulder had suddenly grown a face. He seemed to have more chins than Cody had fingers, with the largest drooping almost to his chest.

When the monstrosity of a man opened his mouth, Cody expected to hear a ferocious, booming roar. To his surprise, the enormous man's voice was rich and almost gentle. "Welcome, most noble Keeper of the Book and follower of the Orb."

The behemoth offered his hand, which was the size of Cody's head. Cody accepted it and was hauled to his feet. Cody looked at the giant in awe. "Who are you? Why are you in the Mouth of the Great Garganton?" The man dropped backwards to sit on the floor, causing the whole pit to rumble. Even sitting, the giant had to look down at him.

"Why am *I* in the mouth? A peculiar question, seeing as though I couldn't be anywhere else."

"Why is that?" Cody asked. The large man laughed so loud the whole pit reverberated with his voice.

"Because I *am* the Mouth of the Great Garganton! The Great One's appointed spokesperson. Or so they say. Guess *the Tongue* didn't have the ring to it." He chuckled again.

"You speak for their stone god? Wait a second..." Cody paused, letting the man's words settle in. "What do you mean, *or so they say*. You don't believe in the Garganton?"

"Ah, you mistake me, boy," he said, his laughter fading. "I worship the Great One for the mighty god he is. But I have enough sense to realize *I'm* not a god. We live in the Great One's mouth; if he were to truly speak, the sound of his voice would annihilate us! Makes it impractical for the two of us to share private conversations, wouldn't you say?"

"Then why do you keep pretending? Isn't it a lie?" Cody asked. The man shrugged his mammoth shoulders.

"I suppose for the same reason the Mouths before me did. The Garga need a leader. Better I lie knowing the truth than let another tell the truth while believing a lie. " Cody scratched his head.

"You're not what I expected. I thought you would be more...well..."

"Savage? Speak only in grunts? Snack on the still-beating hearts of children?" He grinned. "Who says I don't? Just be thankful I've already had my dinner." The giant held out his fist, opening and closing it like a beating heart. Cody didn't know whether to laugh or scream for help.

"They say the Garga are deadly warriors," Cody said finally.

"And so we are! But here's a riddle. We Garga have never stepped foot outside our allotted territory. So where do these tales of fearless combat come from?" Cody was stumped.

The giant provided the answer. "The Garga are attacked. Your General Levenworth has led raid after raid after raid on us. We've made him pay in blood, make no mistake, but over the centuries we've been pushed farther and farther into these mountains."

"But if you don't leave your territory, why would Atlantis attack you?"

The Mouth grunted in disgust. *"Fear.* We all fear what we don't understand. You can either try to understand the unknown or you can destroy it. The Garga used to be as plentiful as the skygems above; now fewer than ten thousand remain, and less than a third of those are warriors. *Hmph!* And they call *us* savages!"

Cody lowered his gaze. "I'm sorry. I didn't know." He looked up with fierce determination, a new idea forming in his mind. "Let's put old rivalries aside. I will speak to the Queen on your behalf. Atlantis *needs* you. If your warriors are as fierce as their reputation they could turn the tide of the war." The giant stood, dwarfing Cody once again.

"Ah, but you mistake me. I have no desire to turn the tide of any war."

Cody felt a chill overtake him. "But the Golden King will not stop. After he conquers Atlantis he *will* turn his gaze to the Garga."

"Perhaps...and when he does, the Garga will fight and the Great One will grant us a glorious victory. If the Garga and El Dorado are destined to fight, let Atlantis weaken the enemy first. When El Dorado is bloody and ragged of breath, the Garga will attack from behind and slaughter them."

Beads of sweat streamed down Cody's face. "You're making a big mistake."

"I confess it would not be the first, nor even the second." He made a loud, high pitched clicking sound. A moment later a rope appeared through the haze.

"I have enjoyed your company, young Book Keeper. You have given me many thoughts to chew on, and being a Mouth, I do so enjoy chewing things." He grinned. "Believe me when I say that I am greatly saddened that I now have to kill you."

24

Reality and Fiction

Jade's neck burned where the rope had rubbed the skin raw. She was bound to a stone pillar. All attempts to wiggle free had been abandoned hours earlier. She couldn't move an inch.

Her eyelids fluttered, sliding slowly over her pupils. The binding around her neck pinched again as her body went limp. Immediately, the sharp pain jerked her awake again. She was thankful for the rope. It kept her from sleeping. It kept her from dreaming.

The waking world offered little reprieve. The image of the half-full water glass in the bathroom haunted her in both dream and reality. Her thoughts drifted to Cody. She had been separated from him and Tiana after Cody was shoved into the steaming pit; she'd seen neither since. Even so, she refused to embrace the possibility that both were now dead leaving her, once again, alone.

Her eyelids fluttered.

She was tired.

So tired...

Jade opened her eyes. Glow-in-the-dark stars illuminated above her bed. She smiled. It had been so long since she'd last seen them. She tried to sit up in her bed but the covers hugged her tight, pinning her arms to her side. She pushed against them and with a final kick she knocked them off the bed and stood.

She looked out her window. Strangely, instead of Havenwood there was only an endless desert stretching out as far as she could see. *I'm dreaming.* She pinched her cheek. *Ouch!* The spot burned. She didn't wake. *I must be in a deep sleep.*

She opened her bedroom door and walked into the kitchen, where she saw her father marching down the hallway toward her. He smiled, ruffled her hair, and continued past her.

In the kitchen she was surprised once again. Cody sat at the table slurping a towering bowl of cereal. He looked up from his cereal just long enough to unleash a large belch. *Disgusting boy!*

Jade opened the fridge and found only fist-sized stones and half-full glasses of water. She grabbed the largest stone and slammed the fridge door. *Calm down, girl. It's just a dream...*

She looked at the rock in her hand. It was painted black with two red eyes. A chill spread through her. Cody's slurping continued behind her. The sound was grating. She had to make it stop. She had to make it *all* stop. She turned, raised the rock above her head, and swung it down toward Cody's skull.

Cody looked up at her, startled. "Jade?"

Instantly the kitchen swirled and faded away. She was now staring at Cody, who was bound to a stone pillar. She traced Cody's bulging eyes upward. In her hands lifted above her head was a large stone. It was smeared with blood.

She dropped it and backed away in horror. Cody continued to look at her as though she were a ghost.

"Jade? What are you doing? How in the world did you get free?" She looked around at the unfamiliar surroundings. She had no memory of freeing herself or locating Cody. Where were the warriors who had been guarding her? *The blood on the rock...*

She shuddered. "I...I don't know. I was sleeping and then..." *The half-full water glass.* Her entire body trembled. *What is going on with me?* "Never mind, it doesn't matter how I escaped, just that I'm free now. They threw you in that pit. I thought you were dead."

Cody scrunched his face, wiggling his nose. "No—not yet anyway. Luckily for me the Garga don't execute people at night. They don't want to disturb the Great Garganton's slumber. But unless we get out of here before the morning they'll make brain-stew with my skull."

Jade's heart skipped a beat at the comment. What would have happened had she brought the rock down on Cody's head? *No, it was just a dream...But the blood? And the water glass?*

She pushed the thoughts away. "Hold on, I'll cut you free. Where's Tiana? We need to..." Before she could finish a knife appeared at her throat.

A voice whispered into her ear. "If either of you makes a sound you're dead."

25
Sightless

The world was blurry shapes and rolling shadows. Tiana blinked rapidly, but the misty scene refused to focus. Her surroundings were completely void of sound.

She was abandoned and alone—or perhaps her hearing had been eradicated with her vision? One thing she *did* know: she was dying.

Her memory remained in only fragments. Whenever she tried to determine her whereabouts, the thoughts danced away just out of reach. She remembered a junkyard, and a hole in the ground.

Wait, was that a sound? She heard it again, this time louder. As the noise came closer it became clearer: people were shouting.

Tiana tugged at the rope binding her arms and ankles but they were too tight and she lacked the strength to fight. Although, with the absence of vision, she would be no better off free. The yelling grew louder. The sound was now loud enough to distinguish the words: "THE PRISONERS HAVE ESCAPED! KILL THE INFIDELS!"

She tugged at her bindings again. It was no use. *Run, Cody! Run, Jade! Orb protect you...* Screams became even louder, and then stopped. Although she could not see it, she felt a presence and realized that wherever she was— she was no longer alone.

Silhouettes floated toward her like spirits from another realm. They came close enough that Tiana could smell the perspiration on their skin. One of the shapes stretched toward her; she felt the touch of a hand against her cheek. Between slow breaths Tiana asked, "Cody? Jade? Is that you?"

The hand slapped her face. "You filthy little heathen," said a hard voice. Terror consumed her. She couldn't move a muscle. Bellows of "KILL THE INFIDELS!" had resumed in the distance. More blurry formations closed in toward her.

"Ahh!"

The wail was not hers. Other screams followed the first as the shadows fluttered in front of her. The frenzy lasted only a moment.

Then, once again, there was silence.

She felt another hand stroke her face. Tiana flinched, her terror returning. This time, however, the voice was familiar. "Ti, it's me." The sound of Cody's voice was the most beautiful thing she had ever heard. She was safe. Her eyes slid closed. *Everything is going to be okay.*

Slowly, the world drifted away and all was black.

26

Ugar-Rir-Nugar

Rantan detested crowds. His venomous eyes cut a path through the mob in front of him, sending civilian and refugee alike jumping aside. He scrunched his pointed nose. A foul odor hung over the city. The ceaseless infusion of refugees into the Capital and the inability of the bathhouses to accommodate them seemed to intensify the smell daily.

The Prince scowled. The legends always told of valiant warriors and noble deeds. Those tales neglected to mention the stench; the long nights studying food inventories; or the squabbles in the streets between tired, hungry, and frightened common-folk. *If El Dorado doesn't attack soon we'll defeat ourselves.*

Despite his brawn, General Levenworth matched Kantan's brisk pace step-for-step like an obedient dog. A loud gong droned over the city.

Dooong—Dooong—Dooooong.

As the last ring faded, the air was reclaimed by the regular clamor of the Mid-City. As had been the case for weeks, there was no kneeling, no chanting the Hymn of the Orb, no recognition of the gong whatsoever. The ringing was ignored like familiar, and unwanted, white noise.

"My lord, it is bad for morale when people see their leader refuse the Orb's call," Levenworth challenged. "If Silkian were to see you..." Kantan irritably waved off Levenworth before he could continue.

"The Hunter can take Silkian and his Enforcer goons for all I care. My father encouraged such nonsense and now he's dead. Look at the mess such actions have left me." Levenworth nodded and did not push the issue further.

Riiiiiiiiiiiip!

The air above their heads suddenly wrinkled. Levenworth grabbed Kantan and dove to the side. The next instant four bodies appeared through a portal in the air, crashing to the ground where the two men had just been standing.

The General was the first to his feet. At the sound of his bellowing voice, a dozen soldiers rushed in, encircling the four intruders. Kantan rejoined Levenworth's side. "What is the meaning of this ... wait... *Book Keeper*?"

Cody raised his arms. "Stop! It's just us!" Jade knelt beside him cradling the lifeless head of Tiana. Kantan spoke with stunned slowness, "This is a most welcome surprise. We thought you were dead." In all the time Cody had known the Prince he could not recall an expression on his face other than contempt. Yet now he saw a look of pure relief. "And who is this fourth member of your party?"

The solace vanished from Kantan's face as the stranger stood. The man was a Garga warrior. "Guards, seize him!"

The soldiers lowered their long halberds. In a flash the Garga produced two serrated stone knives. The guards hesitated, looking uneasily between the intruder and their General.

Levenworth pointed to the Garga. "Kill him!"

"Stop!" Cody jumped between the opposing fighters. "This man is with me." The furrows in Levenworth's brow increased by several deep ridges.

"What is the meaning of this, boy? You have brought a Garga into Atlantis? This has never happened before—and for good reason. No doubt this savage is an assassin."

"No. I vouch for him," said Cody. "He aided us. The Garga were going to sacrifice us but he came to our aid and freed us. He will *not* be harmed."

Kantan snickered. "This is not the first time you've vouched for a traitor. Tell me, where is Sir Randilin now?"

Cody's voice faltered. "Has he not returned? He must have been captured."

Kantan dismissed Cody with a wave of his hand. "Or he's sitting at the right hand of the Golden King laughing about how he played you like a fool. You've lost your right to testify for traitors. This man's fate is not yours to determine." The Prince shoved Cody aside. "Speak trespasser. Identify yourself."

The stranger locked eyes with Kantan. "I am the one called Ugar-Kir-Hugar."

General Levenworth drew his massive blade. "Kill this man immediately! That's an *order*!"

"Wait!" said Cody.

"Do you *know* him?" Levenworth's eyes narrowed and he squeezed the hilt of his sword until the color drained from his thick knuckles."Kir-Hugar...It means *son of Hugar*. This man is the son of the Mouth. You've brought the Garga Prince into our city!"

27

A Voluntary Prisoner

Ugar-Kir-Hugar grinned, revealing his stone teeth, as the outcry erupted around him. His body remained motionless, his eyes never leaving Levenworth.

Kantan raised his hand and the commotion died instantly. "Son of Hugar, you betrayed *your* people to rescue *our* Book Keeper? The only thing I trust less than a Garga is a Garga traitor. As such, I am inclined to let Levenworth remove your head. So believe me when I say I won't ask twice—*why*?"

Before anyone could react, Kir-Hugar tossed his daggers into the air. Catching them by the blades he flung them forward. *Thud. Thud.* The knives buried to the hilt on both sides of Levenworth's feet. "I have come to surrender."

Levenworth's voice faltered from its usual calm. "And why would you want to do that?"

The Garga responded without hesitation. "To make amends for the sins of my people, of course." Kantan had not moved. He continued to scrutinize the enemy prince.

The crowd waited patiently as Kantan performed his silent examination. Kir-Hugar's grin did not waver.

Kantan spoke at last. "You will be escorted to the Outer-City dungeons. I will not allow a Garga in the Inner-City, even as a prisoner. There you will stay until this war has ended. When that time comes, I will grant you the privilege of making amends by sending you to the gallows."

Cody started to object on behalf of his rescuer, but the Garga prince offered a deep bow. "You are most gracious." He presented his wrists to Levenworth. "Will you be binding them? I would not wish to frighten your civilians on my way to the dungeons."

Levenworth frowned. "Is this all a joke to you?"

"There is nothing funny about repentance, noble General." Despite his words, amusement colored his voice. Levenworth motioned to the guards who stepped forward and bound the prisoner's wrists.

As Kir-Hugar was led away he whispered into Cody's ear.

"Thank you."

28
Unexpected Reunions

Cody watched as Tiana was shuffled away toward the hospital, praying it wouldn't be too late. The escort disappeared into the festering mob that now encircled them. Word of their return had spread like wildfire through the city. The people did not look particularly happy to see him.

"Your secret departure to El Dorado was not well received," offered Kantan by way of explanation.

"Just wait until the Golden King comes knocking. They'll change their tune quick enough. People only hate something until they need it. You'll be a hero again in no time," said Levenworth.

Was I ever a hero? Cody wanted to ask. His escorts cut a path through the crowd as Cody followed the group toward the Inner-City. In every direction tattered shelters had been erected, congesting the streets. The area where the marketplace had once been was now a substantial shantytown.

Cody felt a strange sensation. It was soothing and familiar. He pushed his way through the throng toward the source of the feeling. He found Eva standing at the fringe of the assembly. Cody's face lit up. She curtsied and mouthed, "Hail!"

Cody returned a silent "hail" before throwing his arms around the young princess. "Eva, it's so good to see you again! I'm so sorry I stopped writing. I lost my half of *The Speaking Sands* when we escaped El Dorado."

The Princess' face looked more haggard than the last time he had seen her, but her tender smile was as comforting as always. "My heart is warmed to see you as well."

Eva startled Cody by pulling him into another quick hug. She pressed her face to his ear and whispered, "We need to talk...like we did the first time." She released him and vanished back into the crowd.

Cody watched her disappear into the multitude. Her message could not have been clearer. *Like we did the first time.* The first time he had talked with Eva she had warned him of betrayal.

A moment later Kantan and Levenworth were behind him. "Let's go, Book Keeper." As Cody followed, he peeked behind. Eva was standing on a ledge, gazing over the crowd at him. She looked terrified.

The sickly boy looked as though he had died, only to have the grave spit him back out as unsavory. His eyes were closed as he lay on the bed in the overcrowded infirmary, but his chest rose and fell steadily. That was all that mattered to Cody.

Xerx was alive.

The young monk's light hair now sported a gray chunk in the front, but otherwise he appeared in fair condition. His gurney was positioned beside Tiana's.

Cody felt a yank on his sleeve. It came from a stranger lying on the bed to the other side of Xerx. Cody pretended not to notice. The last thing he wanted was to hear another civilian's displeasure toward his departure. He felt another tug. Taking a deep breath, Cody turned around. "Do you *need* something? I really must be... "

His words jammed in his throat as he stared into the most frightening face he had ever seen. The woman was utterly repulsive. Her skin was grainy, and grotesque boils spotted her brow and chin. Skeletally thin, her flesh was stretched so tightly that every bone was clearly visible.

The woman's swollen lip moved into what Cody took to be a smile and her voice rasped, "I never thought I'd see you again."

Her words startled Cody. "I'm sorry, have we met?" When the woman responded her words were coated in sorrow. "Am I really so monstrous that you cannot even recognize me?" Cody lowered his eyes to look into hers for the first time. They were as desolate as her gaunt body.

There was something strangely familiar about the disfigured lady. Then it hit him. He covered his mouth in shock. The woman was Queen Cia.

29

Dark Clouds

Cody wanted to look away from the repulsive face but couldn't. The Queen's lifeless stare seemed to hold him in place. Suddenly her eyes turned white, her pupils rolling to the back of her head. She gasped for air. Then, with a violent cough, she collapsed back against the bed. She was breathing, but her body had gone limp.

Cody backed away from the bed in horror. Two firm hands gripped him. Cody yelped and leapt three feet into the air. The man behind him chuckled. "If ever you tire of being a Book Keeper you have a future in tournament high-jumping." Cody recognized the voice instantly.

"Dace!" He spun around and flung himself at the Captain. "It's like my greatest dream come true to see you again!"

Dace wiggled free from the tackle and ran his fingers through his wavy black hair.

"This isn't the first time someone's confessed that seeing me was their greatest dream come true. Although it's usually said by young, attractive maidens." He winked. "It cheers me to see you again as well."

Dace's gaze shifted over Cody's shoulder to the unconscious Queen and his playful smirk vanished. Cody asked, "What in the world happened to her?"

Dace shook his head. "I don't know. Princess Eva found her lying amidst a pool of blood in the middle of the Queen's chamber. Fortunately Eva found her soon enough that Master Stalkton was able to save her life."

"But what *happened* to her? I didn't even recognize her. She used to be so beautiful." Cody lowered his voice. "Now she's...well, *ugly*." Dace raised an eyebrow at the comment.

"Trust me, no one in Atlantis knows pretty girls as well as I do. So take my word: not all beauty is found in powdered cheeks and pretty dresses. It seems the assassin's knife was poisoned with venom unknown in Under-Earth. Stalkton contained the poison's spread but the damage had already been done. She'll live; but she'll never heal."

Cody had never felt much fondness for Cia, yet he couldn't help but feel deep pity for her now. *No one should suffer a fate like this.* He shivered. "How did *you* manage to escape El Dorado?"

Dace wrapped his arm around Cody's shoulder and led him from the infirmary. "Would you believe that I challenged the enemy to single combat, defeated their entire army one-by-one, and then rode home on the back of the Hunter with a champion's spoil?" When Cody only grinned Dace's face fell. "I'm hurt by your lack of faith!"

As the two friends made their way toward the Outer-City, Dace recapped the Company's escape from the Golden City, Randilin's disappearance, Chazic's sacrifice, Tat's discovery that his wife may still live in captivity, and lastly how Xerx had managed to create an escape portal, almost killing himself in the process, just in time for the remaining Company to flee El Dorado.

Reaching the Outer-Wall they climbed the steep staircase. Two familiar soldiers greeted them at the top. "Wolfrick! Sheets! I assumed you were both dead!" The two guards laughed, slapping Cody on the back.

"What, and let you steal all the battle glory? Never!" said Sheets.

Wolfrick nodded, "Aye, ol' Nocsic, the Orb rest his soul, sent us back with a final report the day Flore Gub fell. Figured if we were to die defending a doomed city it might as well be Atlantis, with my axe in one hand and a mug of Yanci's finest ale in the other!"

A distant boom of thunder interrupted their exchange. Cody looked out from the forty-foot wall across the vastness of the wasteland. Dark clouds blotted out the horizon, illuminated by sprawling tentacles of lightning.

"The Golden King sends clouds with his armies to demoralize us," Dace said. Another lightning flash ignited the sky. The unstoppable armies of El Dorado were on the march.

Cody gulped. "It's working."

30

An Inadequate Hero

The High Priest Lamgorious Stalkton was naked. The light gleamed so brightly off his pale, and exceptionally bare, backside that Cody had to look away. Not that he resisted, of course.

"Oh, good heavens, Master! Where are your clothes!?"

Stalkton turned and his face lit up. "Great gobs of golly! My apprentice has returned at last!" He twirled his cart and propelled himself toward Cody. "I have missed you more than I ever thought I would!" He scratched his chin. "Although, perhaps that is because I didn't anticipate missing you at all. It was actually quite relieving that day you left. I threw myself a glorious party to celebrate and..."

Cody cleared his throat, bringing Stalkton's attention back to him. "Oh, right. Welcome back!"

Cody cringed as the pale, and still disturbingly fleshy, priest pulled him into a tight, lingering embrace. When finally released, Cody quickly helped the old priest dress. When they finished, Stalkton examined his new robe suspiciously, the way a barbarian war chief might examine a fine china teacup.

At last he looked up with a distasteful expression. "Have you come to tell me about your visit to the Golden King?" Cody took a deep breath, swallowing both oxygen and pride.

"Master, I wasn't powerful enough. He was just toying with me. I gave everything I had and it wasn't nearly enough."

"I tried to warn you," the priest said. "He's the most powerful man in the world and you are well...*not*. Quite frankly, I was betting that you wouldn't return alive. Literally. I lost my prized recipe for earthworm jelly on that miscalculation." Cody pretended not to hear the last bit.

"How can I defeat the Golden King? He will reach Atlantis in a week. There isn't enough time to train with the High Language to match him or even be close to what is required. When I face him again he will kill me."

Stalkton nodded matter-of-factly. "Indeed. Most likely a prolonged, excruciating death. That tends to be his preference." Cody had been hoping for a different response.

"Master! I'm doomed then."

Stalkton nodded again. "Oh, most definitely."

Before Cody could pout further, Stalkton added, "Unless you start using that tiny gray blob inside your skull." The priest bopped himself on the head to clarify his point.

Cody stared wide-eyed at the priest in silent confusion. Stalkton proceeded to pound himself on the head several more times to drive his point home.

"I *get it*, Master! You want me to use my brain. But I still don't understand how my brain will defeat the Golden King."

Stalkton cleared his throat. "Let me tell you the tale of the seven-legged spider and the horse who forgot his name. Once upon a time..." He stopped and scrunched his nose. "Wait...that's the wrong story. This story is about the mighty warrior and the shrewd librarian." Stalkton whacked himself on the head once again for good measure, and then began.

"Once there was a Librarian and a Warrior. The Librarian was short of stature while the Warrior was of legendary size and had never been bested in combat. The Warrior became increasingly arrogant of his invincibility. He would bully anyone who crossed his path until they bowed down and honored him. While passing through a small town the Warrior demanded all inhabitants worship him by offering all their possessions. Everyone in the town reluctantly agreed—except for the Librarian."

"The Librarian said he would happily hand over his possessions to the mightiest warrior in the land. But, having read so many books about legendary warriors, how could he know *this* was truly the mightiest of them all?"

"The Warrior was enraged and boasted that he could *prove* he was the mightiest. The Librarian suggested that if he were really as mighty as he claimed, he could lift the heaviest book in the library without breaking a sweat. The Warrior laughed. He found the thickest book in the library and tossed into the air like a feather, so high that it didn't land again for three days."

"The Librarian was impressed, but pointed out that just a single book was not conclusive proof that he was *really* the mightiest warrior. He said a true warrior could lift several *stacks* of books without breaking a sweat. The Warrior laughed. He found the three largest stacks of books and began juggling them effortlessly. Then he tossed them into the air like a feather, so high that they didn't land again until the next day."

"The Librarian was very impressed, but pointed out that even three stacks of books were not conclusive proof that he was *truly* a mighty warrior. He said a true warrior could lift every book in the *entire library* without breaking a sweat. The Warrior laughed. He reached down, pulled the library from the earth, and lifted it above his head effortlessly. Then he tossed the library into the air like a feather. However, the library didn't go very high. It landed on top of the Warrior and killed him."

Cody squeezed his lips together to prevent a laugh from exiting. The story was one of the most ridiculous things he had ever heard. "So I'm supposed to defeat the Golden King by dropping books on him? Maybe the seven-legged spider will help?"

The look of disappointment on Stalkton's face made Cody wish he could retract his words and melt into a puddle. The pale priest shook his head. "Apart from my riveting narration, there is a point to the story. The moral is this: Only a fool fights his enemy in the arena and manner of his enemy's choosing. You will never be as powerful as the Golden King with the High Language, so you'd be a fool to fight him with it. Use *your* strengths and use the Golden

King's pride against him and the arrogant King will defeat himself."

Cody felt something he had not sensed in weeks. *Confidence.* Hope began to emerge cautiously from the dark depths he had banished it to for the last few weeks. Maybe he *did* have a chance. Maybe he *could* defeat the Golden King. "Do you really believe that, Master?"

Stalkton burst into laughter. "Golly! Absolutely not. But you have to admit, it was a pretty good pep-talk, wasn't it?" Cody sighed, letting the hope retreat to its hiding place. *At least I didn't have to hear about the horse who forgot his name...*

31

Through the Heat

A flash of lightning ignited the sky as angry clouds loomed overhead. The expanse of smoldering waste-land stretched in all directions as far as even the keenest eye could see. Intense heat vapors rose from the scorched, red soil of the Fiery Plains. The temperature was unbearable. Randilin Stormberger ran his stubby fingers through the sticky knots in his hair.

"Bloody heat." He punctuated the grouse with a few of his favorite curses before turning away from the burning landscape. The sight behind him was no more pleasant: the expansive El Doridian war camp. The gold platelet armor fused into the soldiers' skin was glowing orange. "Bloody armies," Randilin grumbled. The rising heat had put the whole camp in a bitter mood—he *most* of all.

A monstrous shadow crept over him like a spider. Randilin looked up at El Dorado's High General. As always, the titan was covered head-to-toe in his polished, midnight black armor. Only his mouth remained exposed. *For all the bloody good it does him!*

The General was known by many names: *The Impaler*, The Spider-General, or simply *The Spider*. Randilin was one of the few who knew him by an older name; a forgotten name—Kael the Invincible. As Randilin looked at the monstrous specimen he remembered why such a name was well-earned.

The General thrust a piece of parchment into the dwarf's hand then departed without a word. Randilin skimmed the letter. *You've got to be bloody kidding.* Somehow things had managed to get even worse. Randilin called to the nearest gilded soldier. "Prepare the ruddy men, Spider-Head says we're marching out." The soldier frowned.

"With all due respect, *little man*, despite what the Lord of Lights may think of you, you have no rank out here to issue orders, nor do you have any love among these men. Why should we listen to a traitor?"

"Because I *am* a traitor. Or is your brain made of the same tin as your armor? I have no love among *any* men. That makes me a very dangerous individual." Randilin flashed an ugly grin. The soldier fidgeted.

"I see, Sir Randilin. I will try to remember."

"Ruddy right you will! Don't get me wrong; I'd be as far from this blasted place as possible if it were up to me. If ol' Tin-Man had let his General keep his tongue I *would* be. I'm just here to speak for the General, nothing more."

The soldier scanned left and right to confirm The Spider-General was gone, then leaned forward. "Why *did* the Glorious One remove *The Impaler's* tongue?" Randilin grabbed him by the collar and pulled his face close.

"Because words are more dangerous than muscles. Ol' Kael was once the mightiest warrior among the Alac-icacs tribe. Aye, and firstborn heir to his namesake, the bloody Chief. His father had a problematic, unquenchable appetite for death. When enemies weren't around, his own people would suffice to be beheaded or gutted." Randilin sliced his hand across the soldier's belly, causing him to cry out.

"Eventually the tribe became weary of their leader's vicious hobby. The Butcher Chief was overthrown and eviscerated by his own advisor—Uscana. Realizing the former chief's heir, Kael, posed a threat, Uscana ordered him executed as well. It was Uscana's youngest son, known now as the Golden bloody King, who intervened, suggesting that they wished only to remove possible uproar, not lose their champion warrior. Uscana agreed. In his *grace* Uscana amended his order and allowed his son to remove only Kael's tongue. Bloody hard to lead a revolt if you can't speak."

Randilin shoved the conscript away. "What the ruddy Lord of Tin has done to him *since* that day is a tale too terrifying for a snot-nosed boy like you. So be gone. Rouse the men. Tell them we march in an hour. We're going *through* the Fiery Plaines."

"Surely you jest! That's madness! We cannot withstand such heat. Tell the General we refuse."

Randilin shrugged. "Why don't you tell him yourself?"

The soldier turned to find the immense frame of The Spider-General towering over him. Despite being a grown man, the soldier's head only reached his superior's chest.

"Lord General... "

The General grabbed the subordinate by the neck and lifted him off the ground so his feet dangled helplessly. *The Impaler* leaned in and opened his mouth. The soldier's face went white as the exposed mouth of The Spider-General contorted and expanded—and two claw-like pincers emerged.

"What in the world *are* you...?" The pincers tapped together as they stretched toward the victim's face.

The anguished screams could be heard throughout the entire camp.

32

Strategy and Smiles

The boisterous discussion died instantly as Cody entered the room. Seated around the circular table were Kantan, Levenworth, Silkian, Dace, Tat, and a well-postured man with a thick mustache dangling past his chin. Cody guessed the stranger to be the new Captain of the Mid-City Guard following Captain Eagleton's terrible death by *The Impaler*.

Every eye fixed straight on Cody as he took a seat beside Dace. Directly across from him, pale-faced Sli Silkian peered at him while drumming his long, bony fingers together. Cody looked away but could still feel the AREA leader's slimy gaze as the interrupted debate resumed.

"I say let them come," boasted the mustached stranger. "Atlantis has walls forty feet high, sixteen feet thick with just one diagonal gate. *Ha!* Let us not forget that a moat, fifteen feet wide with a thirty-foot drop encircles the entire wall. Should the dolts attempt to cross, we will baptize them with boiling tar from the thirty towers. *Ha!* Let the tin brains crash against the wall. Let them die score by score! *Ha!*" He unsheathed his dagger and slammed it into the table to add an exclamation mark to his challenge.

An unexpected, stern voice sounded from the doorway. "Captain Yaru, you are a juvenile fool whose knowledge of war ends at playing with wooden toy swords." The Captain's face flushed bright red and he yanked on his mustache. All eyes turned to the doorway. In the entrance stood Queen Cia.

Kantan stood. "Dear sister, we were not expecting the honor of your presence. You should be resting."

Cia waved a hand to silence him. "The enemy has stolen my father and my beauty. I will not lie around in self-pity and let them steal my city as well. The next time I rest I will be using the Golden King's head to prop up my unbalanced bed." She sat at the head of the table, sizing up the attendants, silently daring anyone to question her. None did.

Captain Yaru was still red-faced from the slight. "My Queen, I was just saying..."

Cia turned away from him. "I have already heard more from you than I care to. I require wisdom to cleanse your stupidity from my palate. General Levenworth, what have you to say?"

Levenworth stood. "I admire Captain Yaru's confidence, but only a fool lets himself be blinded by pride. Atlantis has been infiltrated once before. We must be aptly prepared if we wish to prevent the same outcome as the First Great War."

"Will we fill the moat with water?" Cody suggested, trying to contribute. He noticed several others nod in affirmation of his idea. Cody sat up straighter, rather pleased with himself. Levenworth shook his head.

"No. A water-filled moat is a romanticized notion. Water allows the enemy to counter with pre-constructed rafts and logs; an empty pit requires our enemy to undertake the laborious task of filling it with dirt while being barraged by our archers. Furthermore, it will not take long for the moat to become a rank cesspool. The moat will be filled with sharpened poles instead."

Cody's shoulders slouched as he sank back into his chair. Apparently reading *King Arthur and His Knights* had not prepared him to plan against a castle siege.

"What do you propose, General?" Cia's tone signaled that further suggestions by others were unwelcome. Levenworth stroked his thick beard.

"As impregnable as the Outer-Wall would seem, our best defensive position lies with the Second Wall. The Outer-Wall is too expansive to adequately fortify with the soldiers we have available. We will be spread too thin. Against the Second Wall the enemy loses the advantage of their siege engines. We must resist as long as possible, but the Outer-Wall, however strong, *will* fall. We must be prepared when it does."

Cia looked around the table, but no one spoke. The incident with Cody had discouraged any from daring to challenge the legendary tactician's strategy. "My father never doubted you, General. There was no one in Atlantis he trusted more. I give you my father's trust. How then shall we prepare to keep the Second Wall?"

Levenworth turned to Dace, the General's face blank as a statue. "We tear down and burn everything in the Outer-City district."

Dace jumped to his feet. "We can't! What of the people living there? The refugees? My soldiers? The beggars? You speak as though we are discussing colored chips on your war map."

"Thatched roofs can be re-thatched and walls rebuilt," Levenworth responded firmly. "Even the scum-hive you call Yanci's Pub can be rebuilt. When the enemy breeches the First Wall it will raze the district to the ground without mercy. If it must burn, let it be to our advantage. With the buildings demolished the enemy will have no cover..."

"Creating a killing pit." Dace finished, plopping back into his chair.

"Precisely," said Levenworth. "Newly appointed *Captain* Shunbickle has been given command over the archer regiments. When the enemy pours into the killing pit, our bowmen will rain arrows down from atop the Second Wall, killing them by the scores."

The pain on Dace's face was great. "It is a sound strategy. I request permission to tell the people and personally oversee the demolition. They are my people; it should come from my mouth."

"Permission granted." Levenworth placed a map of the city onto the table. "Furthermore..."

For the next several hours the Council plotted various defensive strategies for withdrawing between walls, resisting catapult fire, and establishing troop and reserve rotations.

The newfound ability for the enemy's Dark-Wielders to create wormholes presented a major obstacle. It was determined, as Tat first suggested, that the contents of every building, especially the Royal Palace, were to be rearranged daily and the guards within the city doubled so that no location could be recalled from memory, and thus no portals created behind the walls.

As the discussion dragged on, Cody found himself tuning out. Instead, his attention turned to the AREA leader. Throughout the meeting Silkian had not uttered a single word. His eerie stare had remained transfixed on Cody. As Cody locked eyes with the man, Silkian's thin, worm-like lips rose into the slightest of smiles.

Cody jerked his head away. Eva's warning came back to him. *Atlantis is not safe.* The moment the Council dismissed, Cody jumped and hurried toward the exit. He could feel Silkian's sinister gaze on his back the entire way. Cody could not shake the troubling thought: all the defensive strategies in the world might protect them against the enemies outside the walls—but what about the enemies *inside*?

33

Bad Dreams

The ground grew smaller and smaller as Jade was raised into the air. She grabbed the railings for support as the rickety elevator continued its slow ascent. Beyond the city's walls the violent storm now wholly blotted out the mountain backdrop. *It's spreading fast.*

As the elevator rattled to a halt Jade stepped off and scurried across the balcony toward the Monastery. She stepped hesitantly through the door. "Hello? Anybody here?" There was no response, other than her own voice echoing in the large, oval chamber.

She ventured deeper inside where cobwebs and dust had laid claim to the dingy, abandoned monastery. *"Hello?"* Her voice became increasingly timid with each shout.

Creak. Creak. Creak.

Jade twirled around. The hallways were empty behind her. The squeaking continued. The noise seemed to come from nowhere and everywhere all at once. *"Is anyone there?"* Her voice was a whisper. Abruptly the noise stopped, leaving only the sound of her uneasy breathing. A ghostly white hand reached from behind and grabbed her.

Jade screamed and spun around—and then screamed even louder. The man behind her was a monster. His skin was colorless from forehead to toe; at least it would have been if the man *had* any toes. His legs ended in two rounded stumps above where his knees should have been. A black scar sliced diagonally across his face.

The terrifying specter sat in a wheeled-cart. He propelled himself forward with a long oar-like stick. "I always knew you'd show up one day, you two-timing, false-faced scoundrel!" His seething voice was as creaky as the wheels of his cart.

Jade's gaped at him. "Master Stalkton? Is that *you*? Wait—why would you call me a scoundrel?" The man launched himself toward her, flailing his arms as though swimming through the air.

"You lost that spider-racing bet fair and square, Gelph! I may be losing my mind, but don't think I've forgotten. You owe me a dozen rock cakes, extra burnt, just as we promised!" He paused, scratching his pointy chin. "Or did *I* lose? I'm sorry, am *I* the scoundrel? Wait...am I *Gelph*?! I can't remember anything these days!" He continued muttering to himself, listing all the things he had recently forgotten. The words *bathing* and *underpants* surfaced. Jade was awestruck. *Cody wasn't joking, this guy is bonkers!*

"Wise Sir, I'm afraid I don't know if you're a scoundrel or not. My name is Jade. I'm Cody's friend from Upper-Earth." Stalkton's face lit up like a Christmas tree, starting at his mouth and moving up to his eyebrows.

"You're a girl?" The albino combed his bleach-white hair behind his ears. "Two female visitors in *one* day! Golly, that hasn't happened to me in over a hundred years. Not since my mother brought the nurse to examine the mountainous wart forming on my..."

"Pardon me, Sir," Jade interrupted. "You've had another visitor today?" On cue, Jade heard quiet footsteps approach and Princess Eva appeared from the corridor. She looked weary and a dark purple bruise covered her lower face. At the sight of Jade, the young princess quickly rolled up the torn piece of paper in her hands and shoved it into her pocket.

"Oh, my gosh. Are you okay, Princess?"

Eva gave a weak smile. "The sight of you well and returned to Atlantis warms my heart, Lady Jade." She gently took Jade's hand in both of hers. "Don't forget who you are." Without another word she was gone before Jade could call after her to ask what she meant.

Behind her the albino was continuing his ramble. "Was it spider-racing or were *we* racing?" His self-contained debate had become heated, with several insults being volleyed back and forth. Jade wondered how long it would take him to realize she was gone if she left. He seemed to be a man well accustomed to talking with himself. But crazy or not, he was the one man who might have the answers she needed.

"Master Stalkton, I need your help." The old priest looked up.

"*Told you so,*" he muttered to himself, apparently settling the debate of his identity. "Your friend Cody always *acts*; you are a wise girl to come with questions and not answers. It's rather refreshing not to have such a dim-witted pupil for once. What troubles you, dear child?"

Jade took a deep breath before answering.

"Dreams."

34

A Bad Idea

Something had died behind Dace's glassy eyes as they stared ahead. His finger mindlessly traced the rim of his untouched mug. Cody's heart broke for the youthful Captain. The decision to burn down the Outer-City had been devastating for him.

Tat, Wolfrick, and Sheets rounded out the table in the corner of Yanci's Pub. The usual rambunctious activity of the tavern had been subdued by the hard news. The others dropped equally void stares at the drinks before them.

Finally Wolfrick grunted. "Well...suit yourselves, lads." He scooped the mugs to himself and set to the solemn task of downing them.

Dace spoke without lifting his eyes. "With the number of refugees arriving each day our food supply won't hold long. If the siege stretches out as long as Levenworth foresees, we'll all die from starvation rather than steel. Before the battle begins, a third of our city will be demolished. We all know that El Dorado has infiltrated our city. We have a mole. They know our every plan. Yet, all we can do is sit, wait, and burn our own city to the ground."

Tat was twirling an arrowhead across his knuckles. "Perhaps there's another way." His voice dripped with mischief. Even Wolfrick lowered his ale to listen. Tat scanned his companions. "Perhaps it's time to fight fire with fire." All five heads leaned in. "If they can have moles why can't we? I say we infiltrate *their* war camp."

"I'M IN!" shouted Wolfrick gleefully, slamming his mug on the table.

Dace grabbed the soldier's braided beard and pulled him back into the huddle. "Don't be foolish. It's far too risky. If we were discovered, our capture would only provide the enemy with valuable hostages."

Tat shrugged. "Then we make sure we're not discovered. Where's the *old Dace* I heard so many tales about back in Flore Gub? *Captain Rule-Breaker* is what they used to call you out on the Borderlands. You're starting to sound like the General."

Dace grinned slightly, but shook his head. "Your taunts are transparent. I know you desire to find your wife, Rali. I don't blame you for that; but trying to locate one woman amidst two hundred and fifty thousand soldiers, plus half that again in camp followers and cooks, is madness."

"What about Chazic? Surely the noble Dace Ringstar has had sleepless nights over the sacrifice of a holy man?"

"Chazic did his duty so that we could live long enough to do ours," responded Dace firmly; however, his tone seemed to confirm that Tat's taunt had hit the mark.

"Isn't it our *duty* to protect our city in any way possible? Like you said, finding one person among such a force is a near impossible task. We should slip in, learn all we can about the enemy's plans, and return to Atlantis. No one will be the wiser." A long silence ensued.

Then the slight hint of a grin appeared on Dace's face. "I'm in."

"I'm *still* in," said Wolfrick.

"I'm in," echoed Sheets.

"I'm in, too," said Cody, but Dace shook his head.

"Out of the question. That is where I draw the line. You are not coming, Cody. We've nearly lost you already. Atlantis *needs* its Book Keeper. Your place is here."

"But *you* will need me," Cody pleaded. "Your best chance of sneaking in and out is with a portal. The only three people in Atlantis strong enough to create wormholes with the High Language are Xerx, Master Stalkton, and me. One's in a hospital bed and the other has no legs. Face it. I'm your only choice. I'm coming."

Tat nodded. "The boy is right."

Dace grimaced. "I don't like it, but you're right. You can come." Before Cody could celebrate, Dace added, "But you leave the Book here."

"No! I can't!" The Book was a part of him. Dace might as well have asked him to leave his left foot behind. The leather-bound tome was all that separated Cody the powerful Book Keeper from Cody the ordinary nobody. "I *need* the Book."

Dace wouldn't budge.

"Either the Book stays or you do. I will not be the one responsible for handing our enemy *The Code* on the eve of battle." It took every ounce of his willpower for Cody to nod in agreement, unable to muster the words aloud.

Dace turned to the others. "Sheets, you will stay behind. You will select four of your most trusted men. Choose *only* from the Outer-City Guard. I don't trust anybody else. The five of you will keep the Book hidden here in Yanci's Pub. We will not speak of it; not even amongst ourselves. Understood?" Mutters of affirmation rounded the table. Dace stood.

"We leave at nightfall."

35

The Infirmary

The light pierced through her pupils and pounded against her brain. Her thoughts were a scrambled, incoherent mess. She felt as though she had been asleep for weeks. *Where am I?*

Tiana pushed herself to sit up, her muscles as stiff as wooden planks. The first sight she saw was the wide, anxious eyes of Xerx. He was staring at her so intensely she thought his head would burst. His lips quivered, teasing a myriad of unspoken sentences. It was a pitiful sight. Tiana decided to put the young monk out of his misery.

"So I guess I didn't die?" Her words served to remove the invisible cork plugging his mouth. Xerx began vomiting out each of the foreshadowed sentences. Amidst the verbal barrage Tiana identified *hospital, worried sick*, something about Master Stalkton, and a sappy sentiment about "willing her back to health."

"*Whoa*, boy, rein in the horses. Can't a girl come back from the dead in peace?" She surveyed the room, hoping for intervention, but found, to her displeasure, that she and Xerx were the only two in the room. *Just my luck.*

"Master-Stalkton-was-able-to-heal-your-infection-in-time." Xerx took a deep breath. "Had-you-been-even-a-few-hours-later-it-would-have-been-too-late. I'm-supposed-to-make-sure-you-rest," he finished, speaking in double time.

"Slow down! Are you my caretaker now?" Xerx nodded eagerly, missing the sarcasm in her voice.

He stopped, blushing as he realized her intent. "By Master Stalkton's orders, of course." His face was now so red Tiana wondered if she could chop it off and pawn it as a ruby. *Hmm, what would I do about the eyes and mouth, though?*

Xerx continued to bumble, each word more flustered than the one before. "You've been in a coma for several days now. I've been watching you the whole time."

Well, that's downright creepy, Tiana thought, but she forced herself to say, "Thank you." If his face had beamed any brighter they would have to build another Sanctuary of the Orb around his head.

A rush of nausea overtook her and the room seemed to spin around her. She laid her head back on the pillow. The last sight she saw was Xerx's concerned eyes.

Xerx watched as Tiana slept peacefully. He cradled her limp hand in both of his own. He dared not do so while she was awake, but her low, steady breathing suggested it was safe now. He felt his own eyes weighing heavy.

By all accounts he should still be in a hospital bed as well. He had used several High Language words to skew the healers' tests and convince them he was well. He didn't want any healers focusing on him instead of Tiana. Besides, he was already feeling much better. The news that Tiana had returned to Atlantis and was alive had given him a boost.

He reached into his robe and retrieved a faded blue stone. His fist closed tightly around it. Armies were preparing for war and death all around him, but for at least a moment Xerx allowed himself to feel truly happy.

He remained at her bedside for several more hours, until his own eyelids began to sag. He wavered briefly before tumbling forward, his face buried against Tiana's shoulder.

In the secret of the shadows, two eyes watched as the young boy and girl slept soundly. All day he had waited as people entered and exited the infirmary, oblivious to his presence. He had remained absolutely still. However, while the others came and went, the devoted boy had not left the girl's bedside. Eventually the boy would leave. It was inevitable. When that moment came, the observer would make his move. Until then he would be patient.

Waiting...

Watching...

36

Warnings

Eva Morningstar was sitting alone on her bed looking down at a single, crumpled piece of paper when Cody entered.

"Welcome," she said, slipping the piece of paper into her dress.

Cody stepped inside. "You said we needed to talk?"

Eva smiled, and motioned to the door. "What I have to tell you is best not heard by wandering ears."

Cody took the meaning and pulled the door closed behind him "It's so good to see you again, Eva. I have missed your company." His eyes explored the room. Reflecting its occupant, the room was startlingly simplistic. The room felt more like a dungeon cell than a princess' royal chamber.

He spotted Eva's half of *The Speaking Sands* beside her bed. His eyes moved to the window. Startled, he saw subtle traces of dried blood staining the window ledge. "What happened? Are you okay?"

"A story for another time," she said. "Please, sit." She motioned her hand to a chair and Cody complied.

"You said I was in danger."

"We are *all* in danger. However, it is not *you* of whom I speak."

"Then who?"

"The ones closest to you." The words hit Cody like an avalanche.

"Excuse me...what did you say?" The words in his nightmares came back to him: *The one closest to you must pay that price.*

"There is no redemption without sacrifice. No victory without bloodshed."

Cody felt his entire body being pulled into a tight knot. "It's Jade. Jade has to die..." It was the first time he'd spoken his fear out loud. Somehow verbalizing the words acknowledged their truth. Eva put her soft hands on his.

"A sacrifice that is easy is not a true sacrifice. You cannot do anything to prevent what is destined to be."
"You're wrong," Cody snapped. But as quickly as the rage surfaced, it drained out. "I'm sorry. I didn't mean to talk to you like that. It's just, I don't want...it doesn't...I can't..."

"I understand." Somehow those two simple words brought instant comfort. He believed her. She *did* understand. She was perhaps the only person in the world who truly understood his recent fears.

"How can you know these things?"

"Has anyone ever told you what happened to me?"

The unanticipated question made Cody uncomfortable. "I was told there was an accident. They say that's why

124

you're so..." Cody bit his tongue in horror when he realized what he was about to say.

"Crazy?" Eva laughed. "I have been called worse things than that. In a world full of plotters, schemers, and power mongrels, *innocence* must appear an oddity."

"I don't think you're crazy," Cody said, and he meant it. Not even Jade had ever offered the comfort and assurance that the simple princess had.

Eva's face lit up at the comment. "There's something I need to tell you. Something known by only one other living being. I am going to tell you about what really happened the night of *the accident*..."

Suddenly the light outside the window was extinguished. Nightfall had come. Cody jumped to his feet without thinking. Eva looked up at him, surprised.

"Oh, Eva. I'm so sorry. I have somewhere I need to be. They will be waiting for me."

Eva smiled gently in understanding. "Go and do what you must. We can finish this conversation when you get back."

Bidding her good-bye, Cody rushed out the door toward Yanci's Pub. The ebony night sky magnified the brilliant flashes of lightning. Thunder exploded, rattling the ground. The storm was approaching. A storm he was running *toward*. The time had come to infiltrate the enemy war camp.

37

Losing One's Mind

The light from the candle illuminated the priest's white face, giving it a haunting, spectral glow. "Tell me about these dreams." He whispered almost inaudibly, even though he and Jade were the only people in the room.

Jade took his lead, dropping the volume of her own voice. "I keep having the same type of dream every time I close my eyes."

"And, is this a good dream? Or a bad one?"

"A bad one," she answered. "A *very* bad one. The worst nightmare imaginable."

Stalkton nodded, almost impatient, as though the question had been a formality and Jade's answer expected. He motioned for her to continue.

Jade took a deep breath. "The dream is always different, but still somehow the same. I am in different places, some real, others impossible. But they all end the same. Before I wake from the dream I..." Jade paused for just a moment before finishing, "I kill someone."

Stalkton's eyebrow-less forehead furrowed and his nose wiggled as though catching an unsavory scent. "And, do you know the victim? Or is he or she a stranger to you?"

Jade hesitated again, but realized she had already shared too much to stop now. "I know him. He is someone close to me."

"And you have strong feelings for this person?"

Jade nodded. "Yes. I care about him very much. More than anyone else in the world."

Stalkton examined her face. Jade wondered what was going on behind the priest's probing eyes. *Is he judging me? Does he know I'm talking about Cody?*

"Do you *love* this person?"

Jade was taken aback by the question. *He's just a friend,* she thought; yet she heard herself answer, "Yes."

"Curious," muttered Stalkton, gazing intensely at his long, fidgeting fingers as though the answer to the mystery lay within them. "Curious indeed..."

"There's more," Jade said. "I think, somehow in ways I don't understand, these dreams are starting to become real." There were a number of responses Jade expected after her confession, but the one she received was not one of them.

"*Of course* they are real!"

Jade frowned. *Did I miss the punch line?* "I'm sorry, but I don't follow..."

"*All* dreams are real," Stalkton explained. "A dream is merely the reality that has yet to become realized. In dreams our imagination stages a dress rehearsal of our deepest desires and fears. Reality is born first in the imagination." With every word Jade felt more confused.

The cryptic priest continued, "If you look hard enough, hidden beyond the surreal, otherworldly masquerade, you will find truth. A dream never lies."

His words disturbed Jade. "So dreams reveal the truth about us?" she asked.

"In a manner of speaking, yes. Do you have reason to be angry toward this person you love?" Instantly the memory surfaced of Cody abandoning her in the battlefield to chase after the Book. Next came the recollection of the way he had humiliated her when she had put on make-up and a pretty dress to impress him. All while he shamelessly drooled over Tiana.

Through clenched teeth she admitted, "Yes." The image of the half-full glass of water came to her mind; the feeling of elation she had experienced plunging the jagged glass into Cody's heart. "I don't want to be bitter. I don't want to hate him!"

Stalkton shrugged. "Then don't."

Jade's irritation continued to grow. "I don't have a choice! I'm having horrible dreams and you just told me that dreams reveal the truth."

Stalkton stroked his narrow chin and nodded. "Indeed I did, but we *always* have a choice. Dreams tell us the truth about ourselves, but who tells our dreams what to dream?"

When Jade didn't respond, Stalkton said, "Just remember who you are. Dreams are treacherous. The day we lose control of our own mind is the day we die. Your *thoughts* are a creation that should always be your own. In the end, *you* choose what you believe and what you don't. Don't ever forget that. Your life, and the lives of those you love, may depend on it."

38

Behind Enemy Lines

Cody crept through the darkness. He couldn't help noticing the irony of his situation. *For the great hero and
savior of this city, I seem to spend half my time sneaking around
at night trying not to be seen.* But on this particular night,
evading notice was imperative. In a city where no one
could be trusted, being spotted by roaming eyes would
compromise the Book's hiding spot, and the entire war as a
result. Fortunately, few people were as masterful at sneaking as he was.

Slipping through the city, invisible to all, he came to a
crouching stop. Directly across from him was Yanci's Pub.
No lights were glowing within, as was expected. Cody
scanned behind him to confirm that he had not been followed.

Like a gentle breeze Cody glided to the tavern. He
slipped through the door and inside the unlit building.
"Psst! Dace? Tat?" He heard sounds and saw dark shapes
stirring. "Guys...is that you?" The shapes moved toward

him, emerging from the shadows—they were golden golems.

The largest golem grasped him, pinning his arms to his side. The huge soldier's breath reeked of ale. Cody scrunched his eyes. "Wolfrick?"

As his vision adjusted he realized the men were not golems after all. Like Wolfrick, both Dace and Tat wore matching gilded breastplates. Gold platelet armor concealed the greater portion of their faces. "We took the armor from the soldiers slain during the funeral ambush," explained Dace as he dumped a heavy bundle into Cody's arms. "In daylight it will be evident to all that the facial platelets are not truly melded into our skin. However, under the dark of night no one will be able to discern the difference."

Cody hoped Dace was right, but there was only one way to know for sure. He put on the disguise. Next came the moment he'd been dreading all day. He squeezed the Book against his chest before handing it over to Sheets. "Promise me you'll keep it safe for me."

Sheets quickly hid it from sight. "You have my word. And the word of Sheets is good, *regardless* of what Wolfrick might tell you." Wolfrick muttered something under his breath.

Dace called the group into a huddle. "We'll infiltrate El Dorado's rear force. I have no desire to have tea with the Golden King or his Spider. Prince Hansi is no smooth-skinned boy but he lacks war experience and even Levenworth would have his hands full to maintain order in a two-hundred-thousand-man force. The four of us should be able to blend in as long as we keep our heads down and our wits about us."

Dace tossed his sword back and forth between his hands, swirling it with a powerful *whoosh*. "At first sign of light we return. *No exceptions.* Am I understood?"

Wolfrick banged a fist against his chest. "Well, if that's all good and settled, what are you lousy mama's boys waitin' for? Let's go get ourselves bloody killed!" Dace grinned and flipped his sword so the hilt extended toward Wolfrick.

"Don't take it personally, but I already added your notch to my sword-hilt after we left you in Flore Gub. That makes you a dead man walking." Wolfrick gave a hearty laugh. Cody wished he shared the soldier's good humor rather than the tingling sensation of nerves. He dared not laugh for fear of throwing up instead.

"Whenever you're ready, Book Keeper," Dace said. Cody took a deep breath. *Here goes nothing.*

"*Spakious.*"

The portal rippled in front of them. The blurry scenery of the Under-Earth wasteland was faintly visible, like they were looking to the bottom of a murky pond. "Remember, we stick to the plan." With that final command, Dace stepped through the portal, disappearing to the other side. Tat and Wolfrick followed after him.

Cody stepped through the portal.

The world shifted.

The walls of Yanci's Pub morphed into golden tent flaps. The air was filled with chattering and scurrying about. Dace, Tat, and Sheets were waiting for Cody at the mouth of a tent. Dace spoke in a whisper. "Split up. Meet back at this tent *before* daybreak." Without another word they stepped from the tent and departed in different directions.

Panic struck Cody as he emerged from the tent. There were thousands of soldiers in every direction he looked, completely blanketing the rolling sand dunes.

"Gai di gasme."

The Portal closed behind Cody. Until daybreak he was trapped behind enemy lines.

39

Up to No Good

Night had fallen over the city of Atlantis. Despite the late hour Jade was in no hurry to retire to her bedchamber. Not after the conversation she had just had. Her head was still spinning from all Master Stalkton had told her.

Little of the priest's words had even remotely made sense to her. However, she could still hear him saying: *All dreams are reality*. Those had been the albino's precise words. If what he said were indeed true, Jade realized she could never let herself fall asleep again. She would let herself die of exhaustion first.

As the platform of the pulley-elevator neared the ground she watched the crowds scurrying toward their beds. Dotting the streets were blazing fires erected by clusters of refugees attempting to stay warm through the night.

Jade was eager for a distraction to keep her from dwelling on her already heavy eyes. She turned and headed toward the infirmary. Jade never thought a day would come when she would go to *Tiana* for comfort; but desperate times called for desperate measures.

As she rounded a corner a man brushed past her. Their shoulders collided causing Jade to stumble against the wall. She glared in irritation and caught only a quick glance of his face before he had dashed away. That one glance had been enough. Jade had no doubt. The man had been the Garga Prince—Ugar-Kir-Hugar.

He's supposed to be in Outer-City Dungeons. What in the world is he doing wandering free though the Inner-City streets at night? Whatever the reason for the Garga's nighttime stroll, Jade knew one thing for sure: *He was up to no good.*

Pulling her hood down to conceal her face, she trailed after him. The Garga moved like a ghost. Jade caught only brief glimpses of his cloak as he danced upstream of the sea of people.

Jade skidded to a halt as an agonizingly slow refugee couple blocked her path. She shoved through them and stopped. The Garga Prince was gone.

Blast! Where could he have gone? Jade jumped, scanning over the heads in the crowded street, but Kir-Hugar was nowhere to be seen. He had vanished like smoke to the wind. *That slippery little fish.* Giving up the futile chase, Jade turned to leave. As she did she spotted the tail of a gray coat as it disappeared over the top of a building. *Slippery fish, indeed...*

Jade broke free from the crowd and took off down the alley. She caught glimpses of the Garga as he sprang from rooftop to rooftop. It took all Jade had to keep pace as she weaved between buildings. The Prince leapt from the roof, somersaulting to ease his landing. Without slowing he dashed forward. For the first time Jade realized where the fugitive was heading: the Royal Palace.

Jade trailed him at a distance as they circled around the back of the Palace. Glancing both directions, Kir-Hugar descended a hill toward the building. Jade watched him from the cover of a large heap of refugee trash.

The Garga Prince moved across the base of the wall and stopped at a small tunnel. The rusted grating that had once barricaded the narrow opening now lay discarded on the ground. Kir Hugar reached into his belt and pulled out a jagged, stone dagger. *He's going to enter through the sewer.* Suddenly, the Garga's head shot back, scanning behind him. Jade ducked, covering her mouth with both hands and holding her breath.

Her heart pounded as she waited. She didn't dare check to see if the Garga was still looking. Several excruciating seconds passed until she mustered the courage to move. She peeked around the side of her hiding spot.

The Garga was gone.

Jade glanced up and down the wall but there was no trace of him. *Did he enter the sewage drain? Or...* Jade felt a sickening knot form in her stomach. She twirled around, throwing up her hands.

She exhaled. There was no one in sight. *He must have entered the palace. I need to warn people.* She briefly considered running to alert the City Guard. *No, it will take too long.*

Before she could talk herself out of it, Jade ran down the slope to the opening. She extended her arm into the tunnel and watched as her hand was completely blotched out by the pitch darkness. *I've become as reckless as Cody,* she thought. She entered the sewer.

Her feet made light splashes in the ankle-deep water that carpeted the sewer floor. She traced her fingers down both walls of the narrow tunnel as she blindly entered deeper and deeper into the abyss. The drainpipe twisted and turned like a slithering python. With each step she further regretted her boldness.

Whoosh!

A gust of air brushed the back of Jade's neck. She spun around, swinging her fist through the air, but hit nothing.

Whoosh!

Another blast of wind came from the other side. Jade couldn't hear or think over her own heavy breathing. The next instant a stone dagger was pressed against her throat.

"I do not appreciate being followed."

40

An Unexpected Visitor

Haunting chants swelled in the air. The dark cloaks of the crystal-bodied Dark-Wielders swayed as they perched like ravens atop the peaks of the highest sand dunes surrounding the war camp. Above them, black storm clouds churned. Their heads swiveled slowly, peering watchfully over the valley.

Cody felt the Dark-Wielders' penetrating inspection pass over him. He shivered from head to toe. The wormhole had opened on the fringe of the enemy encampment. Cody headed toward the central section of the camp, guided as much by the stench as the noise.

As he ascended a sand dune, two golems appeared from the other side. Cody dropped his gaze as he passed by. At last he reached the top. He looked down over the enemy camp—and his hope died.

El Dorado's army stretched like an endless, flooding river, cutting across the terrain and fading into the distance. He had never seen so many men in one place. The innumerable tents and fires had accumulated in an oozing mass at the base of the dunes. *What chance does Atlantis have against a force like this?*

A rough voice broke Cody's trance. "What's the problem, soldier?" Cody's muscles tensed. "I asked you a question, you filthy worm."

"I...uh...I was just resting for a moment." Cody winced as the words left his tongue. The speaker grabbed Cody's shoulder and shoved him to the ground.

"Resting? Is this a war camp or a ruddy day spa? The Radiant One has no use for *resting* soldiers." The golden golem unsheathed his sword. "You'll have eternity to *rest* when you're worm food." Cody didn't have time to react as the soldier brought down the sword to his neck.

Clang!

A second sword appeared from nowhere, parrying the blow. "There's enough dirt and worms here for two," rasped the newcomer. The first soldier maintained his furious gaze, before deciding the dispute wasn't worth the time.

"If you're still alive after we take Atlantis I'll hunt you down and kill you." Lobbing a gob of spit at Cody's feet, the golem departed. Cody sighed, but his relief was short-lived. His rescuer yanked him to his feet and pressed the tip of his blade to his throat. "Better start acting like a soldier or you'll be killed by one," he hissed.

The voice was familiar. "Dace?" Cody gagged as the sword pressed harder against his Adam's apple.

"Say my name aloud again and *I'll* kill you. Now go and stay focused." Dace shoved Cody and vanished into the camp. Cody looked around and realized that several people had stopped to watch the ruckus. However, deciding there was nothing more to see, they turned away one by one and returned to their tasks. Cody wiped the sweat from his forehead. He couldn't afford another close call. Not lingering, Cody descended the dune. Something in the distance caught his eye. The torrent of campfires split into two smaller streams then converged again farther on. In the clearing between the two diverging branches, several odd, triangular buildings had been erected to form a tight circle.

As good a place to start as any, he supposed. He set off, keeping his head lowered. Thanks to the small, mousy appearance of all the Under-Earth residents, Cody was roughly the same height as the soldiers. However, his scrawny, boyish stature stood out like a neon sign against the broad-chested, battle-hardened troops. Cody quickened his pace. If he kept his feet moving perhaps the patrols wouldn't notice the contrast. At least he *hoped* not.

He spotted Wolfrick sitting among a band of soldiers beside a campfire, a mug of ale in his hand, bellowing some surely fabricated tale of bravery. *So much for subtlety.* For just an instant Wolfrick's eyes rested on Cody before passing on. The message was clear: *I'm doing my job, so go and bloody do yours!*

Cody took the hint, resuming his trek toward the strange tents. Several soldiers seemed to eyeball him curiously. With his face still downcast, Cody walked right into a Dark-Wielder. The crystal fiend hissed, but paid him no more attention. Without further incident, Cody arrived at his destination.

There were thirteen pyramids in all. The surface of the peculiar objects had a smooth, almost metallic texture. Each one stood no less than fifteen feet tall. The structures formed a ring, obscuring any view of what might lay within the circle.

A barricade of warriors lined the perimeter. Cody felt a chill. They were not just warriors, nor were they entirely human. They were *creatures*, manufactured to be killing machines and animated by the souls of unfortunate victims. They were *The Rephaim*.

Their white, plastic-hued flesh rendered them the appearance of silent maggots; their hollow, cavernous eyes peered straight ahead. Despite their empty eye-sockets, Cody had the sickening sensation that their haunting surveillance missed nothing.

The hair on his neck and arms tingled. Cody felt their invisible scrutiny on him. He couldn't stay. He needed to put as much distance between himself and the nightmarish *Rephaim* as possible. Before he could leave, he heard something that stopped him cold.

"Hail, Lord Hansi!"

The chant echoed around him, and the statuesque El Doridian Prince appeared, strolling through the soldiers toward the metallic pyramids. His muscular physique filled out his polished, chain-mail armor. He removed his golden helmet, which was adorned by more jewels than any grown man could cup in both hands, and ran his fingers through his golden hair.

Cody suddenly realized that he was the only soldier still standing. In panic, he dropped to his knees and bowed his head. The Prince stopped only a few yards from his position. *If he sees my face, I'm as good as dead.* Cody stopped breathing.

Cody heard a sound, like that of tearing paper, and recognized it instantly. A wormhole. He lifted his eyes just as it opened. Emerging from the portal was the Golden King, the Hunter close beside.

41

Sinister Words

Jade's throat burned as the knife's sharpened edge began to split the epidermis of her neck. Her arms throbbed where the Garga's tight grip held her captive. He pressed his face against her cheek, his musky breath bathing her ear.

"You've been shadowing me since the market. Why?" The Garga's voice lacked any trace of patience. "I asked you a simple question. Kir-Hugar doesn't ask twice."

"I...uh...I..." Jade stumbled over her words. Her mind raced to conjure up a workable lie; but all she could focus on was the sharp blade against her jugular. "I was...I thought..." Kir-Hugar's stone teeth rubbed together, the grating sound causing her to shiver.

"So be it. May the Great Garganton be ever merciful..." He grasped her mouth. Jade squirmed helplessly as the Garga prepared to cut her throat.

Pat...Pat...Pat...

Jade gasped for air. The knife against her neck was gone. So, too, was Ugar-Kir-Hugar. He had vanished without a word or sound. Jade rubbed her skin where the Garga Prince had nearly opened her throat. *What just happened?* Then she heard the faint sound again.

Pat...Pat...Pat...

It was the sound of feet trekking through the water-filled tunnel. *Someone else is down here. I need to warn them about Kir-Hugar!* She raced blindly toward the splashing.

Pat...Pat...Pat...

Torchlight bounced off the walls at the end of the tunnel. Hushed voices were speaking around the corner. *There's more than one person.* Jade was about to call to them, but hesitated. For the first time, the oddness of the situation hit her. *What are they doing roaming the sewers in the middle of the night and speaking in whispers?*

Jade was now close enough to hear the strangers' words. "What you suggest is treason of the most despicable nature," said a gruff, commanding voice. It belonged to General Gongore Levenworth.

"*What I suggest* is the only hope for Atlantis," replied Sli Silkian in his familiar smooth cadence. "I have studied the prophecies. There is no mistake. Deep down in that heart of stone you know my words have the aroma of truth."

"I smell only the stench of deceit."

"Perhaps, but a necessary deceit."

After a pause the General responded, "You are certain of what must be done?"

"Oh, yes. It is simple. Jade must die."

42

A Hound with a Scent

The Hunter's shrilling howl reverberated through Cody's bones. Instant silence settled over the camp. Cody's legs wobbled as he maintained his uneasy kneel. He didn't dare move or draw attention to himself as the El Doridian rulers converged twenty feet away.

Prince Hansi approached the Golden King. "Father, what a pleasant surprise; I was not expecting you or your... *pet.*"

"Keep your lies," the King said flatly. "My coming is neither pleasant nor welcome."

Hansi's face reddened. "My father will *always* be welcome in my camp. I would never..." The Golden King silenced him with a penetrating stare.

"*Your* camp? Do the sheep welcome the shepherd to his own flock?" The King's ruby eyes perused the campsite. Cody dropped his face as the King's eyes passed over him. "Your men are rowdy and lax."

"They are only restless, Father. Eager to fight in your honor," said Hansi defensively.

"They are spineless louts who have grown too comfortable. Comfort is a sign of poor command. It's a sign of disrespect. Your men must *fear* you, and a fearful man is never comfortable."

"And how do I make them fear me?"

"You kill them." Hansi's face flashed clear displeasure.

"Kill them? What for, Father?" The King's golden hand slapped across Hansi's face with a *clang*.

"I've already given you a reason—*Fear*. A man is most obedient when his life depends on it. When next I come I expect to smell the stench of fear a thousand leagues away." The Hunter snorted, as though in affirmation of its master. "However, I didn't come to lecture. Take me to the prisoner. We have much to...discuss."

Cody's leg muscles burned. He wobbled, fighting to maintain his bow. *Just a little longer.* With a stout nod, Hansi and the Golden King departed, trailed by the Hunter. *That was too close,* Cody thought in relief.

The Hunter paused.

It lifted its large snout and sniffed the air. Cody's palms became clammy. *It's me. It senses me.* The Hunter's snake-like eyes scanned the crowd. Like a silent jaguar the Beast began stalking in Cody's direction.

In that very moment Cody's fears were realized. He lost his balance. He tumbled forward only an inch, but that was all it took. The Hunter's glowing red eyes fell upon him.

43

A Hospital Visit

Tiana lay completely unmoving. She could hear the breathing from the boy in the visitor's chair. Xerx's unwavering presence and concern was touching. At least it had been at first. Now his constant, smothering shadow was a massive annoyance.

She had made a habit of feigning sleep every time she heard the young monk enter the infirmary. Xerx would brush the hair from her eyes and sit beside her bed holding her hand for an hour or two before reluctantly leaving. But he was never gone long.

That the boy loved her there was no question. The spark in his eyes when he looked at her was the same as the day he had ludicrously offered her that gaudy gemstone and asked for marriage. *Foolish boy.*

She peeked through squinted eyelids. The blurry silhouette in the chair remained. *You're nothing if not consistent, boy.* As much as she hated to admit it, it *was* flattering. She had never experienced such devotion from a boy before. There had been Cody, but that had all been a farce.

She had pulled his strings like a puppet and he had predictably danced to her tune. At least that's how things had started...

An itch assaulted the tip of her nose. She scrunched her face, but the itch only grew worse. She sighed. *Okay, you win, Xerx.*

She sat up in the bed to scratch. She looked to the visitor's chair—and screamed. The man sitting at her bedside was not Xerx.

Tiana gasped. *"You!"*

44

Old Prisoner, New Prisoner

Cody ran for his life. All notion of stealth was abandoned in his desperation to escape the monstrous creature chasing him. He pushed his way through the mob of soldiers. He heard the tromping of the Beast's taloned feet.

Splitting a pair of golems, Cody looked up just in time to see the blazing campfire blocking his path. Without slowing Cody leapt, the flame singeing the soles of his feet, before landing unsteadily on the other side. He veered sharply to the right, trying to lose himself in a congregation of soldiers.

Several men hurled obscenities at him as he pushed past them. Their vulgar words were quickly replaced by frightful gasps at the sight of the Hunter in close pursuit. Cody didn't dare look back to find out just how close that pursuit was.

High atop the sand dune the Dark-Wielder sentries were scanning the camp, their penetrating gaze drawn to the commotion of the chase. *I need to get out of sight,* Cody realized. He sprinted around the edge of a tent and skidded to an abrupt stop. The Golden King and Hansi were coming directly toward him. He could hear the startled cries behind as the Hunter neared.

I'm trapped.

He glanced around, desperate for any solution. He found one in the form of a tent entrance. The guards had abandoned their post to inspect the disturbance. Cody ducked inside.

He crouched behind the entrance flap, trying to catch his breath. He knew that if he didn't keep moving, the Hunter would find him easily. He peeked outside the tent, but jerked his head back as two men appeared. The guards had returned to their post.

Cody backed away. *What do I do?* He could create a portal and return to Atlantis, but to do so was to leave the others to certain capture or death. The silhouette of the Hunter's domed back projected against the side of the tent. The sound of its sniffing could be heard through the thin fabric of the tent wall. *I'm doomed.*

"Cody? *Cody Clemenson?*" Cody spun around at the sound of the woman's voice.

"Sally?" The plump diner-owner sat at a table in the center of the tent. "What in the world are you doing here?"

"*Shhh!*" Sally put her finger to her mouth. "They're coming."

Cody heard the rattle of armor and the thumping of footfall approaching the tent. "You need to hide! *Quickly!*"

"Where?"

Sally stood from the table, sending her mug crashing to the floor. Behind her chair was a cedar chest. Opening it, she frantically emptied it of the clothes within.

"Quick. Get in." There was no time for hesitation. Cody climbed in, pulling his knees against his chest to fit into the small box. The next moment an icy voice sounded from the tent's entrance, "Lady Sally, I do hope I'm not interrupting anything." Cody's blood went frigid. The Golden King was inside the tent.

Sally cast Cody an anxious glance. "Of course not. I only hoped to wear a more elegant dress, better befitting the presence of the Lord of Lights." With a final nervous glance Sally turned, allowing the lid of the chest to fall closed—trapping Cody in silent blackness.

45

A Dead End

———————

"*It is quite simple. Jade must die.*"

The words lingered on the stale air like a toxic gas. Jade remained still, her back pressed against the cold sewer wall. The two long shadows of Levenworth and Silkian stretched like deformed wraiths on the wall. The two men were standing just around the bend of the drainpipe. If they took a dozen more steps she would be seen.

Jade's head was pounding. *Why would they want me dead?* Eventually Levenworth broke the tense silence.

"Why would I betray the city I have given my life to defend?"

"Not to *betray*—to *save*," Silkian said. "Your loyalty is precisely why I have chosen to share my secrets with you. You and I both want the same thing—a better Atlantis. The Queen is frail and your beloved Kantan is cunning, but his father he is not. I have powerful allies..."

Jade leaned forward. *What does this have to do with having me killed? I need to warn Cia...*

"Of what allies do you speak?" asked Levenworth. "El Dorado? The Garga? I'll chop off my own head before I sell my soul to either of them."

Silkian laughed. "There will be no need for decapitation. El Dorado and the Garga are nothing. They are little more than irritating fleas compared to my new friends."

"Who?" Jade found herself leaning forward in anticipation as Silkian answered.

"An entity known as...CROSS."

The revelation blared like a trumpet through the sewer. Jade grasped her mouth with both hands, silencing her startled gasp. *What in the world does CROSS have to do with this?* She leaned forward, but her foot slipped on the smooth floor.

SPLASH!

Jade toppled face-first into the polluted water. She pushed her drenched hair out of her eyes—and looked straight into the vexed faces of Levenworth and Silkian.

"Weren't you ever taught that it's unfitting for a lady to eavesdrop?" Silkian's voice was shrill. The two men stepped toward her.

Jade was on her feet in a flash and running blind through the dark tunnel. The light followed behind her and she heard the splashing of the two men giving chase. She twisted and turned down the sewer's labyrinth. She didn't know or care if she was taking the correct path. All that mattered was escape. Her arms swung like wild pendulums, propelling her forward.

"Umph!"

She thudded into something solid. She had reached a dead-end. She heard noises echoing down the tunnels behind her. *I'm trapped.*

She felt dizzy. She grabbed her forehead as a jolting sensation tickled down from her head and spread through her whole body. *What's happening to me?* She collapsed to the floor. As she did so, her body began to violently convulse.

46

Improvising

---

uffled voices sounded in the dark. Cody remained deathly still, as much by choice as by the fact that the small chest restricted all movement. The walls of the box muted the words beyond distinction. Cody waited anxiously as the time passed.

Then, without warning, the lid of the chest was opened. Torchlight blinded Cody's adjusting eyes as someone grasped his collar and pulled him from the chest. Before he could scream Sally's hand smothered his mouth.

"Quiet boy! They're gone." She released him. "But they will be back. I don't know what in the world you're doing here but it's not safe. You need to get out of here. *Quickly.*"

"What *I'm* doing here? Since when did you become an El Dorado Lady?" The last time Cody had seen the feisty woman she had been returning to her diner in Upper-Earth the day of Randilin's near-hanging. Whatever had happened in the months that followed had transformed her. Her frizzy braids had been tamed and she wore a lavish gown. Most noticeable of all was the doused fire in her eyes. She looked broken.

"Since they separated me from the man I love. It's a long story." For an instant some of the old flame flickered in her eyes. "But you need to *go*. You can slip under the back of the tent."

"Come with me." He held out his hand toward her. "It's almost morning; I need to rejoin the others before daylight comes. Come with us."

Sally shook her head. "You don't understand. I *can't* go with you. If I escape they'll do something to Randilin. Something horrible." The clanking of armor announced the night patrol as they passed outside the tent. Cody ducked down against the wardrobe chest, hiding his silhouette from view.

"Randilin's a clever man. He can handle himself. Please Sally. This may be your only chance to escape." Cody looked at her in a silent pleading until at last Sally gave a determined nod.

"We have no time to waste." She foraged through a pile of clothes she had emptied from the chest until she found a plain brown robe. She pulled it on, tugging the hood down to cover her face. "We need to hurry. My movement throughout the camp is not restricted, as they see no threat to escape on foot. But I am constantly monitored. It won't take them long to discover I'm missing."

Cody glanced around the tent, his mind racing as fast as his heart. "I have an idea." He moved to her desk and whispered. *"Gadour."* What happened next was one of the oddest sights either had ever seen. A small pebble, no larger than a sunflower seed, appeared on the seat and began to rapidly grow. It was like watching an infant morph into an adult. Within fifteen seconds they were looking at an exact stone replica of Sally.

Cody placed the candle in front of the statue. "It won't fool anyone looking inside. But maybe the silhouette will buy us some time."

Sally grinned. "Clever boy. Now let's *go*." They darted to the back of the tent. Cody pulled up the bottom of the canopy, looked left and right, and then motioned Sally ahead of him. He rolled out of the tent after her. *Now for the hard part,* Cody thought.

They encountered their first problem immediately. When Cody had arrived at darkfall the camp had been bustling with activity. Now, on the brink of day, the camp had become a near ghost colony. Before Cody could voice his concerns, Sally whispered, "I know. Just keep moving."

They moved through the camp as fast as they could without attracting too much attention. Even so, several of the night patrol cast curious glances their way as they passed. Cody nodded in salute without slowing, to avoid a clear glimpse of his face. "It's working..." Cody said under his breath. By some miracle they had made it halfway to safety without incident. Unfortunately, their luck did not hold.

WahOoOoOoOoOoOoOoOoOoOoOoOoOoO

The jarring blast of the horn pierced the air. Soon horns all over the camp echoed with droning bellows. Lights sporadically ignited inside the tents as soldiers were roused by the alarm. Cody squeezed Sally's arm. "That didn't take long. Hurry!" They quickened into a near sprint, no longer concerned over drawing attention; the time for that had just ended. The tents continued to illuminate and the vigilant voices of soldiers joined the blaring horns.

WahUo0o0o0o0o0o0o0o0o0o0o0o0

Cody sensed a presence behind them and instantly knew they were being followed. He could make out the jingle of armor and the clanking of footfall as the shadow fell into matching stride with them. Sally sensed it too. They increased their pace.

Cody felt warm breath against the back of his neck. A gold gauntlet reached for Cody's shoulder. Cody flinched; but before he could react further the shadow pressed his mouth to Cody's ear. "*Shhh.* Just keep moving." The voice belonged to Tat.

Cody exhaled in relief. Tat whispered, "Who is the woman?" Cody turned to answer but Tat's pinched his arm. "Don't turn, just keep walking. What the blazes are you doing with her?"

"Improvising," Cody said. "I didn't think we'd set the alarm off so quickly."

Tat huffed, "I don't think you did. For that we can thank Wolfrick, the Master of Stealth himself."

"What do you mean?" Cody turned around. Tat and Wolfrick stood behind him; each held the arm of a lifeless man between them. "Who is that?" Tat grabbed the man by his thick hair and lifted his head, revealing his face.

"You've got to be kidding me," Cody said in disbelief. "Are you guys *insane?* You've kidnapped *Prince Hansi!*"

Wah0o0o0o0o0o0o0o0o0o0o0o0o0

158

The horns continued to blow as the camp awoke and soldiers came streaming out of the tents hollering, with swords raised. There was a flash like lightning, illuminating the sky—morning had come.

"RUN!"

47

Out of Time

The brilliance of the Orb shone like a spotlight upon the band as they fled through the enemy camp. All at once Cody felt the gaze of a thousand soldiers fall on him. Sally tugged his sleeve, and the next moment they were sprinting up the sand dune.

The eyes of a soldier bulged at the sight of them. He waved his sword in the air and bellowed. "I've found them! I've f..." A slash from Tat's dagger silenced him. However, others picked up the alarm. Like an agitated beehive, the camp was stirred to action.

As Cody ran he looked to the highest hills—the Dark Wielders were gone. Their disappearance could only mean one thing. *They're coming for us.* The thought gave Cody a second jolt of adrenaline. *We're almost there...*

They reached the top of the sand dune. Their designated meeting place was directly in front of them and the only people around were unarmed camp workers. By some miracle they had made it.

A sickening feeling overtook Cody as he looked around. "Where's Dace?" The Atlantian Captain was nowhere to be seen. "We can't leave without him!"

Enemy soldiers were now swarming up the dune toward them. Several Dark-Wielders joined the ranks of the golden golems as the mass closed the gap. Tat shouted, "If we wait any longer we're *all* dead!" It looked as though all of the camp's two hundred thousand soldiers were rushing toward them at once. Still, Cody lingered.

Tat urged, "Dace gave the order himself. Anyone not at the meeting point by first morning's light must be left behind. *No exceptions.*"

The truth of Tat's words made his message no more palatable. He nodded his reluctant agreement. "*Spakious.*" A portal appeared behind them. Tat and Wolfrick tossed the captive Prince Hansi through before following after him. Sally stepped toward the wormhole, but turned back to Cody.

"You, too, sweetie. It's the only way." Then she, too, disappeared. Cody watched as the soldiers stampeded up the hill toward him. He took another step toward to the portal and stopped. He looked back and waited.

Please, Dace, hurry!

WahOoOoOoOoOoOoOoOoOoOoOoOoOoOo

Dace cursed as the sound of horns rang over the war camp. It could mean only one thing: one of their party had set off the alarm. *But who? And why?* Daylight's unwelcome arrival had worsened their dire situation.

He had to reach the rendezvous point. The others would be heading there as well. *Unless they've been caught.* Dace dismissed the thought. *Please don't let them catch Cody. Orb keep him safe.*

As Dace neared the designated landmark he heard the cry of an El Doridian sentry. "I've found them! I've f…" The man's shouts ended with a gurgle. Dace smiled. *The others have reached the apex.*

He began his ascent of the dune. He could see the rippling air of the wormhole. Dace's legs burned as he climbed. He caught sight of Cody standing alone in front of the portal.

A sea of golden golems was flooding the slope. The sheer volume of the soldiers slowed them. Dace knew he would win the footrace. He waved his arms and shouted. "Cody!" But just then another horn blared and drowned him out. Dace dropped his head and directed all his strength into his legs. *Almost there…*

Pop.

The noise stopped Dace cold. He knew that sound. There was no need to look, but he forced himself to anyway. His fear was confirmed. Both Cody and the portal were gone.

The mass of soldiers closed in and swallowed the dune's peak. Dace grasped the hilt of his sword; his fingers felt numb with the chilling realization.

He had been left behind.

48

A Stranger's Couch

The man's face was haunting. Tiana's skin crawled and her mouth became as dry as the Under-Earth wasteland at the sight of him. She could never mistake that face. She had seen it a hundred times, whenever she closed her eyes—a simple action that the stranger could not share.

The old man's long, stringy hair hung in patches over his face and his large, lid-less eyes peered through the gap, pinned directly on her. He did not flinch nor move a muscle as Tiana recoiled.

Tiana knew she was brave. Even death did not scare her. Yet, under the weight of the man's stare, she felt utterly terrified. She wanted to yell for help but held her tongue. *Screaming is for little girls who still play with dolls.* Instead she sat still as the hermit's boney hand reached toward her.

The coarse skin of his fingers brushed against her cheek. With blinding speed his other hand reached out. He clamped both sides of her head. The world seemed to explode and vanish before her eyes. So, too, did her courage. Tiana screamed like she'd never screamed before.

49

Stolen

Cody emerged from the portal to the sight of a dozen spearheads pointed at him. He skidded to a stop, nearly impaling his face on the nearest blade.

"Lower your weapons! It's me, Cody Clemenson. *The Book Keeper!*" Yet the soldiers did not stand down, but kept their spears leveled at Cody and the others. "Did you not hear me? What is the meaning of this?" Cody demanded.

The soldiers parted, allowing Cia, Kantan, Levenworth, and Silkian to step through. Levenworth raised his hand and the soldiers stepped back in unison, retracting their blades. Kantan's face was an amalgamation of surprise and fury.

"I ask the same of you. Appearing unexpectedly through a portal in the middle of the city disguised as enemy troops is inviting a quick death. In such occurrences, our men have been ordered to kill without question. Had El Doradian golems stepped through, hesitation would have led to the slaughter of our men. So I ask you again, what is the meaning of this?"

Cody brushed the dust from his clothes. "We were conducting a stealth mission into the enemy camp."

"Odd, I don't recall commissioning such an endeavor," Cia said coldly. The skin on her face sagged like gobs of tar ready to plop to the ground, adding to the frightening sternness of the Queen's gaze.

"Dace thought secrecy the safest path to take," Cody said. Levenworth grumbled.

"I should have known. This madness has Dace's stench all over it. And where is the foolish Captain?" Cody's eyes began to water.

"Unfortunately he was...left behind." The words were painful to force out. The shocked and angry clamor his answer produced blurred into white noise as Cody thought of Dace trapped alone behind enemy lines.

Cia motioned to the two hooded members of their party. "Who are these others?" Her voice had a surprisingly firm calmness to it.

"Well...let me explain..." Cody's explanation was interrupted as Sally threw her hood back.

"Gatekeeper Sally?" The stout diner lady gave a respectful bow to each of the dignitaries until she reached Kantan, offering only a spiteful glare instead.

"I have much to tell you from my time as captive to the Golden King."

Cia stroked her sagging chin. "We will be glad to hear all you have to say, Gatekeeper. Perhaps some good can come from this insanity after all. And who is the other?"

Tat pulled off the stranger's hood. If the faces of the Inner-Council had been surprised to see Sally, they were in full shock now.

"Prince Hansi? You captured the Golden King's only son! How is this possible?"

"Because we're bloody heroes, that's how!" huffed Wolfrick.

Cody paused. "Wait a second..." He looked at the crumbling thatched roofs of the homes around them. "What are *you four* doing in the Outer-City at this time of night?"

Levenworth answered. "We've had a troubling report."

"Trouble?" Cody's voice wavered and he felt his body deflating. "Where?" Levenworth eyed him curiously.

"At your beloved Yanci's Pub."

Cody didn't wait to hear more. He took off running toward the tavern, his hands shaking. He instantly sensed something odd in the air as he reached the pub.

It was deathly quiet.

Yanci's Pub was a lot of things, but it was never *quiet*. A rank smell wafted through the front door—the grisly odor of death. Cody kicked the door open and stepped inside. The sight that greeted him was horrific.

Five bodies lay spewed across the room. Everywhere Cody looked he saw puddles of blood. "They're all dead..."

Wolfrick shoved Cody aside. "Sheets? Sheets? You stinking piece of dung, where are you?" His eyes widened when he saw the red-haired soldier sprawled on top of a table. "It *can't* be..." He ran to him and turned his friend over. Sheets' eyes were lifeless and his throat had been cut.

"NOOOOOOOO!" Wolfrick's howl shook the tavern's walls. "How dare you die on me!" Wolfrick pounded his fist on the man's chest, tears and snot flowing as one from his face.

Cody broke from his trance and his eyes darted around the bloodstained room. His face went pale. "It's gone..."

Cia caught his eye. "What are you talking about?" Cody fell to his knees and grabbed his forehead.

"They've stolen the Book."

50

A Cold-Blooded Killer

Jade woke.

Rubbing the back of her scalp she found a tender bump where her head had hit the stone sewer floor. *What happened to me?* She could remember running. She had reached a dead end—and the next instant she had been carried away by another nightmare.

As usual, Cody had been in the dream. She had found him alone in a dark room. He was muttering in an almost inhuman voice, repeatedly saying, "I chose the Book over you. I chose Tiana over you." The next instant Jade had been holding a dagger, unsure of where it had come from. The knife had a solid gold hilt with two ruby gemstones embedded in it. She had not wanted to harm Cody, but his incessant chanting had made her so angry. *It was only a dream...*

She massaged her eyelids as her pupils adjusted. *Did I pass out?* She had become used to the violent dreams, but never had one come while she was still awake.

Suddenly she heard shouts all around her. She realized that there were lights in the room and that she was no longer in the sewers. *How did I get out?* She slowly pushed herself into a sitting position.

Someone in the room shouted, "Jade?" The next moment a dozen shocked faces were staring down at her. Among them was Cody.

"Cody! What's going on?" Cody shook his head.

"I was going to ask *you* the same question..." He extended his hand and helped her to her feet. Jade instantly recognized her surroundings. It was the same room where she had found Cody in her nightmare.

Only then did she notice the five dead men covered in blood. "Oh, my gosh! What happened here? How did these people die?" She felt vomit rising in her throat.

"They were murdered," said Prince Kantan.

"*Murdered?* Who did this?" Jade watched as all eyes drifted downward. She dropped her own gaze. Both of her hands and her dress were completely drenched in blood. She frisked herself but there was no sign of a wound. The blood was not her own. She looked up in horror. Kantan's voice was firm.

"*You* did."

PART THREE:
THE BRINK OF WAR

51

A Disturbance

The earth rumbled, dislodging an avalanche of debris from one of the large spires of junk. The Garga scouts Kagar-Kir-Jaqcin and Ygar-Kir-Togo froze, opening their ears to the earth's vibrations. The ground shook again, sending more scraps crashing to the dirt.

Kir-Jaqcin motioned to his comrade, who returned a silent affirmation. Crouching low, they disappeared into the maze of rubble. Kir-Jaqcin stopped and pressed his ear to the ground. Violent tremors pulsed though the soil like the pumping of the Great Garganton's heart. The vibrations were originating from the water portal. *Has the Great One feasted again?* It was not unusual. The Great One had an enormous appetite; but never had it caused such a disturbance. He quickened his pace.

Kir-Togo's signal came down from his position atop the highest peak. Kir-Jaqcin nodded and expertly scaled his own mound, without loosening any of the debris. Reaching the top, he spied down on the source of the disturbance—and frowned. He was an elite Stone-Warrior, not some smooth-skinned member of the Pebble-Guard; yet he had never seen anything enter the Great One's mouth as he now saw.

There were thousands of oddly dressed warriors. Sliding between the rows of soldiers were large metal beasts. Rocks shattered beneath their serpentine legs as they moved across the ground like queen magma-worms. There was a booming *crash* as another of the metal monsters emerged through the water portal, and then another...and another...and another...

The Mouth must be told. Kir-Jaqcin whistled to Kir-Togo, who echoed the sound. Kir-Jaqcin prepared to leave but was stopped by a clanking sound. One of the metal beasts was turning its head, pointing its long, tube-like snout toward Kir-Togo. *A noisy hunter always goes hungry,* he thought, recalling his father's favorite proverb.

Boom!

Fire burst from the metal beast's mouth. There was a low whizzing sound just before Kir-Togo and the junk tower he stood on exploded in a haze of fire and smoke.

When the air cleared, half of the tower's peak was gone and Kir-Togo was nowhere to be seen. Kir-Jaqcin looked to the metal beast in disbelief. *What sort of fire-breathing demon is this?* The monster pivoted its head. Kir-Jaqcin stood in place, too shocked to move.

Boom!

The blast was followed by the same whizzing noise— and then an explosion.

52

Accusations

Cody stared wide-eyed at Jade. Fresh blood still soaked her hands. "Jade, what happened here?" She gaped in horror at her dripping hands.

"I...I...I don't know," she muttered.

Wolfrick shoved Cody out of the way. "I'll tell you what happened. Your girlfriend spent too much time in El Dorado and now she's *one of them!* She's a traitor! She *killed* them! She killed Sheets! I'm going to make her pay!" Wolfrick lunged forward, but Levenworth caught him around the neck and tossed him aside effortlessly.

Queen Cia placed her hand under Jade's chin and tilted her face up. "Tell me what happened here. *Everything*. And for your own sake, don't try to lie to me."

Jade looked to Cody for help, but Cody was still frozen in shock. "I...don't know what happened," she said slowly, squeezing her eyes shut and grabbing her temples. "I was somewhere else. And then I started having a dream, although I don't think I was asleep when it happened. I don't know how to explain it. In the dream I..." Her voice faded.

"In the dream you *what?*"

Jade's body was trembling. "In the dream I killed someone. And then the next thing I remember is waking up here and seeing all of you." Kantan perched beside his twin sister.

"So you had a *waking dream* that you murdered someone. And then next thing you know you wake up in the middle of a murder scene?"

"Give her some space," Cody barked. He stepped forward, shielding Jade from the crowd. "Jade, I trust you more than anyone in the world. But are you sure it was a dream?"

Jade pushed him away. "I know what a dream is! Trust me, I have dreams like this all the time."

Cia raised an eyebrow. "You frequently have dreams about murder?"

"That's not what I meant!"

Cia sighed, and motioned to the guards behind her. They stepped forward to seize Jade.

"I didn't do it!" Jade hollered.

There was a high-pitched cough behind them as Sli Silkian lifted his fist to his mouth and cleared his throat.

"Fishy as this seems, it is highly improbable that this slender girl could overpower and slay five seasoned soldiers." He paused for another wheezing cough. "Furthermore, the stolen Book is not in the girl's possession. If nothing else, she was not working alone."

Kantan nodded. "Silkian speaks truth."

"The Garga Prince! Ugar-Kir-Hugar!" Jade shouted. "I saw him earlier. He was sneaking around the city and he had a knife!"

Levenworth shook his head. "After I heard the report of what happened here I went straight to the prison. Our Garga Prince is right where we left him, chained up in the Outer-City dungeon where he belongs."

Kantan narrowed his eyes. "Another waking dream, perhaps?" Jade's face reddened.

"It was *real*. I *saw* him!" Jade pointed toward Levenworth and Silkian. "I saw them, too. They were meeting secretly in the sewer tunnels beneath the palace. I eavesdropped on them and heard them conspiring to kill. How else would they have known to come here so fast?"

Levenworth grunted. "So you're a spy *and* a murderer? You are quick to point a finger at others when it's *your* hands stained with blood."

"Enough!" Cia raised her hands to silence them. "Until a proper investigation is made there will be no haughty accusations." She motioned to the guards. "Escort Lady Jade to her chambers. I want a constant watch on her door. She is *not* to be harmed, but is not to leave her room until this mess is resolved."

As the guards ushered Jade from the building Cody grabbed her hand and squeezed. "I will get this cleared up. I believe you."

Jade closed her eyes. *Did she believe in herself?* She remembered the nightmare in the Garga camp. She had awoken holding a blood-smeared rock. She refused to think of what happened that night.

She looked at her crimson hands and the words of Master Stalkton came back to her. *All dreams are real.* The sickening realization came over her. Maybe she *did* do it.

53

Becoming a Monster

Cody stood immobilized by shock as he watched Jade leave. His head ached. In the blink of an eye it seemed everything had changed. Dace was gone. The Book was gone. But it was the sight of Jade's blood-soaked hands that hit the hardest.

Something had changed in his best friend. The girl he had traveled across the wasteland to rescue was not the same one he had returned to Atlantis with. There was an ever-present danger that seemed to lurk just beneath the surface, threatening to burst forth at any moment.

Yet, at the moment, the only thing about Jade that concerned him was her safety. No amount of evidence could convince him that his best friend since the third grade had committed such atrocious evil. Cody turned at the sound of someone shouting his name. Tiana was running toward him. Her skin still had a grayish tint and her expression was troubled. "We need to talk."

"I was told you wouldn't be let out of the infirmary for several more days."

"I *wasn't* let out," Tiana sucked in a deep breath and wiped the perspiration from her forehead. "We need to talk. Jade has to live."

Cody nodded in annoyance. The recent events had left him in a foul mood. "Of course she has to live. She's my best friend and she's innocent." He paused. "Wait, how do you know something happened to Jade?"

Tiana shook her head. "I have no idea what you're talking about. But you don't understand. She *has* to live."

Cody waved Tiana off and turned away. "I really don't have time for this..."

"The man without eyelids told me," Tiana blurted. Cody swung back around.

"So you *have* seen him. I knew it!"

Tiana glanced both directions before pressing her mouth to his ear. "I haven't just seen him...I've *talked* to him. And you're going to want to hear what he had to say."

NO! NO! NOOOO!

Jade slapped herself across the cheek. The drowsiness was becoming harder and harder to fight. She would not allow herself to doze off. Terrible things happened when she let herself sleep.

The shower had washed clean the bloodstains, but the sickening sensation had remained. The terrible images of Yanci's Pub were constantly before her, as though the scene had branded itself onto her corneas.

Her head began to sag again. She jerked herself back awake. *Don't give in. Don't give in. Don't give in.* She stood from the chair. She had refused to go near her bed but now even the stiff chair was becoming too alluring.

She staggered to the bathroom and splashed cold water onto her face. She massaged the chilling water against her eyelids. *What have I become? A murderer? A monster?* She looked into the mirror and screamed. It was not her face staring back. It was the hog-like face of the Hunter.

54

Frightening Reflections

Cody paced back and forth, his hands opening and closing into fists. "He is called The Watching One," he said to Tiana who was perched with her feet on his chair. "That's what the eyelid-less man was called in a history book I read in El Dorado's library. According to the book he has inhabited Under-Earth since before The Twelve arrived." Cody hesitated, trying to gather his scattered thoughts. "There's more. I saw him in Havenwood. He was in Upper-Earth. It's like he's following us."

"He always seems to show up at just the right moment," agreed Tiana. "I never told you how I escaped the cave in El Dorado." She recapped the events of that night. How the strange hermit had effortlessly guided her through the pitch-black tunnels and removed the gold platelet fused to her mouth.

"That's how you knew Jade was in danger from the Golden King at that precise moment. He told you, didn't he?" Tiana nodded. "You said he spoke to you again today in the infirmary. What did he say?"

"It's more complicated than that. He didn't *speak,* at least not with words. I don't think he's capable of speech."

"How else does one speak?"

Tiana reached out her hand and palmed Cody's face. "Like this," she said. "He touched me and, it's hard to explain, but I *saw* things."

"Like a vision?" suggested Cody, but Tiana shook her head.

"No, it wasn't that clear. It was more like quick flashes. Smells. Sounds. Images. I know it doesn't make sense, but somehow I understood what it all meant. The man, this Watching One, told me that Jade *must* live. That if she doesn't live until the two become one then all is lost. She must live for The Prophecy to be fulfilled."

Cody felt a tight knot forming in his stomach. Tiana's words were confirmation of his worst fears.

Jade must live...so that she can die.

Jade screamed. As she did the Beast in the mirror reared its grotesque head and squealed. The feeling of disgust slid down her body like slime. She *was* the Beast.

She shut her eyes. When she opened them again it was once again her own face looking back. *I'm going crazy.* Her forehead throbbed. Each pulse of her heart was like a gong against her brain. She clawed at her face, forming thin red lines with her nails as she tried desperately to remove the strange sensation of fur.

She didn't know what to think anymore. Her senses had become untrustworthy. Like a viper eating its own tail, Jade no longer knew where the old her ended and the new monster she had become began.

Her skin tingled and a foul smell filled the room. She heard a soft purr behind her. She looked to the mirror and saw two glowing scarlet eyes peering at her. But this time they did not belong to her.

She spun around as the Hunter stalked out from the shadows toward her. Its serpentine eyes illuminated the room like torches as it glided forward. Jade stumbled backwards. Her back pressed against the wall. *This isn't real. I'm sleeping. This can't be real.* She could no longer see the room's only exit over the demon's humped back. She was trapped.

The Hunter's breath was hot as the hoggish snout sniffed at her face. Its nostrils flaring, the Hunter rose onto its back two feet, towering over her. In that moment Jade came to a solemn realization. *I'm not sleeping. This is real.*

55

A Waking Nightmare

The musky smell of wet fur wafted through the window. The potent stench halted Cody in mid-sentence. His eyes shot to Tiana. She had already jumped from the chair and was dashing toward the door. "The Hunter."

"Jade's in danger!" Tiana kicked the door open and they dashed down the corridor toward Jade's chamber. They flew around the corner. "Oh, no!" The two guards who had been posted at Jade's room were gone and her door had been torn off its hinges.

"Jade!" Cody ran into the room and stopped.

Jade stood alone at the window. She was petting the air and whispering to herself, "My beautiful pet…"

Cody cautiously approached. At the sound of his footsteps Jade's head perked up. She spun to face him. Her trademark green eyes were gone; in their place were two glowing, scarlet orbs.

Her face contorted, appearing almost inhuman. The pure rage in her expression forced Cody back a step. Jade bared her teeth and hissed. Cody heard Tiana draw her knife.

Jade charged.

Tiana braced herself with her dagger, but Cody pulled her arm down. "No! She won't hurt me." *Would she?* Jade dropped to all fours and pounced at him. Her arms grasped him, the vice-grip squeezing the air from his lungs.

"Oh, Cody," Jade nestled her head on his shoulder. "I was hoping you would come," she whispered. Cody exhaled and returned the tight embrace.

When at last they released, Jade's green eyes were damp and black rings sagged beneath them. No trace remained of the glowing scarlet that had burned in them a moment earlier. "Jade, are you okay?"

She shrugged. "As okay as a girl can be who has been accused of murder." She spoke with indifference, seemingly oblivious to what had just transpired.

"What happened in here?"

Jade gave him a quizzical look, as though he had just asked if she had grown a tail.

"Nothing," she said sharply. "I was just dreaming again. At the time I thought it was real, but it obviously wasn't. I was dreaming of..."

"The Hunter?" Tiana asked.

Jade looked at her in astonishment. "How did you know that?"

Cody and Tiana exchanged quick glances.

"Jade, the two guards that were outside your door. Do you know what happened to them?" Jade shrugged.

"How would I know? I've been..." She seemed to notice for the first time the door hanging off the hinges and the deep claw marks cut into the wall. "I don't understand. It *had* to be a dream. If it wasn't a dream then that means the Hunter was really here. That means I was...no, it's impossible."

Tiana voiced what Jade could not. "That means you were *petting* the Hunter." Tiana frowned. "That doesn't make sense either. You were alone when Cody and I entered. Unless..." Cody stepped in before she could voice any more hypotheses. He took both of Jade's hands in his.

"Jade, I think you're sick. Something has happened to you; I don't know what, but you aren't yourself right now. You need to let Master Stalkton look at you. All the tension we've been under, and the lack of sleep. Silkian was right; none of this makes sense. You didn't—you *couldn't*—have killed those men."

"What if I *did* do it? I've done it before, at the Garga camp."

"That was different," Cody insisted. "You were fighting for your life."

"I broke free from my bindings and killed skilled Garga warriors with nothing but a stone. That doesn't make any sense either, but it happened. Face the truth. I'm a killer." Jade's voice was saturated with bitter acceptance.

Cody chewed his lip. His worried expression revealed the concern his words were trying so hard to mask. "You're my best friend. I know you better than anyone. You're *not capable* of doing evil like this."

Jade released Cody's hands. "I'm not the same person. Something's changed. I don't know what to believe anymore!" Tears began rolling down her cheeks. Cody wrapped his arms around her again, but she shoved him away.

"It's *your* fault!" she shrieked. "Get out of my room!" The moisture in her eyes was gone, dried up by the burning hatred he now saw in them. "Get out or I will kill you, too."

Before Cody could leave, Jade's arms were wrapped around his neck and her tears were streaming down his shoulder. "I'm so sorry," she said between sobs. "I didn't mean that. I don't know what's happening to me. I need help. Please, help me."

Cody had never hugged Jade so tightly as he did in that moment, stroking his fingers through her charcoal hair. Even Tiana had placed a tender hand on her shoulder. "I will," Cody said with iron determination. "I promise." This time it was Cody's turn to let anger overtake him. "The Golden King will pay for what he's done to you. I promise you that."

56

A Slap to the Face

"**W**e're doomed! I'm lost without it! I *need* that Book!" Cody threw up his hands in frustration. "El Dorado is closing in, Jade needs my help, and now the Book is *gone*."

Master Lamgorious Stalkton sat with a plate of earthworm and *de-fossilized* cucumber sandwiches and listened patiently as his pupil despaired. "How can I face the Golden King without the Book?"

Munch...Munch...Munch...

"How could I have been so *foolish* to leave the Book behind in the first place?"

Munch...Munch...Munch...

"I feel so *naked* without it!"

Munch...Munch...Munch...

Cody's rant died as Stalkton's chomping began to drown him out. "Master, are you even *listening* to me?" The albino priest looked up from his plate with a surprised expression, giving testimony to the negative.

"Come here." Stalkton motioned Cody toward him. "No-no-no, closer. Come on, here." Cody stopped a foot from the priest. "Very good, now please hold this." Stalkton handed him the plate of crumbs. Cody took it reluctantly.

SLAP!

Stalkton's hand whipped against Cody's cheek. "Ouch! What was that for?" Cody grabbed his throbbing face.

SLAP!

"Ouch! Stop it!" Cody pulled his head back before a third blow could connect. Master Stalkton retrieved his sandwich plate and, licking his finger, set to devouring the crumbs.

Munch...Munch...Munch...

Cody's face reddened with anger. "Why did you hit me?"

Stalkton speared his gnarled finger toward Cody's chest.

"Because you need to snap out of it! Stop being a baby. You want to know what it's like to *feel naked without it*, try misplacing your entire wardrobe for two months, as I have done on three different occasions."

"How can you be so calm? They've taken *The Code*! If El Dorado now has both Books of Power, we're doomed."

Stalkton prepared to deliver another slap but Cody backed away.

"Surface-Dwellers have brains like underlings, do they not? The Golden King had *The Code* in El Dorado once before and then let it go. It is not the Book itself that he desires. Have you forgotten your training so quickly? What does the Book *do*?"

Cody answered without hesitation, "It funnels the Orb's energy to me."

"Exactly! It's a tool. On its own it is nothing more than leather, paper, and gibberish. It is the Orb that gives you power, not the physical book. As long as you remain Book Keeper you still have unequaled access to the Orb's great power."

"But doesn't the Orb's flow grow weaker the farther I am from the Book?"

Stalkton shrugged. "Absolutely. What of it?"

"So I need the Book close to me," Cody said hotly, as though being forced to defend that two plus two still equaled four.

"Utter nonsense," Stalkton chastised. "Banish the Book to the farthest known ends of the world and the Orb energy flowing into you would still be enough to do limitless wonders. Hear me clearly; the only limitation to what you can do with the power is *you*. Don't limit yourself."

Cody nodded, still skeptical, but too confused to argue further. He *wanted* to believe Stalkton's claims, but couldn't dispel the thick shroud of doubt. Unlike Jade, who would not believe her own nose was there if she couldn't touch it, Cody had never found it hard to accept the unseen. His wild imagination had instilled in him a longing for the existence of supernatural forces. However, there was a vast gulf between *believing* in something invisible and *staking your life* on that unseen truth.

"Master, do you have faith in me?"

Stalkton burst out laughing, slapping his stumped thigh. His jovial cackles faded as the priest wheeled himself away, leaving Cody alone in the dim room.

57

In Search of Answers

Time was running out. Each passing day brought the unrivaled armies of El Dorado closer to Atlantis, the coming and going of daylight acting as a ticking time-bomb for war. Although, of late, the festering storm had blurred the distinction between day and night.

If Cody were to unravel the mysteries and save both Jade and Atlantis, he needed to do so quickly. For the eight-thousandth time Cody stared transfixed by the ruby pocket watch. The colored clock hands rotated in slow, counter-clockwise paths.

Three hands. Three colors. Cody knew there was a crucial piece to the puzzle still eluding him. *If only Chazic were here.* The tattooed Enforcer had known more about The Prophecy and The Earthly Trinity than he had let on, perhaps more than Chazic had even realized himself. However, he, like everyone else important to Cody, was gone. If Cody were to find the answers he would need to do so alone. He looked to the stone tablet on the table. He knew the words by heart:

THE POWER OF FULL DIVINITY,
RESTS ENCODED WITHIN EARTHLY TRINITY
WHERE SACRIFICE OF THE PURE ANGEL WHO FELL,
IS THE WAY TO RETRIEVE THE PEARL WITHIN THE SHELL.
WITH HUMBLE HEART AND GOLDEN KEY,
THE UNIVERSE'S MOST POWERFUL FORCE IS REVEALED TO THEE.

Cody grunted in frustration. *What good is a Prophecy that doesn't make any sense?* According to Gorgo Tallsin, the Resistance leader in El Dorado, the Golden King was convinced that the words *EnCoded* and *Golden Key* referred to the two Books of Power, *The Code* and *The Key*. The line *"Sacrifice of the Pure Angel who Fell"* caused Cody's stomach to tighten. *I won't let them take you, Jade.*

A familiar voice spoke behind him. "Don't you wish the world made more sense?" Cody turned, clenching his fists. Dunstan was reclined in a chair, his fedora resting on his lap. There was a sardonic grin on his face.

"How dare you come here!" Cody said, his blood boiling. Dunstan grabbed his heart, feigning an expression of hurt shock.

"Good heavens! What has ol' Dunstan ever done to deserve such a terrible threat?" If looks could kill, laser beams would have shot from Cody's eyes and disintegrated the CROSS agent.

"Besides shoot Tiana in the head and almost kill Jade? Or keeping us prisoner in your master's house? Should I continue?" Dunstan tilted his head like a curious puppy.

"Keeping you prisoner? Is that what you think? Tell me, how is it that you ever managed to escape? Or possibly locate the Table Room where your precious Book lay..." Cody hesitated; he had walked blindly into one too many of the Englishman's ensnaring webs not to tread cautiously.

"Do you expect me to believe that *you* unlocked our door and allowed us to escape? Or that you led me past that opened door *on purpose?*"

Dunstan held his hands out. "Have I ever lied to you?"

"You've done far worse things than that," Cody snarled.

Dunstan nodded. "Perhaps, but I've never *lied*, which is the vice of importance at the moment." Cody bit his lip and remained silent. It took every ounce of restraint not to use the High Language and turn the British gentleman into a bonfire. However, like it or not, Dunstan was one of the few people who might hold the answers he desperately needed.

"Very well. Say what you came to say, and if I like it I may let you live."

Dunstan grinned. "How courteous of you, my old friend." He sat up in the chair and folded his hands onto his lap. "Shortly before you departed on your rescue mission to El Dorado, I sent a colleague to you to share some advice. Do you remember?"

Cody nodded. "The answer to questions not yet asked waits at *the place where it was discovered*. Find the northern caves where The Thirteenth dwells; there you will receive understanding."

"Precisely," said Dunstan. Cody waited for the CROSS agent to elaborate, but he said nothing more.

"I've already been to the Caves of Revelation," Cody said in frustration.

Dunstan leaned forward. "Indeed, but did you find understanding?" Cody looked at the man with newfound curiosity.

"Are you trying to tell me I need to go back to the Caves?"

Dunstan shrugged. "Far be it from me to tell a Book Keeper what to do," he said through a crooked smile. "I only offer my humble observations. I merely thought you would be interested to know you wouldn't be the first Book Keeper to return to that location."

"The Golden King has been to the Caves? When? Why?" Cody realized for the first time that he was sitting on the floor at Dunstan's feet, listening.

Dunstan stood, fitting his fedora atop his head. He grinned. "No idea." He offered a slight bow. "Oh, and don't think I've forgotten. You still owe me that favor." Then he was gone, disappearing through the door, leaving only the aroma of his strong cologne.

Cody looked out the window; the horizon was blotted out by the approaching clouds. Somewhere out in the storm were the Caves—and answers.

58

What Was Taken

"Are you crazy?" Tat Shunbickle looked up from the arrow shaft he was whittling with a small knife. "You want to leave the city *again*? And you expect me to come with you?"

"Yes," Cody said with forced confidence. "I must return to the Caves of Revelation and I need your tracking skills to see if there have been others in the Cave. It's crucial."

"It's *crucial* that you stay alive," Tat said with surprising irritation. His grip on the knife tightened and there was a *crack* as the arrow shaft splintered.

"I thought you would be happy to go on another dangerous adventure."

"That was before we got Dace killed."

"We don't know..." Cody began, but Tat shook him off.

"No man can survive those odds."

"But Dace is not an ordinary man," Cody said firmly. To his surprise, Tat grinned.

"No, I don't suppose he is." He drove the knife into the wooden table and tossed his quiver of arrows over his shoulder. Cody was taken aback by the sudden action.

"Where are you going?"

Tat grabbed his bow. "To do something foolish with a foolish boy." He inspected the bow, snapping the bowstring. "Well, what are we waiting for?"

The gaping mouth of the dark cave swallowed all light or warmth from the rocky cliff-side. Despite the dozens of other entrances, invisible forces drew Cody to this particular opening. It appeared somehow darker and more ominous than the others.

Tat stood after examining the ground. "Footprints, no more than a day or two old." Cody bit down on his lip. *Dunstan was telling the truth.* "It's interesting. There are two different sets of prints."

"How can you tell?"

Tat pointed to the ground. "Many ways. The shape or depth of the print and so forth. But this time it is much more straightforward. The man who made the second prints was bare-footed."

"Garga?" Cody asked.

"Perhaps, but Garga scouts work in pairs, never solo. Either way, we need to act quickly." He looked up to the cave entrance. "Are you sure this is the same cave? If you enter the wrong one..."

I'll be lost to wander in the endless tunnels as I slowly die of starvation, Cody thought, but banished the notion from his mind. He traced his fingers along the rock until he found what he was searching for: A small engraving. An upside-down arrow surrounded by a sun. The sign of The Earthly Trinity. "This is the one."

Tat grabbed his bow and scanned their surroundings. "Then make haste. I will stand watch." The scout grabbed Cody's shoulder. "Be careful." Cody nodded, and stepped into the cave.

"Illumichanta."

A light globe materialized, floating several feet ahead and guiding him down the tunnel. The light beams struggled to penetrate the abysmal black as Cody ventured deeper and deeper. He moved slowly, one foot after the other, until the light from the entrance had vanished.

After an endless number of steps, the tunnel opened into a familiar hollow. The shelves that had once contained the countless inscribed tablets had been pulled down and stone chunks were scattered like rubble across the floor. In the center of the room, framed by the light above, was an empty space. The body of The Thirteenth was gone.

Did the Golden King take him? What use is a dead body? Cody examined the wreckage. *Why had the Golden King come here? What was he looking for?* The violent manner in which the cave had been trashed filled Cody with timid hope. *Perhaps the Golden King hasn't solved the mystery of The Earthly Trinity either.*

Cody approached the fragile wooden table against the far wall. The surface was coated in a thick blanket of grime. The faint outline of a rectangle could be distinguished where the dust was not as thick.

What used to be here? Did CROSS take it? Or did the Golden King?

Cody used the table for leverage as he stood. As he did, the table's legs wobbled and snapped, sending Cody tumbling forward, face-first against the wall.

He rubbed his throbbing forehead as he sat up from the ground. The table had splintered into a pile of rotted kindling. Cody squinted as a beam of light blinded him. He stood slowly. The light was coming from the wall. Rather, it was coming from *behind* the wall, through a small crack created when Cody's head had struck.

There's something on the other side of the wall. Cody grabbed two stones and flung them.

CRACK!

The wall crumbled like dry leaves, revealing a narrow passage. Cody grinned and set off down the tunnel to discover whatever awaited him.

59

A Man and His Promise

The tunnel stretched on for what seemed like infinity. Cody could see nothing apart from the faint light glowing in the distance. No matter how many steps he took, he never seemed to get closer to the light.

Cody began to second-guess his decision to enter it. The last time he had uncovered and entered a hidden entrance he had summoned a monster. However, his spiked curiosity and the weight of Jade's request for help compelled him forward through the narrow channel.

The tunnel's end arrived abruptly. The secondary cave was the same size as the first. The only objects occupying the small grotto were three podiums atop an elevated platform. Both platform and podiums were made of one seamless, smooth stone. Cody examined the room. *What was so important about this place that The Thirteenth kept it hidden?*

Before Cody could approach the platform he heard noises coming from the tunnel. *Is that Tat?* Cody felt panic rising up within him. *Has the Golden King come again?* Cody looked for somewhere to hide but knew it was no use. He was caught against an anvil and could do nothing but wait until the hammer struck.

He waited, watching for any sign of light piercing through the black—but none came. Cody's palms were clammy. *Where are you?* A man emerged from the dark as though appearing from thin air. It was not Tat *or* the Golden King—it was The Watching One.

The pupils of the hermit's wide, lid-less eyes made no adjustment as he entered from the dark into the light. Cody stood dumbfounded as the peculiar man came toward him. "Who are you? Why have you been following me?" The man remained silent, ignoring Cody's questions. He reached his hands toward Cody's neck. Cody flinched as the man's rough fingers pressed against him.

Cody grabbed his neck, but the hermit was gone. The room was the same but somehow different. His eyes scanned the cave until they stopped at the podiums. The empty stone podiums were empty no longer. His skin tingled. Upon two of the podiums were the two Books of Power. His heartbeat quickened at the sight of the familiar leather-bound book with the scarlet 'A' embroidered on the cover.

He hurried toward the Book. *I've found it!* Cody stroked his fingers along the leather surface. Oddly, he didn't feel anything. The customary surge of energy never came. He grabbed the Book and tried to lift it but it wouldn't budge. Using his foot to brace himself, he heaved with all his strength; but the Book didn't move. Cody shook his head. *I don't understand...*

He spun to face the entrance. Someone was coming down the tunnel toward the cavern. *Is it The Watching One again?* The sight of the man stole Cody's breath.

"It's you! The one they call The Thirteenth—Boc'ro the Wise. You're supposed to be dead." The man scurried forward without acknowledging Cody's presence. With his head downcast, The Thirteenth walked straight into him and passed through like a ghost. Cody yelled and grabbed his chest as the man reappeared behind him.

The man was muttering to himself. "I made a promise. I made a promise. I made a promise." He carefully inspected the two books on the pedestals; using his fingers he delicately adjusted them, assuring they were perfectly aligned.

A sound resonated from the tunnel and caused both Cody and The Thirteenth to crank their head anxiously. Boc'ro the Wise turned back to the books. "They must not know. Not yet. I made a promise."

Finally satisfied with the books' alignment, he backed away. He began speaking a string of words Cody did not understand. Boc'ro grasped at the air, scooping it toward himself. In the next instant, as though pulled from beneath an invisible curtain, another book appeared. It had a smooth ivory cover, with rounded ridges like a seashell.

Boc'ro the Wise continued to mumble, "I must preserve the Truth. I made a promise." He gingerly set the ivory book on the remaining podium, positioning it as carefully as he had the prior two. When he was finished, he stood at the apex of the three books. "I made a promise. Boc'ro keeps his promises."

The peculiar man resumed his incoherent muttering, his words becoming faster and louder. Cody squinted as a white light appeared. In amazement, Cody realized that it was Boc'ro himself who was shining. He began to glow brighter and brighter and brighter. Cody had to shield his eyes as the entire room filled with the blinding light.

A sucking noise, as though all the air in the room was being vacuumed, sounded in Cody's ear. The light flickered before being snuffed out, hurling the cave back into complete darkness.

Boom!

Light exploded in a churning pillar toward the ceiling. The force of the burst threw Cody from his feet. The light pillar twisted, drilling into the cave's ceiling. Then, as quickly as it had begun, it was over.

Cody opened his eyes cautiously. The pillar of light was gone, although all three Books had a faint, shimmering glow. Boc'ro's skin retained a glimmer as well. "It is done. The Truth has been preserved. Only when the two become one can the one become two."

He continued to ramble about making a promise as he lifted his gaze to the cave's ceiling. Cody's eyes followed. The light-beam had scorched a circular marking into the rock like a laser. Only the spots where the podiums had blocked the light were not seared.

Cody tilted his head as he examined the odd etchings. The three rectangles where the podiums had blocked the light were arranged in the shape of an upside-down arrow. The symbol was centered in the rough, sun-like shape around it. It was the sign of The Earthly Trinity.

"Cody! Snap out of it!"

The cave blurred like a rippling pond. When it came back into focus, the three Books and Boc'ro the Wise had vanished. Cody looked around, momentarily disoriented. The eyelid-less man was gone as well. In his place stood a distressed Tat Shunbickle. Cody glanced around the cave. "There was a man here. Did you see him? He can't have gone far..."

Tat shook Cody's shoulders. "Perhaps not, be *we* should. We need to get out of here." Before Cody could question why, he heard footsteps and saw light leaking from the tunnel entrance.

Cody looked back to the three empty podiums. "I just need a few more minutes. There are answers here..."

"We don't *have* a few more minutes," Tat urged. A man emerged from the tunnel. Cody and the man traded surprised stares. It was the Golden King. Before the King could speak, Cody said, "*Spakious.*"

A portal opened in the center of the cavern, severing two of the podiums in half. The Golden King opened his mouth but Cody never heard what he planned to say. He and Tat dove through the opening.

"*Gai di gasme.*"

The portal closed.

60

The Beautiful and the Ugly

Prince Hansi lifted his head at the sound of the dungeon door opening. There was a click as the door was quickly shut. Hansi tracked the visitor with his eyes as she approached. "Lady Cia," he said politely. "An honor to meet you at last, dear cousin. Tales of your great beauty are well known even in El Dorado."

"Then El Dorado tells dated tales, " Cia said flatly. "Now, if we are finished with empty flattery, let us move on to more important matters."

Hansi grinned. "It appears your sharp tongue is as worthy of tales of its own." His laugh was not returned. Cia remained stone-faced until the Prince finally sighed.

"Very well, what is it you wish to talk about?"

"Why five of my soldiers are dead."

Hansi shrugged. "Many soldiers die during wartime."

Cia's eyes dissected him, searching for a hidden truth beneath his flesh. She appeared content to wait for a confession. Hansi shrugged again. "Why do you accuse me of doing this evil?"

Cia responded instantly. "Because your father is the Golden King." Like a needle drawing blood, the comment drained Hansi's good humor.

"Is the color of a man's soul painted by his father? Your father was called the *Good* King yet your heart seems black as wet dirt."

Cia's eyes narrowed. "You will quickly find yourself *beneath* six feet of wet dirt unless you give me the answers I seek." She leaned closer. "I ask again, why are five of my soldiers dead?"

Hansi matched her gaze. Despite the swollen flaps of skin causing her to squint, there was a fiery determination in the Queen's eyes.

"My father has plotted to gain control of the *The Code*." Hansi smirked. "And I assume he was successful. Otherwise you would not have barged in as you did."

Cia raised her hand as though to slap the Prince, but thought better of it. "You had our Book Keeper and *The Code* in El Dorado for over a week and did not take the Book. Why go through the elaborate plotting to steal it now?"

Hansi raised his eyebrow. "I didn't say anything about *stealing* the Book. I said my father has plotted to take *control* of the Book. That, my dear cousin, is a mighty difference."

"And how does my uncle presume to *take control* of the Book?"

"He doesn't. *Your* people have done that for him."

Cia stood. "You're lying."

Hansi shrugged. "Perhaps."

Cia's face hardened at the jest. She turned and departed. Reaching the door, she hesitated. A moment later she was back before Hansi.

"Who?" she demanded.

Hansi grinned. "I knew you'd warm up to me." *Slap!* This time there was no hesitation as Cia's hand whipped across the Prince's cheek. Hansi waved his finger at her. "Temper, temper..." Cia's arm cocked for another blow.

"Very well..." said Hansi. "You want to know El Dorado's great plan for gaining control over your Book? Isn't it obvious?"

"Tell me!"

"The answer comes down to just one simple word," Hansi's lips curved. *"Jade."*

61

Putting the Pieces Together

Jade wanted nothing more than to strangle Cody. Her face burned with anger. "Are you *crazy?*" Even her best friend's bashful, puppy-dog face was powerless to douse her fury. "You left Atlantis alone, based on the advice of a man who tried to murder us, to go to a location where you knew the Golden King might be? How does that not compute as a horrendous idea?"

Even free-spirited Tiana seemed slightly stunned. Only Xerx appeared mildly amused. Cody shook his head. *What is the world coming to when Xerx is my only ally?* "In my defense, I *wasn't* alone. Tat was with me."

"I don't trust Tat," said Jade and Tiana in unison. Cody plopped himself onto the floor of Jade's chamber with the others. He glanced to the door. Since the still-unexplainable disappearance of the guards, Cia had tripled the watch. Cody dropped his voice to a whisper.

"I admit I may have acted a bit rash, but it was worth it." He heard Jade mutter something about dumb luck, but continued, "The Prophecy about The Earthly Trinity—I think there is a third Book."

Xerx frowned. "That doesn't make sense. Everyone knows the history. The two Books of Power were made after the First Great War as a peace treaty, to divide the Orb's power between Atlantis and El Dorado. Two cities. Two Books. So why a third?"

Tiana nodded. "And why create a third Book only to keep it hidden?" She had a point. Although, the Book's creator, Boc'ro the Wise, had also kept *himself* a secret until recently. Cody closed his eyes, conjuring up the vision he had witnessed.

"There was something else. Something odd The Thirteenth said. Something about *only after the two become one could the one become two.* Does that mean anything to you guys?" He was answered by three blank stares. "Yeah, I didn't think so."

"What about this part?" Jade pointed to the stone tablet on the floor between them. "This mumbo jumbo about a pure angel and a required sacrifice. Do we know any more about what this means?"

Cody went cold. He exchanged a quick glance with Tiana. "No." His abrupt, forceful answer made Jade examine him curiously. He could feel beads of perspiration forming on his forehead. Mercifully Xerx bailed him out.

"Could there be a connection with the object you found in Jade's father's office?" Cody was glad to shift the discussion.

"Perhaps. Although the object CROSS has is made of wood. If there really is a third Book, it has a seashell cover. Besides, when the Golden King and I brought our two Books together they *connected* somehow. I saw a vision. Nothing similar happened in Mr. Shimmers' office."

The four drifted into silent contemplation. Somewhere amidst the muddled riddles were the solutions they sought. Yet, even their combined intellect proved insufficient. Cody sighed.

"At least we're getting closer to figuring this out."

"I hope so," said Xerx. "Because we also have less time than ever before." He pointed to the last phrase of The Prophecy: *The Universe's Most Powerful Force is Revealed to Thee.* "The race to crack this code is winner-take-all. There's no prize for second or third."

Cody's resolve drained. "And I keep getting the feeling that right now we're a distant third in that race."

62

A Secret Weapon

He should be dead. It had been three days. Three long days of evading death. Yet, whether by fate or inexplicable luck, Dace was still alive. He knew, however, that you could only roll the dice for so long until eventually luck would forsake you. He prayed that time had not yet come.

Dace kept his eyes downcast as he marched. Golden golems flanked him on all four sides. The sound of four hundred thousand feet shook the earth as the army advanced across the wasteland. Every step brought them closer to the walls of Atlantis.

The thick storm clouds following the army were both a blessing and a curse. While they shrouded the camp in a constant dreary aura they also helped keep Dace's identity secret. As long as he didn't draw undue attention to himself he could blend in. He did so by constantly moving. The army ranks were in such disorder no one questioned his coming or going. He spent each night at a different campfire, sitting silent and listening.

Due to the constant blanket of clouds, time was nebulous to Dace. The army marched until told to do otherwise. His feet throbbed by the time the day's march was finally called to a halt and the men made camp. As always Dace selected the night's campfire based on volume. If his friendship with Wolfrick had taught him just one thing, it was that there was no greater mine for extracting secrets than a blowhard soldier.

On this night he found his target in the form of a soldier with facial hair so profuse it consumed his eyes, nose, and mouth. Below the hairy globe was a rotund body, inflated more by hot air than muscle. The hair where his mouth should be jiggled as he boasted.

"I've said it before, and I'll say it again. If it were up to Yours Truly I'd storm Atlantis myself with one arm tied behind my back and still clear the Outer-Wall in time for breakfast! Fortunately for them, the Lord of the Lights thinks my talents are better served by allowing my valor to rub off on the likes of you lousy new recruits."

Dace inwardly groaned as the others around the fire inhaled the man's fluff with beaming admiration. The only thing worse than an arrogant soldier was an arrogant commanding officer. Before he could think better of it Dace blurted, "Don't forget about that Captain Dace Ringstar. He's sure to be on the Outer-Wall. I have heard it said that he's the greatest swordsman who ever lived." The hothead's laugh was mimicked by his admirers around the fire.

"*Ha!* Dace is a wrinkle-less boy. I could best him with my bare hands! But we all know that *The Impaler* has claimed the boy-captain for his own. *The Spider* takes it personally when people challenge his title as greatest swordsman."

How flattering, Dace thought. "Surely as one of the Golden King's chosen you must know his plan for breaching Atlantis' forty-foot walls..." Dace let the comment dangle over the campfire as bait. As he had expected, the egotistic officer bit the lure. He leaned forward.

"Aye, I've heard whispers. It seems the Lord of Lights has someone *inside* Atlantis' royal palace!" A skinny soldier to his left waved his hand, "Is that all, Gote? Everyone knows *that*. I thought you had something juicy." Only the thick carpet of facial hair hid the flush on Gote's face.

"That's not the *half* of it," he declared. "The other day I heard it from the mouth of the Radiant King *himself* that he has a *secret weapon* to breach the First Wall." Dace tilted his head. *Now we're getting somewhere...*

"What is this secret weapon?"

Gote frowned and turned to Dace. "Do you think I eat off the King's golden tray? Ain't much of a secret if he went around telling everyone, is it? Although I'll give up my sword and become a priest if that ain't what's being kept hidden in those pyramid buildings. The hollow-men guard it day and night. But, enough of this. Did I ever tell you boys about the time I defeated an entire Atlantian legion just by staring at them? Well, it all started when..."

As the man entered into his tale Dace looked down the valley. As Gote had said, a circle of *Rephaim* warriors surrounded the pyramids. For all the officer's nonsense, he was right about at least one thing: whatever was being hidden at the center of the camp was important. The soldiers, hypnotized by Gote's farcical story, didn't even notice Dace's departure or his discreet movements toward the camp's nucleus.

63

The New Brotherhood

_____

_____

Cody hesitated at the Monastery door. He had decided to share his experience at the Caves with Master Stalkton. However, now that he had reached the Monastery he wasn't sure he was in the mood for the pale priest's cryptic lectures or tactless remarks. Cody took a deep breath. *For Jade's sake...*

He stepped through the doors—and into chaos. Thunderous noise shook the Sanctuary. He heard screaming. Cody's pulse accelerated. There were no more monks. That could only mean...

Master Stalkton!

Cody dashed up the staircase, clearing three steps a stride. The sound of shouting echoed against the large, dome-roofed room. Suddenly the walls of a corridor lit up and a ball of fire shot out of it, crashing against the far wall.

"Master!" Cody dashed toward the hallway as it spat out flames. A moment later he had to dive out of the way as a flood of water billowed from the entrance. The instant the surge had passed Cody was back on his feet running.

"Umph!"

Cody crashed into someone running toward him. He grasped onto the person to keep from falling. To his surprise it was Tiana; her hair was frizzled and her skin was covered in grime. She was sobbing. Cody pulled her close. "What's going on? I need to get you out of here!"

Cody paused. Tiana wasn't crying—she was *laughing*. He stared at her in dumbfounded confusion. More laughter came from the hallway and a stubby figure waddled into view.

"M-m-m-my apologies, my lady," the stumpy man croaked. "It's my stutter. E-e-e-every time I try to say the correct High Language word my stutter turns it into the wrong one." Cody's confusion leapt to new heights.

"Poe?"

Poe's eyes bulged the size of apples at the sight of Cody. "M-m-m-master Cody...I-I-I'm glad to s-s-see you..." Poe's terrified expression called his own bluff. After all, the last time Cody had seen the pear-shaped servant he had tricked him and left him locked in a prison cell.

Cody rubbed his forehead. "What in the world is going on?" Another *boom* shook the floor. When the trembling ceased, Tiana took Cody's hand. "Come, I'll show you." She led him down the corridor as Poe waddled after them. The passageway opened into a large atrium. Cody was astonished. The room was crowded with people.

The packed room contained the oddest assortment of individuals Cody had ever seen. Elderly people stood alongside youth, both men and women, nobility and vagrant. Most in the room were strangers; however, he recognized several familiar faces, such as *Under-Earth Rumblings* reporter Fincher Tople and Gelph, the beggar. Even frizzy- haired Sally Peatwee was present, making Cody feel instantly guilty for not having checked in on her since the rescue.

At the front of the assembly, elevated on a platform, stood Xerx. His hands danced through the air as he spoke. "The Orb's power is limitless, but *we* are not. Never forget that. The more time you spend practicing the simple High Language the easier it will become. Of course, you will not become as powerful as Master Stalkton overnight! And furthermore, you must always..."

Tiana leaned toward Cody. "He's calling it the *New Brotherhood*. All the old monks were killed during the King's funeral ambush so Xerx had the idea to re-open the Monastery to anyone willing to learn."

The crowd applauded as Xerx demonstrated a new High Language word. Tiana eagerly added her own clapping to the ovation. "Xerx had assumed Master Stalkton would train the new recruits but the priest had other plans. Stalkton is taking a temporarily leave to handle some unfinished business. He's given Xerx charge over the Monastery and the New Brotherhood until he returns. Xerx has been doing a fantastic job so far."

Cody noticed her fair cheeks turn pink. He smiled but held his tongue. Xerx continued his lecture, "The aim of using the High Language is *not* to show off how powerful a creator you are, it is to be effective and make a difference. Simple is best. And *never* forget..."

Xerx's voice faded as he caught sight of Cody. He looked uncomfortable. He motioned for Cody to come to the platform. Cody understood. *He feels awkward teaching when the Book Keeper is here. He wants* me *to teach.*

Cody waved him off and winked. Xerx grinned, returned a slight nod, and then resumed the lesson. Cody slipped into the back row and spent the rest of the evening practicing alongside the new recruits. It was refreshing to return to the basics of training. All other fears and worries dissipated as he was swept away in the joy of creating, a joy that he had lost somewhere along the way.

Tiana had spoken truly; Xerx *was* doing a great job. *I may be the Book Keeper, but Xerx is who Atlantis truly needs.* There was no anger or jealousy in the realization. He was genuinely happy for his former rival.

When Xerx announced it was time to spar in pairs, Cody's face lit up. Before Xerx had even finished speaking Cody pushed through the crowd and claimed Fincher Tople as his partner. The pure horror on the journalist's face was something Cody hoped never to forget.

Tonight is a good night.

Lamgorious Stalkton listened to the sounds of the practice. *Oh, to be young again,* he thought. *At least I still have my good looks.* He rolled his cart away from the door, humming one of his favorite tunes. He suspected he had written the song himself, although he wasn't quite sure. Of course, it was his habit to claim any expression of brilliance as his own, as it undoubtedly must have been.

He snatched his walking stick from against the wall. He wiggled his leg stumps and knew he had no real need for the stick; yet, it seemed morally wrong to depart on an adventurous journey *without* a good walking stick. He placed it in the back of his cart beside his bag brimming with three-dozen blackened-earthworms and *de-fossilized* cucumber sandwiches. *All the essentials,* he thought, hoping it would be enough.

"The time has come!" He spun his cart to face the far wall. *"Spakious."* The wall morphed into a portal. A gust of heat seeped through from the other side. "And so my adventure begins..."

64

The Correspondent

It appeared on the horizon with the day's first light as though inexplicably built overnight. In the distance, across the sprawling desert wasteland, rested the majestic walled-city of Atlantis.

Randilin gazed longingly across the sand dunes at his home. He wanted to run to it, but knew there remained several long marching days until they arrived. The clamor of fifty thousand soldiers behind him dulled his eagerness. *I return home bringing only death. Atlantis will fall.*

Randilin turned to depart but his face collided with something as solid as a brick wall. He looked up into the helmeted face of *The Impaler,* his insect pincers bulging against his cheeks as he towered over the dwarf. Randilin stumbled backwards.

"Kael, you scared the stinking snot outa' me!" The Spider-General produced a shrill hiss at the sound of his birth name, as he did every time Randilin used it. Randilin couldn't bring himself to use any of the man's new titles;

if not for respect of the man, for honor of the man he had once been long, long ago.

The Impaler thrust his fist at the dwarf, opening it to reveal a crumpled piece of paper. Randilin retrieved it. "New orders, eh?" His irritation turned to surprise. "Bloody blazes of bogar! They've gone and kidnapped the pretty Prince himself!" The Spider hissed again. Randilin shooed him with his hand. "Oh, simmer down. Go catch a fly or something."

He skimmed the rest of the dispatch. Each line he read lowered the temperature of his blood by a few degrees. *This is not good news.* "I'll deliver your orders straightaway." With an exaggerated bow he set off toward the tents. The moment he was out of earshot from The Spider-General, he exhaled. *The second they realize you're afraid, you've lost,* he reminded himself for the thousandth time.

As he reached the camp he looked over his shoulder to confirm that he wasn't being followed. With a quick glance the other way, he slipped into his tent, pulling the flap shut. He ran to the back of the tent and began frantically digging through a mound of belongings until he found a chest. Unlocking the latch, he opened it and retrieved a round object.

Randilin unfolded *The Impaler's* dispatch on the table. *I need to be quick.* He set to rapidly copying the orders written on the paper. He hoped his correspondent would get the message in time. He heard noises outside his tent. Sweat poured down his face as he relayed the final line. A waft of air washed over him as his privacy was breached. "Hello, my old friend."

Randilin cursed to himself and turned to face the Golden King. "If you're my friend than I'm Under-Earth's most eligible bachelor." The Golden King smiled, an icy gesture devoid of any humor.

"So...what is so important that you felt the need to delay delivering my orders by rushing into this tent?" The King's ruby eyes narrowed and his voice took on the intensity of an overdue volcano. "Did I catch you at a bad time?" Randilin huffed.

"I entered this tent to relieve my terrible gas from tonight's foul supper!" He waved his hand in front of his nose. "So you'd be wise not to linger; and while you're going anyways, you can deliver your own wretched orders to the men." Randilin wadded up the paper and tossed it at the King.

They stood, their eyes locked in an uneasy stare for several tense moments. Finally, the King grinned again. "Come, let us walk together." Without further words the King ducked out of the tent. As Randilin followed he glanced over his shoulder at the bowl sitting on the table.

That was too close.

65

A Deadly Plot

For the first time in weeks Cody felt hopeful. The training session with the New Brotherhood had put a skip in his step and neither the dark clouds above nor the unpleasant aroma of the overcrowded city could dampen his mood. As it turned out, using Fincher Tople as a practice punching bag had been the perfect remedy.

He had worked up a sweat during the practice and was eager for a bath. He stopped at the door to his chamber where his eyes wandered to Jade's closed door. Her drastic transformation and enraged outbursts were an unrelenting weight on his shoulders. If, as The Thirteenth claimed, the *one closest to him must pay the price*, then he decided it best to keep Jade at arm's length. However, he had not foreseen her condition. For once in his life, she needed *him,* and he wasn't going to let her down.

Cody began to approach Jade's door but a nauseating waft of his own stink suggested a bath was still first priority. As soon as his body no longer smelt like spoiled milk he would visit his best friend and start putting the pieces of his life back in order; and this time he wouldn't let anything get in his way. Satisfied with his new resolve, he opened his door—and found Tat Shunbickle sitting on his bed.

The scout raised his head as Cody entered. "About time you returned. Come on, there's no time to waste. We need to go." He stood and made his way to the door. "We have a situation."

"The bad kind?"

Tat nodded. "The worst."

"The Golden Knife has been unleashed."

The Queen's words generated instant fear, passing from face to face around the war-room table. Even the inscrutable Gongore Levenworth looked uneasy at the announcement. The terror was contagious. "What is the Golden Knife?" Cody asked. "Does the blade have special power?"

"The Golden Knife is not a *what*, it is a *who*," Kantan said.

"An *extremely lethal* who," Levenworth added. "The Golden Knife is El Dorado's elite force for making people... *disappear*." There was no confusing the General's meaning.

"So they are assassins," Cody concluded, his fear growing with his understanding.

"Yes, but not just *any* assassins. They are the best," Levenworth said. "The Golden Knife consists of five, never more, never less. There are five golden daggers. The only way to join the Knife is to kill one of the existing five mem-

224

bers and claim his gold dagger. They are the best of the best. We have no record of the Golden Knife ever failing to eliminate their target."

Cody gulped. "And these assassins are coming *here*?"

Kantan nodded with a grim countenance. "My sister Eva claims to have contact with a mole inside the enemy's camp." Cody immediately thought of Dace. *Could he still be alive?*

"Who is Eva's source?" The question brought a frown to Levenworth's face.

"The princess has refused to disclose his identity. It seems she suspects that even our Inner-Council is not safe from the Golden King's spies. She refers to him only in code as—the Keeper of the Fishbowl."

Cody barely managed to suppress his grin. *Randilin.* So the ugly dwarf was alive after all; and if anyone was suited for life as a traitorous double-agent, it was him. "Did the source reveal the target?"

Cia shook her head. "He did not. It could be any one of us around this table." Cody glanced at each face, knowing they were doing the same toward him. One of them was going to be assassinated.

"When will the Golden Knife strike?" All eyes fixed on Cia as she answered.

"*Tonight.*"

66

An Uneasy Wait

Few things are more difficult than trying to go about your day with a smile on your face all the while knowing that at nightfall you could be the target of the world's deadliest band of assassins. It seemed a swarm of butterflies had taken residence in Cody's stomach. Everything he looked at, be it man, building, cloud or rock, seemed to morph into a golden dagger.

The Inner-Council decided it would be best to keep the impending assassination attempt secret. If rumor spread to the already fragile public that the legendary Golden Knife had been loosed it would ignite panic. And there was enough of that already.

It had also been decreed that the potential targets would be divided into pairs and hidden in various parts of the city under guard. No group would know the whereabouts of the other groups. In this way, they stood a better chance of evading the Knife's strike or at the least they would prevent exposing all of the Royalty and prominent leaders to a single devastating massacre. Cody suspected there were other concerns at play as well. Although no one verbalized it, the prevailing suspicion and the conviction that a mole may have infiltrated their inner circle may as well have been scribbled in large print on the wall.

After much discussion, the arrangements had been finalized and the pairings determined. Now came the hardest part—the waiting. Cody was eager for any distraction. He decided to join the New Brotherhood for another training session. However, despite admirable improvements in the new recruits' abilities, the impending threat had soured Cody's mood. After all, what good was one week's training against a legion of Dark-Wielders? Or when facing the Golden King himself?

Cody tried to push the thought from his mind. The only person in Atlantis who needed to be prepared to face the Golden King was him, and that notion was much too depressing to ponder at the moment. *It won't matter if I don't live through today*, he acknowledged gloomily.

From across the training room Tiana shot him an annoyed expression and pointed to her face, suggesting that pouting faces were unwelcome. Cody frowned even deeper. He decided it would be easier to leave than to fake a smile. He departed without waving goodbye.

He walked, paying no heed to where he was going. When he became aware of his surroundings he was standing at the entrance to the garden. *Solitude.*

So much time had passed since he had last visited the garden. He noticed right away that he had not been the only one to ignore the location. The plants were either overgrown, dying, or both. It appeared that following

Prince Foz's departure the plants had been left to die. *Like the city around it.*

"Cody?" In the quiet garden the voice seemed a roar. Cody followed the voice to a bench where a woman was sitting. It was Sally Peatwee. "I'm sorry to startle you."

Cody took a seat beside her. "What are you doing here?" Sally looked around, plucking a wilted purple flower.

"Solitude," she said with a wry smile. For a while they both sat in quiet, enjoying the peace. With the city's over-crowding, Cody had almost forgotten what it was like to experience silence.

"You still haven't told me how you ended up in that tent."

"You still haven't asked," Sally responded. She plucked another flower. "I had only returned to Upper-Earth for a day when my diner was invaded. I was captured by CROSS. It seems I was to be used as leverage for some scheme of theirs. I don't know how long they kept me, but eventually I was delivered to the Golden King."

"Wait, CROSS is working with El Dorado?"

Sally shrugged. "That I don't know. But I do know what the Golden King wanted me for. To use Randilin." She took a deep breath. "I need to tell you something about Randilin. You deserve to know the full story. The truth of *Randilin's Dark Deeds.* I..."

Dooooooong!

The abrupt clang of the gong caused both of them to jump. The gong sounded six more times. The closer the black storm clouds came to the city the less distinct day and night became. Seven rings of the gong signified night had come.

Cody jumped to his feet. "Blast! I need to go. I'm sorry. I don't have time to explain. We'll finish this conversation another time. I promise." Sally nodded in understanding. Cody ran from the garden, adrenaline raging through his body. The wait was over. The Golden Knife was coming.

67

Shadows in the Night

The night air was uncommonly quiet and a nipping chill swept down from the black clouds above. The frosty breeze had sent the citizens of Atlantis retreating to shelter. Even the refugees had abandoned the open streets in search of asylum from the cold.

Horne Stalwarg peered uneasily into the shadows; his frenetic mind conjuring visions of what ghosts and creatures may be lurking within them. General Levenworth had warned his night patrol to be on high alert but had done so without explanation. The ambiguity had become the breeding ground for a dozen nightmarish possibilities.

Horne's route crossed with fellow night watchman, Boras Uptar. The elder soldier's face displayed the same apprehension. The entire patrol had sensed it: something was going to happen that night. Something dreadful.

Horne stopped. A strange popping sound was coming from the gloom. He strained his ears but the sound was gone. *It's just my imagination,* he thought. He looked over his shoulder but Boras was already out of view and earshot. He hesitated, and then moved cautiously around the corner.

He called into the shadows. "Who goes there?" There was no answer. His eyes darted from side to side as he inched deeper down the dark alley. His fingers squeezed tighter around the handle of his halberd.

Click...Click...Click...

"Ahh!" He spun around, blindly thrusting his weapon toward the sound but the alley was empty. He backed away, pivoting left and right as his heart pounded like a hammer against an anvil.

Click...Click...Click...

Something moved behind him. He twirled, slicing through the shadows with his axe. There was a loud *clang* as his blade ricocheted off the stone wall.

Click...Click...Click...

He screamed and spun around again. The last sight Horne Stalwarg saw was the glimmer of the gold dagger as it sliced down at him.

68

Waiting for the Pinch

Cody peered out the window at the empty streets below. A foreboding tension hung thick on the air as though the city itself was holding its breath in apprehension. Somewhere out in the night, scuttling through the dark alleys like unseen vermin, the assassins were closing in.

A husky voice from behind him ordered, "Get down from there!" Cody pulled his head from the slim window opening. Wolfrick knelt beside Cody on the floor. "Watching for them won't make 'em come any quicker," the large soldier said, "and if they see you, our location is blown."

Despite Wolfrick's caution Cody had the nagging impulse to peek back through the narrow window. The waiting was unbearable. Even Princess Eva's calming presence failed to slow his frenzied nerves. Cody had personally requested the princess as his pairing and Wolfrick to head the trio of soldiers that was assigned to them. He prayed the other groups were still safe. None more so than Jade.

They waited. Time never moved slower than when waiting for something terrible to happen. Eventually Cody couldn't handle the anticipation. He rose to his knees and crawled back toward the window. "Quiet!" Wolfrick ordered. Cody halted. Wolfrick cupped his ear and motioned toward the door. Cody held his breath and listened.

Click...Click...Click...

His face went pale.

Someone was coming.

Jade stared unwavering at the staircase winding up toward the exit. It was not the desire to go up the stairs that overwhelmed her; it was the hope that no one would come down. She wondered how Cody and the others were faring.

Unlike the others, Jade was not privileged with a friend to wait out the storm. Suspicion over her involvement in the Yanci's Pub massacre and the Book's disappearance was still prevalent, so she had been escorted to the deepest dungeon and locked in a cell, alone. Well, *almost* alone.

"Lady Jade..." She flinched at the sound of her name, chomping down on her tongue. In the adjacent cell, with all four limbs chained to the wall, was Ugar-Kir-Hugar. The Garga Prince was looking at her with startling intensity. "You must remain calm."

Jade frowned. *"Calm?* I will be *calm* when I know Cody is safe."

Kir-Hugar examined her with a blank face.

"Safety for Cody...But not for yourself?"

"I deserve no safety," Jade said. "Not after the terrible things I've done. I've killed men. I'm a monster."

Kir-Hugar stretched his neck toward her. "We have a saying amongst the Garga. *Some men build, others tear down, yet all dwell within the Great Garganton's mouth and live according to his mercy.*"

Noticing Jade's puzzled expression, Kir-Hugar explained, "Good or bad, we are all unworthy in comparison to the Great One. We all rely on his goodness. That puts all of us, even the *monsters*, in the same place, no matter how much good or evil you have committed."

The Garga Prince's words should have been comforting, yet the recent recollection of his stone dagger against her throat dulled such a sentiment. "Thank you," she muttered. They both settled into wordless waiting. With no windows it was impossible to know if night had arrived, but Jade was sure it must have. That meant that at that very moment the Golden Knife was roaming the city on its deadly hunt.

Jade's senses heightened as a noise sounded from the top of the staircase. The sounds were muffled and indistinguishable. Kir-Hugar's chains clanked as he stood. His demeanor was calm, but Jade could sense his fierce readiness. The noise continued from the stairwell.

Thump...thump...thump...

Jade braced herself. She rattled the locked door of her cell, knowing it was a useless gesture, but feeling obliged to try anyways. Kir-Hugar stood motionless.

Thump...thump...thump...

Two shapes tumbled down the stairs into view and onto the floor. It was the two prison guards—both had their throats slashed. The sound of footfall descending the steps followed.

I'm the target. They're coming for me.

Three tall, cloaked men appeared at the base of the stairs, gliding toward her like wraiths. Jade backed away until her back pressed against the cold stone of the cell wall. Kir-Hugar was shouting but the three assassins paid him no heed. They reached Jade's cell. With a clang the lock fell to the ground and the cell door opened. The front assassin pulled out a solid gold dagger, and entered.

69

Inside the Walls

Click...Click...Click...
Cody crouched behind a chair, his stomach churning and his eyes transfixed on the doorknob. *They're coming for me. I'm the target.* Wolfrick pressed his ear to the door.

"There's someone on the other side." Wolfrick and the two guards drew their weapons. Cody grabbed Eva's hand and squeezed it tight.

Click...Click...Click...

Wolfrick motioned to the two guards. "Quickly. Barricade the door." The two soldiers sheathed their swords and set to blockading the entrance. The chair hiding Cody was pulled away and used to jam the doorknob.

"There's no way anyone can break through that. We're safe in here," Cody whispered, as much to himself as to the others, knowing it was a fat lie. If the assassins wanted to breach the barrier they would—and he had no doubt that was what they *did* want. Cody listened anxiously for the clicking noise but the sound he heard next was unexpected.

DONG!...DONG!...DONG!

"The sanctuary gong," said Cody, his voice rising with panic. "What does that mean? Is it morning already?" Wolfrick moved swiftly to the window and glanced out.

"No lad, seven rings signals morning. I heard only three."

"What do three chimes mean?" Wolfrick turned back to face him.

"Three chimes is an alarm. The Golden Knife has struck."

Cody jumped to his feet. "Where? Who? We need to go. They need our help!" He started for the door but Wolfrick's large hand grabbed him and held him in place.

"No. If the Golden Knife has struck then we're already too late. Besides, you don't know where the others are hiding."

"I know where Jade is," Cody insisted, but Wolfrick didn't release his grip.

"It might be a trap to draw us out. It's far too dangerous. We stick to the plan." Cody bit down on his lip so hard his teeth met. He looked helplessly out the window as Atlantis woke under the gong's dreary drone.

Please be safe, Jade...

Randilin stared at the Atlantis skyline. Faint torchlights twinkled like tiny fireflies in the distance. Even so, he could hear the monotonous toll drifting across the desert. The harbinger of death.

He had managed to send word to Eva that the Golden Knife had been dispatched. He had done all he could. However, he knew forewarning did not guarantee safety. *No matter how brave a face you wear, or how hard you flex, a knife will still puncture your skin.*

"Is something bothering you, my foul little friend?" The words announced the arrival of the Golden King. Randilin realized he had been holding his breath. He quickly exhaled and relaxed his shoulders.

"The only thing bothering me is that you keep bloody sneaking up on me," Randilin growled. The Golden King's ruby eyes narrowed.

"An odd comment from one who has been creeping around this camp for days." The remark startled Randilin. *Does he know? Surely not. He couldn't.* Randilin kept his gaze straight ahead, disguising his worry and deflecting the accusation.

"The Golden Knife is five, no more, no less. Everybody knows that. Yet I counted only three that passed through the Dark-Wielder's portal."

"You wonder about the location of the other two?" A self-satisfied snigger formed on the King's face. "Did you think I would yield my prized Knife on a whim?"

Randilin's body went rigid as the realization hit him. "The other two assassins were already in Atlantis."

"They infiltrated Atlantis weeks ago under the guise of refugees. In that time they have been positioning themselves and waiting." The King rapped his long fingers together. "Oh, yes. They are *very* good at what they do—and what they do is *kill*."

238

Randilin cursed inwardly. *I must warn Eva!*

As the King turned to leave, he looked back over his shoulder with a mocking grin. "Oh, and the sound of the gong means it is too late to rush off and alert your little friends through that sand bowl."

He knows.

Randilin's lips bumbled, trying without success to form a suitable lie. The King merely sneered. "It's time for the Golden Knife to strike—and my Knife never strikes late."

The two sentinels in Cody's hiding room confirmed that their barricade was virtually impenetrable. It would be near impossible for anyone to get in—or *out*.

The torches lighting the room flicked before dwindling out. The two men reached to their belts and pulled out daggers.

Daggers made of solid gold.

70

A Bloody Night

The whistling of the gold dagger cutting through the air was the only warning Cody had. He flung his head back but not quick enough. Blood spurted as the tip of the blade sliced open his right nostril. *"Ahh!"*

Cody grabbed at his gushing nose and backed away. The two assassins moved with inhuman speed. Cody glimpsed the flash of another knife. *"Sellunga!"* A steel sword sprouted up from Cody's hands just in time to parry the blow.

Clang!

The giant frame of Wolfrick jumped in front of him. He twirled his large axe in a powerful sweeping motion, parrying two blows at once. "Cody. Eva. Get the blazes out of here! I'll hold them off."

The wraithlike shapes of the assailants danced around the room in a blur of movement. Cody pointed and yelled in warning, "Behind you!" Wolfrick spun, bringing his axe up just in time to deflect the attack. Before Cody could give another warning the second assassin appeared from the other side and plunged his golden knife up to the hilt into Wolfrick's back.

"Noooo!"

Wolfrick stumbled to one knee. He groaned as the assassin landed three subsequent blows into his back. Cody stood frozen in disbelief. The assassin brought the knife up for a final killing slice. Then, to Cody's astonishment, Wolfrick began to laugh. "Dace says I'm already a dead man walking—dead men don't die so easily."

Wolfrick pushed himself from the ground and swung his head back. The head-butt crashed into the assassin's chin. Spinning around, Wolfrick raised his weapon and with his final breath of life brought the axe head down on the stunned foe.

The remaining assassin lunged forward over the two dead bodies on the floor. Cody opened his mouth to launch a High Language attack, but his adversary was too quick. The assassin's hand grasped Cody's mouth, suffocating his words.

There was a sudden pounding on the chamber door. People were shouting from the other side and ramming against it, but the barricade held. *They won't break through in time. He's going to kill me.* Cody watched the golden dagger rise, waiting for it to plunge into his heart—but it never did. The assassin's gaze fell upon Princess Eva, still curled against the wall on the other side of the room.

Pop.

The air split like a zipper as a wormhole opened in the middle of the chamber. Cody felt faint hope return. *Please be Xerx and Tiana coming to rescue us.* Those hopes died a swift death as two hooded men stepped through the portal into the room.

Both of them wielded solid gold daggers.

71

A Welcome Friend

The two reinforcements towered over Cody; both scanning the room with vulturous eyes beneath their deep hoods. Their gaze passed over Cody, still held captive by the first assassin, and stopped on the young Atlantian Princess. The taller of the new arrivals, standing well over seven feet, moved toward Eva. As he did he removed his hood, revealing a head comprised entirely of crystal. It was a Dark-Wielder.

The Princess' eyes widened in terror at the revelation, yet she didn't flee as the Dark-Wielder approached. The Wielder clutched Eva's neck with one hand and lifted her off her feet.

Cody thrashed helplessly against his captor's grip. He chomped down on the man's hand as hard as he could, drawing blood. But the man did not so much as flinch. The futile barrage continued outside the door as the Dark-Wielder carried Eva toward the portal.

The second newcomer had remained perfectly still at the mouth of the wormhole. Then, in a blur of motion, he raised his golden knife and sent it flying through the air across the room.

CRACK!

Cody shielded his eyes as crystal shards rained down on him. Half of the Dark-Wielder's crystal head had been shattered. The creature dropped to the floor, releasing Eva in the process. The grip on Cody's mouth vanished. He gasped as he sucked air back into his lungs.

Sparks flew as the two remaining Golden Knife assassins pirouetted around the room. Cody had never seen two combatants move with such speed and grace. The gilded daggers sliced through the air as each fighter lashed out in a furious attack.

There was no time to question why his enemies had turned against each other. Cody forced himself to look away from the transfixing contest. He helped Eva to her feet and dashed to the door, the pounding continuing from the other side. Cody pressed his palm to the door. *"Duomi."* The blockade exploded, launching the debris across the room with such force that it burst through the stone wall.

In ran Levenworth, followed by a dozen armed soldiers. Tat Shunbickle emerged holding his bow. He notched an arrow and let it fly toward the back of the closest assassin.

At the *twang* of the bowstring the assassin pivoted, slicing his blade down and severing the arrow shaft in two. Then, twirling around, he resumed his battle against his comrade. Tat fitted another arrow. But before he could release it one of the assassins launched himself across the room and dove headfirst through the newly formed hole in the wall. Cody dashed after him, looking down four stories to the ground below, but the man had vanished.

Tat shifted his aim toward the remaining assassin and released the arrow. The man rolled to the side, dodging the projectile. The other soldiers cut off the escape routes. The hooded killer threw his golden dagger to the floor and raised his hands. "Wait!"

The men hesitated. The assassin removed his hood to reveal a familiar face. "What the blazes...Captain Ringstar?" Dace's face was coated with crusted blood and his handsome features were gaunt.

Cody rushed toward him. "You're alive!" He flung himself on his friend. General Levenworth stroked his bearded chin. "You have much explaining to do, Captain Ringstar." Dace nodded wearily, his eyes fixed on the bloody back of Wolfrick crumpled on the floor.

"Indeed, I do, General. But not now. I have horrible news." He turned to Cody with an anguished face. "I am so sorry. I know you will never forgive me for what I've done, but I had to make a quick choice and I did. Now I must live with consequences. I'm sorry."

Cody melted under the weight of Dace's words. "What do you mean? What have you done?"

Dace took a deep breath. "The Golden Knife intended to cause a diversion. Once the alarm sounded we were to meet up with the others and eliminate the actual target intended all along. Each member of the Knife knows only part of the mission; only that part which is essential to carrying out his objective. I did not know what—*whom*—the diversion was until we were there. I didn't know what to do. If I had tried to save her I would have given up any chance of saving the real target. So I did nothing. I left her—I left her there to die."

A single tear slid down Dace's cheek. Cody backed away. "What are you talking about? Who did you leave to die?" Dace hung his head.

"Jade."

72

Another Killer

Cody ran faster than he had ever run before. Voices shouted after him, giving heed that the assassin was loose in the city. He ignored the warnings. He *hoped* the assassin was still out there. If Jade had been harmed in any way El Dorado would pay dearly for it.

He shoved through the crowd. The constant ringing of the gong drowned out the electric clamor of disturbed citizens. The alarm had ignited frenzied chaos throughout the streets. Cody shoved people aside as he dug his way through the mob toward the dungeon cells.

He felt nauseous. Why had he ever agreed to let Jade out of his sight? Ever since The Thirteenth had prophesied, *"The one closest to you must pay that price,"* he had been playing a high-stakes chess game against Fate, with Jade's life the prize. Time and time again Fate was proving to be the more skilled player.

When he reached the prison entrance he found a crowd already clogging the entrance. Cody didn't slow his pace. *"Byrae!"* A wall of wind crashed down from above, parting the multitude. Cody ran through the gap and down the stairs, clearing four or five steps with each stride.

At the bottom two guards lay lifeless on the ground. He stepped over them and scanned the dungeon. Both cell doors were wide open and empty.

Oh, please, no…

Cody started forward, but his foot stubbed into something he hadn't noticed. On the floor was a third body; or rather, the *shape* of a body, as it resembled a human form in silhouette only. The lump had been scorched as black as coal.

Too big for Jade, he concluded. Cody didn't hear the others arrive behind him. Tat knelt down beside the charred corpse and pointed to its hand. "Look here." The hand was coated in a golden cap. "This was the fifth assassin. The intense heat melted his gold dagger."

A soft sound emanated from the shadows of the cell. It was the sound of quiet sobbing. "Who's there?" Dace demanded. "Expose yourself."

The sniffling continued. Dace inched forward and then his sword arm dropped. "Impossible. It's Jade!"

Cody needed no further invitation. He shoved through the guards and darted into the cell. Jade huddled in the corner with her knees pulled tightly against her chest. She looked up as Cody entered, her green eyes glistening. Cody wrapped his arms around her.

Levenworth appeared at the entrance of the cell. His face registered the usual mixture of suspicion and annoyance. "We have no time for sentimentality. What happened here?" He scanned the adjacent cell. The chains hung loosely on the wall. "Where is the Garga Princeling? Where is Ugar Kir-Hugar?"

"He's gone," said Jade, her voice distant. "I let him go." The General's face reddened.

"You did *what*? Have you lost your mind, Surface-Dweller? It's bad enough to have a member of the Knife still loose in our city *without* Garga savages roaming as well."

"Speaking of the Golden Knife," Dace interjected, kneeling beside the blackened body on the floor. "What happened here? What happened to this assassin? Did Kir-Hugar kill him?"

Jade stood and walked toward the dead body. The soldiers stepped away as she approached. She looked down on the blackened body with complete indifference.

"No, Kir-Hugar did not kill this man—*I* did."

73

No Time to Rest

"Impossible," said Levenworth. "An unarmed little girl from Upper-Earth defeated one of the famed Golden Knife? Nonsense." All eyes were focused on Jade, although she seemed oblivious to the attention. She stared at the burnt body like a painter admiring her latest masterwork.

Cody reached out hesitantly and touched her arm. "Jade...how did you do it?"

Jade shrugged. "I don't know. I became...*angry*." A flash of rage flickered in her eyes and then was gone.

Cody turned to Levenworth. "I demand Jade's freedom. She has more than proved her innocence."

Levenworth huffed.

"*Proved her innocence*? The only reason she has thus-far avoided the gallows is because it seemed utterly implausible that she could have killed five trained soldiers." He motioned to the body on the floor. "An alibi that no longer carries any weight."

"Why would the Golden King send his most deadly killers to eliminate his own undercover agent?"

Queen Cia appeared from the crowd, her breath heavy from her dash to the cell. "Perhaps she just happened to be in the wrong place at the wrong time? They may have been trying to free Prince Hansi, assuming he would be in the dungeons."

"Possible," mused Levenworth. "Yet a band of skilled killers smart enough to position themselves as Cody's own protective guard would hardly make such a miscalculation. Hmm…" They waited as the General pondered the situation. After a moment he nodded. "Very well, the girl is free to go. I am placing her under your watch, Captain Ringstar. If I hear even rumors of a rumor of suspicious activity the girl will hang within the hour. Understood?"

Cody exhaled as Dace nodded his acceptance of the responsibility. It appeared that Fate had not won the game just yet. Queen Cia seemed relieved as well. "We are deeply saddened by the loss of several honorable soldiers. Yet, by their sacrifice, we remain fortunate. Our Book Keeper is safe and for the first time in history the Golden Knife has failed."

Cody recalled the scene in his mind. It had been a blur and he remembered only fragments, but it was enough. The Golden Knife *had* failed, but not because he had survived. He was sure of it. For some inexplicable reason the assassins had been targeting Princess Eva. Cody felt a newfound eagerness to finish his conversation with the youngest Royal child. However, such desires would have to wait. In the early morning came the report they had all been dreading: the enemy forces would reach the city by nightfall.

74

Advancement and Responsibility

―――――――――

A spreading terror followed the disconsolate storm clouds as they stopped above the city. The thick gloom almost entirely swallowed the Orb's light. Everyone understood what the long-anticipated arrival of the clouds signified. The enemy was upon them.

The tension in the War-Room was no less suffocating. Never had time been so needed or so scarce. Cody's shoulders were rigid, pulled almost to his ears. News of the enemy's imminent arrival had numbed any joy felt in enduring the Golden Knife's attack.

Queen Cia exuded fierce determination as she stood at the head of the table and addressed the Inner-Council. "Captain Ringstar's brash and unauthorized infiltration of the enemy camp may be of some benefit after all. Report."

Dace stood, offering a quick salute to the others around the table. "While behind enemy lines I gathered much that may aid us in impending siege. Foremost, that the Golden King has prepared a secret weapon."

Levenworth grunted in disapproval. "Of *course* he has a secret weapon. Cowards always do."

Sli Silkian produced a high-pitched cough before speaking. "Did you uncover the identity of this weapon, perchance?"

Dace shook his head. "Unfortunately not. I traced its location to a cluster of strange pyramid structures at the heart of the enemy camp. However, *The Rephaim* guarded the structures and I was prevented from getting close. I did, however, catch brief glimpses of civilians moving between the tents."

Captain Yaru barked, *"Ha!* What care we for El Dorado's common folk!"

Dace looked toward Tat. "I did not say they were El Doridian. Their dress confirmed that the civilians were our own."

"Prisoners of War? From Flore Gub and Lilley?" suggested Prince Kantan.

Tat leaned forward eagerly hoping for news of his wife but Dace shook his head.

"I agree with Kantan's conclusion, but I recognized no faces."

Levenworth paced around the table, his hands clasped behind his back. "We must remain vigilant, but without greater knowledge of this secret weapon we cannot prepare for it. We *can,* however, prepare for what we know for certain; and what we know for certain is that by nightfall two hundred and fifty thousand enemy soldiers will lay siege to our city. So, let us begin..."

The discussion moved from defensive formations, to patrol and reserve shifts, to strategies to repel siege engines and ladders, to accommodations for the civilians and refugees if the First and Second Walls fell and so on. Cody listened quietly, having nothing to offer such discussions. He was once again astonished by General Levenworth's grasp of tactics. The man's brain was like a supercomputer programmed for battle strategy. As long as Levenworth led the defense there seemed to be a chance, however slim, of holding the city. The preparations lasted several hours until Cia finally called an end to the meeting.

Dace joined the other attendees in filing out of the room. As he reached the door General Levenworth grabbed his arm. "Wait." Dace obeyed, waiting until the others had vacated the War-Room. When the final person had departed Levenworth closed the door. He turned to face Dace, inspecting him up and down. "I'm worried about you, Captain Ringstar."

Dace had expected as much. The General was a machine, and machines did not respond well to rash impulse. "I have no doubt, Sir. You have been worried about me since my promotion to Captain, Sir." The curt response had more snark than Dace had intended. If the reply angered Levenworth it didn't show on his stern face.

"Indeed...But I *did* promote you."

"To the Outer-City," said Dace, "as far from the Royal Palace as possible."

"And as close to the front line," Levenworth said with a glare that silenced Dace. "I've entrusted the gates of Atlantis to you and your ragtag force. You dislike me, but don't be blinded by your spite. Along with *The Impaler* you are one of the two greatest swordsmen in Under-Earth..."

"I am *the* greatest, along with no one," Dace corrected.

"Perhaps. My point, boy, is that the enemy will soon be at our gates. I've placed my trust in you to keep them out. From this moment forth you are my second-in-command."

The announcement caught Dace by complete surprise. "Me? Surely you are jesting! What about Yaru?"

"Yaru is an arrogant fool, as was Captain Eagleton before him. You inspire confidence in the men, and right now confidence is in short supply."

With any other man Dace would have waited for the punch line, but if there was one thing Levenworth had never done in his long life, it was joke. Dace bowed. "I'm honored, Sir. But I am also confused. You said you were worried about me. Why?"

"The incident with the Surface-Dweller girl." Dace cringed at the reminder. The image of Jade's wide eyes as he had abandoned her to die would be forever branded into his memory. He had felt a part deep within him die that moment he had turned away from her—the last residual of his innocence.

"I was forced to make a quick decision, Sir. I went with my gut. I chose to save the Book Keeper instead of the girl. I will always be haunted by the choice."

Levenworth jabbed his thick finger between Dace's eyes. "Exactly! *That* is what worries me." Dace frowned, pulling his head away from the finger.

"I don't follow."

"You were faced with a conundrum but the action you took was clearly the correct choice. You could only save one, so the wisest option was to rescue the one who would be of greatest advantage for Atlantis in this war." Dace could feel the temperature of his body climb at his superior's callous words.

"So I shouldn't be upset that I abandoned my friend to death?"

"Be upset or don't, what of it? But if you dwell on your emotions they will cloud your judgment. Our city is outnumbered twenty-five to one; we can ill-afford military leaders with clouded judgment. Leave emotion to the poets."

Levenworth took a deep breath and reclined against the wall. "Most people don't like me. They look at me and they see a soulless monster. Yet the distasteful qualities that people loathe about me are what won us the First Great War and secured their freedom. People desire charismatic leaders, but what they *need* are leaders who make the right choice even at the expense of their popularity. Do you understand me?"

There was something different about the General. For the first time Dace saw the erosion that centuries of carrying the heavy burdens of the city had taken on the man. Above all else, Levenworth looked tired. Then, in the blink of an eye, the General pushed himself back to his feet and his face once again resumed its stoic state.

"Before this war is over you will be faced with many more difficult decisions. There is never a clean winner when playing this awful game of life and death. So I need to know right now, when the time comes, can I count on you to make the right choice?"

Dace thought once again of Jade's face and his gnawing guilt. In his mind he thought, *I'm sorry, but I can't do it again,* but with his lips Dace heard himself say, "Yes, Sir, you can."

75

Every Able Hand

The city was burning.

The intense heat beat against Cody's face. He looked at the solitary dwelling before him. Somehow the building had evaded the spreading flames. Cody cleared his throat. *"Fraymour!"* Fire burst from his hands like a harpoon. Within seconds, the simple house was consumed.

"A sad day," Dace said, appearing at Cody's side. His face was coated in grime. Cody nodded, his own eyes burning from the billowing ash. All agreed that Levenworth's strategy to raze the Outer-City and create a killing ground was wise, but that knowledge made it no easier to watch people's homes reduced to mere soot.

It was Dace who hurled the first torch, and Dace who comforted the distraught Yanci as the flaming projectile ignited his beloved pub. Cody watched in silence. He was grateful to watch the building swallowed by the inferno. He was eager to burn away the image of the mauled soldiers and Jade's bloody hands.

Dace gave Cody's arm a firm squeeze before departing to supervise the rest of the operation. Cody didn't think he could stomach any more and his stinging eyes were becoming unbearable. He headed toward the gate to the Mid-City district, but was paralyzed by the sound of shouting:

"THEY'RE COMING!"

The call had come from one of the lookout towers. Terror gripped Cody. *There's still daylight. It's too soon! We're not ready!*

"THEY'RE COMING!"

Cody found himself running back through the fire and ash toward the Outer-Wall. A mob was rushing toward the wall like a herd of cattle, as people fought for a glimpse of the approaching force. Cody was swept up and carried in the crowd without his feet ever touching the ground.

Reaching the wall, Cody spotted Dace and Tat standing together halfway up a staircase looking over the crowd. Cody squeezed his way forward and called to them. "What's happening? Are we under attack?" He ascended the steps and surveyed the wastelands. A mass of torch-bearers marched in neat rows toward the city.

"OPEN THE GATES!'

Cody was stunned. *"Open* them?" A loud cranking sounded from the lowering drawbridge. It took three guards to pull open each of the iron doors. Dace motioned with his head toward the entrance. A hush came over the mob as a column, five-people wide, marched through the open gateway and into the city. The procession continued as hundreds of the newcomers poured into the Outer-City. They were children.

Cody looked to Dace in disbelief. "Are they here from the *Ageing City*? Was the city attacked? Have they come here for safe-keeping?" The procession of children continued to flow through the gate.

Dace shook his head. "Yes and no. The *Ageing City* was sacked only a few days after it had been evacuated. However, they have not come just to hide behind these walls."

"Why else would they be here?"

"To fight."

"You can't be serious! They're *children*!"

"So are you! Most of those *children* were born a hundred years before your great-great-grandfather. I admit I don't like the idea any more than you. But in Levenworth's eyes they are able bodies to patrol the walls and wield spears; and that's a commodity we lack."

Cody watched as the parade continued. Each child strong enough to hold a spear was handed one upon entering. Continuing down the assembly line, the children were fitted with various pieces of armor. For most, the oversized armor dragged on the ground. No child received a full suit; to one a rock-mail breastplate, to another a helmet, to a third only a set of gauntlets or greaves.

Tat read Cody's thoughts. "The ones who survive the initial assaults will be fitted more fully." Cody didn't need to ask where the additional armor would come from. The thought sickened him. *Has it really come to this?*

He would not have to wait long to find out. As they had been forewarned, at the break of nightfall, the alarm sounded over the city

El Dorado had arrived.

76

Before the Walls

The earth trembled as the endless swarm of torches, stretching far off into oblivion, closed in on the city. The dark clouds, vanguards to the colossal force oozing forward, had now firmly settled above Atlantis. Only the rhythmic stomping of five hundred thousand marching feet swallowed the roaring crack of thunder overhead.

Cody and Jade stood side-by-side upon the wall watching and waiting. In eerie contrast to the clamor that rang outside the walls, Atlantis itself was a noiseless morgue. Not one person spoke. Following the implicit code of silence, the entire city seemed to hold its collective breath.

Cody wedged his clammy fingers between Jade's. The rapid pulsing of her heart called the bluff of her composed face. Cody was oddly comforted by it, feeling less ashamed by his own poorly concealed trepidation. Colored chips on a war map had held sparse meaning until now, when they had grown savage faces and wielded sharpened blades.

Farther down the wall Cody spotted Xerx. Members of the New Brotherhood, including Poe and the beggar Gelph, flanked the monk. Tiana had been irate when assigned to the South Wall, wanting as always to be in the frontline. As Cody looked at Xerx standing straight and poised, he wondered if Tiana's desire was more complex than that.

Lightning flashed overhead as the approaching mass continued its forward march. Cody's hand unconsciously searched for the Book in his backpack, but found nothing. The Book was gone. The one thing that elevated him from ordinary to extraordinary had been ripped away; and as the inexhaustible enemy army closed in around them he wasn't sure if ordinary would be enough.

Dace rested a hand on Cody's shoulder. "Be calm, my friend. Flinching doesn't dampen the pain of the knife." On this day, Captain Dace Ringstar looked every bit the warrior, standing tall in a full suit of polished armor. His presence exuded confidence.

"Aren't you going to give a rousing speech? That's what the leaders always do in the stories."

Dace unsheathed his sword. "I've never been the speech type. My blade speaks more elegantly than my mouth. The men will feel inspired when foe start dropping beneath this sword." He rotated the blade exposing a fresh cut in the hilt. No explanation was needed. *That one's for Wolfrick.*

All at once the ground stopped shaking and the thunder ceased. El Dorado had arrived. Cody could see faces lit by torches. The horde stretched in all directions farther than he could see. Atlantis was like a ship lost in an endless ocean with no land in sight.

Three men emerged into the clearing. Cody didn't know if he or Jade had squeezed first, only that their hands were now locked in a vice-grip. On the right was *The Impaler,* his black armor rendering him near invisible in the lightless night. On the left was Randilin. The dwarf's eyes were downcast as he approached a half step behind the other two. Centering the trio was the Golden King.

When the King spoke, his voice boomed with unnatural resonance. "Greetings, my Under-Earthling brothers and sisters."

General Levenworth shouted back. "If you've traveled all this way to seek a conversation, I'm afraid you will be greatly disappointed! Unless you care to talk to my axe!"

The Golden King scanned the wall and smiled when he located the grizzly General. "You always were a bold one, Gongore."

"And you always were an arrogant fool! I see some things never change. You're still half the man your brother was. Hail the Good King Ishmael!" The cry, *Hail the Good King Ishmael*, was echoed along the wall.

The Golden King's humor drained. "I see you are eager to watch your city bleed—and bleed it shall. Here are my terms. You have until the first sign of light to surrender and open your gates. The two Surface-Dwellers and Lady Eva will then meet me in the Sanctuary of the Orb. All others will have their lives spared and be welcomed into El Dorado's kingdom. If you refuse..." He paused, his grin returning. "If you refuse, every man, woman and child behind those walls will die." The sky exploded as lightning cracked.

"Choose wisely."

The Golden King's ultimatum broke the spell of silence. Murmurs spread up and down the wall. Cody could feel hundreds of hungry eyes cast in his direction. Dace's hand lowered to his sword hilt as he stared down the grumbling men. Several soldiers nearby began moving slowly toward him. Cody could sense that the situation was about to get out of hand.

Levenworth's booming voice brought instant silence. "I'll sit and have a bloomin' tea party with *The Impaler* before I give in to the whims of that tin-headed oaf. If he wants our Book Keeper, let him come get him!" At their General's words, the defenders on the wall raised their weapons high and released a unified war cry. Levenworth pointed his sword toward the King. "How's that for your bloody answer?"

The Golden King smiled.

"So be it."

77

Murderous Intentions

The imagination can play funny tricks on a fright-ened mind. As the night stretched on, the wayward thoughts of the defenders atop the wall strayed to un-speakable nightmares. Every few minutes their eyes would drift toward the tall, spherical structure at the city's center, knowing that the Orb's light could appear at any moment. They also knew that when the light *did* shine it would rep-resent the last morning many of them would ever see. Yet, despite the frequent glances the light did not yet appear, and so they waited.

With thoughts awry, no one noticed the figure mov-ing through the shadows below. He drifted down the al-leys like a light breeze, undetected by the night's patrol. He stopped at the base of a tall, stone wall and listened to the nervous chatter of the guards above. Using the voices as a gauge, the figure pinpointed the guards' location. He moved along the wall until he came to the targeted place. Then he scurried up the wall like a spider and jumped off the other side, rolling into a soundless landing. Without slowing he continued his swift pace until he arrived at his intended destination.

Looking up the building's wall he located a window on the third story. The man held his knife in his teeth and began to climb, scaling the steep wall with remarkable ease. Reaching the target, he propelled himself upward, through the window, and into the room. He spotted a bed at the center of the room. Taking the knife from his teeth he stalked toward it.

The first thing Levenworth saw as he woke were the murderous eyes of Ugar-Kir-Hugar. The Garga Prince's stone teeth were clenched and he held a knife to the General's throat. Levenworth remained completely still, unblinking as he stared the intruder straight in the eyes. If he were going to die, he would do so with his honor.

For a time neither moved. Levenworth could see confusion in the young warrior's eyes. "If you're going to kill me then get on with it! If not, let me return to my sleep, I have a war to fight in the morning."

"I was sent by my father to kill you, Garga-Slayer." The Prince's words oozed with venom.

"Then you are doing a poor job, because I still live. By the quivering in your hand my guess is you've never had to take a man's life." Kir-Hugar pressed the blade in slightly, drawing a bead of blood.

"Don't mock me, Garga-Slayer. You have slaughtered my people. Stolen our lands. Dishonored the Great Gara-ganton."

"A pox upon your ruddy stone god. Will killing me bring him honor? Is that the god you serve? Will my death heal the enmity between our people? Nobody wins when death begets death."

Kir-Hugar shifted uncomfortably. "What would you have me do Garga-Slayer?"

Levenworth's laugher was a deep rumble. "So now *I* give you orders? Do as you feel wise, but be prepared to live with the consequences." His eyes fell to the knife still against his throat. "But for the love of the bloody Garagan-ton, decide already! I'm not as young as I once was and you're stealing my valuable sleep."

Kir-Hugar squeezed the knife hilt, sweat dripping from his palm. Then, with a piercing, guttural war-cry, he raised the knife over his head and brought it swinging down. *THUMP!*

The hilt wobbled as the knife was buried halfway up the blade. Kir-Hugar turned and jumped from the window, disappearing back into the night.

A few moments later the door to the bedroom opened and Sli Silkian stepped in. "General? Gongore? I heard screaming." The AREA leader found Levenworth propped up in his bed, a stone dagger jutting out from his bedpost beside his head. Levenworth stood and pulled the dagger free.

"The Garga Prince tried to assassinate me but he lacked the courage. He was going to cut my throat with this." Levenworth handed Silkian the knife and walked to the window. "He escaped out of here."

Silkian twirled the blade between his narrow fingers "Cowardice is so unbecoming of any man." He stepped toward the window to join the General. "What has our world become when assassination attempts are becoming the norm?" Then, in one fluid move, Silkian grabbed Levenworth's head and cut his throat.

78

Lies and Bad News

"**D**ead!"

With the shocking announcement of General Levenworth's death the hope in the room deflated into frantic despair. Sli Silkian tossed a dagger onto the table. It slid to a stop in front of Queen Cia, leaving a trail of smeared blood.

"Murdered. By the fugitive Garga Prince, Ugar-Kir-Hugar." The AREA leader cast his beady eyes to Cody. "It appears he was less trustworthy than we were led to believe." Cody opened his mouth to protest but no words found their way out.

Kantan lifted the blade, inspecting it with glazed eyes. "And the location of the murderer?"

"Unknown, my lord," said Silkian. "I set my Enforcers to search the city the instant I discovered this horrible deed. But he has thus far evaded us. I will continue the hunt."

Kantan slammed the dagger into the table. "Don't bother. He is gone. He accomplished what he came to do and has no doubt returned to his people. We cannot afford to hunt after ghosts when two hundred and fifty thousand soldiers surround our city."

Cia ran her finger across her deformed lips. "I agree. The absence of Levenworth's brilliant, tactical mind is a harsh blow on the eve of battle. With one cut of the knife we have lost our one true advantage—but we can lick our wounds after this war is over. Captain Ringstar, I am told you were recently named Levenworth's second-in-command. Is it so?"

"It is, My Lady."

Cia nodded. "Good. I hereby appoint you High General of Atlantis. From this point forward you will assume responsibility for our city's defense."

Dace's face fell. "Your Majesty! I beg your pardon, but I am a swordsman not a tactician. I cannot hope to fill his shoes."

"Then I suggest you depart immediately to study Levenworth's notes," Cia responded curtly. "We are on the cusp of the greatest battle our world has ever known. This is our defining moment. You have no choice, *General* Ringstar."

Dace stood, displeasure clear on his face, and bowed. "Very well, Your Majesty. I will do my best." He turned to the others. "My first act as General is to appoint Tat Shunbickle my second-in-command."

Captain Yaru slammed his fist on the table. "A *scout*? By succession of command that title belongs to me!" Dace gave him a stare so intense the Mid-City Captain bit his tongue.

"If you question my command again I'll have you stripped of all rank and scooping horse waste by morning, is that clear?" Yaru nodded his head dumbly.

For the first time since his return to Atlantis, Cody saw Queen Cia smile. "You are a quick learner, General Ringstar."

Dace stepped away from the table. "With all due respect, I must retire to my chamber and prepare. Time is short. Morning is soon upon us." The others of the Council departed after Dace, although Cody suspected no sleep would be had. They, like him, could think of nothing but the unstoppable coming of morning—and doom.

79

The Dam Breaks

The Golden King gazed hungrily at Atlantis. Standing beside the King like an obedient hound was *The Impaler*. Randilin slowly approached the two from behind, stopping at the King's side. The Golden King welcomed him with an exaggerated bow. "A lovely night, wouldn't you say?" Randilin ignored the remark.

He looked up at the towering walls of Atlantis. The bright flashes of lightning illuminated the terrified faces of the city's defenders. Randilin grumbled, "Did you wake me from my beauty sleep just to enjoy some bloody sightseeing with you?" The Golden King stepped forward, stretching his arms out as though to embrace the city.

"I have waited a long, long time for this moment. As you have been such an invaluable help to me over the years, it would be discourteous not invite you to witness this glorious moment with me." The King's mocking grin deepened like that of a child with a naughty secret.

"And what bloody moment is that?"

"Victory." The King said. At the sound of his voice a dim light appeared from the city, only a few rays breaking through the dark fog. Morning had come.

The Golden King turned to his mute General. "Let your siege begin. Unleash our *secret weapon*." The Spider-General nodded and departed in submission. The King lifted his palms to the sky. "Time to set the mood. *Seamour*." Thunder roared, rattling the earth, and fierce rain began pouring down, pummeling against the city walls. Randilin's matted hair drooped over his eyes. His body began to shiver.

The he heard it—the sound of chanting. It started soft, then gained volume, spreading throughout the camp. Soon two hundred and fifty thousand voices had joined in chorus.

"BLEED! BLEED! BLEED! BLEED! BLEED!"

The soldiers stomped in a stationary march, causing the ground to quake; even the lofty walls of Atlantis seemed to sway to the rhythm. The manic chanting grew louder and louder.

"BLEED! BLEED! BLEED! BLEED! BLEED!"

Several legions separated from the horde and began marching toward the city gates. The moment Randilin saw them his courage abandoned him. He recognized instantly that he was staring at the King's secret weapon. "That's... impossible."

The Golden King watched with beaming pride. "Impossible for lesser men but not for one who has mastered *The Creation-Which-Should-Be-One's-Own*." The Golden King sneered. "I hope you enjoy the show."

Randilin's hatred for the man burned more intensely than ever before. He looked on helplessly as the legions moved like a spear toward the city's gates.

Atlantis is doomed.

Cody watched silently as Dace pored over the stack of notes and maps on Levenworth's desk. Cody and Dace shared matching black bags under their eyes. "Levenworth was brilliant," Dace muttered. "His tactics were flawless. I couldn't hope to read and process a tenth of these battle plans in a year, let alone a single night."

"This city believes in you," Cody insisted, but his attempt at comfort fell flat under the frightened waver in his voice. Dace dropped his head to his hands in exhaustion.

BOOM!

The room shook violently, sending the papers on his desk soaring into the air. Cody looked to Dace in terror. "What was that?" Dace held up his hand to silence him. "Listen."

The room swayed as they listened to a faint sound in the distance. A multitude of voices were chanting as one.

"BLEED! BLEED! BLEED! BLEED! BLEED!"

Then came the deafening ringing of the gong.

DOOOONG!

DOOOONG!

DOOOONG!

"The alarm..." Dace jumped up from his desk and grabbed his sword. "Hurry! It's happening! We're under attack!"

The final battle for the Orb had begun.

PART FOUR:
THE BATTLE
FOR THE ORB

80

A Prodigal Son Returns

"Master. It has begun."

Mr. Shimmers turned, his hands clasped behind his back. "Right on time." The CROSS leader pivoted, resuming his stare across the Under-Earth wastelands. The distant tumult of battle was a faint whisper on the air. The Master closed his eyes and sniffed the air, savoring the moment.

Dunstan turned to depart but Mr. Shimmers' voice stopped him. "Faithful Dunstan, do you love me?" Dunstan frowned at the unexpected inquiry.

"Master?"

Mr. Shimmers turned, a trace of anger creeping into his icy eyes. "It was a simple question. Do you love me?"

Dunstan hesitated. The question had the distinct tone of a dangerous trap. He answered cautiously.

"I have great respect for you, Master—but I do not love you." Dunstan met his Master's stare and awaited his response.

"Good," said Mr. Shimmers without emotion. "I was loved once, adored by many. But then the world moved on. The people shared glorious stories about me to their children and their children's children, all the while stripping the crown from my head to melt down in their machines of industry. I learned a valuable lesson—love fades. Respect does not."

Dunstan studied his Master as though regarding a stranger. Here was the man who had taken him in as a boy and reared him in his own manor. Unsure how to respond and fearful to trek deeper into a snare, Dunstan simply nodded. "Yes, Master."

Mr. Shimmers appeared amused by his second-in-command's discomfort. "You have a question on your tongue." The directness of the statement implied a demand and not an inquiry.

Dunstan shifted. "Master, do you love *me*?" A wicked smile grew on Mr. Shimmers' face.

"Like a son." He turned toward the distant rumble. "So be a dutiful son and fetch me the ancient garments."

"Master, are you sure? Is the timing right? Would it not be wise to wait until..."

"No," Mr. Shimmers declared. "I have waited long enough. It is time the world looked upon me once more in the full glory of who I truly am."

"Yes, Master." Dunstan departed to obey the command. Mr. Shimmers licked his upper-lip, lapping up every drop of the moment and savoring its sweet taste. Everything was going according to plan. Thousands of years of anticipation all led to this. His moment of glory was close at hand. *The Day of Reckoning* had come.

It's time for the prodigal son to come home.

81

The First Wave

"**B**owmen ready! Fire at my command!"
The appearance of the assault's first wave set the wall abuzz. The defenders dashed in all directions, getting into position as Tat Shunbickle bellowed orders. Like a whooshing gust of wind, several thousand archers retrieved arrows from their quivers and nocked their bows in unison.

Amid the archer regiments stood Jade. She joined the others, pulling her string until it brushed the tip of her ear. She tried to recall everything Hansi had taught her about bowmanship. She squinted, gauging the distance of the approaching enemies who were almost in range. Tat looked to Dace for the cue to unleash the rain of death onto the enemy ranks.

The first wave of attackers continued its steady advance. Several siege engines including three forty-five-foot towers and an armored battering ram accompanied the infantry.

Cody's heart pounded out of control as he watched. *I could have stayed in Havenwood,* he thought gloomily. For the ten thousandth time he yearned for the electric power of the stolen Book. He looked up at Dace's sword pointed skyward. When the blade came swinging down the bloodbath would begin.

Dace frowned as he scanned the invading force. "Something isn't right. This first assault is far too small in scale to make sense. They're bringing the siege instruments and ladders, but without more foot soldiers to cover them they will be massacred by Tat's bowmen before they come within two hundred yards of our walls. The siege engines will be torched and wasted. *The Impaler* is too cunning not to realize that."

It was true. At the current distance it was hard for Cody to distinguish individuals, yet there couldn't have been more than five hundred, and half of those were responsible for moving the towers.

Cody bit his lip. "Maybe it's a trap?" Dace laughed humorlessly.

"It's *always* a trap. But it's about to be a dead trap." His sword quivered in the air. "Defenders of Atlantis, brace yourselves!"

Tat shouted, "Bowmen ready! They're almost within range..."

The wheels of the immense towers creaked as they approached.

"FIVE...FOUR..."

The enemy was now close enough to see distinct faces, clothing, and weapons.

"THREE..."

Jade's arm trembled under the tension of her drawn bowstring as she prepared to loose her arrow.

"TWO..."

"Wait!" Tat screamed. Dace turned to see his second-in-command rushing toward him and waving frantically at the archers. "Stand down! Stand down!"

"Captain Shunbickle, what in the world are you doing? We cannot afford a delay. Ready your bowmen! That's an order!"

"No wait," called another voice from the wall. "Look!"

Dace inspected the attacking force again. There was something odd. Something *familiar.* His stomach clenched in realization. A man to his left shouted, "It's the Lillians! The people of Lilley live!" A boisterous cheer erupted from the defenders. "Lilley lives! They're returning the prisoners!"

Tat searched the approaching mass anxiously. "That's her! That's my wife. My precious Rali! She lives!" Cody followed Tat's frantic pointing to a pretty dark-haired woman at the front line.

Cody noticed that Dace had not joined the others in voicing celebration at the surprising turn of events. Instead he stared with calculating, unblinking eyes and muttered to himself, "Why would the Golden King return his prisoners just to kill them? And why send the siege engines? Unless..."

Cody watched as alarm stole Dace's expression. He thrust his sword back into the air again and brought it swinging down. "Bowmen FIRE!"

Tat drowned him out with countering orders. "Hold position!" He grabbed Dace's sword arm. "What the blazes are you doing? Those are Atlantis citizens down there. My *wife* is down there!"

Dace pushed past the frenzied Captain and continued to shout. "Fire! It's a trap!" The Lillians were almost at the wall now. Close enough for Cody to see their glazed and lifeless eyes. Instantly he knew Dace was right: The Lillians were El Dorado's secret weapon.

The archers on the wall stood in confused stillness, disoriented by the conflicting commands of their superiors. That brief hesitation was all the enemy needed. Rali Shunbickle was the first of the Lillians to reach the base of the wall. She raised a crossbow as Tat looked down at her in stunned confusion. The weapon rattled as the projectile was launched.

Thud.

The bolt slammed into Tat's chest.

82

Friendly Fire

Wave after wave of crossbow bolts bombarded the wall of defenders. Pained cries resounded in a spine-tingling chorus of death as arrow-ridden soldiers tumbled from the battlements. Countless soldiers were slaughtered before the shock of the attack passed.

Dace ducked as an arrow soared by his left ear. Weeks of preparation had been cast aside as confused chaos overtook the men. The final words of General Gongore Levenworth rang in his mind: *"Before this war is over you will be faced with hard decisions. There is never a clean winner when playing this awful game of life and death. Can I count on you to make the right choice?"*

For the first time in his life, Dace understood the late General's hardened face. He raised his sword. "Bowmen, ready...!" He heard groaning at his feet. Tat was trying to push himself to his feet as blood pumped out of the arrow wound above his heart. Tat's pleas were drowned in the gurgling blood filling his mouth.

There was no time for delay. Already the defense was crumbling. Dace needed to make a quick decision. Suddenly the image of Jade flashed in his mind. In that moment he realized what he had to do. "Orb help us..." He turned to his men. "Fronor, Baggs, Lewen, I want your battalions with me to the gate! Xerx, have the New Brotherhood provide cover. We're going to take the Lillians alive!"

The commanders nodded and set off to obey without question. Tat was still writhing on the ground. Dace scanned the archer lines and found a familiar face from his Outer-City Guard. "Hoffin, you are now in charge. Ignite the arrows. Torch the towers. *Only* the towers."

Dace didn't wait to see if his orders were followed. Instead he grabbed Cody's shoulder. "You're with me." Cody followed as they dashed down from the wall toward the city gates. The passive uncertainty that had dominated the soldiers was gone.

The officers and their troops were already assembled at the gate when Dace and Cody arrived. Dace acknowledged the soldiers. "We must act quickly. When the gate opens we rush out and take as many of the Lillians as we can manage. I don't know what dark sorcery the Golden King has used on them but they are not trained soldiers. Subdue them and bring them into the city. You may see familiar faces. Do not be fooled. They will not recognize *you* and will kill you without a second thought. The Spider-General will pounce at the sight of our opened gate so we must make haste. We will not be able to save all of them. When I give the order to fall back it is imperative that you obey without hesitation. Understood?"

The soldiers nodded their affirmations. Dace sighed. "Here goes nothing. OPEN THE GATE!" The gate creaked as it was pulled slowly open like a curtain. Cody gulped as the frenzied battlefield was unveiled. Bodies of attackers and defenders alike littered the ground. Ash swirled in the air from several of the giant towers, which had already been ignited into burning pyres. Dace yelled, "Men, at the ready!" Cody inhaled a deep breath, wishing once more for the feeling of the Book against his back. "Charge!"

The soldiers stampeded out of the gates, abandoning the safety of the walls. Arrows, screams, and blood came from all directions as Cody ran into the heart of the battlefield.

83

A Crushing Defeat

She was pretty. No older than fourteen, her dress was without embellishment; she wore an enchanting smile and a neat braid draped over her right shoulder. She was also trying to cut off Cody's head.

The young girl lunged forward, swinging an axe almost as tall as she was. Cody ducked as the blade glided over his head, trimming his shaggy hair. The girl released a high-pitched banshee wail and unleashed another savage chop that penetrated the ground at Cody's feet.

"Dastanda! Seamour! Hustanda!" The High Language combination resulted in thick, tar-like substance bubbling onto the girl's eyelashes. The heavy goo pulled down her eyelids, blinding her. A moment later she was being carried on the shoulder of a soldier, thrashing all the way toward the city gates. Cody turned his attention back to the battlefield, seeking another target. A specific target.

Boom! Boom!

Two of the siege towers had reached the wall. Their heavy ramps had been lowered and latched into place. Cody looked back to the El Doridian battle lines. They remained unmoved. It didn't make sense. They had gained the Outer-Wall yet still held their ground. Cody knew as soon as the Lillians were cleared out of the siege towers the towers would be torched. *So what are they waiting for?*

An instant later Cody had his answer.

POP...

POP...

POP...

The sound was horrifyingly familiar. Cody's heart stopped as

wormholes began popping open all across the battle-field. The next instant, horde upon horde of golden golems and Dark-Wielders spilled out from the portals. Cody realized in horror what El Dorado's plan had been. *We took the bait and got caught in the trap.*

He could hear Dace yelling. "BACK TO THE WALL! RETREAT! FALL BACK!" The clanging of steel on steel filled the air. Cody ran, arrows and swords whizzing through the air all around him. In his periphery he saw Xerx and several New Brotherhood monks racing the opposite direction toward two approaching Dark-Wielders. Cody didn't see the outcome of the clash as he continued his dash toward the wall.

The city gate was still open and a congested mob fought to squeeze through the narrow entrance. The diagonally constructed gateway, designed to slow attackers from entering, was now acting against the defenders, trapping them outside the walls. Dozens of golems had already reached the opening and were trying to break through. A flood of golems and Wielders charged forward to reinforce them.

They will reach the wall before the gate can be closed, Cody realized in dismay. Nor could Tat's archers offer much aid without taking down their own comrades. The realization had not been lost on Dace. "Men of Atlantis, to me! Form lines! Protect the gate!" Dace led the charge, followed by several dozen remaining Atlantian troops. The small band crashed into the wall of approaching enemies like a wave against a cliff. The two forces morphed into a single congregation of hacking swords. Cody rushed to Dace's aid, sending a flurry of High Language attacks into the mass.

All the while wormholes continued to open, each one spilling forth streams of fresh foe. For every enemy Cody eliminated, two more appeared to take his place. *This isn't enough. We can't hold them for much longer.* Dace's band of soldiers was already crumbling against the relentless assault. Just when it seemed the battle couldn't get worse one of the Atlantian soldiers hollered, *"The Impaler!* The Spider-General has taken the field!"

The El Doridian General, clothed in midnight-black armor, stepped through a portal. He drew his immense sword and walked straight toward them. The Atlantian defenders looked to their General for orders. Dace squeezed the hilt of his sword. Cody could read his friend's intentions like a map. He grasped his arm and pleaded, "Dace *don't.* Right now these men need your leadership more than your sword. There will be another time to face *The Impaler."*

Dace hesitated, and then nodded. "You're right." He turned to his men. "FALL BACK!" As they turned to flee they realized the wormholes had begun opening behind their barricade, cutting them off from the city. "Hurry!"

Fighting their way back toward the city Dace and his men hacked through the golems as though cutting through dense jungle foliage.

The golems were now flooding up the remaining towers and ladders the Lillians had placed as the battle had oozed onto the wall. Men, both friend and foe alike, were falling off the ramparts and filling the moat with bodies and blood. Cody did not need to be an expert tactician like Levenworth to realize they were losing.

"FALL BACK! TO THE WALL!"

As Cody reached the base of the wall he finally caught sight of the target he had been desperately seeking—Rali Shunbickle. There was no time to second-guess himself. Cody veered off from the retreating soldiers and ran toward her. She loosed a crossbow bolt that dropped another soldier from the wall.

She loaded another bolt, cranking the lever to prepare the bow. At the sound of Cody's approach she spun to face him. Cody dove at her at the same instant she launched her arrow.

"Dastanda Scato!"

The arrow splintered into a thousand particles, deflecting off Cody like a fistful of sand. His shoulder slammed into her chest, sending them both to the ground. Her head whiplashed and slammed against a discarded helmet, knocking her unconscious.

Cody scooped Rali onto his shoulders; her malnourished body was almost weightless. To his dismay, he realized his delay had been costly. The City Gates were now completely overrun by the enemy as golems poured undeterred through to the Outer-City. Cody's only entrance inside was now blocked.

An intense wave of heat washed against his cheek. One of the deployed siege towers erupted into a pillar of fire. Screaming golems ran out of the tower, their gold platelet armor glowing red. Cody dashed full-speed toward the billowing tower.

"Byrae!" Two small whirlwinds spiraled up from the ground, flinging the fleeing golems out of the way. *"Colania! Seamour Frazen!"* A chilling aura materialized around him as a torrent of frost formed on the ground, charging ahead of him to swallow the crazed flames. Cody, with the lifeless Rali still draped over his shoulders, darted into the tower.

He danced around several unfortunate golems who had been consumed by flames. Despite the spreading frost, sweat poured off Cody's brow from the lapping flames. He climbed the winding steps toward the top. The structure began to wobble. Then, with a loud *crack*, the tower collapsed. Cody jumped.

He slammed onto the wall with a grunt as the tower crumbled behind him. Picking himself up, he lifted Rali back onto his shoulders. The Outer-City was now completely over-run. From somewhere amid the carnage he heard Dace's commands. "RETREAT! FALL BACK TO THE SECOND WALL! FALL BACK!" And so it happened, on the first day of the siege, the First Wall fell.

84

Only the Beginning

He had watched it all.

Not an ounce of the bloodbath had escaped his senses: The sight of lifeless bodies; the sound of screaming; the clangor of steel; the smell of blood and smoke. He had witnessed every moment of the slaughter. He received no choice in the matter. His body was immobilized; the paralyzing substance known as Dytalisia pumped through his veins.

His captors had been courteous enough to position him facing the battle. They had granted the privilege of watching as his people were butchered. What his captors overlooked was the fact that he *had* no people. He had never had people. He had come into the world alone and with each passing day of captivity he grew more certain he would depart in like manner.

He heard men approaching but was unable to turn toward the sound. Long crystal fingernails stroked his cheek as the Golden King circled in front. "Good morning, Chazic." The Enforcer didn't honor the King with a response, even though his mouth was the only unaffected portion of his once massive, but now emaciated body.

On this morning, however, it seemed the Golden King was content to merely gloat. "Such a remarkable victory is only dampened by my brother's absence. A pity he could not be here to see in the flesh who the greater leader turned out to be."

"The greatest leaders in history are awarded their status not by the leaders themselves, but by the history," Chazic remarked.

The Golden King laughed coldly. "Perhaps. But the leader who survives, great or not, is the one that writes the history. As such, the victorious leader is always great." He pressed his face next to Chazic's. "Although what interests me at the present moment is not my legacy, but rather, what is inside this large head of yours."

The King pressed the tips of his nails against Chazic's forehead, as though to burrow inside and physically harvest the desired thoughts. Chazic could do nothing to resist. "I'll ask you once more... where did the tattooed markings on your back come from? The ones in the sign of The Earthly Trinity."

"I don't know," said Chazic truthfully, for what must have been the hundredth time. And for the hundredth time the Golden King was displeased with his answer. The King pressed his fingernails deeper.

"A pity. I suppose I will have to entice the information from you in other ways. Shall we begin?" Chazic fervently prayed to the Orb that the paralysis drug would numb the pain.

It didn't.

Randilin Stormberger was in a fouler mood than usual. Throughout the entire stroll to his tent he muttered curse words in a rhythmic, almost melodic chant. Had he known of the Golden King's scheme with the Lillians he would have sent advance warning to Eva. Instead, he could do nothing but watch as the First Wall fell.

History taught that Atlantis' true strength came from the Second Wall; yet to yield a third of the city on the first day of the siege would demoralize the defenders. Randilin felt sickening guilt. There had been two Great Wars, and both times he had played a role in allowing the enemy to breach the walls. It was a sour thought. Even his profuse cussing provided little comfort. He experimented by combining the first few letters of one vulgar word with the last few of another. The amalgamated curse was surprisingly soothing. Feeling slightly better, he pushed through the flaps of his tent—and found the Golden King waiting for him.

Randilin put his newly minted word to good use. "Is my eyesight poor? Because I don't recall seeing a sign outside my tent that reads *bloody hotel, please come the blazes in*."

The Golden King grinned in amusement. "So cranky, and after such a beautiful victory."

"You think you're bloody clever. Your victory came as the result of your precious secret weapon. Your brother would have won through smarts and courage, not lies."

The Golden King's amusement faded and his face darkened. "You had best rephrase that to *our victory*, or I may be forced to have my Spider behead you for treason. However, my ugly little friend, you are mistaken. Using the Lillians on the front line *was* entertaining, but you are wrong to think I would squander my secret weapon on the first day of this siege."

Randilin could sense the conversation heading in a direction he wouldn't enjoy. "Well, then what the blazes is it? Are you going to drop your pants and blind them all when the Orb reflects off your shiny golden backside?"

The Golden King smiled again. "I wonder if you were given such charming wits to counter-balance your ugliness? However, I'm afraid I must disappoint you. It would be unwise to talk of a *secret* plan to the King of Traitors himself. But know this, the prisoners from Lilley were but the first of three...*surprises*. Three secret weapons to obtain The Earthly Trinity; poetically fitting wouldn't you say?"

"I got a poem for *you*, but it ain't child friendly," snapped Randilin.

"Perhaps another time," the King said, taking a final sip from his goblet as he stood. "I'm afraid I have a war to win. Today was a glorious day, but it was only the beginning."

85

Licking Wounds

The final count was in: Three thousand dead. In one bloodbath the enemy had removed almost a third of Atlantis' defenders. The people of Atlantis had lost more than just men. The greatest casualty was Hope.

From their view atop the Second Wall the remaining defenders watched the El Doridian forces making camp on the Outer-Wall. The same fortification that countless had died upon to keep the enemy out was now being used by that same enemy to keep *them* in. Despite the valiant fighting they had failed to make even a dent in the attacking force.

Cody rested wearily against the wall. He looked down at Tat; blood still trickled down his chest from his wound. The barbed arrowhead had narrowly missed the heart. However, to withdraw the arrow meant risking a nick to Tat's heart, so the medics had cut the shaft and pushed the bolt through and out his back.

Tat's wife lay beside him. She had awakened only briefly, and immediately began thrashing, attempting to strangle Tat before being subdued again.

In all, they had managed to capture almost two-thirds of the Lillians; the remaining third were either killed in the conflict or stranded. The Lillians who had been rescued were tied up and put into the dungeons until a means of healing could be found. Several jailers had been killed in the process.

Cody sat down beside Tat. Tears glistened in the older soldier's eyes. Were they tears of joy at his wife's return or pain at her condition? Cody wasn't sure but he suspected a mixture of both. Tat fingered two pieces of a heart pendant in his hand and mumbled, "I don't understand. Rali is a gentle soul. She'd never harm anyone. *How*?" The last word was voiced as a desperate, helpless plea for understanding.

"I don't know," Cody said. "The Golden King did something to them. I don't know what, or how, but it's the only explanation. She wasn't herself." Cody's words seemed to provide no comfort to his distraught friend.

"What chance do we have when the enemy can turn our own loved ones against us?" Tat stroked his wife's hair, sobbing, "My precious Rali, my precious Rali."

Cody took leave, at a loss of what to say. He found Dace walking amongst the men. As he passed he would touch their shoulders. The men returned the gesture with a silent head nod.

When Cody reached Dace he noticed that the hilt of his sword had been chipped away to almost nothing. The handsome features of the newly appointed General were distorted by sorrow. His face was hardened and worn. At the sight of Cody, however, Dace's countenance improved slightly. "Come. Walk with me."

Cody's feet fell into stride with his friend. For a while they ambled along the wall in silent companionship. Cody didn't know where they were heading; he suspected Dace wasn't sure either. After a time Dace abruptly broke the silence, verbalizing the middle of a conversation that had apparently been taking place in his head. "Three thousand men were killed to rescue three hundred. We lost the Outer-Wall on the first strike and our morale will never recover. Levenworth warned me. I promised him..."

Dace's words faded. Cody was at a loss for words, so he said nothing. *Jade would know what to tell him. She would be able to comfort him,* he thought. A while later Dace resumed speaking as though he had never stopped. "A good leader must make difficult decisions. I should have ordered the archers to shoot. I should have held the wall. But what good is staying alive if it costs your soul? We couldn't kill our own. We couldn't."

Cody finally realized what the conflicted General needed to hear. "Dace, you made the right decision."

The simple affirmation worked. The pained shroud vanished from Dace's face and was replaced by fierce determination.

"We have lost one wall but two more remain. We still have the killing ground. We must regroup and redeploy our defense. Armor must be stripped from the dead and given to the living. Weapons that were dulled against the golems armor must be sharpened or replaced. There will be time to mourn later. For now we prepare. *The Impaler* will not wait long. He knows our morale will be fragile. He will strike again soon, and he will strike hard."

Dace's words were prophetic.

El Dorado's next attack came at morning light.

86

The Killing Ground

They came in full force. Hundreds, perhaps thousands, of golden golems burst into the Outer-City. They seeped through the gate and over the Outer-Wall in a moving mass of glinting armor and drawn steel.

Jade's arm trembled as the fletching of her arrow brushed against her earlobe. She could hear her own heavy breathing and worked to steady it. She relaxed her muscles, starting at her toes and working slowly up her body to the cramp in her neck. As the enemy stampeded toward the Second Wall she could smell their sweat and hear their violent war cries. The mob pressed forward impetuously, spurred on by their comrades.

Jade could now distinguish faces among the mass. Her eyes locked onto a warrior with his tongue hanging out like a rabid dog. He howled and beat against his chest in berserk ecstasy. The ground rumbled like thunder as the enemy surged. They were almost in range. *Just a little closer...*

Dace Ringstar's voice boomed across the wall. "FIRE!"

Jade released her arrow. She watched as it cut through the air and landed with a *thump* into the canine warrior's neck. The golem dropped and was trampled by the herd. Using the form Hansi had once taught her, Jade whipped another arrow from her quiver, fit it to her bow, and launched it. Another golem tumbled as her projectile found exposed flesh between platelets of armor.

As the rabble pressed forward, the necessity for accuracy was abandoned in favor of raw speed. It was impossible to miss, like hitting a lake with a pebble. Jade fired blindly, each of her arrows bringing quick death to a faceless foe. By the time the skewered golem fell, a dozen subsequent shafts had found him.

Jade fired again, and again, and again, and again, and again. She settled into a steady rhythm—*hand to quiver, arrow to string, string to ear, release, repeat.*

Members of the New Brotherhood sprinted behind the archer ranks, refilling depleted quivers. A second band of monks created new arrows with the High Language.

Jade didn't know how long the carnage had been going on. Her body had gone numb some time back. She knew she should feel tired and hungry but she didn't. Her only thought was the endless jingle—*hand to quiver, arrow to string, string to ear, release, repeat.*

The casualties had begun to pile up, at some points reaching almost a third of the height of the wall. Yet the assault continued, the arrows continued to soar and the enemies continued to die. No one spoke. There was no need. Each defender on the wall knew their role. The only sound was the whizzing of arrows and reverberating bowstrings.

Then it was over.

Jade felt dizzy as her legs wobbled beneath her. Before she could collapse, a firm hand helped her. "You did well. You did well." Tat lowered her gently to the ground. All at once fatigue hit her. Her entire body ached.

A few tired cheers sounded, scattered along the wall, but most had no energy in reserve to join the victory celebration. There would be a time for celebrating, but now was the time for rest. For the first time in weeks, even the threat of nightmares couldn't prevent Jade from laying her head against the wall and drifting into a deep sleep. Her final thought before fading was the repetitious intonation—*hand to quiver, arrow to string, string to ear, release, repeat.*

87

A Scarcity of Friends

"**W**hat do you mean he's still gone?" The emphatic victory at the killing ground had restored some confidence among the soldiers, but not for Cody. He had been a bystander to the battle, allowing Jade and the others to do their duty. He knew his own responsibility was still looming: To fight and defeat the Golden King.

He had returned to the Monastery seeking counsel from Master Lamgorious Stalkton only to hear from Xerx that the High Priest was still missing. "Where in the world did he go? How could he leave me on the onset of battle?"

Cody's skin tingled as an anxiety attack threatened to hijack his body. First the Book had been stolen and now his mentor, perhaps the only man alive with the knowledge to help him defeat the Golden King, had abandoned him. Every day brought him closer to the imminent rematch against the Golden King; yet, it seemed every day the odds of success dwindled.

Xerx held out his arms. "I don't know. I really don't know." The young monk's tone was laced with concern. "I understand what you're feeling Cody, I really do. But hope is not lost. You're not alone in this."

Tiana appeared from behind Xerx. She wore the same frown as when Cody had seen her last, when she had been deployed to the south wall. She didn't cast the slightest glance toward Xerx, nor did Xerx acknowledge her arrival. Cody was perceptive enough to know when, for the sake of self-preservation, not to interfere. When Tiana spoke, her voice communicated the same displeasure as her face.

"That's life. People betray and abandon you. The sooner we all accept it the better." She plopped down and sat cross-legged in the middle of the floor. "Speaking of which, Randilin looked right at home standing beside the Golden King earlier. At this point, I can't say I'm too surprised."

Cody shook his head. "No, it's not what it seemed. Randilin is our friend. He's been spying on the Golden King and warning us about El Dorado's next moves."

"Has he? Because I don't think anyone was ready to be attacked by the Lillians."

"Maybe he didn't know."

"Maybe he didn't care," Tiana countered. "Does anyone know why the dwarf didn't rendezvous with us the night we escaped from El Dorado?"

"What are you implying?"

Tiana shrugged. "I'm just saying, he seems to be getting pretty comfortable in that gold-trimmed robe. He was practically eating off the Golden King's own plate. Isn't it curious that the whole Company escaped the city except for him?"

"That doesn't mean he double-crossed us..."

"It also doesn't mean he *didn't*. How do we know?" The last thing Cody needed was to be betrayed by another friend. Suddenly his head snapped up.

"Yes, we *can* know." He headed for the exit. "Follow me."

Sally's eyes were downcast and her brow was scrunched up like an accordion. She refused to meet Cody's interrogating stare. "Randilin betrayed us, didn't he? The night we escaped El Dorado." It was not a question. Cody knew the truth of the statement the instant it exited his mouth. Had any doubt remained, the weight of Sally's posture would have erased it. "How could he do such a thing? He was our friend."

Sally looked up slowly. "I know it's hard for you children to understand. Randy has always done what his heart tells him to. Sometimes that has led him to do some bad things; but Randy is *not* a bad man."

Tiana huffed. "What else would you call a man who has repeatedly forsaken the people he calls friends?"

Cody raised a hand to calm Tiana's outburst. "Why?" The simple one-word question conveyed the core of Cody's conflicting emotions; feelings he had harbored since the first fateful encounter with the dwarf in the Las Vegas hotel room.

Sally sighed and motioned for them to sit. "Best get comfortable." They grabbed cushions from the sofa and sat on the floor in front of her. The diner lady inhaled another deep, reluctant breath. "I'm going to tell you a story; although I'm afraid it's not a pleasant tale."

88

A Sad Love Story

———————

"**R**andilin's story is one of tragedy and sorrow," Sally said, beginning her tale. "He was the youngest member of The Twelve..."

"Thirteen," Cody corrected. "There were *thirteen* who discovered Under-Earth." Sally frowned, her plump cheeks glowing in irritation.

"Twelve, thirteen, thirty-two, four-thousand-and-a-half, what does it matter? Now *shhhh*! This is difficult enough without being interrupted."

Cody bit his tongue and recoiled from the stout lady's wrath. Once again content with her captive audience, Sally folded her hands in her lap and continued. "Randy was never considered exceptionally talented and lacked the physical gifts to become a great warrior like Levenworth or Kael, *The Impaler*, or whatever name that monster goes by these days. Nevertheless, the fact that he was the only child of the Alac-icacs to survive the long desert march is a testament to his resolve."

"It was a lonely time for him. He was a child in a grown-up's world. As the adults claimed the new land and drew borders, Randy was left to play alone. However, eventually babies were born and Randy was sent with the first wave to the *Ageing City*. It was there, during those early years, that Randy first met a young girl named Arianna."

Cody clapped his hands together. "Arianna! That's the girl from the pictures!" A cold glance from Sally silenced Cody once again.

"The two became instant friends. They were inseparable. Every night they would sneak from their beds and meet on the highest rooftop. There they would rest, count the skygems, and talk through the night about what lay beyond the city's blue bubble. They made a pact that one day they would run away and explore every corner of Under-Earth and beyond."

Cody leaned forward. "Did they?"

Sally shook her head. "No. Before they had a chance the Second Wave arrived from Atlantis. Among the newcomers were the Good King Ishmael's firstborn twins, Kantan and Cia. Their royal blood entitled them to several special privileges. They were granted accelerated growth...and grow they did. Prince Kantan grew to become a staggeringly handsome boy. He was quick-witted and overflowing with charm..."

Cody raised an eyebrow suspiciously but Sally ignored it. "Poor Randy. He didn't realize it at the time, but the day Kantan arrived was the day he started losing Arianna. Kantan's charm had Arianna in a trance. Arianna still spent most of her time with Randy, but their relationship was different. She was no longer interested in exploring and playing. Her thoughts and dreams had shifted to a new horizon. Almost overnight, Randy's childhood playmate had become a woman."

"The day they returned to Atlantis as full-grown adults they were also free to marry. Under-Earth customs required a suitor to retrieve a skygem and attach it to a necklace. The necklace represented the unending unity of the covenant and the skygem the heights to which the husband will go for his jewel."

"Randy's physical stature made such an act difficult. He tried many times and many times he failed. Despite his setbacks he refused to give up. Others offered to retrieve the jewel for him but Randy would have none of it and at long last he succeeded. He harvested a rare silver gem. He then enlisted the legendary rock-worker Gorgo Tallsin to cut it into a beautiful piece of jewelry. A flower with heart-shaped petals.

"The moment the necklace was ready Randy hurried to present it to Arianna. However, it was *she* who sought out *him*. She, too, had exciting news to share. As Randy fumbled over his words, Arianna couldn't contain herself. She revealed that that very morning the most marvelous thing had happened. She was betrothed to marry Prince Kantan.

"Randy presented his necklace, but he was a day too late. He was devastated. The Twelve had always looked down upon him, save for the Good King himself, and now he had lost his only true friend. He watched from afar as Arianna relished palace life but his love for her never died. Sadly, he never realized that Arianna felt the same."

"You see, Arianna was the only daughter to Gongore and Tamarah Levenworth. To strengthen the union with their beloved King, the Levenworths had arranged with Ishmael for their children to wed. It was duty, not love, which sealed the marriage union between Arianna and Kantan. Arianna had observed a darkness lurking beneath the charm and handsome features of her betrothed. Ordained to spend her immortality with a man she did not love, Arianna pretended to be overjoyed, vowing never to reveal the secret of her true feelings. She hoped in doing so she would set Randy free to love another. In hindsight, the opposite was true. Randilin was imprisoned by a love that could never again be realized.

"After the wedding Randilin saw her far less frequently, even though he thought of her constantly. So much so that when the First Great War began, Randy feared, above all else, for Arianna's life. As wife to the heir of Atlantis and the only daughter to the High General, Arianna was a prime target for the Golden King. As the armies of El Dorado marched toward Atlantis, all of the women and children were smuggled out of the city and hidden deep within the Caves of Revelation. It was the last place anyone would ever look. They should have been safe there.

"As the First Great War continued it appeared inevitable that Atlantis would fall. It was during those despairing days that the Golden King appeared to Randilin. He offered his old friend a simple bargain. If Randy would open the gates of Atlantis and allow El Dorado's forces in, the Golden King would repay him by allowing him and one other to escape and live out the rest of their days in peace."

"The Golden King gave his word, swearing upon the grave of his father Uscana. Randy hated the Golden King and he was as loyal to the Good King as any man in Under-Earth; yet his love for Arianna was greater than all. He agreed to the pact."

"Randy opened the gates then he fled to the Caves to rescue Arianna. But this had been the Golden King's plan all along. The evil King didn't truly need aid breaching the gates, but he had been unable to locate the women, including his brother's wife, Queen Naadirah. The Golden King sent a legion of his best soldiers to follow Randilin. Without realizing it, Randy led the enemy right to the hiding place."

"The women were trapped. It was a massacre. In what is now known only as *Randilin's Dark Deeds*, the enemy began slaughtering everyone in the cave. Randy was helpless to stop it. Arianna was pierced in the heart by a spear. She took her final breath in Randilin's arms."

Cody pictured the skeletons scattered about the cave floor. "You were there, too, weren't you?"

"Yes, I was there," Sally said distantly. "I will carry those horrors to my grave. I requested of King Ishmael the duty to become a Gatekeeper on Upper-Earth because I had to put distance between myself and the memories of those caves. Arianna was my closest friend."

"How did you survive? And Randilin, too?" Tiana asked.

"We should have been killed along with the rest. I retreated deep into the caves until I reached a dead end. I waited for the inevitable—but it never came. A band of

Garga warriors descended upon the El Dorado legion and dispatched them. In exchange for their aid they asked only that Atlantis would grant them more land. Levenworth responded by attacking them soon after the war was finished, which happened to be that very night.

"Randy was dragged back to Atlantis as a traitor. He was the most despised man in all of Under-Earth, surpassing even the Golden King himself. Kantan and Levenworth set the blame for Arianna's death on his head and he was sentenced to death. But the Good King had compassion. Mourning the death of his own wife, he refused to spill any more blood upon the already crimson-soaked ground. Instead he banished Randy to Upper-Earth. I am one of the few still alive who was there to see the look in Randilin's eyes on that awful night. The night he died inside.

"He is not a bad man. He is a broken man, and oftentimes broken men do bad things; but that does not make them bad. I love him. I love him as much as he ever loved Arianna. I love him not in spite of his brokenness, but *because* of it. Underneath his decaying shell remains the same eager, tender-hearted boy that loved to explore and used to dream of running away.

"This brings me to what you call *Randilin's betrayal of you* in El Dorado. The Golden King used me to pierce an old wound that has never healed. When faced with losing me as he had once lost Arianna, Randy couldn't bear it."

Tiana reached over and wiped Cody's eye. He felt guilty for blaming Randilin. Would he have done anything different if it had been Jade's safety in question? Had he not let men die so that he could rescue Jade from El Dorado?

313

"There is something else. Something I vowed never to tell anyone. A dark secret I've carried with me every day since the awful nightmare at the Caves. A secret I've held tight for reasons you may never fully understand."

"What is it?" asked Cody, Tiana, and Xerx in unison. Sally's face was contorted as she forced herself to speak.

"On the day Arianna was murdered...she had delivered a child."

Cody's jaw dropped. "She was pregnant! Did Randilin know?"

Sally shook her head. "Randilin never knew about the child and I hope he never does."

"Arianna's baby lived?" asked Tiana.

Sally nodded. "Yes. I was the midwife who delivered the child only moments before the ambush." Tears began to stream down Sally's face. She slowly lifted her hand and pointed her index finger. "Tiana—*you* are that child."

89

Not Alone Anymore

Tiana said nothing. Her face was stoic, as though oblivious to the shocked stares pinned on her. She reached to her pocket and retrieved a glimmering object: a tarnished silver necklace with heart-shaped petals. She pressed the necklace against her chest.

Cody did not share the same restraint. "That means... oh my gosh, that means Tiana is a *princess*. The heir to the throne of Atlantis!" No one looked more astonished by the revelation than Xerx. His mouth opened and closed several times wordlessly.

Tiana remained silent, gazing straight ahead at the wall. The necklace trickled through her fingers and fell to the floor. Then Tiana turned and left the room.

My mother's name was Arianna. Tiana repeated the name over and over in her head: *Arianna. Arianna. Arianna.* For as long as she could remember she had wanted nothing more than to know that name. To know why her parents had abandoned her. Now she knew.

Tiana didn't know whether to scream, cry, laugh, or do all three. *Arianna,* she thought once more. She wrapped her arms around her tucked knees and pulled them toward her chest. Rain poured down on her but she didn't notice. Her eyes looked out at the enemy camps on the fringe of the city but her mind wandered elsewhere. *I have a family. I'm not alone...*

"You're in my spot."

Tiana looked up, pushing her rain-drenched hair from her eyes. Standing before her was a young girl. The girl's oversized helmet covered all but her small chin. She lifted it, revealing a petite freckle-spotted nose, two large brown eyes and an irritated countenance.

Tiana couldn't help but smile. "It's a large wall, but this *is* a nice spot. Perhaps there's room for two?" The comment seemed to please the girl. She plopped down beside Tiana, pulling her knees to her chest in a mirror image of the other.

"Well," the young girl said as she raised her eyebrows.

Tiana frowned. "Well, *what?*"

"Well, *what's your name?*" she said with exaggerated vexation.

"My name is Tiana. What's your name?"

"Elena. But my friends call me Ellie."

"Am *I* your friend?"

"Do you want to be?"

"Sure," said Tiana.

Ellie's face lit up. "Good. Then you can call me Ellie." She opened her mouth, hesitated, and then closed it. A second later she seemed to reconsider, and blurted, "That thing I just said, about my friends calling me Ellie, I made that up. I just always wanted a nickname."

"What *do* your friends call you?"

Ellie shrugged. "I don't know. I don't have any friends." The comment stirred an old pain deep within Tiana. Memories of her time in the *Ageing City* flickered before she subdued them.

"Why don't you have friends?"

Ellie answered nonchalantly. "The other kids at the *Ageing City* are boring. They can't keep up with me."

"Even the boys?"

"*Especially* the boys." Ellie rolled her eyes. "They can be such dim-witted, dirt-brained fools. You have no idea."

Tiana sighed. "Oh, I understand perfectly. Trust me."

Ellie raised an eyebrow, conveying suspicion rather than trust. Despite Tiana's aversion to making friends, she was taken with this feisty girl. "Did you arrive with the other children? Where are you parents?"

Ellie fidgeted. "Yeah, I just arrived. My mom died in a rockslide when I was a baby. My dad was a brave, heroic warrior."

"Was?"

"Yeah. He killed lots of bad guys on the First Wall yesterday, but one of those gold-skinned ones got him. Now he's dead. But don't worry about me. I'm tough. I'm used to being alone."

Although it was Elena's mouth that moved, Tiana heard the words with her own voice. She had played that act too many times not to empathize. She understood the hurt and confusion that lay beneath the facade. She gently wrapped her arm around the little urchin. "You're not alone. Not anymore."

Tiana wasn't sure at what point Ellie fell asleep against her. She could feel the peaceful rhythm of the girl's rising and falling chest. The world didn't understand misfits like Ellie, but *she* did.

Tiana felt a sense of guilt. She had sought a quiet spot, feeling sorry for herself over just now discovering her heritage, while, with every passing day of the siege, others were having their families torn away. Ellie coughed and repositioned her head, burrowing it into Tiana's lap. Before long both were in a deep slumber. For several hours the two kindred spirits were lost to their dreams beneath the rainy sky.

Their tranquility was demolished by the jarring blare of an alarm, signifying another El Dorado charge.

Elena jerked awake, terror gripping her face. Tiana stroked her hair. "Don't worry. I will stay with you. The attack will be just like before. We will repel them as we have before." Elena was comforted by the promise. At the time Tiana had no way of knowing just how false that promise would prove to be.

90

Those Who Feel No Pain

Captain Yaru stepped onto a crenellation and banged his fists against his chest in defiance. "Come on ya' stinkin' tin-heads! *Ha!* I got some pointy arrows anxious to make acquaintance with your pretty glittering faces!"

A rousing cheer erupted from the wall. The heavy fatigue they all felt was numbed by the sweet taste of their latest overwhelming victory. Since the initial charge on the Second Wall, El Dorado had made two ensuing pushes. Both had ended in routs. The killing ground had more than earned its vicious name. In fact, many were now calling the battlefield the crimson bathtub.

Jade cracked her knuckles. She retrieved her bow from her shoulders, robotically rehearsing, *hand to quiver, arrow to string, string to ear, release, repeat.*

"THEY'RE COMING!"

The *whoosh* of a thousand drawn bowstrings filled the air. Jade found the waiting to be the worst part. She had lived through the horror three times already, yet waiting

319

for the charging enemy to appear was still unbearable. The familiar sickening feeling seized her stomach.

"THERE THEY ARE..."

They came slow and silent, approaching like a glacial trudge. A hush spread over the wall, the earlier courage seemingly sucked in with every breath. There was something awry about the attack. It was too slow and lacking urgency. Too confident. Too fearless.

The horrible realization hit Jade just as someone else yelled.

"IT'S *THE REPHAIM!*"

Panic gripped Jade. El Dorado had unleashed its monsters—profane warriors fueled by the harvested souls of innocent victims. The hollow beings plodded forward, their eye-sockets like gaping caverns and their thin black lips locked in mocking grins against their pale, maggot-like skin.

Tat Shunbickle bellowed, "FIRE!"

A thousand arrows pummeled down on the enemy like a hailstorm. The barrage pierced and tore at the hollow men's artificial flesh. Pointed shafts passed clean through the chest and emerged out the back. But, still, *The Rephaim* trudged relentlessly ahead.

Jade heard several shocked curses. "They didn't even slow down or cry out in pain! We fight not men but *demons!*"

"Unless your words are killing enemy soldiers then keep your mouth shut," Tat ordered. "FIRE!" The arrow waves continued to drub the hollow beings to no avail. The enemy had almost reached the wall.

"INFANTRY TO THE WALL," shouted Dace above the whizzing of arrows. "WATCH FOR LADDERS!" Soldiers rushed forward wielding long halberds. They braced themselves for the enemy ladders—but none came. *The Rephaim* reached the base of the wall—and began to scurry up like grotesque spiders.

White, gangly hands appeared, followed by a face as the first hollow-man pulled itself to the top of the wall. Cody rushed forward. *"Fraymour!"* The creature fell to the ground, engulfed in a ball of fire. An instant later the hollow-man was back on its feet staggering back toward the wall, its unnatural skin seared and melted.

Cody stared in disbelief. *How do you kill something that isn't alive to begin with?* More and more *Rephaim* reached the top of the wall. The waiting Atlantian axe-men hacked away, severing limbs, and mowing the creatures down. Yet, impervious to the pain, the haunting attackers continued their relentless ascent.

One of the axe-men screamed as he was hurled from the wall and swallowed by the zombie mob below. For every *Rephaim* repelled, two others reached the top of the wall. The creatures laid claim to several strongholds, allowing others to file up behind them undeterred.

"Cody, look out!" Cody twirled around as a *Rephaim* closed in from behind. The surreal being was missing an arm and had no head. Cody could see clear through several holes in its chest revealing nothing inside but a swirling black mist. The decapitated fiend reached for Cody, its lone hand grasping tight around his throat. Before his wind was cut off Cody uttered, "*Colania...*"

The Rephaim lifted him into the air by the neck. Cody felt the bones in his neck bending. He also felt a nipping chill exuding from the creature's hand. An instant latter Cody gasped for air, having finally been released. *The Rephaim* had been frozen into an icy statue. "*Duomi.*" The statue exploded into a thousand shards.

Farther down the wall Dace was battling against two hollow men at once. "We can't hold them much longer. We'll be overrun!" Dace brought his sword down, adding to the pile of severed limbs at his feet. Even so, the pieces of the dismembered *Rephaim* were twitching, still unwilling to give up the fight.

Dace was glazed in sweat. "We can't afford to surrender the Second Wall. We can't lose the killing ground!" The second *Rephaim* charged. Dace sidestepped, letting the creature impale itself onto his extended blade. With a grunt Dace heaved on the blade and severed the hollowman clean in half at the belly. The creature's upper torso clawed at Dace's feet. With a firm kick Dace sent the gruesome remains soaring over the wall.

Cody and Tat reached Dace at the same time. Tat's leg was bleeding and five deep fingernail scratch marks were cut across his face. "General, you *must* signal a retreat! We can't hold much longer." Cody looked around. The enemy was gaining hold of more ground every minute. Soon the Second Wall would be entirely overrun.

Dace grimaced. On the heels of losing the First Wall, a second defeat would be crippling. But if they stayed they all would die. Dace opened his mouth to signal the retreat but Cody cut him off. "What in the world is *that?*"

The ground began to rumble. An immense, indistinguishable mass was careening straight toward the city. Cody squinted his eyes before widening them in astonishment. "I don't believe it. It *can't* be!"

91

Smooth Sailing

Acolossal deluge of lava raced across the wasteland with staggering speed. The fiery substance billowed over forty-feet high at its peak; and every gallon of lava was headed directly toward Atlantis.

"We're doomed." Tat muttered in disbelief as the wave approached. The battle on the wall slowed to a standstill as the soldiers turned their attention to the new threat, helpless to do anything but wait for its arrival.

Cody clenched his teeth. "It has to be the Golden King. Only a master creator could produce and sustain a wave that large." The lava approached like an immense, slithering serpent, swallowing the sand dunes in its path. Dace looked around frantically.

"Xerx! Your New Brotherhood better do something to stop that! And quick!" Xerx appeared, followed by three Brotherhood monks. His terrified face hardened at the sight.

"General, it's too big. With only new recruits...I can't...I'm...I'm sorry, Dace. " They braced themselves as the wave rose up like a giant tentacle ready to come crashing down on them. At its apex it seemed to freeze in place, hovering over the wall. The next moment brought forth the most unexpected sight—a ship.

The boat's hull crested the peak and glided down the lava as the wave broke. Suddenly cries of terror turned to joyous applause. Cody looked close and realized why. The ship riding the lava wave was not just *any* ship. It was *The Igg*.

Standing tall at the helm, and stark nude as the day he was born, was the one and only Captain Igg K. Stalkton. High above him in the tottering crow's nest was his brother, Master Lamgorious Stalkton. He was swaying back and forth while chanting and waving his hands, conducting the lava like an orchestra.

"The Stalkton brothers!"

As the lava wave seemed to hover over the city Lamgorious Stalkton called down, "Dear brother, shall we?"

Igg grunted. *"Shall we,* you ask? Were grandma's ears furrier than a wild pack of blue-nosed desert moles?" Apparently, Grandma Stalkton indeed had hairy ears because the wave came collapsing down. The lava splashed as it poured over the wall, filling the Outer-City district like a bathtub.

The Rephaim fled, their plastic skin melting under the intense heat. The elder Stalkton continued to chant, using his boney fingers to select specific *Rephaim* atop the Second Wall. As he did, the lava would lash out like a whip, wrapping around and dragging the hollow-men to a smoldering end.

The Igg sailed into the Outer-City as the lava continued to pour over the wall. The retreating *Rephaim* were nowhere close to the city gate when the lava cut off their only escape. Most were reduced to a melted mass even before the boiling substance drowned them. Several of the hollow-men clung to the side of the ship to escape the rising lava. Igg spotted them crawling over the railing onto the deck. He growled. *"No one* comes onto *The Igg* unless Igg says so."* Twirling the helm, Igg veered the ship sharply to the left. The sudden change of direction sent several of the stowaways spilling over the edge.

Only three hollow-men remained. They closed in toward Igg. Lamgorious Stalkton called down to his brother. "Dear brother, allow me..." He spoke the High Language in a melodic song. As he did two geysers spouted from the lava and landed on the deck in front of the *Rephaim.* The puddles fizzled as they morphed into the shape of humans. At Stalkton's command the lava men charged forward, making short work of the enemy.

In the span of several minutes, what was once an inevitable defeat had become a miraculous rout. The wall defenders stood and watched the enemy annihilated as though viewing a theater performance. Never before had anyone seen two war heroes so unexpected, so deadly, or so explicitly unclothed as the Stalkton brothers.

92

Things Done for Love

The Stalkton brothers were heroes. Tales of their magnificent rescue were already spreading through the city. Some said the brothers had spit the lava from their own mouths; others said they swam through the lava like dolphins. But *all* agreed on the fact the two were heroes.

As Cody watched the admirers mobbing the day's unlikely saviors of Atlantis, he tried to determine what amused him more: Lamgorious Stalkton's puffed out chest or the startled expressions of the women at discovering Igg's state of undress. Already the two brothers were being referred to as the Naked Knights.

Atop the First Wall Dark-Wielders had set to the task of draining the Outer-City of the lava. For the time being, however, the Stalktons had bought much-needed reprieve from battle. Cody scanned the crowd in search of Jade. Instead he spotted Tat Shunbickle. "Mighty Book Keeper," Tat said in greeting as he strolled over to him.

"A Book Keeper without a Book," Cody muttered, the joy of the moment already wavering. Tat shrugged and slapped Cody on the shoulder.

"I saw you fighting *The Rephaim*. I'd say the Book Keeper is remarkably powerful even without the Book."

Cody noticed an odd demeanor in his friend. The compliment had the intonation of a question. Tat stared at Cody, apparently awaiting a response.

"The Book still funnels the Orb's energy to me from wherever it is. At least that's what Master Stalkton keeps trying to tell me."

Tat nodded, seemingly pleased with the answer. "Well that Stalkton is a great place to learn wisdom. Just as long as you don't start taking fashion cues from those two crazy brothers," he said with a wink. Tat turned to walk away, but stopped for a second, and turned back. "Actually, do you have a moment?"

Cody glanced around but still found no sign of Jade. "I suppose so. Did you need something?"

Tat shrugged. "I was wondering if we could finish the conversation we started weeks ago on the journey to El Dorado." Cody instinctively fingered his pocket. His finger pricked the point of the arrowhead. He had kept the trinket on his person at all times.

"Of course."

"Splendid. Come, my chambers will give us a quiet place to talk away from the Naked Knights' victory parade."

Cody's muscles groaned as he walked. They had held their peace during combat, but now the soreness and fatigue hit all at once.

"When last we talked you were a conflicted, love-sick boy." Cody blushed at the memory. Tat continued. "You were torn between, how did I put it, the wild lightning storm you desired and the steady mountain you needed? Did you make your choice?"

Cody's blush deepened. "I chose the mountain and then got obliterated in a rockslide."

Tat laughed. "Young love. If it were not messy it wouldn't be worth it."

Cody struggled to see any humor in the situation and quickly reversed the focus. "I'm so happy you've finally found your wife. She is just as beautiful as you said she was. Don't worry. We *will* figure out what the Golden King did to her and the other Lillians."

Tat nodded, but said nothing. They reached Tat's chambers. He fumbled with the lock; his hands were shaking.

"I'm sorry Tat, I didn't mean to upset you." Tat finally managed to steady his trembling hands long enough to unlatch the lock. He turned to Cody.

"Do you remember what I told you that night? When I told you the moment I realized that Rali was the woman for me?"

Cody recalled the night. It seemed so long ago. "You told me it was the day you realized you couldn't live without her. That a life without her *wasn't* living." Tat nodded silently and pushed open the door. Cody was greeted by two glazed eyes staring back at him. In the lone bed in the center of the room was Rali Shunbickle, ropes binding her hands and feet to the bed.

"Tat, what's going on here? Dace ordered all the Lillians to be kept in the dungeons until a cure could be found. You're not supposed to have her here...Tat?" There was a click as the doo r closed and was latched. Tat blocked the doorway.

"Can you fix my Rali?" Cody backed away slowly. Madness lurked in his friend's eyes.

"I don't know. I don't think it's safe to try. I..."

Tat pulled a dagger from his belt. "That wasn't a request."

Tat stalked forward. "I'm so sorry, Cody."

93

The Price of War

The knife flashed, catching him in the throat. His final expression was fear before he died. The violence was the price of war, turning innocent dreamers into ruthless killing machines. Tiana shook the vision from her mind. Since that first time, several years ago, she had killed more enemies than she cared to remember. The face of every victim still haunted her.

Little Ellie stared ahead with bug-eyes. Tiana felt pity for the girl. The child had just created the first haunting face of her own. *But she lived.* The southern wall had not faced the intense offensive that the northern wall had, and none of *The Rephaim* had been present; but the fighting had been fierce nonetheless.

Suddenly Elena smiled. "We did it, Ti...and you didn't leave me."

Tiana smiled back. "I promised, didn't I?" She inspected her. "But we must do something about your armor. You could fit four-and-a-half of you inside and still have enough room for provisions to last the rest of the siege."

Elena's face lit up at the proposition. "And get me a *real* sword! Not this girly little knife."

"You *are* a girl."

"*So*," Elena said.

Tiana laughed. "You couldn't even lift a real sword."

"I could, too!" Tiana reached down and grabbed a broadsword from a dead golem and tossed it to her. Elena caught it and there was a *clank* as the blade hit the ground, pulling her forward with it. She flushed as she heaved on the weapon to no avail.

"Told you so," Tiana teased. "Boys always like big, gaudy swords to make them feel manly. I've learned to let boys be boys. While they struggle to lift their swords I'll cut their throat with my knives." Tiana tensed the moment the words left her mouth. She was not used to speaking with children. However, Elena was grinning from ear to ear.

"You *do* need armor though. Let's see if we can find you a nice, girly pink breastplate." Elena's eyes went large. She ran after Tiana, protesting the whole way.

The city streets were considerably less congested than they had been several days prior. *How many lives have already been lost?* Tiana didn't really want to know. They turned a corner and stopped. Walking the opposite direction toward them was Prince Kantan.

"Quick, hide!" Tiana said, grabbing Elena and yanking her into an alley.

"Hide from the Prince? Why? I always thought he was so handsome."

"He's...never mind, I'll explain later. Come on. In here...." She jiggled a doorknob but it was locked. "Blast."

Using the point of her dagger she fidgeted until the lock popped open. The two girls ducked inside and pulled the door closed.

"I still don't get it," Elena said. "Why are we hiding from the Prince? Isn't he..." Tiana cupped a hand over Elena's mouth, silencing her. Tiana pointed down the hallway of their refuge. There were no lights, but they could hear hushed voices coming from the other room.

"We're not alone," Tiana whispered.

They were tiptoeing toward the exit when one of occupants said, "You have killed Gongore Levenworth..."

Tiana's heart rate increased. She motioned for Elena to stay put, and crept down the hall toward the mystery voices.

"Gongore Levenworth was too loyal to be persuaded. He had to be silenced." There was no mistaking the glib voice; it belonged to AREA leader, Sli Silkian.

Silkian killed Levenworth?

"I see," said the first speaker. "It matters not. The final phase is underway. The King is coming home." Tiana craned her neck. *King coming home? Is this a spy from El Dorado?* Tiana rose to the balls of her feet and inched closer, but froze as a man appeared before her. His back was to her, but he was close enough to reach out and touch. Tiana held her breath and locked her muscles.

Dangling from the stranger's belt was a crescent-shaped blade. *Not from El Dorado after all—this Agent is from CROSS!* But why was a CROSS agent talking to Silkian? The enemy agent had also mentioned the return of a King. *Has CROSS been aiding El Dorado all along?*

"My payment?" asked Silkian.

"In good time. When the Master arrives you will receive your reward. The Forbidden High Language will be yours. You have one final task."

"It will be done tonight."

Cody's eyes were fixed on the gleaming dagger in Tat's hands. "A dungeon is no place for a lady like Rali," Tat spat. "I will not have my wife treated like a thief or murderer."

Cody backed away slowly. "What do you want from me?"

"I want you fix my wife."

"I already told you, I don't know how," Cody pleaded.

"Enough! It was Orb sorcery that did this to her so the Orb should be able to remove it." Cody's backed toward Rali's bed.

"And if I can't?"

"Then I will be forced to do things I don't want to do." The way Tat twirled the knife left no doubt what he meant by *things*. "I meant it when I told you life wasn't worth living without her."

Cody scanned the room for an escape. He wondered if he could use the High Language quicker than Tat could hurl his knife. The penalty for losing such a gamble was obvious. "This isn't like you, Tat. There's another way. You will be no different than the evil men who did this to your wife."

Tat took another step forward. "I will die without her."

"All men die."

"A peculiar Upper-Earth idiom that poorly translates to a world of immortals," Tat said.

"Rali wouldn't want this of you," Cody said.

"If my sweet Rali had her way right now she'd take my knife and cut open my throat. So it is what *I* want that we will act upon at this moment."

"Is this the price of war? The Golden King has already turned the Lillians against us. Now he is turning the rest of us against each other. If I try to help her I could damage her mind. I could kill her!" Cody took a deep breath and straightened his posture. "I won't do it. Kill me if you must, but I won't do it. I only pray that when Rali *is* healed she still recognizes the man she used to love."

Tat's face contorted at the comment. "I'm sorry..."

He threw his knife.

94

Plans Within Plans

———————————

Cody flinched as the knife hurtled toward him and landed with a *thud*. Cody grabbed his chest, but the dagger had missed him by several inches and pierced the wall instead. The rabid fury had drained from Tat Shunbickle's face. He seemed to have aged fifty years in the span of several seconds.

"I'm sorry," Tat said. "You're right. I've lost my mind." He staggered and fell back against the wall, his hands on his head. "I can't think straight. I almost ruined everything. Rali will be ashamed of me."

Cody exhaled in a mix of relief and sympathy. "No, she won't. She will see a man who traveled from one end of Under-Earth to the other to find and rescue her. One who would do anything to save her. A husband who loves her." Tat slid his back down the wall and sat on the floor.

"Please forgive me, Cody. I have disgraced myself. When you tell Dace what I have done I will be stripped of my command and thrown in the dungeon where I belong."

"Tell Dace what?" Cody said with a slight smile. "All I remember is that we finished an enjoyable conversation about love. I suspect the General has more pressing matters to attend to than the romantic chatter of his men."

Tat grinned wearily. "I suppose you're right. Thank you, Cody."

Cody helped Tat to his feet. "No, thank *you*. You risked your life to help me rescue Jade from El Dorado." He looked back at Rali; she was still in a drug-induced slumber. "It's my turn to help you. I'll help you get your wife back. I promise."

"I need to search the Monastery libraries," Cody declared to Xerx. "This war will not be won by swords and arrows. We've fought valiantly, but Atlantis can't hold much longer. I must face and defeat the Golden King. It's the only way. I need to find whatever I can about The Earthly Trinity. I'm convinced that it is the key to everything."

Xerx's brow furrowed. "There are hundreds of thousands of volumes in the library. It would take years to find what you're looking for." There was no need to remind each other that they might not even have *days*.

Cody recalled his discoveries in El Dorado's library. He had found the desired page on The Earthly Trinity only to discover it had been ripped out with the scribbled words *find the fallen angel* in the book's margins.

"*The Ancients*," he said, remembering. "That was the room housing the books in El Dorado. Atlantis must have a similar section. That's where we need to go." Without waiting for confirmation, Cody set off toward the Monastery. After several steps he stopped, realizing that Xerx had not followed. "Come on. What's wrong?"

"Those books...they're gone."

Cody stomped back. "What do you mean, *they're gone*? Gone where?"

"Transferred out of the Monastery."

Cody's body shook in irritation. "Transferred where?"

"They were delivered to the AREA headquarters, under the orders of Sli Silkian. Not two weeks ago."

A sudden, frantic banging sounded against the door. Xerx stepped to open it but Cody stopped him. "Wait..." Among numerous other foes, a member of the Golden Knife and the murderous Garga Prince Ugar-Kir-Hugar were still loose in the city. The knocking ceased.

The next instant the door exploded off its hinges and fell to the ground in a mound of ash. Tiana burst inside trailed by a young girl. Xerx looked in dismay at the granular, smoking remains of the door.

Tiana kicked the ash pile, scattering it across the floor. "Why was the door locked and why didn't you let me in?" The young girl at Tiana's heel nodded in support. The last thing Cody had time for was to be caught in the crossfire between Xerx and Tiana.

"I'm sorry, I have to go. I was just on my way to pay a visit to the AREA headquarters."

"You can't," Tiana said with surprising firmness.

"Why not?"

Tiana looked behind to confirm no one was near.

"Because I've just discovered that Sli Silkian murdered Levenworth."

"*What!* Are you sure?" Cody had not trusted the cunning AREA leader from the moment they met. But distrusting someone and accusing them of being a murderous traitor were two different things. Tiana nodded adamantly.

"I'm positive. Not only that, but he's the mole. He's the one who has been leaking the plans from the Inner-Council."

Tiana quickly recapped what she and Elena had overheard. Xerx rubbed his forehead.

"The pieces still don't fit. If Silkian was reporting to CROSS, then how did *El Dorado* discover our plans? Is CROSS informing El Dorado?" Cody hoped not. Despite Dunstan's insistence, Cody refused to believe CROSS was his ally; but could they truly be allies with El Dorado? "Did they say anything about *The Code*? Do they know where the Book is?" For once Tiana had good news to share.

"No. Neither Silkian nor the CROSS agent knows the whereabouts of the missing Book. They seemed troubled by it. There is something going on. Something they've been planning. They mentioned something about a sacrifice and The Earthly Trinity being united. By the way they talked I think whatever they're planning is going to happen soon."

"When?"

"I don't know." Tiana cast another glance at the doorway and lowered her voice. "But I think it is going to happen *tonight*."

95

Fear Itself

L amgorious Stalkton wheeled himself into his room. Had he still had legs he would have danced a ferocious jig. Back in his prime people had always dropped their jaws and stared when he danced. He was sure it had something to do with the magical way his hips swayed from side-to-side.

Making sure no one was looking, he pulled out a flask from beneath his cart, and popped off the lid. *Glump... glump...glump.* He downed every drop before finally pulling his lips away and gasping for air. He tossed the empty flask to the floor. That's what the heroes always did in the stories he'd read. Now that he *was* a hero he would have to act the part.

The feeling of the liquid running down his throat caused him to shake like a wet dog. He looked back and forth again. He was a priest after all, and the flask had not exactly been filled with water.

Adrenaline filled his veins. Well, either that or the strong beverage he had just chugged. Either way, he felt energized. It had been exhilarating to sail on the lava sea with his brother. He grinned. He felt good. He felt *alive*. More than he had in many, many years.

He heard someone approaching. "Igg, is that you? Come to *bathe* in the glory of our victory?" He chuckled to himself. He had been working on that phrasing for a while. "Get it, brother? Because you *don't* bathe!" He turned to greet his brother—instead, it was the two scarlet, serpentine eyes of the Hunter that peered at him from the doorway.

"Oh, my heavens, it's *you* again!" Stalkton pivoted his cart to face the lone doorway as the immense Beast strode inside. "After all these long years, I've had countless nightmares of seeing you again. And now that I do, it all seems much more frightening than my dreams."

The Hunter lapped its black tongue across its lips and stepped forward. Stalkton wheeled his cart back slightly as the Beast approached. "I've pondered that night many times. Why you preyed upon all the Brotherhood monks, but left me alive. Why *me*? How was I different than all the others? But I finally figured it out."

The Hunter paused, tilting its great head, as though curious to hear the priest's answer. "*Fear.*" Stalkton pointed his boney finger at the creature. "You are nothing more than Fear with legs and teeth." The Hunter's lips pulled back to reveal its fangs. "Very *big* teeth," Stalkton added.

"Yet fear only has power over the fearful. *That's* the difference. All the others, they were afraid of you. *Terrified* of you. But I was young and proud. I was calm and self-assured. Fear had no power over me."

The Hunter rose on its back feet, its head touching against the high, domed ceiling. It released a savage, high-pitched wail. If Stalkton's skin had contained any color it would have drained away. He tried to wheel his cart backwards, away from the howling Beast but one of the cart's wheels jammed against the empty flask on the floor. With a loud *snap* the wheel splintered. Stalkton tumbled out of the broken cart, rolling until he crashed into the wall.

The room rattled as the Hunter slammed back onto its front feet and stalked toward the fallen priest. Stalkton propped himself up against the wall. He wanted to run, but the nobs where his legs ended merely wiggled uselessly in the air. "I am no longer so young or so foolish," he said. "I *am* afraid." The Hunter purred, as though it could taste the fear on its tongue already. Its snout leveled in front of the priest's face.

Stalkton took a deep breath. "I have seen many things and had many great adventures. The only great unknown that remains for me is through the door of death and into the afterlife. If you, foul creature, are the vessel to send me on this final adventure then be quick about it."

The Hunter was happy to oblige.

96

A Final Warning

The Golden King stood alone before the gate. His abrupt appearance had sent shockwaves all along the wall. Archers fumbled to ready their bows and swordsmen nervously squeezed their sword hilts. The New Brotherhood monks braced themselves, clearing their throats, ready to use the High Language.

All the while, the Golden King stood patiently, seemingly amused by the frantic display. He was well within range of the bowmen, yet none dared be the first to loose an arrow at the King. By the time Cody had arrived with the others the clamor had died into a tense, expectant hush. He didn't spot Silkian among the crowd. *Where did that worm slink off to?* Also noticeably absent was Jade. Cody couldn't remember the last time he had seen his friend. He was becoming worried about her. However, for the time being, he needed to focus on the threat at hand.

Queen Cia hollered down from the battlements. "Why have you come, Uncle? Speak and be gone. I will not allow you to defile our ears with your silver tongue." At her words, the Golden King slid his tongue slowly across his lips.

"Have no fear, dear Niece. I do not intend to stay long. I have come for only two purposes." Prince Kantan leaned in toward his sister, and whispered just loud enough for Cody to overhear.

"I advise you not let him speak. His words bring only death and discord."

"I will not be bullied," she responded. She returned her attention to the Golden King "You have sixty seconds to speak, no more."

"You are *most* kind." The Golden King scanned his ruby eyes across the wall. "I can smell your terror from here. You have fought valiantly. Each one of you deserves the honor of a bard's song. But here is a riddle...what do you call a valiant warrior with a spear through his heart?" The King paused, a horrible smile forming on his face, before providing the answer. "A *dead* warrior. What good is a bard's hymn if you are decaying beneath the dirt?"

From somewhere along the wall a gruff soldier shouted, "What's your point Tin-King?" Several others grunted in support. In that instant Cody realized the Golden King had just won. The smug, arrogant expression on the King's face suggested he knew so as well.

"Why do you fight?" the King asked.

"Because we have something worth fighting for!" shouted a child from the *Ageing City*, his head too short to even see over the wall.

"A curious expression," the King mused. "Who determines what is and isn't worth fighting for? Even so, there is a vast chasm between *fighting for* and *dying for*. As such, I offer each of you a reward for your bravery. Every man, woman, or child who comes to our camp within the next hour will be spared and welcomed into my Kingdom with open arms." A quiet murmur began to grow.

Cia remained composed, but even Cody could sense that her control over the men was slipping away. She raised her hands to calm the chatter but the noise only grew louder. For the first time a slight trace of fear appeared on the Queen's face. She was forced to raise her voice to be heard over the tumult.

"Keep your empty promises, Uncle. We are not so easily enticed." But the steady murmur of the crowd suggested otherwise. "Your sixty seconds are up and I have heard more of your filth than I care to." Another unseen soldier on the wall interrupted the Queen.

"What was the second reason?"

The Golden King smiled. "I merely wished to see the cowardly faces of the fools who reject my offer when I make this promise: Before the Orb shines again the Second Wall will fall, like the glorious days of old, and most of you will be dead." The King gave a mock bow. "Sleep tight."

97

A Change in Leadership

The fragile courage of Atlantis broke. The sight of comrades dying and the ubiquitous stench of death had chipped away the resolve that had once been so strong. Even the strongest had their valor waver as their fellow soldiers exited the city in droves to accept the Golden King's proposition.

The deserters hustled forward with their heads downcast and their meager bundles of belongings in their arms. Cia and Kantan were forced to jump out of the way to keep from being trampled.

Kantan watched them pass with murderous hatred. "The moment they step outside the city gate they become our enemies. We cannot allow them to join the enemy ranks. Sister, you must signal the archers... "

Cia recognized many familiar faces in the exodus. They were those who had cheered at her coronation and had pledged their lives to serve her and the Kingdom. Now none would even give the courtesy of looking her in the eye as they abandoned her. "Every man is free to choose his path," she said softly.

"But if they join the enemy..."

"Then we will still be hopelessly outnumbered." An edge crept into the Queen's voice. "They have made their choice and we have made ours. I did not watch thousands die in defense of Atlantis just to hand it over to our uncle on bended knee."

Kantan nodded. "Very well. Perhaps it would be wise to interrogate the Golden Prince once more. If he has any knowledge of his father's plans, it would be of great benefit." As the departing crowds thinned, the twins headed toward the palace.

What would my father do? Kantan had seldom thought of his father since Foz had murdered him. He had thought even less frequently of Foz. *What ever happened to you, little brother?* Somehow Kantan knew for certain his brother was dead. *How long can worms like you survive in a raven's nest like El Dorado?* Only scum can co-exist with scum. *Scum like Randilin.*

Even from within the walls of the Royal Palace came unexpected defectors. Kantan peered at those scurrying to gather their possessions. He knew he couldn't deter them; but he at least wanted them to feel guilty for their disloyalty. *They would not have left if my father was still king. The Good King, they called you. They loved you, Father.*

Kantan had ordered that Prince Hansi be escorted to the Great Hall for interrogation. The El Dorado Prince looked up as they arrived. Hansi looked depleted, with no trace of the arrogance he had displayed since his capture. "I know what you would ask, but I have had no contact with my people since my capture. Whatever my father intends will be as much a surprise to me as to you. You have my word."

Kantan was not in the mood for pretense. "If your word were currency I would be begging at the city gates."

"Brother," Cia chimed. "This man is royalty *and* family, not a common thief." *The Golden King has both of those titles as well,* Kantan thought, but now was not the time to quibble. She was correct; the time for petty grudges was long past.

"The Golden King made a peculiar comment. He said, *it will be like the glorious days of old*. What did he mean by that?"

"A reference to the First Great War, perhaps," Hansi suggested. Kantan had concluded as much himself, but it wasn't so simple.

"Your father lost the First Great War. There is no glory in defeat." Kantan studied the Prince's eyes for any slip or hint they might reveal. Hansi was no simpleton. Had they shared a father Kantan might have even grown to like the boy.

"You are jumping ahead of yourself, cousin. During the First Great War a traitor opened the gate of the Second Wall from the inside. Our mutual friend, Randilin Stormberger." Kantan's throat tensed at the name.

"But history tells that the dwarf opened the gate of the Outer-Wall..."

"History is the greatest liar of all. Don't always believe what you're told. That is the answer to my father's riddle.

The Golden King will attempt to open the gate from the inside." Kantan exchanged glances with his sister.

"If this is true we must warn General Ringstar at once." The conversation was cut short by the sound of clashing steel from outside the hall. Kantan signaled to the royal guards who drew their weapons. Cia grabbed Hansi's shoulders, but the Prince shook his head. "I have no knowledge of this. I would not lie to you, Lady Cia." He spoke with an earnestness that was hard to reject.

The doors to the Great Hall burst open. Sli Silkian entered the room. He strutted down the rows of columns with a company of Enforcers at his back. The Queen stepped forward to greet him. "We heard a disturbance."

Silkian bowed low. "Have no fear, my Queen. The disturbance has been righted." Before anyone could react the Enforcers turned and rammed their swords into the chests of the royal guards. The shocking slaughter lasted only a few moments before every guard had been eliminated.

"Are you *mad*! What the is the meaning of this?" Kantan lunged toward the AREA leader but two armed Enforcers quickly blocked his path.

"Madness is a disease diagnosed by those too small-minded to recognize genius," Silkian said. Two Enforcers bound the Prince's arms behind him. Kantan had always known Silkian was dangerous. But *dangerous* and *bold* were two vastly different species of man.

"You gave your word," Cia snapped toward Hansi, but the Prince held his arms up in protest.

"I have no knowledge of this, I promise."

Silkian motioned to the Enforcers who quickly tied Cia's hands. "The Prince speaks truth. El Dorado is inconsequential, a mere annoyance. I have powerful allies." He lifted the crown from Cia's head and fitted it on his own. The beauty of the crown looked a mockery atop his worm-like face. "Bow before the new King of Atlantis."

98

Like the Days of Old

The Golden King was true to his word. Before the first sign of the Orb's light an army of Dark-Wielder's appeared. The crystal beings marched shoulder-to-shoulder in a perfectly straight line. The zealots didn't speak. Even their feet seemed to glide silently across the killing ground toward the Second Wall.

Like the glorious days of old, Cody thought. He remembered hearing the stories of the First Great War. Back when everyone had used the Orb's power for violence. The fighting had been short and bloody. *The Golden King is going to demolish the city...*

Beside Cody, Dace watched the new threat approach. "This contest will not be easily won by sword or arrow." The General's meaning was unmistakable. Cody knew he was right. Xerx nodded his understanding.

"I will gather the New Brotherhood and meet the Dark-Wielders head-on." Xerx glanced to Cody in an unspoken question. Cody nodded.

"I'm coming, too. What good is a Book Keeper if not for moments such as this?" Cody knew he should save his strength for his impending duel with the Golden King, and Xerx's raised eyebrow suggested likewise, but there was no time to argue.

Moments later the Brotherhood Monks had been assembled into formation. In total no more than fifty of the original three hundred brothers remained. Cody recognized only Poe and Gelph. He wondered what had happened to Fincher Tople, but something inside told him that Tople had been one of the first to accept the Golden King's offer and desert the city.

The gates were pulled open and the army of Brotherhood Monks marched out to meet the invaders. The two armies advanced slowly in their collision course. The mouthless crystal faces of the Wielders held no expression; their purple robes flowed behind them.

The Brotherhood Monks locked arms forming a single line of defense. Then someone shouted, the ground exploded, and the carnage began.

Randilin watched the battle from the safety of an Outer-Wall sentry tower. No matter how hard he tried, he couldn't force himself to look away. *I'm a bloody coward.* The fighting was ruthless. With every second the scales seemed to shift drastically. It was like watching an equally matched game of tug-o-war with a pit of boiling oil in between. The dwarf's stubby fingers were bleeding from his frayed fingernails.

He glanced to his left, where the menacing figure of *The Impaler* stood watching the battle unfold. A familiar popping noise sounded from behind, but there was no need to turn. The stairs into the tower had been obliterated. Only one man ever came or left the tower freely.

The Golden King did not so much as cast a casual glance at the raging battlefield below. Instead he reclined in a chair, tapping his fingers on the armrests, and inquired of the dwarf. "Do you have a final count?"

Randilin's eyes remained glued to the battle below even as he answered. "Eight hundred citizens of Atlantis have come to accept your offer. They are being temporarily held in former Lillian tents until proper arrangements can be made, as you decreed." The Golden King had assigned Randilin the task of overseeing the census. Randilin knew full well it had been a cruel and deliberate appointment. He had recognized many of the deserters. They had hidden their faces in shame at the sight of him. The act had almost made Randilin laugh. Who was the King of Traitors to toss accusations at others?

The Golden King nodded absently, as though he had just received a detailed inventory list of armaments. The King motioned to his Spider-General. "Welcome the newcomers into our kingdom with open arms...and then see to it that each of these despicable creatures is exterminated."

"What?" Randilin spun around. "You can't! You promised them refuge!" The Spider-General unsheathed his sword and departed through the portal. The Golden King chortled.

"You of all people should know how iron-clad my promises are. El Dorado has no need of turncoats." Randilin received the warning clearly: tread carefully or find his own neck beneath the Spider's sword. Unfortunately, Randilin had never been known for being cautious.

"By the look of it, you may need to stick some shiny gold armor on the deserters and make bloody soldiers out of them. Your prized crystal pets are being turned to pebbles. I expected so much more after all the hot air you were puffing earlier!" Randilin braced himself for the King's rage. What he received instead was the King's mirth.

"I can only hope the other Atlantians are as foolish and blind as you." Randilin had never cussed so bitterly as he did in that moment.

"You cruel devil. The Dark-Wielders are just a bloody diversion."

The gleam of a dagger flashed through the air. The watchman on the south wall was dead before he even realized he should scream or sound an alarm. Had the watchman been aware, he also would have seen the four Dark-Wielders scale the wall and drop down on the other side. Furthermore, he surely would have seen the large hole that burned through the wall to allow the swarm of golden golems to pour into the city. Unfortunately, the watchman was dead, and saw none of these things.

99

A Promise Kept

The fighting was ferocious. The opening moments of the conflict saw countless casualties on both sides. The beggar Gelph had taken down three Wielders with his final breath and the servant-turned-monk Poe Dapperhio had annihilated an entire cluster before being forced back to the wall, in critical condition.

Cody and Xerx stood back-to-back, sending furious High Language attacks at the crystal creatures. Already the ground had been paved in glittering dust. Then the mayhem ceased as suddenly as it had begun.

Cody and Xerx pivoted, keeping their backs pressed together, while searching for new enemies. Across the battlefield Brotherhood Monks were staggering back to the gate, their robes torn and bloody. Cody counted only twenty surviving monks, and prayed that some had already made it back or were being restored by the healers.

"Well, friend," Xerx said. "Any fool, such as myself, who ever felt you didn't have what it takes to be the Book Keeper has some words to eat. Thank you." Cody savored

the compliment as they returned to the City. Dace Ringstar was the first to greet them as they entered through
the gate.

Dace pulled them into a hug. "You rascals are some of
the bravest men I've ever had the privilege to know. I just
witnessed four hours of the most heroic fighting I've ever
seen..."

"*Four hours?*" Cody cleaned his ears, convinced he had
misheard.

"I jest not. Your small band of fifty just held your ground
for four hours against at least a thousand Dark-Wielders. It
was unbelievable. If the first verse or two of a victory song
has not already been composed in your honor I'll write a
song myself." Dace led them toward the barracks. "Let's
get you two some food and drink."

As they and the other monks walked through the city,
soldiers cheered them on. Xerx grinned. "I can't wait to
hear what the Golden King has to say for himself now. The
whole, *like the glorious days of old*, didn't quite work out the
way he expected."

Dace laughed. "Indeed. I hope he comes crawling on
all fours to..." He stopped short as a bevy of soldiers stampeded toward them. The brigade filled the entire field,
blades drawn and battle-ready. Dace unsheathed his own
sword and the Brotherhood Monks crouched in anticipation. Dace frowned. "Captain Yaru? What the blazes are
you doing here? You're supposed to be overseeing the defense of the South Wall." The burly Captain was wielding
his spiked mace and had a hungry look in his eye.

"Just following orders, General."

"Orders?" Dace asked irritably. "What orders?" Captain Yaru pulled out a crumpled piece of paper and handed it to Dace. It was a dispatch from the Royal Palace. Dace scanned it quickly. It ordered all soldiers from the South Wall to deploy immediately to the front gate to counter the Wielder threat.

Dace's head was spinning. How could the Queen be so foolish? *No, how could we be so foolish.* Dace dropped the orders to the ground. "This was dispatched before the Dark-Wielders even attacked. We knew the Golden King would assault the gate, but he said nothing of the manner of doing so. How is it that this dispatch was possible?" At Yaru's blank stare Dace answered. "Because this isn't the Queen's handwriting, you fool."

Yaru frowned. "But it has the royal seal." That much was true. Yet, in his gut Dace sensed something wasn't right and he had learned long ago always to trust his gut. "We've been deceived. To the Southern Wall! Immediately!" But his orders were already too late.

Horns began to blare. The street where Yaru and his men had come was once again jammed from one side to the other with storming soldiers. This time there were no friendly faces in the onslaught. Golden golems, Dark-Wielders, and *Rephaim* charged at them.

"The Second Wall has been breached!" It took Dace only an instant to scan the scene and identify the enemy's strategy. "Get the Brotherhood Monks to the Third Wall! FALL BACK!"

The attackers had wedged between the Atlantian forces, effectively cutting off the defenders along the Second

Wall from the Inner-City. It didn't take Cody much brain-power to see what would happen. The Second Wall resistance would be crushed from both sides, leaving the Third Wall vulnerable and spread too thin to repel an offensive. Unless they acted quickly they would lose both walls and, therefore the City, with one swift stroke.

Dace grabbed Cody's arm. "Book Keeper, get as many people through the Inner-City gate as possible. Do whatever it takes." He pushed him forward.

"What about you?" Dace was already running the other direction. Cody bit his lip and obeyed, spurring on the monks and soldiers. He used the High Language to clear a path through the crowd.

Dace turned, praying Cody and the others would make it in time. Dace recalled advice Levenworth had once spoken: *The soundest defeat occurs when one is unable to accept defeat.* They had been defeated. The Second Wall would be lost. But if they were going to die they would take as many foes with them as possible, hopefully buying the others time to retreat. He raised his sword.

"Protectors of Atlantis! In the name of the Orb and the glory of the Queen—CHARGE!" Dace ran directly at the sea of invaders. He did not know how many others had followed his lead. Suddenly Captain Yaru appeared at his side matching him step-for-step, his mace swinging in hand. Dace was glad. For all of Yaru's fluff, the man was a ferocious fighter.

Dace raised his sword and shouted as the two sides braced for impact. Abruptly, seconds before the impending collision, the ground began to shake. Dace skidded to a halt. The sand on the battlefield began to spiral as hundreds of sinkholes opened. The Atlantis defenders backed away. From out of the sinkholes poured hundreds and hundreds of warriors.

Orb, help us.

100

What Must Be Done

———

The gate slammed closed. The sounds of clashing steel and death were muffled behind the thick iron doors. Any relief Cody should have felt was numbed by the grim realization that many had been trapped on the other side of the barricade. However, just then his thoughts were of only one person—Jade.

Cody couldn't remember when he had last seen her. He had thought she was merely ignoring him, struggling to deal with her mysterious illness. But, he hadn't seen her atop the Second Wall with her archer brigade. Cody could understand Jade brushing *him* off, but she was far too responsible to abandon her duties. It was very unlike Jade, and that worried him.

The city had deteriorated into chaos. People were screaming and running in all directions. Several buildings were ablaze as men burst out of doors with armfuls of looted goods. At the sight of Cody, the men dropped the bundles and fled. *Oh, Jade, where are you...*

As he trekked through the city Cody overheard rumors that the Royal Palace was now under AREA occupation. In some accounts Sli Silkian had beheaded both Cia and Kantan. In other tellings Jade had been included in the execution. Some said *he* had been executed. One soldier even claimed that Cody had been the *executioner.* Cody prayed each of the accounts was as false as the last.

Cody looked across the clearing to the Royal Palace. A platoon of red-sashed Enforcers stood guard at the entrance. *So it's true.* He felt a sense of dread and wondered what other parts of the rumors might be true.

He took only one step toward the Palace when a strong hand shot out from the shadows and clamped over his mouth, suffocating his startled cry. Cody was yanked violently into the shadows.

Go away! Go AWAY! GO AWAY!

Jade squeezed her temples, scrunching her face. *No more! Go away!* Despite her frenzied pleas she felt the thoughts boring into her brain. She sat alone in the corner of a dark room. She had run from them and hidden, but they had followed her. They stalked her everywhere she went. Mocking her helplessness.

Her eyelids fluttered as drowsiness spread through her body. Jade banged her forehead against the wall. *No-no-no-no-NO! Not again! Please, no!* The room around her started to spin. She was so tired. Her head drooped. She relaxed

her body and, for the first time in weeks, she stopped resisting. Emotions that had haunted her were flooding in.

Jade's eyes burst open. She stood and walked to the
door. It was time to do what must be done.

Cody thrashed against his captor's grip. The stranger
slammed him against the wall, keeping his mouth gagged.
The man had a recognizable stench. Cody stopped struggling. He had only known one man to possess such a putrid aroma.

"Randilin?" The dwarf's crooked, yellow-stained teeth
shone in the dark. Cody was released. "I don't believe it.
This is like..."

"A ruddy dream come true?" Apart from his regular
ugliness, Randilin appeared to be in relatively good condition considering his captivity. The same could not be said
about the dwarf's companion propped against the wall.

"Is that Chazic? He's alive!" The once impressive stature of the AREA Enforcer had deteriorated almost beyond
recognition. Scabbed-over cuts and severe burn wounds
covered the greater portion of his skin. Chazic was not unconscious, but neither did he seem alert.

"*Dytalisia.*" Randilin reported as though reading Cody's
thoughts. "His vocal chords have also been disabled. You
need to get him to the infirmary. Perhaps the healers can
bleed the drug out of his system."

Cody looked at Randilin, still startled by his friend's unexpected reappearance. "What happened? How did you escape?"

"I've been waiting for the right chance. When the chaos started I seized the moment to bust the two of us out." His eyes scanned the courtyard. "I must get to the Palace immediately. I have vital information. The Golden King has a plan to infiltrate the Palace, and I know what it is."

Cody nodded. "I'll come with you."

"No," Randilin said forcefully. "Get Chazic help. I must go alone."

"They won't listen to you. Everybody thinks you've betrayed us to the Golden King again. They don't trust you," Cody said. "But I do. I know what really happened at the Caves."

"What did you say?" Randilin's voice was razor sharp.

"I know you never meant for those terrible things to happen. You were only trying to protect the one you loved. You did it all out of love for Arianna." Randilin's face went ghostly white and deep wrinkles distorted his brow. The dwarf's legs gave out and he tumbled forward.

Cody stepped forward and caught him, pulling him into a hug. Randilin steadied himself against Cody's chest. "Then you will understand why I have to do this," Randilin said. He swung his head forward and landed a firm head-butt against Cody's forehead. Cody crumpled to the ground unconscious. Randilin looked down at him. "I'm sorry, Cody. It's the only way. I have no choice…" Leaving the two lifeless bodies, Randilin departed toward the Palace to do what must be done.

101

An Enemy of An Enemy

The Garga had arrived just in time. Dace had watched in disbelief as the stone warriors appeared through their subterranean tunnels. He had lived through enough during his career that few things still caught him by surprise. Being rescued by the Garga, however, was one of those things.

The surprising reinforcements had altered the battle long enough for Dace to regroup the Atlantians who had been cut off from the Inner-City between the two El Doridian fronts. The defenders, roughly two hundred soldiers and a dozen New Brotherhood monks, had fought alongside the Garga and fortified themselves in several of the Mid-City's abandoned factories. Their new stronghold would not hold out long, but it had bought them some time.

Dace turned as Ugar-Kir-Hugar approached. The Garga Prince was smeared from head to toe in dust and blood. He held a stone javelin; he had fastened two additional spikes to its head to form a trident. "Greeting, blademaster," the

Garga offered in greeting, his voice as stiff as his posture. Both of the Garga's hands remained gripped on his trident.

Dace's hand casually drifted until his knuckles brushed against his sword hilt. "And to you, honorable Prince. You are a most unexpected surprise."

"The enemy thought so as well," he said flashing teeth that had been filed into sharp points. Dace banished any emotion from his face as he met the Prince's stare evenly.

"Forgive me if I sound discourteous, but surely you will understand my caution. Yesterday we were enemies, yet today we fought as allies. Why?"

"Not allies," Kir-Hugar responded. "But rather an enemy of an enemy. I have not lost faith in the Great Garganton. We *are*, in spite of your disbelief, dwelling within the Great One's mouth. However, when I looked into the Garga-Slayer's eyes I saw not a demon, but a human."

"And then you cut his throat, you filthy savage," Captain Yaru said. Kir-Hugar inclined his head toward the hefty Mid-City Captain.

"You are mistaken. It is true my father, the Mouth of the Garganton, sent me for that very reason; to deliver the Great One's justice to the Garga-Slayer. But I did not."

"Why? After all the Garga that have died by Atlantian steel, why come to our aid now?"

"Because we face a common foe. Our peoples may not believe in the same divine force, but we *believe*. The Profaner, this so-called Golden King, believes only in himself and in power. He is without faith or honor, and that makes him a dangerous opponent."

Dace kept his gaze steady and nodded. "Of that we are in agreement. Yet, there is nothing we can do to make up for the many Garga who have died by our swords."

Kir-Hugar nodded solemnly. "A battle fought for the dead is only revenge in disguise. Today we fight for the living."

Dace weighed the Garga's words in his mind before dropping his hand from his sword hilt. "It is an honor to fight and die alongside such venerable warriors as the Garga. You are every bit as fierce as the stories say."

Kir-Hugar grinned at the compliment. "The honor is ours, blademaster. Even among the Garga the name of the legendary Dace Ringstar is held in high regard. It is said there is none who can match you in single combat."

It was Dace's turn to smile. "It appears the Garga are as wise as they are ferocious." Suddenly a soldier burst into the room.

"General! He's coming." Dace turned to face the messenger.

"Be calm, Hoffin. *Who* is coming?" The soldier could not mask his fear as he answered.

"It's him, General Ringstar...The Spider."

Dace spun toward the window and watched as a vast company of enemy soldiers charged toward their factory stronghold, bellowing berserk cries and clanging swords against their shields. Dace's drew his sword from its scabbard.

"Good," he said flatly. "Let him come. I've waited to kill him long enough."

Chazic had watched, unable to voice a warning to Cody as the dwarf tricked him. Chazic had been alert when the soldiers found him lying beside Cody before carrying them both to the infirmary. He had felt every moment of the bloodletting as the healers pressed the sharp knife against his arm to drain the immobilizing drug.

His toe twitched. Then his fingers. His muscles were stiff as his mobility returned. He lunged up from the bed, his arm still bleeding. The healers rushed forward ordering him to lie down. With a forceful shove he sent both healers careening across the room. There was no time to waste. He needed to reach the Palace. He prayed he wasn't already too late.

102
Gateway of the Mind

Xerx shoved his way through the manic crowd. The potent smell of smoke invaded his nostrils and he knew some of the Inner-City buildings must be aflame. But at the moment the only thing that mattered was breaking free of the mob that was pushing against him from every side as the panicking civilians fled in all directions. Xerx spotted several bodies facedown in the sand, trampled and abandoned by the multitude. The gruesome sight spurred him on with increased vigor.

Finally breaking free from the torrent of people, Xerx arrived at the Royal Palace. A line of red-sashed Enforcers formed a blockade before the palace entrance, keeping the rioting civilians at bay. Xerx cocked his head at the unexpected scene. *Since when does the AREA protect the Royal Family? Where are the regular palace guards? Something isn't right.*

Ascending the steps, Xerx flashed the badge of the Brotherhood and lied, "I'm a healer. I'm needed at the infirmary." The preoccupied Enforcers said nothing, but did not deter his path. Once inside Xerx darted in the direction of the living quarters. He turned down the corridor and sighed in relief at the sight of Tiana and Elena. "Thank the Orb! I've been looking everywhere for you two!"

Both registered shock at the sight of him. Xerx looked down, and for the first time realized both skin and clothes were completely coated in blood and ash from his battle against the Dark-Wielders. "I'm okay," he reassured them quickly. "But Atlantis is about to fall. El Dorado has taken the Second Wall."

Tiana wiped the blood from Xerx's face. "We know. There has been fighting here as well."

Xerx's heart skipped a beat. "In the palace?" Tiana's uneasy stare confirmed his fear. Before he could speak further a voice shouted at them from the far end of the corridor. Poe Dapperhio was running toward them. The New Brotherhood Monk was almost entirely wrapped in bandages.

"Poe?" said Xerx in surprise. "Last I saw you were being carried from the battlefield to the infirmary in rough condition." Poe doubled over, placing his hands on his knees and fighting to catch his breath.

"Th-th-the infirmary...H-h-he's there...H-h-hurt...C-c-came fast a-a-as could..." Xerx reached out to steady him.

"Pull yourself together, Poe. Who's in the infirmary? Who's hurt?" Poe inhaled a long breath, composing himself before responding.

"The Book Keeper. He's been attacked!"

Xerx and Tiana exchanged a quick glance. Then, without a word, they were dashing with Elena back down the palace corridor toward Cody.

The doors to the Great Hall burst opened as Chazic entered. Several Enforcers stepped forward to block his path but he paid them no heed. At the far end of the Great Hall, perched on the wooden throne and wearing a polished crown, was Sli Silkian.

Silkian stood in surprise at the sight of Chazic. "I had not thought to see you again so soon, my old pupil." Chazic scanned the platform. To the left of the throne several Enforcers held Cia, Kantan, and Hansi at spearpoint. Silkian cast a lazy glance in their direction. "I have been unable to locate the Book Keeper or Ishmael's youngest brat, the Lady Eva; but I trust I will add them to my collection soon enough."

Chazic shook his head, still dizzy from blood loss and disoriented by the unanticipated findings. "What madness has transpired since I've been imprisoned? When did the AREA's duty change from honoring the Orb's power to seizing power for ourselves? Have you lost your mind?"

Silkian laughed. "That ugly dwarf asked me the same. But I asked him as I ask you now, should not the righteous rule over the unrighteous?

Chazic's senses instantly cleared as he remembered the purpose of his coming.

"Randilin was *here*? In the Palace?"

"Indeed. In this very throne room, not ten minutes ago. He barged in here to inform me of his escape." A single bead of sweat zigzagged down Chazic's forehead.

"What did he say to you? Was he acting unusual?"

Silkian frowned, "Are maggots attracted to rotting flesh? Randilin is a worm. Of course he was acting unusual. Only the Orb knows how a runt like him managed to rescue you from the enemy's camp. He wouldn't stand still. Kept walking around, touching everything and muttering nonsense about Sally and having no choice. He practically flew out of the Hall when I dismissed him."

Chazic's shoulders sagged. "What have you done?" He spun to face the Enforcers. "Go now! We must stop Randilin. He may still be heading toward the gate. The dwarf *cannot* be allowed to leave the city!"

Silkian stood from his throne. "*I* am now the King, so *I* will give the orders here! What is the meaning of this?"

Chazic glared at his former mentor. "It is as I feared. This is why I've come. Randilin *didn't* rescue me. The Golden King *sent* him here."

"That's preposterous," said Silkian. "Why would the Golden King do something as ridiculous as releasing his prized prisoner?"

"Because the Golden King has discovered *The-Creation-Which-Should-Be-One's-Own*." Silkian opened his mouth to interject again but Chazic would not allow it. "He can create *thoughts*. While I was captive he entered into my brain. He saw things; things I don't even remember knowing. He harvested information from my mind as though mining sky-gems."

Silkian shrugged dismissively. "So be it. The Golden King can read the dwarf's mind all night long for all I care. Randilin is no longer my concern."

"You *fool*." Chazic's sharp words caused Silkian's pale skin to color. "Don't you understand? You've just allowed Randilin to walk in here and make a perfect mental picture of this room. With this information..."

"...the Golden King can create a portal directly into this throne room," finished Cia.

"Precisely! We must stop the dwarf at all costs." Chazic was already dashing toward the door. "If he reaches the gate all is lost."

Randilin and Sally sprinted down the street, their hands intertwined. She was still sobbing, as she had been ever since Randilin had found her in the garden. "Randy, you don't have to do this. Please. Not again."

Randilin shook his head sadly. "You're wrong. I don't have a bloody choice. I'm sorry. It's the only way." He looked up. Directly across from them was the gate. "Come on, we're almost there..."

103

A Knife in the Dark

Jade moved silently down the endless corridor. The passage seemed to stretch into oblivion, leading deeper and deeper into thick black nothingness. Despite the stifling dark, something inside her told her she was going the right direction. There was something she had to do. Something important.

She was holding a dagger. She couldn't remember where the knife had come from, as though she had somehow had it the entire time. The blade was familiar, with a solid gold hilt embedded with two eye-like rubies. *Why do I have a knife?* Somehow she knew it, too, was vital for her purpose.

Jade entered a dimly lit room full of white beds. Two men lay sprawled on the floor. The men held no interest to her. She stepped over them and walked forward. At the far end of the room was a single bed. On the table beside the bed was a half-full water glass. In the bed itself, eyes closed, was Cody.

She stopped at his bedside, looking down at his sleeping eyes. He looked so peaceful. So oblivious to the chaos and pain that swirled around him. He looked like the old Cody, before responsibility and power had worn him down. "You should never have touched that Book. You were never meant to be the Book Keeper." Jade stroked his shaggy brown hair. "This is the only way." She raised the knife above her head. "I'm sorry." Jade plunged the dagger into his chest.

Cody's eyes flashed opened, bulging and he exhaled a pained wheeze. A tear rolled down Jade's cheek. "I'm so sorry." She slammed the knife back down into his chest again and watched as the life slowly drained from his eyes.

"Jade! What are you doing?"

Jade opened her eyes. The world seemed to spin back into focus. Tiana, Xerx and a young girl were standing at the entrance. Jade rubbed her sweaty palms against her pants. "I've had another nightmare." She followed the others' stares. Her hands were not damp with sweat—they were soaked with blood.

She backed away from the bed in horror. Cody lay with a dagger plunged into his chest—a dagger with a solid gold hilt and two glimmering rubies.

"Jade...it wasn't a dream."

104

Possessed

Jade had murdered Cody.

She stared at the body of her best friend, blood still seeping from the deep gashes in his chest. Jade rubbed her forehead, coloring it crimson. She staggered, unable to speak. She had not been dreaming. It had all been real.

"Jade, what have you *done!*" Tiana rushed forward toward Cody but Jade stepped into her path. With a violent shove she sent Tiana stumbling back toward the others.

"No. Leave him."

Tiana's jaw dropped. *"Excuse me*? What's wrong with you? He's going to *die!* There may still be a chance to save him. But we must get him to Master Stalkton *immediately!"*

Jade didn't budge. "I'm afraid I cannot allow that."

"What?! Have you lost your mind? *Why?"*

Jade's blood-stained face morphed into a chilling smile. "Cody was weak. This is what he deserved." Jade spat the words with unfiltered hatred. "I will live beneath his overgrown shadow no longer. The world will know that *I* am the most powerful!" Jade laughed. "That old fool Uscana was wrong! It should have been *me*! It was *my* right! I will take back what is mine!"

"That name, Uscana," said Xerx. "He was the father of King Ishmael and the Golden King. He's been dead for centuries. Why would Jade…"

"Jade is not Jade," Tiana said. "She has been poisoned by the Golden King." Tiana braved another step toward Cody who was still pumping blood from his chest. "Jade, *listen* to me. This is *not* you! The Golden King has done something terrible to your mind. *Please.* You need to let us to fix you." The flash of rage that stole Jade's face made it clear that it had been the wrong thing to say.

Jade shrieked. "Nooooo! He told me. The Lord of Lights told me. He told me the truth. He said that all of you feared me because I saw through your lies. He warned me you had used the Forbidden High Language to tamper with my mind. The Golden King *saved* me!"

Xerx took a step forward, joining Tiana's side. "The only one who knows the Forbidden words *is* the Golden King. Search your heart. I would not lie to you. We are your *friends.* Cody is your *friend.* He traveled across Under-Earth to *save* you."

"I'm no damsel in need of rescue," said Jade bitterly. "Ishmael never understood, he was too much like my father. Too *weak.*" Jade's body began to shake.

Tiana took another cautious step. "Your name is Mari *Jade* Shimmers. You are a Surface-Dweller from Upper-Earth. You grew up in the small town of Havenwood with your best friend Cody Clemenson. Jade, don't forget who you are…"

The last words of the plea disarmed Jade. She looked around the room quizzically as though waking from a long hibernation. "My name is Jade. Havenwood. Cody..." she muttered to herself. "My name is Jade. Havenwood. Cody..."

Her eyes stopped at Cody. Instantly the fire in her eyes reignited. In that instant Tiana realized they had lost her. Jade's face twisted into a grotesque shape. "No...they lie. It's all lies...LIES!"

Debris began to fly across the room as Jade waved her arms through the air and screamed. Tiana and Xerx linked hands, funneling their combined strength to fling a large orb of energy at her.

Jade waved her hand indifferently as though swatting away an irritating housefly. The orb instantly dissipated. "That's impossible," Tiana uttered.

Jade thrust her hands toward Tiana and Xerx, launching both of them across the room. As they struggled to get up Jade's shrilling cackle filled the chamber. "No more lies! Liars deserve only death." She raised her hands again to carry out the death sentence.

"Jade?" The pained whisper was barely audible. The voice belonged to Cody. Jade spun around.

"Cody?" For an instant Jade's voice was her own again—but only for an instant. "You're supposed to be dead." She screeched and lunged toward him. "I MUST KILL YOU!"

Thump!

Jade collapsed to the floor. A bulge was already forming on the back of her head from where Elena had whacked her with a chair. The others finally regained their footing.

The threesome circled around the gurney. Cody was drifting quickly.

Tiana took charge. "Ellie, here." She guided the young girl's hands to the pulsing wounds in Cody's chest. "Push down hard. Try to contain the bleeding. Xerx and I will fetch Master Stalkton. He's our only chance." Elena nodded without question and without fear. Tiana realized then just how much she loved the little urchin. "I will come back for you, Ellie, I promise."

There was no time to waste. They sprinted from the room to fetch the only hope for Cody's survival, the whole time hoping it wasn't already too late.

105

In the Garden

She screamed.

Her throat was raw as she writhed on the floor, thrashing out against the invisible pain. Her hands grasped at her chest. Yet the unbearable pain persisted. So, too, did the screams.

Ever since *the accident* the spells had become an accepted part of her life. However, the attacks recently had become more frequent and vicious. She had known as much and had prepared for it. But the foreknowledge had done nothing to lessen the anguish.

She had only experienced such torture on one other occasion, the night she had felt the invisible fangs tearing into her body. She had thought it was the most debilitating pain possible. She was wrong.

She cried out, a desperate release of agony, not a call for help. She had come to the garden to *hide* from people, and knew no one could hear her wails. As always, she would suffer alone.

Eva raised her eyes. Several inches from her were light blue leaves spotted with vibrant yellow and orange.

Derugmansia—or *Soul Snatcher* as it was called. The same poisonous plant that had sent her father to his untimely death. Eva gazed at it longingly. One small touch of the beautiful leaf and she could be reunited with her father. There would be no more pain.

No. Not yet.

She pushed herself from the ground. She needed to endure a little longer. She still had a purpose. Her time had finally come.

106

Gateway Through the Mind

The fate of Atlantis rested on the winner of the footrace. Sweat drizzled down Chazic's neck and back and the tattered rags of his captivity swayed as he ran. Where once his wide shoulders had bulged against the garments, fabric now hung loose. *It's slowing me down.* Without breaking stride he tore the tunic and tossed it aside, revealing the peculiar tattoo markings he was always careful to hide. At that moment, however, speed was his only concern.

The Inner-City was overcrowded, the result of three districts corralled into one. Even in his weakened condition Chazic retained some of his exceptional strength. He used his arms like giant cleavers to slice his way through the crowd until he arrived at the wall. The dwarf was nowhere to be seen. *I'm too late.*

He refused to accept defeat. He bounded up the stairs to the top of the wall. His chest heaved in and out as he scanned the Mid-City. Dace's band was under heavy siege in their factory stronghold. *Their sacrifice means nothing if the dwarf isn't stopped.*

He spotted him.

Randilin was already a fair distance from the wall and moving toward the enemy line. *There's still hope.* Chazic blindly grabbed the nearest bowman and yanked him forward. The man resisted, "Get your hands off of me... *Chazic?*" Tat Shunbickle ceased the struggle and threw his arms around the Enforcer. "You're alive!" Chazic shook him off. The joy of reunion was eclipsed by the realization that Tat was the greatest archer in Under-Earth. *Hope is not lost!*

"There's no time," Chazic said. He pointed to the fleeing dwarf. "Take him down! If he reaches the enemy line then we're all doomed." Tat glanced the direction of Chazic's finger.

"I can't. These arrows were mass produced and poor quality. My range is reduced to maybe three hundred and forty yards, if I'm lucky."

"Now!" This time Tat didn't hesitate. He planted his foot against the rampart for support and closed his left eye, gauging the distance. The *plunk* of the string was followed by the graceful *whizz* of the arrow.

The arrow soared through the air in a slow arc before tilting and gliding down toward the fugitive dwarf. Chazic watched as the arrow shaft vibrated on impact. The arrow had landed several yards short.

"I knew I could count on you," the Golden King said. "Although I'll admit, even *I'm* astonished by your continual willingness to betray those you love."

Randilin's face was gaunt. "Just do what you have to bloody do and let me go. You gave your word. Sally and I go free."

"Indeed, my ugly friend. And you know I *always* keep my promises." The Golden King grabbed the sides of Randilin's head. The dwarf cried out in agony as the King took control of his mind and learned the state of the Palace.

"Such a destitute court, so ill-fitting for royalty," the King mused. He released Randilin. "Farewell, my old friend."

Bitter tears swelled in the dwarf's eyes as he grabbed Sally's hand and they fled. The Golden King watched them depart, then turned to look at the Royal Palace visible over the top of the Inner-Wall. He closed his eyes.

"*Spakious.*"

107

A Horrible Discovery

The tumultuous furor of battle resonated from the Third-Wall. As Xerx and Tiana were lifted up to the Monastery of the Brotherhood, they had full view of the black mass of El Dorado still stretching into the distance, veiling the landscape like a sinister shadow.

"So much fighting, so many dead, and we haven't even made a dent in their army," said Xerx. "And now Cody..."

"*Don't*," Tiana said, silencing him. "Cody is not lost to us yet." The word *yet* resounded like a trumpet blast. "We can still save him if we reach Master Stalkton in time." Xerx knew better than to challenge her. The rickety elevator continued its laborious ascent. "We don't have time for this!"

Xerx couldn't agree more. "*Byrae.*" A powerful gust of wind caught the platform from below, launching it upward to the top. They dove onto the balcony and dashed to the Monastery, aware that every second they wasted lowered the odds of saving Cody.

Xerx detonated the Monastery door with the High Language, allowing them immediate entry. Tiana grabbed Xerx's shoulder, stopping him. "*Wait*...Something isn't right." Xerx sensed it as well. The Monastery was always tranquil, but there was something amiss about the current silence.

They ventured into the large, domed room. Nothing seemed to be out of place, yet their sense of foreboding intensified with each step. A foul stench lingered in the stifling air. When they reached Stalkton's chambers they found his door ajar.

They also discovered the genesis of the odor that wafted vigorously through the open crack. Xerx dropped to his knees and retrieved an object from the floor, twisting it in his hand. It was the splintered remains of a wheel from Stalkton's rolling cart. "Oh, no...Master!" Xerx kicked open the door and vomited at the sight.

The body of Lamgorious Stalkton lay in a mangled heap in the corner. "Oh, Master..." Xerx fell against the nearest wall, struggling to stay upright as his stomach twisted, another surge of bile climbing his throat.

He felt Tiana's arms around him. "I'm so sorry, Xerx." Xerx couldn't bear to look. When Wesley had fled to Upper-Earth with the Book, the quirky albino had become a father figure to Xerx. Intense fury welled up within him. *He didn't deserve to die this way.*

"Xerx, look. What are *those*?"

Hundreds of strange objects covered the floor. "Are those what I think they are?"

Xerx took a slow step backward. "We need to warn the others immediately." Before they could act on their panic, they heard a soft sound from behind. It was a low, hungry purr.

The wicked red eyes of the Hunter peered at them from the entrance of the chamber. Its immense, domed back filled the doorframe, blocking the duo's escape from the room. The taloned demon flared its nostrils and prepared to pounce.

"*Duomi!*" The wall exploded at Xerx's command. A cascade of rubble came thundering down in front of them, completely blocking the entrance. They could hear the Hunter's feral shrieks from the other side.

Xerx examined the blockade, wheezing from the barrage of dust. He turned his attention back to the room to where hundreds and hundreds of glossy black oval objects lay. The Hunter's presence had removed any doubt as to what the peculiar objects were.

They were eggs.

108

From Death to Life

The Golden King stepped into the Great Hall. Scores of golems and Dark-Wielders followed through the portal behind him. The Enforcers guarding the throne raised their weapons half-heartedly but none moved to inhibit the intruder's path.

The King's voice filled the room. "I waited and waited for my invitation, yet none arrived. Surely the children of my only beloved brother would not withhold common courtesy from their dear uncle." Every word dripped with mockery.

Cia stepped forward, undeterred by the Enforcers' presence. "You will *never* be welcome in my court, you murdering, traitorous devil."

The Golden King wagged his finger. "*Tsk tsk*. Did your manners run off with your beauty? After all, it appears this isn't even *your* court any longer." The King reached the platform and climbed the stairs. Hansi stepped in front of him.

"Father, I've..."

The King's golden hand slapped his son across the face. "Do *not* ruin this moment for me. You've already disgraced me enough. I curse fate for not giving me a daughter. Perhaps a woman would possess enough cunning not to get herself captured from her own camp. Don't spoil things more than you already have, boy. This moment must be *perfect*." A flicker of madness registered on the King's face but he immediately regained his composure.

"Now," said the Golden King. "Time to deal with this rubbish sitting upon my throne." His ruby eyes lowered to Sli Silkian. The AREA leader was squirming like a fish on land.

"You would be wise not to underestimate me," Silkian said. "I have powerful allies. They *are* coming. They *told me* they were coming..." His voice faltered. "I can make a bargain..."

"Those with unlimited power have no need for powerful friends. I'm afraid I must respectfully decline your offer."

Silkian's eyes bulged. His face was an exhibition of unbridled terror. "When my allies arrive..."

"When they arrive I will offer them your sincere apologies that you were unable to receive them."

Silkian sank deeper into his seat. "I will serve you faithfully! I know things! I will..." The AREA leader was still bumbling when the Golden King said, *"Moltria Grima Dastanda."*

Sli Silkian was turned to dust. His body disintegrated into millions of granules, pouring off the throne and onto the floor. The Golden King brushed the remaining dust from the seat of the simple, wooden throne. *"Sellunga Golanda."*

A bubbling, golden liquid appeared in the center of the seat and spread like spilled ink over the wood, then hardened into a gleaming surface. The King sat on his newly gilded throne, turning to face the crowd that had amassed before the platform.

"Anyone who throws down his weapon will be granted the right to live out the rest of his miserable, immortal life as a servant in my palace. Anyone foolish enough to decline will provide the dust for the others to sweep." The sound of a hundred weapons clattering on the stone floor filled the Great Hall. Only Kantan and Cia remained defiant. The King raised an amused eyebrow as a third figure joined the Atlantian Royals. "Hansi? Will you betray your own father?"

"You are no father to me," Hansi declared. The King shrugged in indifference.

"Suit yourself." He scanned the crowded chamber. "Is this all? Only three lonely souls possess the courage to stand against me?" He let out a shrill, grating laugh. "Not even your cowardly Book Keeper dares resist his rightful King!"

He returned his attention to the three opposing him. "I *am* going to kill you; but before I do, I want you to look around." The King motioned to the assembly behind them. "I want your last living thought to be the miserable realization that you died so very alone." He snarled. *"Moltr..."*

A sudden shout carried across the Hall. "They are *not* alone!" The crowd parted. Standing at the entrance was

Cody. In his hands was *The Code*. "If you want to take Atlantis you'll have to get through its Book Keeper first."

"Splendid." The Golden King smiled. "I was hoping you would show up."

109

Stronger Than Before

Cody stared across the Great Hall directly into the blazing ruby eyes of the Golden King. Cody's face radiated with a slight glow as the rejuvenating energy of the Book coursed through his veins. His skin still tingled where the Book's power had closed his wounds and saved his life.

Surely the Orb had spared him for this very moment. The waiting; the training; the angst—all of it converged into the now. On the inside he remained the same terrified small-town boy from Havenwood; but what was required was a brave Book Keeper. Atlantis needed a hero. He would be that hero.

"I see you have found your lost toy," the King said, motioning toward the Book. "The men I dispatched to steal it were disappointed to discover it had already been taken." The King stood from his throne and descended the platform steps. "I'm curious—who was it? Who stole the Book? A jealous rival? An ambitious commoner? Your precious Jade, perhaps?"

Cody shook his head. "Your greatest flaw is that you can't comprehend that not everyone is driven by selfishness like you. The Book was not *stolen*. It was taken and hidden; kept safe until it could be returned at the proper moment when I needed it most, when my life depended on it. Kept by someone immune to the snare and obsession with power." Stepping out from behind Cody was the diminutive Princess Eva.

"*Ah*, so it was Ishmael's little lamb," the Golden King said with a chortle. "It seems she's also immune to *death itself*. Odd that *she* would be the first to survive my precious Golden Knife. And how could we forget *the Accident*. To fall from so high..."

Cody stepped back in front of the young princess, shielding her from the Golden King's mockery. "This quarrel is between us. Book Keeper against Book Keeper."

The King threw back his head and burst into a crazed fit of laughter. "Are you truly so eager to die? Have you already forgotten our first conflict? How pitiful to watch you give everything you had, only to realize that everything you had wasn't close to enough." The King's taunts bored into Cody's chest like a drill. It was true. Cody's best had *not* been enough.

"I'm stronger now," Cody declared. "Having the Book taken from me taught me a valuable lesson. I've finally realized that to be a true Book Keeper, you must find the power in both the Book *and* the Keeper. I am not afraid of you anymore." The words caught Cody by surprise; yet, even as his lips spoke them he realized they were true. He *wasn't* afraid anymore. For the first time since the discovery in Wesley's bookstore so many months earlier, he was at peace with his role as the Book Keeper.

The humor in the Golden King's face was gone. He stared at Cody loathingly, his lips curving into a snarl. "Then you are a fool..." Cody barely had enough time to dive out of the way before a ball of fire exploded against the spot where he had been standing. He rolled to the side, as the entire chamber seemed to ignite in wild flame.

The battle of the Book Keepers had begun.

110

Battle of the Book Keepers

If he stopped moving, even for a second, he was dead. Cody jumped aside as a lava waterfall poured down from the ceiling. He felt the heat singe his skin. Unlike last time the two Book Keepers had dueled, the Golden King was not playing games. His attack was relentless.

The crowd pressed back with frightened cries, forming a circle around the perimeter of the Hall. Cody rolled away as another fireball exploded. Springing back to his feet, Cody caught a flash of movement to his right. A boulder covered in jagged spikes rolled toward him. *"Spakious!"* Cody leapt through a wormhole as the boulder hurtled past.

Cody reappeared behind the Golden King, but before he could attack, the King vanished, dropping through the floor as though through a trap door. Cody heard a *pop*. He spun around and shouted. *"Eleagu!"* An electric current formed a dome around him. The shield crackled as a spray of stone projectiles deflected off of it.

The ground beneath his feet suddenly vanished. The next instant Cody found himself free-falling through a wormhole from the high ceiling of the Great Hall. A bed of serrated icicle stakes waited for him below. With a single word the icicles melted into a sizable wave of water that broke Cody's fall. He rode the wave and took off running the moment his feet touched the floor. He scampered behind one of the giant stone columns, fighting to catch his breath.

He had lost his bearings on the Golden King's location. He peeked around the side of the pillar—another fireball hurtled toward his face. He yanked his head back and the meteor collided with the pillar. Flames streamed from both sides of the column. Sweat soaked his body as intense heat roasted the stone.

Cody realized he was running on borrowed time. He was no match for the Golden King in this contest. As it had done a hundred times, the cryptic advice of Master Stalkton replayed in his head

"Only a fool fights his enemy in the arena and manner of his enemy's choosing. You will never be as powerful as the Golden King with the High Language, so you'd be a fool to fight him with it. Use your strengths and use the Golden King's pride against him and the arrogant King will defeat himself."

Cody scanned his surroundings. Stalkton's advice had seemed simpler when giant fireballs weren't flying at him. *What is the Golden King's weakness?* The heat against his back had become unbearable.

Cody abandoned his cover. He scurried on all fours and hid behind the next column in the row. He could hear the

Golden King's gloating laugh. "Are you afraid *now*? Did you truly think you could best me? A Surface-Dweller? One so weak, so cowardly, so...*imperfect.*"

Cody's head jerked up. *That's it! That's the answer.* He now knew exactly what he needed to do. Cody inhaled, braced himself, and stepped out from his concealment. The Golden King stood in the center of the Great Hall grinning. "Finally ready to accept the inevitable?"

"The only thing that is inevitable here is your failure." Cody thrust his arms forward. "*Duomi!*" A pillar on the far end of the Great Hall exploded.

The Golden King sneered. "You missed. It would appear your accuracy is far from perfect as well."

Cody grinned. "Precisely." He darted forward, weaving his way through the remaining columns. At his command several of the gems decorating the pillars shattered, their shrapnel raining to the ground.

"Do you think this is a game, Book Keeper? Come fight me!" Cody ignored the challenge. He continued sprinting throughout the room and shouting the High Language. In a trail behind him, the mosaic floor tiles began to shift colors, spoiling the symmetrical, sprawling patterns.

"What are you doing?" The Golden King's eyes followed Cody's sporadic movement. Cody paused for just a moment, spreading out his arms and meeting the perplexed gaze of the King. "*Trembor!*" The Great Hall quaked, sending people stumbling off balance. Every piece of décor ornamenting the throne room walls had been disrupted and now hung crooked.

The Golden King's head swiveled back and forth as he regarded the disarray with repulsion. "What have you done? Stop it..." Suddenly the color drained from the King's face. He staggered back a step. He looked back to the fractured remains of the pillar, the lone flaw in the symmetrical column rows. The remaining jewels adorning the pillars exhibited patterns as disjointed as the multi-colored floor tiles. It was all wrong. It was *imperfect*.

"Stop it!" The Golden King grabbed his head. *"Gadour!"* The fragmented column was instantly mended with new stone, restoring the symmetry. But at that same moment a pillar on the other side of the room crashed to the ground. "I said, STOP IT!" For every restoration the Golden King made, Cody tarnished the décor elsewhere, always a step ahead or a second faster.

Cody watched with delight as the Golden King shrieked, running frantically around the room trying to set things right. *You were right, Master Stalkton.* Cody walked up behind the unhinged King. The insane ploy had worked. Cody had to speak but one word and it would all be over. One word and El Dorado would be defeated. One word to end the war. Cody opened his mouth...

BOOOOM!

The entire Palace shook, knocking Cody to the ground. "What on earth?" He tried to stand but was tossed back once more.

BOOOOM!

A deep fissure climbed up the wall, branching across the ceiling. A fragment of the stone from overhead broke free and crashed to the floor. The people below jumped out of the way just in time.

BOOOOM!

More cracks began spreading up the pillars toward the ceiling. Cia shouted from her hands and knees. "Cody, what are you doing? Cody?" Cody rolled aside, narrowly avoiding a plummeting chunk of debris.

"It isn't me! I'm not doing anything!" He noted that the Golden King was just waking from his trance. "It's coming from *outside* the Palace." The explosions abruptly stopped. Several more stone pieces crashed from the ceiling as the Great Hall stabilized.

Cody pushed himself to his feet. *What's happening?* Then he heard it—loud crackling noises sounding in the distance like fireworks. It was a sound never before heard in Under-Earth. It was the sound of gunfire.

111

The Return

BOOOOM!

B The wall erupted in an inferno, hurling stone chunks a hundred feet into the air. When the smoke had thinned a section of the barricade had been completely obliterated.

Dace watched in disbelief as debris continued to rain down. They were well out of range of El Dorado's trebuchets and catapults. *Dark-Wielders?* Dace knew even the combined strength of the Wielders would be unable to maintain such a devastating offensive. *What demonic, black power is this? Has Hell itself declared war on us?* Whomever the attack had come from, with just one strike, they had reduced a forty-foot solid stone wall into heaps of smoking rubble.

BOOOOM!

One of the sentry turrets flanking the Inner-City gate was demolished by another debilitating hit. "General!" A young messenger ran toward him, his unrecognizable face coated in soot. "General Ringstar, I don't know where they came from, but a new army has taken the field. An army with iron carriages."

The wormhole appeared in the exact spot through which the Golden King's embassy had entered moments earlier. Its sudden materialization drew tense anticipation from every head in the Great Hall. For several long seconds the portal remained idle, as though it had been opened by mistake. Then, with jarring abruptness, a lone figure stepped through the wormhole.

The man wore a purple velvet robe that hung from his shoulders and fell into a flowing cape. In his hand he held a tall, polished sword, and atop his head rested a jeweled crown. Despite the elegant garb, it was his deep green eyes that demanded the room's attention.

Mr. Shimmers smiled. "Good evening, Gentlemen."

112

Suffocating

The cramped room seemed to sway uneasily. The air was thin with only a remnant of oxygen remaining. Xerx cast a tired glance to the caved-in entrance. The blockade was both a blessing and a curse. It was perhaps all that separated them from the bloodthirsty Hunter. However, it also effectively cut off their lone source of fresh air.

Xerx squeezed his eyes shut, fighting to keep the lightheadedness at bay. Even so, he could still feel the ominous presence of the innumerable black eggs sharing the room.

Both he and Tiana had attempted various High Language words to obliterate the eggs, but to no avail. The eggs, like the monster that had produced them, were indestructible. The dismal notion added to Xerx's queasiness. He still couldn't grasp how the nightmarish creature had given birth to whatever unsightly horrors waited inside the inky ovals. Whether by some unholy act of the Beast's creator or, birthed by Fear itself, they were simply the embodiment of fear spawning in the current time of terror,

Xerx knew one thing for certain: when the eggs hatched the world as he knew it would cease to exist.

Tiana coughed; her sickly blue-toned skin hung leaden on her face. "I promised Ellie I'd never leave her, the way I'd been abandoned." She chuckled, a wheezing single burst of joyless laughter. "Turns out I'm destined to die on her like those closest to me died."

Xerx lifted his head from the wall. "What are you talking about? Don't worry. We *will* get out of here. I won't leave you, I promise. By now the Hunter must have left, so it's safe to break out of here. I can..." Tiana's curt laughter cut him off.

"No more lies, Xerx. I'm tired of lies. Even from you. *Especially* from you. The truth is that by now Cody will have bled out; the only man with the power to heal him is also dead; and the Enforcers have likely found Ellie. Atlantis is going to fall. If we must die, here is as good a place as any." She was seized by another coughing fit.

Xerx peered at her and sighed. "I've kept it you know, all this time. I've thought about throwing it away a million times, but I've never been able to do it. I guess I'm a fool."

Tiana pushed herself up on one elbow. "What are you talking about?"

Xerx reached into his pocket and pulled out a small object. It glimmered, although not as brightly as it once had. Had any air remained in Tiana's lungs, the sight would have snatched it away. "You've kept the skygem necklace? You're right; you *are* a fool. Why have you kept it?"

Xerx shrugged. "I guess it's because I haven't given up hope. You moved on, but I never did. I keep it because...

well...because I still love you." The words knocked all expression from Tiana's face.

"Xerxus, you stupid boy." She backhanded him across the face. "You are the most witless boy I've ever known." He winced as Tiana's hand cocked for another blow. She swung again.

CRACK!

The sound caught both off guard. Xerx grabbed his cheek, checking for broken bones. Tiana inspected her hand. "I didn't mean to..."

CRACK!

As the noise repeated they both realized their mistake. It was the sound they had been dreading.

CRACK! CRACK! CRACK!

The eggs were hatching.

113

The Once and Future Ring

CROSS had arrived. The assembly was held captive by the imperious presence of Mr. Shimmers as he strolled down the center of the Great Hall. His emerald eyes examined the battle-ruined room with distaste. The CROSS Master's commanding aura blinded the room to the three others who had entered through the wormhole after him. The man with the circular blades along with the seven-foot, bearded titan trailed close behind their leader. Assuming the rear, several steps behind the others, his pistol unholstered, was Dunstan.

Mr. Shimmers held his arms out in greeting. "I do hope I'm not interrupting anything important."

"You!" said Cody.

"You," snarled the Golden King.

Cody turned to the King in surprise. "You *know* this man?" His question was ignored. The Golden King's eyes narrowed, focused only on the CROSS leader.

"I thought you long dead."

"And I thought you still human, son of Uscana," said Mr. Shimmers. "Yet I see you have turned yourself into a golden idol. You always *did* worship yourself."

Cody's head swiveled back and forth, following the frosty exchange between the two surprisingly familiar adversaries. The leaders remained deadlocked in a stare-down, each sizing up the other. They were two titanic forces on a collision course, and neither was willing to budge.

Cody looked to Mr. Shimmers. "Who are you? Who are you really?"

It was the Golden King who provided the answer. "He is, or *was*, one of us. An Alac-icac from the ancient days. He is one of The Twelve."

Mr. Shimmers raised his eyebrow at the explanation. "Is it only Twelve now, and not Thirteen? Was it I you erased from your history or that old fool, Boc'ro?"

Cody's mouth seemed to arrive at the proper conclusion before his brain. He blurted, "You're the Undecided One." His mind flipped through what he knew of Under-Earth's history. "When Atlantis and El Dorado divided Under-Earth, The Twelve were forced to choose sides. But there was one who refused to choose, and left, never to be seen again. That was *you. You're* the Undecided One."

Mr. Shimmers snickered. "Such a clever boy. No wonder my daughter fawns over you like a lovesick puppy. But *the Undecided One* is such a derogatory title; I *did* choose. I chose the path of eternal glory. While the rest of my tribe squabbled like spoiled children, I returned to our home-land. What glory is there in subjugating a useless cave in the Earth's center? I desired more. To do what Chief Uscana, and Kael the Butcher before him, had failed to do. I wanted to conquer the world."

From the corner of his eye, Cody noticed that the CROSS agents were encircling them as their Master continued his tale. "When I entered the Wishing Well I was but a man— but when I re-emerged, I was a god. With the power of the Orb I accomplished wonders the world had never seen before. I rescued humanity from the dark ages and ushered them into an age of unprecedented prosperity. A time of peace. A time of progress. A time of *magic*, or so people called my creation power. I was a good and fair ruler. My people loved me."

A murky cloud swirled in the CROSS Master's narrowed eyes. "And then it all changed. I was so blinded by the glorious light of my reign that I failed to recognize the cloak of darkness that was descending upon humanity. A wretched age of disbelief. Magic was abandoned in pursuit of cold, soulless reason. My reign was slipping through my fingers."

"Betrayed by those closest to me and abandoned by the ones who had loved me most, my kingdom slowly washed away like a sand castle during high tide. It became but a myth, a silly story for children. Over time I was forgotten—but I never forgot. I vowed to rise again and reclaim my stolen throne."

"I bided my time, awaiting the proper moment to rise. I became a faceless wanderer. Thus was the beginning of the *Reclamation Of Supremacy Society*. For near two thousand years I prepared. I infiltrated governments; started wars and finished others; made useful friends and eliminated potential enemies. CROSS was invisible but it was never dormant. Now, at last, I will lay claim to the one power that can return me to glory. The awesome power of The Earthly Trinity."

"My search for the Trinity has led me to return my attention to Under-Earth, where my former people were still sparring after all these centuries. It was all too easy for CROSS to infiltrate both of your cities. The tension and blind hatred between your people required but a nudge to plunge you into cataclysmic war. You obliged like the faithful puppets you are. I found great pleasure in watching your two kingdoms reduce each other to rubble. And now the time has come to take back my rightful glory."

As the narrative concluded Cody felt like he was emerging from a sleepwalking trance. There was something vaguely familiar about Mr. Shimmers' story. Even the Golden King stood motionless and silent, although Cody suspected a High Language word rested loosely on the tip of his tongue. There remained one unanswered question.

"CROSS is an acronym," Cody said, thinking out loud. "The *Reclamation Of Supremacy Society*—R.O.S.S. But what about the C?" Mr. Shimmers looked down his slanted nose at Cody and shook his head.

"Have you still not figured it out?" he said. "With your lips you ask, yet in your heart I suspect you already know the truth. The C represents my kingdom; the greatest kingdom the world has ever known and will soon know once more." He paused, savoring the long-awaited moment, before finishing.

"The glorious kingdom of *Camelot*."

114

The Earthly Trinity

Camelot.

The revelation resounded like thunder. All the stories and legends whirled through Cody's mind in one jumbled vortex. Tales of chivalrous knights and magic. He recalled the map room in Mr. Shimmers' mansion and the ancient, round table within it. *Could it really be?* Jade had never been sure of her father's role in the British military. Her father, Mr. *Arthur* Shimmers.

In his heart Cody knew it was the truth, but the revelation still felt more fairytale than reality. "If you're the King of Camelot then that makes you..."

"A man worthy of your obedience," snapped Mr. Shimmers. "As you will soon learn." He held out his hand. "Dunstan..." The British subordinate appeared at his master's side and presented him with a wood-covered book. Mr. Shimmers lustfully caressed the cover.

The Golden King remained perfectly still, his eyes unmoving and transfixed on the book. Cody was no less captivated. He remembered the first time he had brought

The Code near *The Key* and the almost unbearable energy surge that had overtaken his entire body. In contrast, he felt nothing at the appearance of this wooden book. The eyelid-less man had shown him the vision at the Caves. A vision of an *ivory* covered book. A slow grin formed on Cody's face. "You're lying. There may be a third Book of power—but that's not it."

Mr. Shimmers tilted his head. "Is that so?" He dropped the book to the floor and raised his sword above his head. The abrupt move caused Cody to flinch. Mr. Shimmers slammed the blade into the center of the wooden cover. Instantly the wood began to peel back like paper tossed into a fireplace. Mr. Shimmers reached into the withered outer-casing and retrieved the object contained within: a book with an ivory, seashell cover.

Instantly, Cody felt a harrowing sensation, one that he had experienced only once before. He had been beneath the blue dome of the *Ageing City* and the flow of the Orb's power had been cut off.

The startled look on the Golden King's face revealed the ivory Book was having the same effect on him. "Enough!" the Golden King shouted. *"Fraymour!"*

Nothing happened.

The Golden King's rage morphed into alarm. He spouted a furious string of High Language attacks. Still nothing.

Cody felt panic welling up inside him. *"Duomi!"* Instead of the expected devastating explosion, Cody felt power sucked from him like a syringe drawing blood. His panic gave way to full-fledged terror.

All the while, Mr. Shimmers stood patiently, clutching the Book to his chest like a beloved child. "As you two have so aptly demonstrated, the three Books are not equals just as the three of *us* are not equals. Boc'ro called this beautiful book *the Truth*."

Cody thought back to the first time he had spoken to The Thirteenth, when he and the Golden King had connected the Books in El Dorado. The man's final words to him had been *Unlock the Truth*. Cody finally understood the meaning of the cryptic words. *He was talking about the third Book!* "The Prophecy," muttered Cody, half to himself. *"The pearl within the shell.* The universe's most powerful force is within *that* Book."

Mr. Shimmers sneered. "Precisely. While *The Code* and *The Key* funnel the Orb's energy, it seems *the Truth* functions in the reverse. The Book *absorbs* the Orb's power. A useful trick. However, what is of greater interest to me is what is *inside* this wonderful Book. The universe's most powerful force. But there is a small problem." He pulled on the cover with both hands but the Book remained closed. "The Book will not open for me. It appears Boc'ro has placed a lock upon his prize. Whatever am I to do?" His mocking tone implied he knew *exactly* what he needed to do.

Cody answered anyway. *"EnCoded, Golden Key*—the answer is all in The Prophecy. The way to open the third Book and claim the power within is by using *The Key* and *The Code*."

"Indeed," said Mr. Shimmers. "How convenient that you two should bring me precisely what I need as my *welcome home* presents." The three men stood in a circle facing each other, each holding his Book. Three men—Three Books—Three Book Keepers.

"Enough talk. Let us go to the Orb. It is time to unleash The Earthly Trinity."

115

Into the Sanctuary

———————————

The Sanctuary of the Orb. The smooth, metallic surface of the outer walls glistened like a fresh morning snowfall. In ways words were incapable of expressing, the surface seemed to *move*, the gleam dancing elegantly and full of beautiful, vibrant life.

Cody was mesmerized by the gorgeous spectacle. It took the cold barrel of Dunstan's pistol against his neck to reorient him to the situation. Mr. Shimmers and the three CROSS agents had corralled Cody, the Golden King, and the remaining royal children from the Palace to the Sanctuary.

Cody's thoughts went to Jade. She had already vanished by the time Eva had come to rescue him in the infirmary. His mind refused to accept what Jade had allegedly done to him. She needed him now more than ever. He kept looking over his shoulder, hoping to see her. *Please stay safe, Jade.*

He glanced to his left. The Golden King stood uncharacteristically silent. The prideful king had been shockingly submissive, yet Cody knew something was brewing inside his golden head.

With a low hum the metallic walls of the Sanctuary began to slide open. Bright light billowed through the gap, forcing everyone assembled to shield their eyes. The heat from the light drew beads of perspiration from Cody's forehead. The humming stopped.

Another nudge from Dunstan's pistol informed Cody that he was to be the first to venture into the Sanctuary. Cody entered with conflicting emotions of anticipation and fear. He was stepping into a holy place where few had ever been. He would soon stand before the Orb; the immense power that had drastically altered everything that was *normal* in his life; an essence he had experienced, but still did not fully comprehend. As Dunstan urged him forward, Cody had no choice but to continue toward whatever awaited him at the heart of the Sanctuary.

The immense, egg-shaped chamber was comprised entirely of the same smooth gleaming substance as the exterior. Everything about the room was rounded, with no trace of ridges, corners or bolts. The enormity of the chamber made Cody feel pitifully small and feeble.

A narrow balcony encircled the entire perimeter of the chamber. The balcony had no protective railing between its ledge and the enormous chasm below. Jutting out into the center from the balcony was a single narrow walkway leading to a platform that hung suspended over the yawning pit. Three silver podiums rose seamlessly from the platform. Cody was awestruck. Yet, as he perused the majestic sight he had the tugging thought that something was amiss. Besides the balcony, the platform, and triad of silver stands, there was nothing else in the expansive space. The realization came to Cody like a knife to the heart.

There was no Orb.

116

The Spawn of Fear

CRACK...CRACK...CRACK...
All around the room the black eggs were rupturing. Lines zigzagged like lightning bolts across their smooth surface. From within the breaking shells came a chorus of high-pitched squeals.

Tiana backed away, bumping against the rubble that blocked the room's exit. A shard of broken shell was flung against her cheek as the wailing continued.

"We need to get out of here," said Tiana, her voice wavering. Xerx was at her side, his fingers interlaced with hers.

"We're both too weary and short on oxygen to produce a wormhole. Even if we were healthy and rested, the only wormhole I've ever created nearly killed me and you've never created one. We could blow through the rubble, but in doing so we'll unleash these demons on Atlantis."

CRACK...CRACK...CRACK...

A taloned, bird-like hand pressed through an egg at their feet. "Do you really think a pile of stone will prevent these creatures from escaping?"

Xerx squeezed her hand, relenting to the truth. "Then what hope do we have?"

"We just need to contain them long enough. When we blow our way out of here, escape through the door of the Monastery, and then use the High Language to trap the devils inside behind us."

CRACK!

Another shard flew across the room. Two glowing scarlet eyes peered out from within the shell.

"Now!"

"Duomi!" shouted Xerx and Tiana in unison.

The wall exploded.

Tiana wheezed as fresh air rushed into her lungs. She heard the shrills as the creatures took their first breath—hatchlings who now desired their first meal.

"RUN!"

As fast as her wobbly legs would take her, Tiana took off toward the entrance, their only hope for escape. She hoped Xerx was close behind her but didn't dare pause to check. She could hear the sound of a thousand feet ticking across the floor like an army of giant cockroaches.

The Monastery's exit came into view. *Almost there.* Tiana willed her aching legs to press on. The ticking feet of the scurrying creatures filled the room. *How close are they?* Tiana risked a glance over her shoulder. Her legs buckled as she lost her balance. She stumbled then fell to the floor.

Xerx's feet dashed past her, continuing toward the door. Tiana could feel the approaching demons through the vibrations in the floor, knowing that any moment they would descend and tear her apart in a feeding frenzy. She hoped Xerx had escaped.

She felt the pressure of the first bite clamp down on her arm—and screamed.

117

A Golden Plan

The Sanctuary of the Orb was empty. Cody moved his hands through the air. He opened and closed them several times. "Jade was right all along. I didn't believe her. I didn't *want* to believe her. The Orb was a lie." The words vomited from his mouth. "I don't understand. I believed it was true all along. I was so stupid."

Suddenly Eva's soothing presence appeared at his side. "What you don't see is only what you expected to see. That does not mean there is nothing there, only the absence of what you expected." The young princess swayed her hand through the air as Cody had done. She held a hand in front of Cody; a bright light streamed through her fingers and illuminated the scarlet 'A' of Cody's Book. "Are you so quick to discount what your intuition tells you is true?"

Cody looked into Eva's tired eyes and knew she was right. Now was not the time to lose faith. He nodded, his determination restored. The war was not lost just yet.

Mr. Shimmers strolled across the walkway to the overhanging platform. He placed his ivory Book upon the middle podium. "If you two gentlemen would kindly place your Books upon the other two stands." The click of Dunstan's revolver made clear it was a command, not a request.

Cody saw no way out of the predicament. He would have to choose his actions carefully and wait for the proper moment. For the time being, he was forced to play along. As he reached the platform he glanced down at the bottomless pit below. The sight made his legs wobble. He placed the leather-bound Book gently down on the left podium, straightening the scarlet 'A' as he had seen Boc'ro the Wise do in the vision. Then he quickly rejoined the group on the balcony.

All eyes turned to the Golden King in expectation. However, the El Doridian King did not move. Then, to Cody's surprise, the Golden King reared his head and let loose a horrible, haunting laugh. "You are all fools!" He turned his gaze to Mr. Shimmers. "I'm disappointed in you. After all these long years did you truly believe I could be so simply played?"

He motioned to the man with the circular blades. "From the beginning I knew better than to trust in your empty promises. I'm dreadfully sorry to inform you that *I* am the one who has been playing *you*." The Golden King closed his eyes and tightened his grip on the Book. The floor beneath them shook. In the blink of an eye, appearing as though from thin air, was the Hunter.

The Golden King ran his fingers across the Beast's hoggish head. "You see, we all have our *tricks*. As it happens, mine is an invincible killing machine." The Hunter released a spine-tingling howl, announcing its presence.

The CROSS agents looked to their Master for direction against the new threat. Mr. Shimmers stood still with an unchanged expression. Yet Cody perceived a trace of concern in his eyes. The Hunter took a step toward Mr. Shimmers.

The Golden King's hollow laughter echoed throughout the Sanctuary. "A Golden King needs a golden plan." The Hunter took another slow step toward the CROSS Master. "Before my pet devours your flesh, I wish to thank you for not only *locating* the Third Book, but also bringing it to me on the day of my victory. You're timing was...*perfect*." A slow smirk formed on the King's face. "There's just one final piece to my flawless plan."

"And what is the final piece?" Cody asked, desperate to buy himself more time to come up with a plan of his own. By way of an answer the Golden King motioned with his head. Cody turned. Behind him, standing at the Sanctuary's entrance, was Jade. Her eyes were glazed with madness and she held a dagger in her hand.

The Golden King sneered. "Your death."

118

Trapped

Tiana's raw throat burned as she wailed. The shrieking creatures scampered all around her. The bite on her arm tightened. She was yanked violently into the air. The vigorous tug forced her eyes open. Gazing back at her were the beautiful eyes of Xerx, his hand grasping her arm.

"You came back for me," Tiana said in groggy disbelief.

"You were right, I *am* a love-sick fool. Now let's GO!" Tiana looked over his shoulder and immediately wished she hadn't. The entire floor slithered as the monsters stampeded forward, hundreds of glowing eyes lighting the room. Tiana felt a tug on her arm and she quickly resumed the mad dash toward the doorway with Xerx at her side.

As Tiana and Xerx neared the exit, two large shapes shot past them. The creatures flapped their wings like grotesque bats, soaring around the room and landing in front of the door. Tiana and Xerx skidded to a halt. Their only escape route had been cut off.

Xerx muttered distantly, "We can't let the beasts into the city."

Tiana nodded. "I know." Taking each other's hand they spoke the High Language in unison. The wall exploded. Rock crumbled down, piling in front of the exit and barricading their only escape route. There was no need to speak; they both understood that they had just buried themselves in their own grave. They prayed their friends on the outside would ensure their sacrifice had not been in vain.

They turned and dashed deeper and deeper into the Monastery as the devilish creatures pursued with voracious hunger.

Cody stared into Jade's raging eyes. She had been his best friend since fourth grade; the companion who had spent so many days exploring the alleys of Havenwood with him—the one person in the entire world who truly understood him. Jade was all of that to him. Yet, as he looked into her green eyes, he saw only raw hatred and confusion.

Her fist was squeezed tightly on the hilt of the dagger and she peered at Cody as though he were the only one in the expansive chamber. Cody returned her gaze. It was like looking at a stranger. His hatred for the Golden King boiled more intensely than ever. "You've brainwashed her!"

"You're wrong," said the Golden King. "I merely *released* her. Do you not wonder why I chose *her* for the task? Why I kidnapped *her* the day of my brother's funeral, and not you? Why it was only with *her* that I finally achieved

The-Creation-Which-Should-Be-One's-Own after hundreds of years of failed attempts?" The Golden King wore a self-satisfied expression. "I chose her because she and I are the same."

"You lie!" The accusation came from Jade. The Golden King flinched, but quickly regained his smug composure.

"Do I? Tell me, when you look about this chamber what do you see? The fingerprint of a divine creator? Or do you see an empty chamber?" Jade didn't answer, but her silence spoke clearly enough. "And did you not feel at home in El Dorado, more than you ever have here in Atlantis or even in your precious Havenwood?" Once again the King's words appeared to strike the target.

"Despite what you may wish to believe, I did not plant anything *new* into your mind. I merely moved your own existing fears, jealousy, and skepticism to the forefront. *This* is who you truly are inside. The true you."

Jade seemed to shrink with the blow of each word. She glanced between the Golden King, Cody, and the dagger in her hand. Cody could see the turmoil in her dazed eyes.

"Why?" Cody thrust an accusing finger at the Golden King. His voice cracked. "Why did you do this to her?"

"It is simple," the King said, basking in his own genius. "In order to unlock the wonders of the universe and claim the full power of The Earthly Trinity, I needed both Books of Power. But I am already a Book Keeper and cannot take claim of a second. Isn't it obvious? I needed a second Book Keeper who was like-minded. One I could control for my own purposes. My own son was too weak and I knew right away you, Master Clemenson, were too diluted by curiosity and imagination to ever join me. But in Jade I saw my own glorious reflection as though looking into a mirror. She was intelligent enough to reflect my brilliance, but too weak to eclipse my glory."

"Having not yet determined precisely how the role of Book Keeper is passed from one to another, I acted upon what I *did* know. When Wesley was murdered it was you who touched *The Code* next and you who became the new Book Keeper. Therefore, I needed my appointed new Book Keeper to kill you and claim the Book. To be honest, I'm surprised to find you still alive. But all things in perfect time." He motioned to Jade. "It is time for you to do what you know deep in your heart you must do."

Jade flew forward with inhuman quickness. Cody stiffened as he felt the tip of her blade at his neck. "Jade, please. This isn't you. You have a choice."

The Golden King screamed. "Do it. Do it NOW!"

Jade raised the dagger over her head, looking between the two men, then brought the blade swinging down.

119

A Battle of the Mind

The dagger clanked as it hit the floor.

"No." Jade stepped forward and stood at Cody's side. "I have a choice. You are right, Your Majesty, you *have* opened my eyes to the truth."

The Golden King's face went icy. "And how is that, may I ask?"

"That I don't *need* to fight who I am anymore. I may never see the world the way Cody does, but that doesn't mean I have to be like *you*. You've shown me my weaknesses, but in doing so, you've unknowingly affirmed my strengths. Mr. Golden King...you have failed."

The room was silent.

The Golden King's glacial glare burrowed into Jade. "We shall see about that." He lunged forward, grabbed her head, and began to squeeze.

Jade cried out in pain.

The Scene Shifted.

Jade stood alone in a vast room. She touched her forehead. It felt as though she had been stung by a bee. A burning sensation branched out from the small wound, slithering around and clutching her brain. She shook her head. She couldn't remember how she had arrived in this place, but a distant voice in her mind warned her to escape.

The entire room was covered from floor to ceiling in mirrors. A myriad of reflections pin-balled around her. The haunting images were of a hideous wretch with a gaunt face, a wart-infested nose, and yellow-stained teeth. No matter where Jade looked she couldn't escape the hag's chilling gaze. Suddenly, she heard the voices of two women, but could not pinpoint their location.

Relieved, she called to them. "Excuse me. I'm lost. Could you please help me find the way out?"

A shrill voice snarled back. "You must be as dumb as you are ugly." Jade went numb. The voice was that of her mother. "Close your mouth; you look like a panting dog. Why couldn't you have been born beautiful, like your pretty friend here?" Then a second voice chimed in.

"She really *is* a repulsive creature, isn't she?" The gibes had come from Tiana. Jade viewed the monstrous lady reflected in the mirrors and realized in horror that the images surrounding her were, in fact, her own reflection.

As her mother and Tiana continued to mock her ugliness, the pain in her forehead pulsated. Jade closed her eyes and covered her ears to block the awful laughter. She couldn't bear it any more.

Then she heard it.

A soft voice from within; a memory lost in the clutter of her mind. She heard Cody's words during their time in El Dorado: *"I've always thought you were pretty, Jade."* She realized that he had meant it. The cackling stopped. Jade opened her eyes and stared defiantly into the mirror. She was beautiful.

The Scene Shifted.

The blistering pain throbbed in Jade's forehead. The sensation spread like tentacles, wrapping tightly around her brain and squeezing. Jade fought to repress the agony. She opened her eyes.

She stood at the edge of a vast crevasse. On the other side of the gulf was her father. He sat on horseback and wore a gleaming crown.

"Father!" He turned his mount to face her. Even from the distance the deep displeasure was visible in his eyes.

"I'm sorry, Mari. I have to leave you."

"But why? You wouldn't abandon me...would you?" Her words trailed off. Her father merely steered his horse around, dug in his heels, and set off in the other direction. "Father? Please! COME BACK!" Jade's voice became hoarse as she screamed after him, but her father did not slow or turn back. His silhouette faded on the horizon.

The pain in her head tunneled deeper. Jade squeezed against it but the hurt would not stop. "Father!" She ran toward him and plummeted off the ledge. The thick darkness of the chasm overwhelmed her. She was alone.

She heard the gentle voice again in the back of her mind. The words belonged to Cody, the moment he had reunited with her in El Dorado and hugged her tightly. *"I've missed you, Jade! You have no idea how much I've missed you!"* But she *did* have an idea. He had traveled the world and risked his own life to save her.

Jade smiled. She knew she wasn't alone. Not anymore. Not ever.

The Scene Shifted.

The Golden King stroked her hair. But every time his hand touched her scalp an intense pain jolted in her brain. Jade pulled away. The King frowned. "Is something bothering you, my precious pet?" Jade opened her mouth to respond but instead of words she heard a low growl. She raised her hand and saw it was taloned. She screamed although, once again, only an eerie howl like that of the Beast emanated from her black lips.

In horror she realized *she* was the Hunter.

The Golden King smiled. *"This* is who you truly are inside. This is the real you." Jade knew the King was right. She had done horrible things. She was a monster.

Cody's voice whispered in the back of her mind. *"Remember who you are. This isn't you. You have a choice."* Jade closed her eyes. *I am who I wish to be. I have a choice.* She laughed. It was the joyful sound of her own voice.

The Scene Shifted.

Jade shrieked. The invisible fingers were prying deeper and deeper into her hidden memories. She stood paralyzed in the center of a battlefield, her joints locked in place as though forged with iron. Across from her, in the center of the courtyard, was a rustic podium. Upon it rested a leather book with an embroidered scarlet *A*.

The ground rumbled as an immense soldier ran across the battlefield straight toward her, his helmet the shape of a giant spider. The warrior raised his sword above his head as he approached. Jade screamed for help. Cody appeared suddenly before her like a mirage. He took a step toward her, but stopped. His head slowly pivoted as though a magnetic force were pulling him toward the Book.

The charging giant was almost upon her. Jade yelled louder, pleading with Cody. Her friend's eyes were downcast. "I'm sorry, Jade, but I don't need you anymore. I've found something better. I've moved on." Jade felt tears welling up. Cody lifted the Book and walked away without a glance back. Tears streamed down Jade's cheeks.

The swordsman was just a few yards away, but Jade no longer cared. She was alone in the world. She was unwanted. It would be better if she were gone...

No. That was a lie. It was *all* a lie.

Suddenly Jade remembered the time she had fallen asleep on Cody's shoulder during their train ride to Las Vegas.

The charging warrior slowed.

More and more joyful memories flooded back to Jade. One recollection pushed to the front: Cody was holding her tight, the waves crashing around them. He was kissing her.

The spider-helmeted warrior stopped, petrified in place.

Jade laughed out loud. It was all a lie. She did *not* hate Cody. Cody loved her; and in the depths of her heart she realized the truth: she loved Cody.

The swordsman wailed in agony. The spider helmet melted away and Jade saw her own face revealed. In that moment everything—the visions, the lies, the pain in her brain—made sense. The Golden King was digging into her thoughts, stirring her deepest insecurities. Jade laughed even harder. At the sound of her laughter the swordsman vanished in a puff of smoke. The Golden King may have the power to show Jade her insecurities, but only *she* had the power, the *choice*, to allow them to destroy her. Jade's tears of sorrow had transformed into tears of joy. She was free.

Jade closed her eyes and pushed back against the tentacles scrounging through her thoughts. Her fearless offensive obliterated the prying, invisible force. She came to a mental barrier at the edge where the Golden King's consciousness linked with her own. Before the King could react, Jade forced herself inside.

The Scene Shifted.

Jade was in a tent. A putrid stench hung heavily in the air. In the center of the tent was a lone bed. A pale, skeletal man lay in it. Two young boys rushed into the shelter. The man waved a feeble hand to them. "Come, my sons." The two boys approached and knelt beside the bed. The sickly man spoke between blood-gurgled coughs. "I will not live to see the morning."

The taller son nodded in solemn acceptance. The father took his hand in his own. "As my firstborn you must be strong, Ishmael."

"I will try, Father."

The second son clenched his fists. "You *cannot* die, Father. This is not how it is supposed to be. You are the Mighty Uscana! Conqueror of the sands! The greatest war chief the world has ever known. The gods will spare you. They *must* spare you!"

"No, my son. You have passion, but you must not lose sight of reality. We do not live in a perfect world."

"Then I will make one!" the boy said. His father's face became sorrowful.

"If you pursue that path you will find nothing at the end but bitter disappointment, my dear Isaac." He coughed violently, his body contorting on the bed. "When I pass into the unseen world, one of you must become Chief. Always, in the history of the Alac-icacs, we have used combat to choose our new Chief. It is said the Chief should be the greatest hunter and warrior in the tribe, full of passion, ambition, and bravery."

Uscana took his younger son's hand. "All of these things are manifested in you. In you I see a clear reflection of my younger self. Yet, you are greater than I ever was. By all of the standards of our people, you are the wisest choice to lead the Alac-icacs."

431

The boy called Isaac bowed, tears in his eyes. "Thank you, Father. I will do my best to lead as you have led."

"That is what frightens me," said the Chief. "Our tribe is in ruin, our empire fallen. At the end of my life I now see what I should have seen from the start. It is not combat skill that we need, but a pure heart. Men like you and I are killers. We can take a life without remorse. What our tribe needs is a life-*giver*." He released the boy's hand. "It is Ishmael our people need; and it is Ishmael that I anoint as Chief of the Alac-icacs."

The boy called Isaac appeared stunned. "Father! You *can't*! You said it yourself. I am the greatest. It is my right to rule!"

"No, my son, it is never anyone's *right* to rule. You two brothers have always been close. Do not break that fellowship. Ishmael will have great need of your passion and cunning in the coming years. Only together can you save our people. Only together can you be whole. Only when the two become one can the one become two."

Chief Uscana motioned his hand and a third man, concealed beneath a hooded robe, emerged from the shadows of the tent. "Boc'ro, long have you been my trusted counselor. It is to *you* I entrust my sons. Watch over them. My dying wish is that you do whatever it takes to keep their union strong. They must never forget the truth. Please, loyal Boc'ro."

The counselor nodded. "I promise."

The Scene Shifted.

120

Consumed By Fear

J ade opened her eyes as though she were looking at the world for the first time. She scanned the room. All eyes were fixed on her. It appeared that the mental battle with the Golden King that had seemed to last for days had, in reality, occurred in only seconds.

The Golden King staggered back several steps, his hand grasping at his forehead. "You filthy little creature! It should have worked. My plan was *perfect*!"

"Have you forgotten?" Jade asked. "If you pursue that path you will find nothing at the end but bitter disappointment, my dear Isaac."

The life drained out of the Golden King's face. "What did you call me?"

"It's not pleasant having someone dig through your memories, is it? That's your name. That's who you truly are inside. Imperfect Isaac."

The Golden King shrieked. "STOP SAYING THAT NAME!" His body convulsed under his uncontrollable fury. "This is impossible. You are just a stupid little girl! *FRAYMOUR!*"

Nothing happened as the power of the High Language was stifled by the third Book, *The Truth.* *"FRAYMOUR! DUOMI! BELZTAR! YOURNI!"* The King's attacks had no impact but he was too enraged to stop. *"Never* use that name! I will kill you! You wicked girl!" Jade continued to repeat the name Imperfect Isaac over and over. Her words were a chisel against the King's sanity. He continued to scream the High Language to no avail. In his blind fury he opened the Book in his hands and began reading the pages like a madman.

The room shook.

The Hunter wailed.

The Golden King laughed. "Nothing can stop me! Not an imperfect new Book! Or an imperfect little girl!" The room stopped vibrating. Anxious anticipation permeated the chamber. The Golden King continued to laugh. "I will show you, Father! You were wrong about everything. It *is* my right to rule!" He pointed to Jade. "My precious pet, kill her!"

The Hunter paced forward but stopped. Sniffing the air, it turned back around to face the Golden King. The King frowned. *"Kill her,* you filthy beast! Your Master *commands* it!" The Hunter took another step toward the King. Fear crept into the King's polished features. "What are you doing? I *created* you! *I'm* your Master, and I'm giving you an *order!*" The Hunter moved in closer. The Golden King looked to Jade.

"What have you done?"

"How long did you think you could control Fear itself?" Jade asked. "Your *perfect* plan was flawed. Cody didn't become the Book Keeper because Wesley died. He became the Book Keeper because Wesley freely chose to give the responsibility to another. While our minds were linked I took it upon myself to release you of your burden as well. I passed the responsibility from you to another."

Cody grinned as he fully realized what his friend had done. "And we know what happens to people who read from the Book when they aren't the rightful Book Keeper..."

The Golden King shook his head in disbelief. "But it was all so perfect..." The Hunter lunged. "Nooooo!" The King threw up his hands as the Beast pounced on top of him. Loud clanging echoed as the Hunter's fangs chomped down on the King's golden limbs.

The two, man and beast, tumbled off the ledge into the void. The sound of the King's agonized screams and the Hunter's wails faded. A pillar of light burst from below. When the light dissipated both the Golden King and his precious Beast were gone.

The iron jaws of the rabid creature snapped, ripping Xerx's robe and digging into his flesh. Tiana swung hard with a book, smashing it into the beast's snout and knocking it screaming back into the hive below.

Xerx and Tiana perched atop a tall bookshelf, bloody wounds covering their bodies. Below, the monsters swarmed the base of the bookcase like a flood rising to swallow them. Several of the winged creatures circled above before diving at them.

Both Xerx and Tiana had completely exhausted themselves with the High Language and had resorted to clubbing the creatures with books. Slim, unspoken hopes of a timely rescue had long since been abandoned.

The beasts scampered over each other's backs, each eager to be the first to taste flesh. They came too fast and were too resilient to repel. Tiana felt a pinch on her thigh and another on her shoulder. The bookshelf was overrun. The demons lashed out with their jaws...

Then they were gone.

One instant the beasts were swarming toward them, the next they had vanished without a trace. Only the bleeding wounds testified that the nightmare had been a reality. Tiana looked around in bewilderment. *We're not dead...*

She launched into a giddy fit of uncontrollable laughter, fueled by the absurdity of having somehow survived. Xerx joined in, cackling like a madman. When at last they quieted, Tiana looked at her companion. He was smiling back at her. She grabbed his face and pulled him forcefully toward her. In the long history of Under-Earth there had never been shared a more passionate kiss.

"Ah!" Randilin tumbled to the ground grasping his forehead. Instantly Sally was there to help him to his feet. The dwarf brushed the dirt from his clothes, cussing as he regained his footing.

He looked down into the valley at the city of Atlantis. Thick pillars of black smoke rose from the crumbling city as the battle raged on. CROSS had arrived from nowhere, their deadly tanks annihilating both Atlantian and El Doridian alike. Randilin sniffed. Whatever happened in the battle no longer mattered to him. He had made his deal with the devil. Yet, no matter how much his mind willed his body forward, his legs refused to obey. He stared transfixed at the battlefield.

"Randy," said Sally softly. "Why do you trap yourself in the man you once were?"

"You were there, that horrible night in the Caves. You should know the truth better than anyone. I'm a bad man."

"Some of the greatest good deeds ever performed were done by so-called *bad men*."

"No. There's nothing I can ever do to amend for the bad I've committed. I can't bring back the ones who died because of me. I can't bring *her* back."

"You're right. You can't. But you have a choice to learn from your past or to repeat it." Sally reached into her dress and retrieved a shiny object. She tossed it and he snatched it from the air. Randilin's eyes went large at the sight of it.

"This necklace...I gave this to Arianna. Where did you get this?"

Sally stepped forward and took Randilin's hands in her own. "It was given to me...by Arianna's daughter." The breath jammed in Randilin's throat.

"Daughter?" His voice was a husked whisper. "Tiana," he said at once, as though he had somehow known it all along. Sally nodded.

"My sweet Randy, you can't change the past, but you have a choice about what future you create. Isn't it time to stop punishing yourself for not being the man you want to be, and start *becoming* that man?" Randilin gazed back down the valley at Atlantis. He brought the necklace to his chapped lips and kissed it.

121

A Willing Sacrifice

The Golden King and his monstrous pet were gone. It was too good to be true. Cody rushed forward and wrapped his arms around Jade. He pulled her head tight against his chest. "You did it. Jade, you did it! Like always, you succeeded where I failed. You defeated the Golden King. *How?*" The scene had been bizarre. One moment the Golden King had lunged forward and grabbed Jade's head and the next he had gone completely insane.

"I remembered who I am. Who I've always been. Who I *choose* to be." Cody bit his lip. Jade's explanation made as little sense to him as the events he had just witnessed, but he didn't care. All that mattered was that by some inexplicable miracle Jade was okay.

"Wait a second." Cody looked at Jade quizzically. "But, if the Golden King was no longer the Book Keeper—then who is?"

Jade smiled. "You didn't think I'd let you have *all* the fun, did you?"

"You? You're the Book Keeper!" Jade's grin deepened. Without thinking Cody pulled Jade forward and kissed her. Realizing what he had done he backed away, his face glowing red. However, Jade merely continued to smile. Slow, hollow applause reminded him that the two were not alone.

Mr. Shimmers slowly clapped his hands together. "This is such a touching moment; however I'm afraid I have unfinished business. But I *do* offer you my deep gratitude for eliminating my greatest threat."

"Father..."

"Save your words, Mari," spat Mr. Shimmers. "I *will* have the power of The Earthly Trinity. And you will be an obedient daughter and help me. Place the Book on the podium." She glanced to Cody for help. Her father frowned. "For every minute you defy me I will have Dunstan shoot one of your friends in the head. I will bleed this city dry if I must, and deep down you will know that *you* were responsible."

Cody gripped her hand. "Do what he says. It's not worth it." Jade lifted the Book off the ground and brought it to the platform. She positioned the Book on the final podium and backed away.

"Good girl," Mr. Shimmers said. "Now, open the Books." Cody and Jade exchanged worried, helpless looks. They had no choice. They reached out and opened the Books.

Cody didn't know what to expect. The last time the two Books of Power had been united he had seen The Thirteenth in a vision. Sharing a final nervous glance they began to read.

Nothing happened.

The ivory Book on the podium remained unaffected.

"It's not working. Something's wrong," Cody said, voicing the obvious. "The last time the two Books were read together they connected. I think the third Book is blocking the connection."

As always, Jade was one step ahead of him. "It is not working because you have forgotten part of The Prophecy—*Where Sacrifice of the Pure Angel Who Fell, Is the Way to Retrieve the Pearl Within the Shell*. The Earthly Trinity cannot be opened unless there is a sacrifice."

A lump dropped in Cody's throat. In all that had happened he *had* forgotten. His greatest fear, the destiny he had fought so hard to prevent, had arrived anyway. He had played a high stakes game against Fate but he had lost. Suddenly, a last desperate solution came to him. *If I sacrifice myself then Jade still has a chance to live.* It was the only way. The words were still forming on his tongue as Jade stepped forward and announced, "I will sacrifice myself."

Cody's own words got jammed in his mouth. He gagged before blurting. "No! Stop! What are you talking about? You don't have to do this."

Jade shook her head. "Oh, Cody, when will you finally learn that I've known you far too long to fall for your lies. When I was inside the Golden King's head I caught a glimpse of a memory. A vision. A vision I think you've seen, too. In the memory I saw a girl falling into the Orb. Do you think I haven't noticed how peculiar you've been acting around me? We both know that *I'm* the Fallen Angel. *I'm* the one who must do this."

Cody's eyes watered. "But I don't want you to..." Jade stepped toward the ledge. Her courage waned as she looked down the bottomless chasm. She turned to face the others, her face a raging battle between fear and determination.

"Jade, no..." Cody lunged forward but was stopped by Dunstan's firm grip. He thrashed, trying to break free and reach Jade. "NO! Don't. Please. Jade. Please..."

"I'm sorry, Cody." Without another word, Jade stretched out her arms and fell backwards off the ledge.

122

A Losing Battle

The battle had become genocide. The sudden arrival of the mystery force had changed everything. The new army showed favor to neither side. The unworldly weapons were pulverizing soldiers from Atlantis and El Dorado alike. Most devastating were the iron carriages with the exploding projectiles that leveled entire buildings with a single fire. The resulting carnage had forced Dace to order evacuation from their factory stronghold. The few remaining Atlantian defenders now fought side-by-side in the open battlefield.

Dace parried a series of strikes before sending another golden golem to his death among the thousands of others who had met their ignoble end. Dace pivoted at the sound of a blade splitting the air behind him. He deftly blocked the blow.

He recognized the attacker as Gote, the braggart commanding officer. Dace could not see the man's expression behind the abundantly hairy face to know if he was recognized in return. The contest lasted only two more strikes before Dace gave the foe a much-needed shave, adding another corpse to the pile.

A booming echo sounded as another portion of the wall crumbled; the debris raining down and crushing helpless soldiers. Dace grimaced. Unless something changed quickly there wouldn't be a city left to defend.

Tat, Chazic, and Kir-Hugar stood with their backs to each other, fending off a cluster of golems. Suddenly the air cracked. One of the golems collapsed, wounded in his chest. Another crack and another fell dead. Dace called to his comrades. "Behind you!"

Kir-Hugar spun, launching his trident as he did. The weapon soared through the air before finding its target in the chest of one of the mystery attackers. The man collapsed, dropping his deadly weapon. Tat yelled over the sound of another explosion as he continued to fend off invaders.

"Dace, we can't fight on two fronts against two enemies. We *must* join forces with the El Doridians or neither of us is going to last much longer against these exploding weapons!" Dace fought his way toward his friends.

Chazic nodded. "Tat is right." He grunted as he slashed his mighty scimitars and shattered a Dark-Wielder's crystal skull. "But as long as their General remains in charge they will fear him too much to listen to reason. The Spider-General is a demon with his blades. I have never seen a swordsman so great..."

"Then you've never seen me," Dace remarked irritably. "But you are right. We unite or we are annihilated. If their General refuses then we must cut off the head of the serpent." The opportunity was not long in coming. He appeared through a cloud of smoke across the field—*The Impaler* had found them.

The armored titan dwarfed all others on the field. Wielding two matching swords he dispatched his foes with a deadly fusion of power and precision. It was as though Death itself were incarnated in the monstrous guise of The Spider-General.

"Come and get some! Today's the day the flies feast on the Spider!" The boastful taunts came from Captain Yaru. The burly soldier raised his mace and banged his chest with his fist. With a savage bellow he rushed forward on the attack.

The brutal conflict lasted mere seconds. The Mid-City Captain fell to the ground in a lifeless, bloody heap. *The Impaler* crossed his blood-smeared swords above his giant spider helmet to mark yet another life taken.

The Spider-General scanned the field for more victims. Dace peered at the monstrous General across the clearing. Their eyes met. They stood staring at each other, oblivious to the wild clamor of battle raging all around them. In that moment only the two of them occupied the field. The two greatest swordsmen of the era. Dace twirled his blade. *Let's settle this once and for all.*

123

Fallen Angel

Jade was gone.

"NOOOOOOOOOOO!" Cody broke free from Dunstan's hold and ran to the ledge. Staggering, he lost his balance and crashed face-first to the floor. Tears coursed down his cheeks. He had failed. His best friend was gone. He slammed his fist against the metallic balcony floor.

Through glistening eyes he saw Jade's spirit floating up from the pit, ascending to heaven. He wiped the moisture from his face. *How am I seeing this?* Cody pushed himself back to his feet. It wasn't Jade's spirit—it was her actual body.

Jade floated like a leaf, as she was lifted out of the pit. She glided gracefully through the air before coming to a gentle rest on the ledge. Cody was speechless. He ran to her, sliding on his knees to her side. He cupped her head in his hands as her eyes slowly opened.

"You fell…you should be dead…I don't understand." He looked around the room in a desperate search for answers. The others looked equally astonished. Even Mr. Shimmers stared at his daughter in bewilderment. Cody continued to survey the chamber before stopping on the young princess, Eva Morningstar.

Eva's hands were outstretched and perspiration bathed her face. Somehow, despite *The Truth's* restriction of the Orb's power, Eva had used the High Language to rescue Jade. "How?" The single-worded question was all Cody could manage to extract from his jumbled thoughts.

But it was Mr. Shimmers, not Eva who answered. "Indeed. It appears there is much more to the youngest daughter of Ishmael than meets the eye."

"Little sister, don't..." said Kantan. Eva stepped forward, ignoring her brother's caution.

She began speaking in a soft voice. "I was only a child during the First Great War. Atlantis was burning and I feared for my father's life. I sneaked into this very Sanctuary to find him in a duel with his brother. My Uncle was about to win the battle, so I rushed forward to help my father. There was a brief scuffle and the Golden King shoved me over the ledge into the pit."

"You're the Fallen Angel," Cody said with full certainty. "You are the one who ripped the page from the El Doridian history book. But, the fall would have killed you."

"It should have," Eva admitted. "But somehow, in ways I have never fully understood, I survived. I remember the sensation of energy surging through me and then waking up in the infirmary three days later. The war was over. My presence in the Sanctuary had distracted my uncle just long enough for my father to overcome and defeat his brother. But my father knew that if the truth of what the

Golden King had done to me were revealed the people of Atlantis would be enraged to the point of a Second Great War. We decided to keep it a secret. We simply called it..."

"The Accident," finished Cody.

Eva nodded. "Yes. I had survived, yet I was different afterward. In my fall I had somehow become intimately connected to the Orb. The High Language would not work whenever I was near. No one understood why but I knew it was *because of* me. I could feel my skin absorbing the energy, in the same way as the ivory Book draws in the Orb's power. That's not the only thing I absorbed. Through the Orb's flow I also soaked in people's emotions, more specifically, their fears and pains. Their deepest hurts passed from them to me."

Cody remembered the calm and peaceful feeling that enveloped him whenever he was near the young princess. Eva read his thoughts. "As Book Keeper you have the Orb flowing intensely through you at all times. As a result I feel your pains above all others. I understand your hurts better than anyone."

The words that had haunted Cody's every nightmare echoed again in his mind: *The one closest to you must pay that price.* He had always understood that the words had only one meaning: Death. Cody's heart slowed. It all made sense. For weeks he had done everything in his power to prevent The Prophecy's required bloodshed from coming true. He had vowed not to let it happen and he had failed. He had been wrong. The Prophecy wasn't referring to Jade at all.

Eva gave him a tender smile in silent affirmation. Her eyes glistened as three tears slid down her cheeks. She stepped another inch toward the ledge, the vast chasm below her stretching out into oblivion. The heels of her feet hung suspended over the ridge. Cody could hear the desperate pleading of Cia and Kantan behind him. Eva wobbled for just a moment before regaining her balance. Her face conveyed both fear and determination.

Cody felt his own eyes moisten. "Don't...there has to be another way...please...." His rasping voice trailed off. His arm stretched out toward her. She raised her hand, the tips of her fingers brushing against his. "I'm sorry, Cody. It's the only way. The price that must be paid." Her voice was gentle but laced with unwavering conviction.

Cody shook his head. "I don't care about The Prophecy. I don't want it. I want *you*. Don't leave me...*please*." He knew every eye in the room was staring at him but he didn't care. He let the tears stream down. She smiled; a smile full of sadness.

"Precious Cody. One day it will make sense. I promise." She took a deep breath. "Be strong."

Then, without hesitation, she spread her arms and stepped backwards off the ledge.

"Noooooooo!" Cody lunged forward. His fingertips brushed against the fabric of her dress—and then she was gone.

Her long hair streamed around her calm face like a halo as she fell. The light illuminated her silhouette with an angelic glow. She was beautiful. She gave one final smile before a pillar of light exploded from the bottom of the chasm to the ceiling.

Cody shielded his eyes from the blinding light. Eva's remaining siblings wailed, falling into each other's arms. A sharp pain pierced Cody's chest. It burned like a furnace. He collapsed weakly to the floor. "I'm so sorry" he whispered, "I'm sorry. It should have been me, not you." The column of spiraling light erupted in a final flash, faded, and vanished. *The price has been paid in blood.*

A soft humming rang in his ears. The sound was followed by a collective gasp. Cody wiped his eyes and looked up at the metallic podium jutting out over the crevasse. The humming increased to a deafening siren. The simple ivory book was glowing, a beam of light shooting up from the cover. The crowd around the Book backed away nervously as a laser scorched an image on the ceiling. An image of an upside-down arrow framed by a sun—the sign of The Earthly Trinity.

The Sanctuary began to shake as the two Books of the Covenant burst into white flame. They burned for only a moment and then the fire subsided, leaving only two piles of dust upon the podiums. A gust of wind came forth from the pit and swirled around the ivory Book.

The Book blew open.

124
The Greatest Swordsman Who Ever Lived

The two legendary swordsmen charged toward each other.

Dace formed a solid two-handed grip on his sword. He could feel the ridges of the notches, bringing a parade of faces and names to his mind.

The Impaler twirled his matching blades. As The Spider-General stampeded toward Dace, his blades lashed out eliminating every man, both friend and foe, in his path.

The Generals closed the distance between them. In perfect symmetry the two combatants raised their weapons. Each launched a forceful blow, seeking to end the contest immediately.

Clang!

Dace deflected the first, bringing his sword up to block a slash from *The Impaler's* second blade. The force of the parry caused Dace to stumble back a step. Instantly regaining his footing, Dace launched himself forward, executing a furious three-strike pattern. The Spider-General deflected each strike effortlessly.

Back and forth they dueled. Neither could gain the momentum of a prolonged offensive. Perspiration cooled Dace's face as he sidestepped a slice, keeping his eyes and blade aimed to El Dorado's General.

The Impaler was tireless. He hissed and lunged. The move caught Dace off guard for only a second; but in this contest even a fraction of a second would be the difference between life and death. Dace winced as a razor sharp edge nicked his leg, squirting blood to the ground. He dropped to his knee and *The Impaler* was on him instantly.

Dace swung his sword up to block as both The Spider-General's blades came down to dissect him. Dace's arms quivered as the larger warrior pressed down his swords, inching closer and closer to Dace's head. *The Impaler*'s mouth opened and two pincers wriggled out, snapping together at their tips. The fiend hissed again as the pincers snapped at Dace's face.

"Ah!" Dace cried out as one pincer caught the flesh of his cheek. He sent a kick that caught the Spider in the knee-cap. The move bought Dace enough relief to crawl free and gain separation from his foe. His wounded cheek burned. Already he could feel the smoldering sensation spreading through the rest of his face and he knew why—he had been poisoned.

The venom from the Spider's pincers was now flowing through his veins. Dace knew that if he didn't end the contest soon the poison would. He charged the monstrous General with reckless abandon. His sword blurred as he unleashed an unrelenting pattern of attacks, each strike dedicated in vengeance to a fallen comrade. A slice to the throat. "For Wolfrick!" A slice at the belly. "For Sheets!" A slice to the left shoulder. "For Nocsic!" Another slice to the neck. "For Kingsty!" A slice to the thigh. "For Lacen!"

Dace stumbled back, his chest heaving and sweat pouring from his forehead. The burning pain had intensified and his vision blurred. Across from him *The Impaler* stood silently, waiting, having effortlessly turned aside every one of Dace's attacks. The realization hit Dace's gut like a rock. *He's better than I am.*

The Spider-General hissed a piercing, mocking sound before he approached. The spreading venom was sapping Dace's strength. His sword lumbered in his hands. *The Impaler* lashed out with tireless speed. Dace parried the first but was too slow to stop the second. More blood sprayed out from his hip.

The Spider had gained the upper hand and knew it. For every two blows Dace turned aside, a third cut his skin. The open wounds tattooing his body stung as his own salty sweat flowed into them. *The Impaler* was slowly backing Dace toward the wall.

The venom was spreading rapidly. Dace mustered his remaining strength and lashed out at *The Impaler's* throat. The Spider deflected the thrust easily, sending Dace's sword soaring through the air and thudding on the ground ten feet away. It was over.

The Spider-General stepped forward to end the contest. Dace, with tortured breath, crawled up the steps toward the top of the wall. *The Impaler* raised his crisscrossing swords with a victorious sneer. Dace had no strength left to climb. He looked down at the points of *The Impaler's* helmet, his vision almost gone. Yes, it was over.

Dace lifted his weary eyes, scanning the crowd of onlookers who had ceased fighting to watch; Atlantian and El Doridian were intermingled. Levenworth's words sounded in his ears: *Before this war is over you will be faced with hard decisions. There is never a clean winner when playing this awful game of life and death. Can I count on you to make the right choice?* Dace had promised he would and Dace was a man of his word. He lunged from the staircase.

The Spider tried to back away but was not quick enough. Dace slammed on top of him. He felt immense pain across his chest and back as the spikes from *The Impaler's* helmet punctured him, passing completely through and emerging out his back.

Dace grabbed the Spider's wrists and yanked them back. *The Impaler* was still hissing as his own swords decapitated him. Black blood spouted out like tar, and the headless Spider collapsed.

Tat Shunbickle rushed forward, flinging himself to the ground. *The Impaler's* lifeless body pinned the Atlantis General against the ground; the blood tickling from his mouth already beginning to crust.

A bemused expression was on Dace's face. He looked unabashedly proud of his victory, but Tat would never know for sure. There would be no final words. Dace Ringstar, the greatest swordsman the world had ever known, was already dead.

125
The Pearl Within the Shell

—————————

The Earthly Trinity had been unleashed. The Orb's light gleamed in Mr. Shimmers' eyes as he gazed lustfully at the open Book. The exposed pages were glowing pure white. He motioned to his henchmen.

Dunstan aimed his gun at the remaining assembly. Mr. Shimmers stepped forward. "Nobody moves. This is *my* moment of glory." He walked out onto the platform.

Cody shouted after him, "No person should have ultimate power. You've had your time. You've had your glory. It's time to let it go."

Mr. Shimmers cast him a furious death glance. "QUIET! You don't understand. They *loved* me! They loved me and still betrayed me. I will make them pay. I will make them dearly regret what they did."

He stopped in front of the podium. "At long last, the power of the universe is *mine!*" His fingers twitched with eager anticipation as he reached down and touched the open pages of the Book.

BANG!

The ear-splitting eruption caused Cody's heart to skip a beat. Mr. Shimmers' body stiffened. A red splotch began soaking through his velvet shirt. He examined the wet mark with stunned curiosity.

BANG! BANG!

Two more crimson blots appeared over his heart. Mr. Shimmers' face went pale. He collapsed to the ground, dead. Cody turned. Standing behind him, holding a smoking pistol, was Dunstan.

126

The Puppet Master

The unexpected turn of events cemented everyone in place. All but Dunstan. The British gentleman turned, raising his pistol.

BANG!

The shot caught the man with the circular blades squarely in the forehead. Before the dead agent hit the ground, Dunstan spun away.

The tall bearded CROSS agent was the first to recover from the surprise. He drew his long silver pistols, but Dunstan was half a second quicker.

BANG!

The shot dropped the titan like a boulder, a bullet wound between his eyebrows. Before anyone else could react Dunstan grabbed Jade. He pulled her toward him, spinning her around, and locking his arm around her neck. He pressed the still-smoking barrel of his gun against her head.

Cody started forward, but froze as Dunstan pressed the barrel of the gun harder against Jade's neck. "I have one shot remaining. If anyone moves, the girl dies."

Cody's fingers twitched at his side. "What are you doing?"

"You are a slow learner, Master Clemenson. Have you already forgotten the lesson I taught you in our chess game? The key to victory is to let your opponent think *he* is winning until the end. Then, at the proper moment, *strike*."

"But, your master..."

Dunstan laughed. "My master? No, Mr. Shimmers was my pawn. He of all people should have learned from history that those you trust the most are positioned the closest to stab you in the back. Or, in this case, shoot you thrice through the heart." He laughed, finding sick humor in his words.

Cody's head was spinning. His eyes fell on the three lifeless victims on the floor. "But why?"

"Don't you see? As a young lad I ran away from my home to find the Holy Grail. All these long years that prize has remained my one driving obsession. CROSS was merely a tool to obtain my goal. You have no idea the joy one feels in watching powerful kings bask in their clever schemes, oblivious that they are but puppets mindlessly performing the script I was writing. Everything, from the very beginning, has happened exactly as I have intended." He eyed the open Book voraciously. "And now I've found it. At long last I've found my Holy Grail."

Using Jade as a shield, Dunstan backed toward the podium and claimed the Book while Cody watched helplessly. Jade's eyes were a silent plea for rescue. After everything that had happened, he wasn't about to lose Jade now.

"Please, Dunstan. You can have the Book. I don't want it. Just let Jade go. Please don't harm her." With Jade still in tow, Dunstan shuffled toward the Sanctuary's exit.

"I like you boy, I always have. That was never a game to me. Deny it all you want, but you and I are similar in almost every way. Two ordinary chaps from the middle of nowhere who are destined for so much more." He cast a fleeting glance at the bloodstained body of Mr. Shimmers. "However, the three bullets through the heart of my former employer testify that trusting others is foolish. I like you boy, but I don't trust you. This girl is my insurance policy. I'm sorry, lad. I really am…" With Jade's neck under one arm and the ivory Book in the other, Dunstan backed out of the Sanctuary and was gone.

127

Dark Deeds Redeemed

Cody dashed after the fleeing Dunstan. Bursting out of the Sanctuary, he came to the balcony encircling the outside of the Orb's metallic casing. Thick black smoke billowed up from the burning city far below. Cody looked both directions and spotted him racing toward the elevator. Cody ran forward but realized he would never catch up in time. *I can't let him leave the city.* He quickly scanned the scene. When *The Code* had vanished, so too had the direct flow of the Orb's energy and any advantage it had given him. He bit his lip then yelled,

"Fraymour!"

With a loud snap the rope of the rickety elevator frayed, sending the wooden platform crashing to the ground far below. Dunstan paused for just an instant, glancing venomously over his shoulder, before resuming his dash across the balcony. Cody didn't know if Kantan or Cia had followed him out of the Sanctuary. He didn't care. All that mattered was rescuing Jade. As Cody pursued, he realized the CROSS agent's intended destination. He was fleeing to where Tiana had once taken him to view his first Under-Earth sunset.

He's heading to the top of the Sanctuary.

By the time Cody reached the end of the platform, Dunstan had already taken the lone elevator to the top and severed the ropes.

"Bauciv Veagum."

At Cody's words thick green vines burst through the floor and began slithering up the side of the wall like pythons. Cody grasped onto one of the vines and was lifted off his feet up the side of the smooth, rounded structure. When Cody reached the top he found Dunstan standing on the far side waiting, his pistol still jammed beneath Jade's jaw.

"This is the end of the road, Dunstan. You have nowhere else to run. The puppet show is over." Dunstan's head turned on a swivel, peering over the ledge to the city far below. He backed away another step toward the ledge.

"Dear boy, I'm afraid we have moved far past the possibility of a clean, happy ending." He raised the Book and shook it above his head. "This Grail is my whole life. I've given everything to find it. Do you really expect me to give it away now?"

Cody took a small step forward. "It is not the Book I want. Please, let Jade go. Keep your prize, but there's no reason for anyone else to get hurt. This doesn't have to end badly."

Dunstan scoffed at his plea. "You must think I'm a fool. I severed the only elevator to this roof, which means you scaled the building by using the Orb's power, which means, despite your Book vanishing, you still possess the ability to create." He sneered. "If my time in the service of Mr. Shimmers taught me anything, it's that only an idiot would underestimate one who can wield the Power. The only thing stopping you from killing me with the Orb's power at this very instant is the fear that you may be too slow, allowing me to put a bullet through Jade's head." Jade winced at the remark, but said nothing. She was placing her life in Cody's hands.

Cody maintained a straight face. Dunstan's words were true. Cody wasn't willing to risk Jade's life. There had to be another way to free her. "Then it seems we're at a stale-mate. You won't release Jade and I won't let you leave this roof. You can't stand there for eternity. The Book won't do you any benefit if you can't open it."

Cody's words were true. Dunstan could not open and read the Book without losing his hold on Jade or removing his eyes from Cody. For just a moment Cody thought he had the upper hand until a crooked grin reappeared on Dunstan's lips.

"You will read it for me." His voice was as smooth and calm as a garden pond. "As the one who killed Mr. Shimmers, the Book is connected to me and me alone. You will read the words and if I suspect even the slightest hint of trickery I'll send Jade to join her father in the afterlife."

Like the chess game two weeks prior, the tables had just been abruptly turned. Once again Dunstan appeared the more competent player. Cody was at a loss, and Dunstan had the look of a man who was rapidly running short on patience.

Cody approached cautiously. His eyes locked with Jade's. Surprisingly, she didn't appear frightened. Instead, she radiated determination and trust. Trust that he would find a way to rescue her. Her courage was contagious. Cody would not let her down.

He took the Book from Dunstan's hands and backed away several quick steps. He ran his hand across the smooth, seashell cover. A war had been waged and thousands of lives lost for the sake of what lay within this Book; the gateway to unleashing the universe's most powerful force. Cody opened the Book.

He skimmed the words on the pages intently. Dunstan fidgeted. "What does it say? Tell me!" Cody turned the page and continued to scan the words.

"This is amazing...."

Dunstan shook Jade, spearing his gun against her jaw. "Tell me! Read it out loud."

Cody looked in Jade's affirming eyes once more, and then began to read, "If you are reading these words, then you have uncovered The Earthly Trinity and the two have become one. Contained within the pages of this tome is the Truth. A force greater than any witnessed in the history of man. An eternal power that has existed even before the creation of the world and will continue on long after the world has passed away. Once released, this immortal power will transform the world forever...." Cody paused. "I shouldn't..."

"You will do as I tell you, boy," said Dunstan, "Keep reading or Jade dies." Cody took a deep breath and turned the page. "Only the Keeper of this Book can claim this power. To obtain godhood, the Keeper must place his right hand upon these pages and recite the following words..."

"Stop!" Dunstan laughed wildly. "I'm no fool. I see what you're doing. You would pickpocket the power from me right before my eyes. Give me the Book. Only *I* will speak the words."

Cody stood without moving, grasping the Book tightly. He looked across at Jade's captor. The jolly Dunstan he had met on the Las Vegas train was dead. The man he now saw was consumed by an unquenchable lust for power. Dunstan's finger tightened on the trigger. "You owe me a favor, Cody. You gave your word. It's time to pay up. Give me the Book." Cody hesitated. "NOW Cody! I will shoot her. You don't have a choice."

"Everyone has a choice," interrupted a familiar voice. It was Randilin.

The dwarf stepped forward, locking eyes with Cody.

"You came back," Cody said, startled by the traitor's unanticipated appearance. "Why?"

Randilin dropped his gaze to his feet. "For the first time in a long, *long* time I realized I, too, have a choice. What value is there to save your life only to lose your soul? When the cost of saving everything is to *lose* everything you sought to save."

Dunstan's last ounce of patience was spent. "Enough! Cody, give me the Book."

Cody squeezed his fingers against the ivory cover. Randilin gave him a knowing look. Cody bit his lip, "As you wish." He held the Book in front of him and stepped forward. Dunstan's eyes grew larger with Cody's every step. His hand trembled in uncontrollable anticipation as he reached out to take his prize.

Just before Dunstan's fingers touched the cover Cody winked. "Go fetch." Spinning, he hurled the Book through the air toward the ledge.

Dunstan shrieked. "NO!" He shoved Jade to the ground and fired his pistol at Cody.

BANG!

Cody grabbed his chest but the pain never came. Randilin hurled himself forward. The dwarf wheezed and collapsed as the bullet struck him in the chest.

Dunstan dashed after the Book as it sailed through the air. The Book landed with a thud and skipped several times across the smooth surface of the Sanctuary roof before bouncing over the edge. Dunstan dove forward, sliding on his stomach, and flying over the ledge.

Cody rushed forward and found Dunstan dangling, the fingers of his right hand latched on to a ridge in the structure's smooth surface where the Sanctuary's walls opened and closed to imitate the rising and setting sun. In Dunstan's other hand he held the Book. The British agent's knuckles were white as he swayed. The muscles of his forearm pulsated as he hung suspended above the ground far below. His fingers were slipping.

Cody lunged forward and grasped Dunstan's wrist with both hands just as Dunstan lost his hold. The weight of the bigger man tugged at Cody, forcing him from his feet. *"Sellunga!"* The metal of the roof rippled, forming a ridge and catching Cody's feet before he plummeted to his death.

Time seemed to stand still as they dangled high above the ground. Cody could feel Dunstan's sweaty hand slipping from his grip.

"Give me your other hand!"

"No. I won't hand over the Grail."

Cody's grasp weakened. "If you don't give me your other hand you're going to fall. Let the Book go. It's not worth losing your life." Dunstan looked down at the Book in his hand. He looked back at Cody with the deranged look of a madman.

"No! The Book is everything!"

With a forceful tug, Dunstan wildly attempted to climb Cody's arm. Cody's balance buckled under the man's weight. Then, tumbling forward, Cody was dragged over the ledge. Dunstan opened the Book and frantically flipped through the pages as he fell. His eyes bulged as he pulled the Book against his chest before disappearing into the black smoke. Cody closed his eyes, feeling the wind against his face.

128

The Universe's Most Powerful Force

When Cody opened his eyes again he was staring straight into the ugliest face he had ever seen. "Randilin?" Cody rubbed his eyes. "Am I?...I mean, are we?...Is this?..."

The dwarf smiled. "No, laddie. We aren't dead." Cody looked at his body in disbelief. They were lying atop the Sanctuary roof.

"You saved me?"

"I did."

"But..." Cody's eyes dropped to the hole in the dwarf's shirt where Dunstan's last bullet had struck. "But...*how?*" Randilin reached to his neck and pulled out a necklace from beneath his tunic. Hanging on the chain was a flower pedant with heart-shaped petals. The pendant was dented. Randilin's lower lip quivered as he gazed upward, speechless.

"Cody!" At the sound of Jade's voice Cody jumped to his feet. Jade ran into Cody's arms. The two best friends held each other in a tight embrace. Cody stroked his fingers through Jade's charcoal hair as she buried her head against his shoulder. "We did it," Jade whispered.

Cody smiled. "Yes, Jade, we did it." Neither could think of what to say next. It would take months, maybe years, to process all they had been through. But that was tomorrow's concern. For the moment, both were content to simply be alive and together.

Jade was the first to let go. "But it's too bad we lost the Book."

Cody shrugged. "What is a book anyways? Just paper and words. The Book was meaningless."

"You can't be serious! After all that has happened to unleash the power in that Book. After the soldiers, and Eva, and..." She stopped as Cody placed a finger to her lips.

"*Shhh,*" Cody said gently. "I only meant that a physical book is only as meaningful as the words written inside it."

Jade stammered. "But what about placing a hand on the pages and reciting the words to claim the power and..." She stopped as a slight grin formed on Cody's lips. She knew that smirk well.

"You made all of that up. You tricked Dunstan."

Cody's lips seemed to climb as high as his shameless pride. "Who says you never learn anything valuable in school?"

Jade couldn't help but laugh. "You are a horrible, manipulative little boy," she chided him. "So what *did* the Book say?"

"In the Book there was only one word."

Jade tilted her head suspiciously, wondering if she, too, was falling victim to Cody's make-believe.

"I'm being serious," affirmed Cody. "Within the entire Book there were *many* words, but they were all the same. The same word written over and over and over in every language there is. Don't ask me how I know, somehow I just did. I could read them all. Every word was the same."

Jade frowned. "And that one word is the universe's most powerful force?"

Cody nodded. "It is."

Jade waited for Cody to elaborate but he didn't. Jade leaned forward.

"Annnnnd...? What is it? What was the word? What is the universe's most powerful force?"

Cody wrapped his arm around her shoulder.

"I'll show you." He led Jade to Tiana's old balcony over-looking the city. Together they watched as the remnants of CROSS were besieged by El Dorado from behind and by the Atlantis and Garga coalition from the front. "What do you see?"

Jade scrunched her face and thought for a moment. "I see enemies fighting side by side to defeat a greater threat." Cody nodded.

"Exactly. The Earthly Trinity was never about the power within the Book, it was about the process of opening it. The only way to claim the pearl in the shell was to set aside differences and work together. *Only when the two become one can the one become two.* That's what the riddle means. Only when differences are put aside and people come to-gether can they ever become strong on their own. Atlantis and El Dorado need each other. They may never see eye-to-eye, but without the other to offer balance, both cities were destined for destruction. Uscana's two sons could never be the great kings their subjects needed them to be unless they learned from each other. The two had to become one before they could ever truly reach their destiny as individuals. It obviously didn't turn out as Uscana or Boc'ro had hoped…but tomorrow is a new day."

Standing hand-in-hand, they watched as the unified Under-Earth forces engulfed the enemy. The ancient kingdom of Camelot had been defeated once and for all. The victorious cheers from the distant battlefield below carried up to the top of the Sanctuary. The Second Great War of the Orb was over.

Jade squeezed Cody's hand. "I know what the one word is."

129

Peace Restored

Three days had passed since the resurgent armies of Camelot had been routed. The war was over and peace had been restored. However, the long and grueling restoration process had only just begun. Over two-thirds of Atlantis had been obliterated and thousands of men and women had fallen in its valiant defense.

In the chaotic aftermath Cody did not learn of Dace Ringstar's sacrifice until the following morning. Dace had been Cody's first and closest friend in Under-Earth. His death was a reminder that peace is never free, and there are no winners in war. Cody's deep sorrow at his friend's passing was numbed only slightly by the knowledge that Dace's heroic death had been the decisive act that united Atlantis' and El Dorado's armies against Camelot. Dace had given his life to purchase the survival of both Kingdoms. Cody wished he could have spoken to the General one last time. He smiled as he imagined the conversation to include some braggart remark about how every pretty maiden in Atlantis would wear all black in mourning until the end of time.

Cody felt soft fingers slip between his own as Jade appeared beside him. She looked lovely. "Let's go. We don't want Atlantis' beloved Book Keeper to be late..."

"*Former* Book Keeper," Cody corrected. The simple leather Book that had so radically changed his life and thrust him into the role of a hero was gone forever. A small part of him missed it, but *only* a small part. He was mortal once again—and that was fine with him.

Cody followed Jade through the sea of people as they made their way toward the Palace. When they arrived a sizable crowd had already assembled before the steps. Standing atop the platform was Queen Cia. To her right stood her twin brother Kantan, and to her left was Hansi. An absence, which seemed to have gone unnoticed by all but Cody, was that of little Eva. Cody fought to maintain his composure. Likely no one would give the gentle child any credit for her part in helping to win the war, but Cody would never forget her.

Cia raised her hands to silence the crowd. For the first time since the poison had ravaged her body she was adorned in the extravagant garments Cody had become accustomed to seeing. The Queen's voice was strong and commanding. "We stand here today not as Atlantians, El Doridians, or Garga, but as the united people of Under-Earth. We may not always see eye-to-eye, but if this horrible war has taught us anything, it is that despite our differences we stand stronger together than we ever can apart. Centuries of animosity nearly brought us all to ruin. Yet here we stand. Many valiant men and women have laid down their lives to allow us this opportunity to start anew. Together we will rebuild. A new age has dawned!"

The crowd erupted in applause. Cia waited until the cheering had died down before she continued. "Our new-found union must not falter. The crown atop my head was accepted reluctantly, but it is with full willingness that I place a crown upon another." She lifted a golden crown. "Kneel, Hansi."

Hansi obeyed, dropping to one knee. Cia placed the crown onto his head. "Now rise, cousin. Rise as the King of El Dorado."

The crowd chanted in unison. "Hail the King! Hail King Hansi! Hail the King!" Cody grinned. It was an odd pairing indeed—a deformed Queen with a perfect King. The two rulers were opposites in almost every way imaginable. But Cody was starting to think that was exactly how the world was supposed to be. That, contrary to the Golden King's delusions, no one person could ever be perfect. Every single person was flawed. Perhaps the key to completeness was not striving for unobtainable perfection, but rather, finding the people who completed you in your imperfection. Cody's eyes drifted to Jade beside him, and he smiled.

130

Saying Goodbye

Igg K. Stalkton celebrated the victory the only way he knew how: with an explicit amount of exposed, heat-burned skin. Cody kept his gaze straight ahead, but was immediately drawn to the cavernous right eye socket. He watched as a fly buzzing around the captain disappeared inside the cavern. Cody struggled not to gag.

"I'm so sorry about your brother," Cody said. "He was one of the greatest men I've ever known." Igg's posture stiffened and he placed his hand above his heart in a solemn salute.

"What will you do now?" asked Jade. "Do you have any plans?"

Igg snorted, "Bah! Did my brother Lammy add roasted toenails to his sandwiches for that delightful, crispy texture?"

Cody answered with a quick, disgusted, "Yes."

"That he did! Always was a food connoisseur, he was. Ol' Igg has sailed *The Igg* over every inch of the Magma

Darling. Igg has a hankering for fresh adventures. Aye, the *Seven Seas,* or so the dwarf says."

Cody felt a surge of terror. "You're going to *Upper-Earth?*"

"Indeed! That Garga Princeling, Ugar-Kir-Hugar has promised to escort Igg and *The Igg* to the portal in his lands. Adventure awaits!"

Cody didn't have the heart to inform the sea captain that above ground people are expected to wear clothes. He grinned. He would let that task fall to some poor, unsuspecting fisherman. Bidding farewell, Cody turned and found Xerx and Tiana waiting for him. The young girl, Elena, stood at Tiana's heel.

Cody wrapped Xerx in a tight hug. The monk stiffened for a moment, memories of their old rivalry lingering, before relaxing and patting Cody on the back. "I will miss you."

Cody turned to Tiana. She was beaming with girlish glee. At her throat was a necklace with a faded sky gem. Sensing Cody's gaze on the jewelry Tiana's face colored to match her ruby lips. Cody smiled. He was happy for her. She deserved some joy in her life. As they hugged, Tiana whispered a simple, "Thank you."

Jade took her turn next, hugging her friends. "What will you two do now?"

Xerx grinned and looked at Cody. "A dear friend once helped me realize that perhaps my destiny was not to become a Book Keeper; maybe I was meant to do something else."

Cody rubbed his nose. "As I recall, it took several bruises and black eyes for those friends to come to that realization."

Xerx laughed. "As I recall, the friend deserved every one of those hits and more." He inhaled a deep breath. "With Master Stalkton gone, I have decided to carry on his work. I will continue to train the New Brotherhood on how to use the Orb's power for the good of Atlantis and Under-Earth. All who desire to learn will be welcome." Xerx slipped his arm around Tiana's waist and pulled her close. "But I won't be doing it alone."

The young girl, Elena, exclaimed, "I'm going to have a new mommy!" Tiana messed the girl's hair, pulling her close. Cody smiled and bade his friends farewell.

Waiting next in line to offer their well wishes were Randilin and Sally. The dwarf's hands were bound with rope. The sight alarmed Cody. "What's going on? Does Kantan still want to have you hanged? I won't allow it. I'll go to him immediately and..."

"Take er' easy, boy, take a ruddy breath," said Randilin. "There will be no hangings." Cody's shoulders relaxed. "Seems ol' Kantan is his father's son after all. War has a way of taking away one's lust for bloodshed. But justice must be given nonetheless. I've been banished, again, from Under-Earth."

"Banished? But you're innocent!"

Randilin snorted at the remark. "Innocent? I'm a bloody traitor, that's what I am. You've got a lump on the side of your head to prove it!"

"But you came back. You saved my life," Cody insisted. "Besides, we don't know what the Golden King may have done to you in captivity. I am betting he tampered with your thoughts the same way he did with Jade or the Lillians."

Randilin shrugged. "Perhaps. But the Golden King only worked with what was already there. He may have been the sculptor, but I provided the stone. There's no bloody use denying it, boy. In my heart I'm a selfish traitor."

"But you've changed so much," Cody said, knowing his arguments were futile.

"Aye, I guess I have. But change takes time." Randilin cast an impish look at Sally. "Besides, I've heard there's a fantastic diner in Upper-Earth that serves the best hot chocolate around. I have a mind to see if they have any job openings."

Sally narrowed her eyes. "Hmmm, that depends. Are you known to be reliable?" Randilin's face fell for just an instant before he caught the grin on her face. Sally planted a wet smooch on the dwarf's rough cheek. "I *suppose* there are some tables with horrendous coffee and mustard stains in need of some scrubbing…"

Cody watched in delight as panic stole Randilin's face. The dwarf mumbled under his breath, "Perhaps it's not too late to change Kantan's mind about the bloody hanging after all…"

Chazic watched the celebrations from a distance. He had never been comfortable in crowds. He turned to find quiet solitude elsewhere when he heard someone shout his name. Tat came jogging toward him. *General* Tat, or so he'd heard.

Tat wrapped his arms around his one-time foe and pulled the former Enforcer into a hug. He slapped Chazic's back and released him. "What will you do now? I've heard Queen Cia means to disband the AREA and allow people freedom to worship the Orb however they wish." Tat stroked his chin for a moment. "Dace's heroic sacrifice grieves me deeply —but it also leaves me with a need to appoint a second-in-command. I know no man in all of Under-Earth more worthy to fill the position than you."

Chazic smiled at the offer. "It would be an honor to serve beside a man like you...yet I must decline. War and battles are not my purpose."

Tat shrugged as though he had expected the answer all along. "Well, my friend, then may the Orb lead you to find whatever and wherever that purpose may be."

Chazic raised an eyebrow. "Better be careful, you're starting to sound like a holy man."

Tat grinned. "Baby steps." With that, Chazic departed. He soon found himself outside the city walls. He had no destination in mind, only the desire to be moving forward. He prayed the Orb would guide him. He turned—and came face-to-face with a strange, gangly man.

The man had a long, matted beard and stringy gray hair that hung past his shoulders. His eyes were gaping, accented by the absence of eyelids. Without a word the peculiar man pulled off his robe. He turned and let the shabby garments fall to the ground.

Covering his back were tattooed markings in the shape of an upside-down triangle amidst a runic sun. It was the sign of The Earthly Trinity. The tattoos were identical to the ones that marked Chazic's own back.

The strange hermit placed his hand gently on Chazic's forehead. Chazic's face lit up in astonishment. The visions he saw rendered him speechless. It was glorious.

Pulling his hand away, the eyelid-less hermit set off toward the open wasteland. Chazic followed.

131

Time to Go Home

In all the books Cody had ever read, even the greatest adventures eventually came to a close. Now his own adventure had reached its end. A journey that had begun with two ordinary kids, in an unassuming bookstore, would end with great fanfare and unforgettable friendship.

The Great Hall of Atlantis was filled beyond capacity. Cody and Jade surveyed the array of faces gathered before them. So much had transpired since their lives had been drastically altered in *Wesley's Amazing Rare and Used Antique Book Store*. However, both knew, without a doubt, that the strongest memories they'd carry back with them were the relationships they'd made. And the friends they'd lost.

Cody recognized so many in the crowd. Tat with his wife, Rali, nestled against his side. Cia looking radiant once again beside the handsome King Hansi. The pudgy Poe Dapperhio. Randilin and Sally standing together at the back of the crowd, her head resting on his shoulder. Cody's eyes paused as he spotted Tiana and Xerx standing side by side with little Elena. A stunning crystal tiara rested atop Tiana's head. She looked every bit the princess. To her other side stood Prince Kantan. The Atlantian royal was almost unrecognizable. The solemn demeanor that once had seemed permanently etched on his face had been replaced by a softer countenance. Yes, Cody had made some dear friends.

Now it was time to return home.

Cody took Jade by the hand and turned to face the portal behind them. They could see the blurred view of small-town Havenwood on the other side. The crowd behind them broke in applause and cheers. Together Cody and Jade stepped through the portal and vanished to the other side. The portal closed at the sound of Cody's voice as he said:

"Gai di gasme."

Epilogue

He opened his eyes. The moonlight shone bright through the window. He groaned. The only thing worse than waking up in the morning was waking up in the night. A piercing wail was coming from the other room. He cringed. Was there a more grating noise than the sound of a baby crying?

He shut his eyes, pretending to fall back asleep. Like a contagious disease, the first baby's war cry was picked up by a second. Then, he felt a sudden sharp pain as the woman beside him released a perfectly placed kick to his shin. "It's your turn," his wife mumbled groggily. He sighed. Why did the woman have such a good memory?

"Yes, dear." He crawled out of bed and staggered into the nursery. He was greeted by two plump bundles of skin. He plucked his daughter out of the crib and planted a kiss on her forehead. "It's okay, my sweet Eva." The infant ceased her crying, staring wide-eyed at him.

Setting her gently back in her bed, he moved to the second crib and was instantly greeted by a foul smell that suggested a large portion of the child's weight came from the diaper. The boy grinned, apparently proud of his accomplishment. "Oh, Dace, why couldn't you have taken after your mother?"

Minutes later the mess had been dealt with and both children were back in their peaceful dreamland. He tiptoed back into the bedroom, cautious not to wake his wife. As he crept around the side of the bed he stopped. The moonlight streaming through the window illuminated a chest against the far wall like a spotlight.

He crept to the chest and removed a mountain of dirty laundry that covered it. He opened the wooden chest. In doing so he unearthed an old object. A smile formed on his face. The sand-filled bowl was the lone souvenir he had brought back with him from an adventure long ago. Various faces flashed through his mind. Old friends he had not seen in a long time. He wondered about them. A powerful yawn forced his mouth open.

He needed sleep. Tomorrow would be a big day. After months of hard work, they would finally launch the grand re-opening of *Wesley's Amazing Used and Rare Antique Book Store.* He quietly crawled into bed and cuddled next to his wife, draping his arm around her. She wiggled, nesting herself against his chest. *Life was good*. He smiled and fell fast asleep.

On the other side of the room the sand in the bowl begin to shift. Had he paused at the bowl a minute longer he would have seen lines drawn into the sand as though by an invisible finger, forming a single word.

Hail.

THE END

Acknowledgments

A journey has come to an end. There are so many people who deserve credit for getting me to the finish line in one piece. To name just a few...

My beautiful wife, Sarah. Thank you for the countless hours you willingly shared with your husband's crazy, fictional characters. Thank you for putting up with my zeal when the writing went well and enduring the gloom when it did not. Thank you for candidly letting me know when my great new ideas were, in fact, not so great.

My editor, Anna McHargue. Thank you for putting up with this stubborn writer for four years and three books. God reserves a special place in Heaven for editors.

My loving mother. Thank you for not only encouraging me to follow a dream, but for willingly sacrificing endless hours of editing and proofing to help me do so. Sorry for killing off all your favorite characters!

Marilynn Blackaby (aka. Grandma!), Greg and Shari Black, Hal and Terry Osgood, Mike Webber, and Robert Eather for their generous contributions to help this book become a reality.

Last, but definitely not least, my deepest gratitude goes out to YOU. Thank you to all the amazing readers who have invested in my story. Writing can be a lonely, frustrating chore. Your support and enthusiasm were a shot of adrenaline that made the process entirely worth it. I can never repay you!

About the Author

Daniel is a fourth generation author. He grew up on the icy plains of western Canada. He has published multiple books in both fiction and non-fiction genres. Daniel is an avid reader, an undefeated Star Wars trivial pursuit player, and a self-professed connoisseur of European heavy metal music. He currently lives in Atlanta, Georgia with his beautiful wife, Sarah.

Follow his writing at these locations:
Danielblackaby.com
Facebook.com.danielblackabyauthor
Twitter@DanielBlackaby

Author Q&A
with Daniel Blackaby

(Warning: Contains Spoilers for Earthly Trinity)

1. **Do you have a favorite book in the trilogy? What was the easiest and hardest books to write, and why?**

   Each book is special in its own way. I have a hard time separating the actual book from the life context attached to each. However, as of now, my favorite is *City of Gold*. The easiest to write was *Legend of the Book Keeper* because I wrote it before I signed a publishing contract (no deadlines!). The hardest was *Earthly Trinity* because of all the loose ends I needed to tie up, without losing momentum in the story.

2. **How did you come up with the original concept for the *Book Keeper*?**

   I always knew I wanted to begin the journey in an old bookstore to pay homage to all the years I'd been swept away on wild adventures by a dusty old book. I wanted a story that toyed with several famous myths, and realized that a powerful, mysterious book could be the thread that connected them.

3. **If you could go back in time and change anything about the trilogy, would you? If so, what would you change?**

I wouldn't change much of the actual story. However, I would polish the writing of *Legend of the Book Keeper*. When I wrote that book I was 22 years old and had never written a book in my life. I'm a far better writer today than I was back then. Who knows, maybe I'll do a 2nd edition one day!

4. **Who/what inspired the main characters?**

Cody is based directly on me. Jade is in many ways a mirror image of my wife, Sarah. In fact, several of their interactions are taken straight from real life events between us. I also tell my little sister the Hunter was inspired by her after-school appetite.

5. **Who was your favorite character to write? What character was the hardest to write?**

My favorite character is Dunstan. My favorite character to *write* was definitely Lamgorious Stalkton. I had a blast with his chapters because there were so many ways I could go with them. He could spout great wisdom at times, and then turn around and do something gross and childish. I looked to him as the glue that holds the whole trilogy together.

The *hardest* character to write was probably Mr. Shimmers, simply because he didn't have a lot of airtime to develop. I wanted him to be more than a stereotypical, diabolical villain, but had limited ink to work with.

6. Did any characters take a drastic turn that even you did not anticipate?

Characters have minds of their own. The best thing for an author is to just hang on for the ride. A couple of examples: Tiana was originally conceived as a minor character that wouldn't even appear in books 2 and 3. It wasn't until the second draft that I finally surrendered and let her develop into who she needed to be. Also, from the beginning of Book 1, Randilin was destined to die and Dace was plotted to live. It wasn't until I started writing the end of Book 3 that their fates were reversed.

7. Were there any particular scenes that were difficult to write?

Yes! Several. I didn't write chronologically. I'd write the chapters I was excited about first. Then, afterwards, I'd go back to all the scenes I'd skipped. Sally's monologue about Randilin's tragic backstory took several attempts until I was happy with it. Also, all of the final confrontations between Cody/Jade/Golden King/Mr. Shimmers in the Sanctuary of the Orb at the end of *Earthly Trinity* were a nightmare. They were also the last chapters I wrote.

8. Do any of your personal beliefs affect the story?

Every writer is influenced to some degree by their own biases and worldview. As a Christian, the themes of faith and redemption naturally became an important question for my characters to wrestle with. The concept of an unseen world came from my own view of the real world.

9. What is the main thing you hope readers get from reading the trilogy?

More than anything else, I hope the reader simply enjoys the adventure. Imagination is becoming a lost art in our pragmatic culture. I believe with all my heart that fantastical stories still have a vital role in our world.

10. What were some books or authors that were inspirational for the trilogy?

I'm an avid reader, especially in the fantasy genre. It's nearly impossible to write fantasy today without being influenced by the giants such as Tolkien, Rowling, Robert Jordan, and G.R.R. Martin. You're either mimicking them or reacting to them by doing the opposite. I also borrowed from the Biblical narratives.

11. Is there anything you wanted to put into the story but didn't/couldn't?

There were several areas of Under-Earth I had hoped to explore but the plot didn't allow for it. I also have a lot more backstory than what is in the books. Some questions were left unexplained or open-ended. In the end, I had to draw a line between telling the best story I could and simply checking boxes to make sure I answered every possible question.

12. Now that the trilogy is complete, do you plan to continue writing?

Definitely. My commitment to *The Lost City Chronicles* has been my primary focus. Now that the trilogy is complete I have a backlog of new story ideas I'm excited to explore. I believe my best work is still to come! Make sure to check out my website (www.daniel-blackaby.com) for news about upcoming books.